THE ADVENTURES OF CORWYN

Chad Corrie

An Aspirations Media Publication

An Aspirations Media Publication
www.aspirationsmediainc.com

Copyright © 2008 Chad Corrie
Cover and Interior Art by Tiffany Prothero
Layout by Jennifer Rowell
Design: Jennifer Rowell and Chad Corrie

LIBRARY OF CONGRESS CONTROL NUMBER: 2008902422

IBSN: 978-0-9800034-2-0

PRINTED IN THE UNITED STATES

First Printing April 2008

Other books in **The World of Tralodren**®

The Divine Gambit Trilogy
Seer's Quest
Path of Power
Gambit's End

Tales of Tralodren™: The Beginning*

The Adventures of Corwyn

*Graphic Novel

AUTHOR'S FOREWORD

I first cut my fantasy reading teeth on the works of Robert E. Howard. I'd read a little bit of fantasy before Howard but after I discovered him I was pulled deeper into the genre than ever before. He had a way at drawing the reader into the story and his action scenes kept a teenage boy more than excited with the visceral detail and emotional pacing that was abundant in his better works.

One thing I also enjoyed was the brevity of his tales. I didn't know then that most of his stories had been published long ago in magazines and had to be under the restrictions of a certain word count. The story collections I'd been reading gave me the impression that Conan and Howard's other fantasy tales were written in a serialized short story or novella format for book publication. Not being as avid a reader as I would become, the stories where just the right length to get me trained for the larger sized fare I would later encounter.

Even after I learned the truth about Howard's work, I thought the concept of short story collections was tremendously fun. Here the hero was getting progressively older and wiser while further exploring his world in a single volume. That was the best part – I didn't have to read five or ten novels or even wait that many years to get the next installment of his adventures. Instead, the next adventure was in the same book right after the current short story I was reading.

This certainly left an impression on me and was part of the reason why I decided to put together a collection of stories for this book. I wanted to offer a new character who could grow in the pages from story to story and help not only showcase **The World of Tralodren®**, but also convey to a new generation some of the same wonder and joy I felt in reading those old Howard tales.

I also wanted to take it on as a personal challenge. I hadn't written a short story or novella in a long time and I wanted to see if I could do it again after previously being engrossed in writing epic-sized books. I think I was able to put forth a decent offering, but I'll let you decide the matter for yourself.

Oddly enough, the character of Corwyn Danther seemed to be a bit more of a challenge in the way he was designed. That challenge, though, helped make for some excellent story opportunities of which I believe I took good advantage. Whatever the case, the bottom line is I hope you enjoy reading these tales as much as I did writing them.

Chad Corrie
2008

To my mother:

You introduced me to the joys of reading.
For that I will forever be grateful.

I haven't a clue as to how my story will end. But that's all right. When you set out on a journey and night covers the road, you don't conclude that the road has vanished. And how else could we discover the stars?

— **Unknown**

It is only in adventure that some people succeed in knowing themselves – in finding themselves.

— **Andre Gide**

Life is either a daring adventure or nothing. Security does not exist in nature, nor do the children of men as a whole experience it. Avoiding danger is no safer in the long run than exposure.

— **Helen Keller**

Table
of Contents

Rainer's Legacy

1

As the sun was sinking into the reddish-orange cumulus canopy of sky, a lone vessel traveled north from Talatheal through the shimmering, lapping waves of the Yoan Ocean. This ship had come from the port kingdom of Elandor and was en route to the colder waters of the Northlands. The large frigate, seasoned in waves far to the west, was called The Phoenix and flew the flag of the nation of Breanna from its main mast alongside a sage flag emblazoned with a golden phoenix in spread eagle display.

The flag of Breanna, home of the gnomes, was pure white with a medium-sized stripe of powder blue sweeping across its snowy surface. Few had seen it this far east and north, for Breanna was one of the lands far to the west. The Mystic West, as some would say; and not many of the denizen who dwelled there traveled too far beyond the familiar waters of their homeland. Only when they had a great compulsion could you ever see a Breannain vessel outside the Western Lands.

And The Phoenix had just such a compulsion. The frigate had left Elandor in fine weather three days ago. It was spring in the Midlands and the fresh winds were just gaining strength as the seasons changed from the harshest winter that many had seen in more then a decade, to a warmer and more inviting climate. The favorable winds from this seasonal change did much to aid the vessel's voyage, cheering the crew. Their labors had been easier due to the fair breezes assisting them in their journey from Breanna some six months ago.

They had been happy, after half a year of travel, to see the coast of Talatheal and even happier to gain some land beneath their heels for a bit of time. The frigate wormed its way around the continent's northern confines until it docked in Elandor to fill up with supplies and gain some rest for the crew for the next stage of their journey.

The Phoenix had been a solid ship when it was first purchased, but the captain had followed a common gnomish practice – placing large projectile weapons in the lower sections of the vessel for added protection. It was an expensive outfitting. Few did it, save the war vessels of the Breannain navy, but the captain of The Phoenix enjoyed the added protection granted by these modifications, for it had come to sail in many different waters for many different reasons. In such cases, a bit more protection was always welcome. The Phoenix had only two such projectile devices, both bastille, hidden below decks with trap doors on each side of the vessel that would open when needed to levy large bolts against any enemy.

The Phoenix's captain and crew were more or less traders and adventurers, who opened themselves up for sale as transport and guide for various clients – taking a share of their clients' profits, in addition to the initial fee for their services. It was a lucrative venture that never failed to net the crew a fine reward; this current voyage was no exception.

The crew itself was a ragtag bunch, as most men of the sea or aquatic-based commerce were. Mannerisms, old prejudices, and ways were often forgotten or suppressed in favor of civility and survival in the cramped quarters of wood, rope, and sail that they called home for months at a time. Though the crew showed a mix of races, many were tall and tawny Telborians with sharp green and blue eyes and leathery flesh lashed by sun and cured in salty surf. Mixed among them were a varied host of dark-eyed and onyx-skinned Celetors who made their way about the ship alongside a few gray-tinted and silver-haired Patrious and even a handful of Napowese – their almond-shaped eyes and jet-black hair accented their soft yellowish-brown complexion.

All of the crew were men. Woman didn't bode well with men on ships. Indeed, many of the crew gathered would consider it a grave invitation to bad luck and strife to so embrace a policy of inclusion encompassing what the bards called "the fairer sex". No, these men were traditionalists to the core. Loyal only to their captain, a powerfully built, dark-skinned Celetor named Hirim Koofehi, himself a skilled and accomplished sailor who had embarked on this recent gnomish venture to the distant north.

Just what this venture involved, though, the captain would not reveal to the sailors. Only his first mates had any inkling of what it was about. This didn't concern them that greatly, however, for Hirim, was trusted by his crew; he had earned it over the years. In many things he was open in his discourse with the men in his employ but in some matters he kept his lips tight. The crew figured as long as they got paid, they really didn't care what this current venture might be. However, they assumed it was something highly profitable if the gnomes were involved. Tales and popular thought spoke of anything a gnome touched as turning to gold and returning a profit with a higher yield than could be imagined. Such were some of the delightful stories that danced in the crewmen's heads as they sailed.

For now, the men were just content to scrub the deck, maintain the order of the ship, and dream of the rich reward that awaited them. Some still dreamed of Elandor and the pleasures they'd had there – keeping them smiling for a few more days, until the doldrums of sea travel returned. As they worked away, the captain and his guests rested in his cabin at the stern of the frigate.

Hirim actually had more than one room that was part of his cabin. He wanted a larger area than most captains, so had some space custom-fitted to meet his likings. None saw these spacious personal quarters but him. The smaller room off this private area, however, was a common hosting area for the captain and his guests (those who had secured the services of the phoenix). Though it was a smaller room, it wasn't too cramped as one might expect, being able to allow comfortable seating for six people around an old circular oak table in the room's center.

It was inside this room where the captain and his guests had taken to, as they had many nights prior. Inside all was awash with bluish-white smoke. It hung above the four occupants' heads, strangling a copper oil lamp that swayed over the center of the table on a stout chain, before it fled out an open, narrow, rectangular window at the back of the room, opposite the door. There were two such glass windows in the room, but only one of them allowed the strongly scented smoke to escape.

"I see you're courting Saredhel now, eh?" Hirim's smile was like a flash of lightning in the starless night sky. His strong jaw clenched a thickly rolled cigar that churned out a wreath of slate-gray, pungent-smelling fog about his shaved head; adding to the hazy halo above the gathered men. Angular eyebrows outlined his dark brown eyes that flirted with mirth. He was dressed like many Celetors of the West: billowing red silken pantaloons, leather boots, and a large khaki shirt opened at the top, just low enough to outline the dark valley between the twin mountains of muscle on his large, hairless chest.

"One does the best one can," an oddly accented voice spoke back in Telborous, the same tongue that Hirim had been speaking as he fanned his playing cards wide before him. It came from Josiah Brookshire, the gnomish representative of the Breannain company that was funding the expedition.

The gnome was dressed in a simple brown coat that covered garb very similar to Hirim's own – save for breeches instead of billowy pantaloons. He also wore a leather vest in whose breast pocket rested a set of spectacles, and when he wasn't smoking it (as he was now), an elegant ivory pipe that had a fruit layered, nutty flavor about its wispy plume.

Josiah was no exception to his race, who were shorter than humans while being similar in height but not in build to dwarves. Josiah was slender and tall for his kin, though not by much;

crossing above a man's belt by a head (giving him just enough clearance at the table to function like his taller companions). His eyes were a deep blue, his smile straight – though a bit stained from pipe smoke and tea – with a face well worn, many a wrinkle forged by a hospitable and kind nature.

"Well, read them and weep, losers," a scruffy looking halfling thrust his cards upon the wooden table, "a full court."

The vellum cards revealed a colorful portrayal, done in profile, of a Telborian king, queen, prince, princess, and priest. Their suits were not matching, however, revealing the five suits of the deck: clashing silver swords, a yellow circular shield, a singular green oak leaf, a bright red heart, and a soft blue four-pointed star.

"Looks like I win." The halfling's bloodshot eyes lusted after the small pile of copper coins in the center of the table.

"Not so fast, Charles," the Telborian beside him smiled.

Charles de Frassel's diminutive figure turned to the bard while grabbing for the loot at the center of the table. "Got something on me then, do you?" His grin was sour, his skin waxen – as if he'd been to the bottle for some time and was only now showing the signs of it. His combed over thin wisps of auburn side hair did little to hide the pale moon that rose behind it, but it made him feel like he was younger. The rest of his face was clean-shaven, though dark stubble was making its way back up to be harvested once again.

He wore a rather simple outfit. Simple that is for a halfling, that was. Charles' pantaloons were of rich, blue silk that ballooned out to double the size of his small legs. His stockings were white, with gold embroidery, and matched his golden, wooden-soled, silken shoes. On his chest he sported a white cotton shirt that was slightly undone to show off his hairy chest. The shirt stretched over a protruding belly, as if it were covering the waist of some expecting woman, and was tied down with a wide black belt.

Like most of his race, Charles stood a little less then four feet tall, and had the look of a man in a child's body. Though similar to the dwarf and gnome in stature, halflings were completely different from them, and each was proud of that fact. Where the dwarf was stocky and muscular, the halfling was thin and frail and possessed an ear that rose to a small point. Collectively, the race was famed for being rude, obnoxious, and selfish in both their wants and dealings with all they encountered.

Most detested manual labor as well, considering such work only worthy of the common beast, and indeed seeing those that did so no better off than such base animals. Instead, they tried to pass themselves off as freethinking men and women of culture and expression – beings of living art and ideas – and therefore above just about all folk they came across.

To a halfling life was a series of pleasures to be enjoyed, but only by themselves, for their *own* glorification. It was no wonder that the race was so disliked and hated throughout the world and was the butt of many a joke both clean and raunchy from east to west, north to south.

"This ought to be good," Hirim stroked his handlebar mustache over his broad, toothy smile. "What you got, Corwyn?"

"The Court of Leaves," the Telborian bard grinned as he displayed his hand to the players.

"Let me see that!" Charles hopped up on his chair and leaned over to have a closer look at the bard's hand. Sure enough, it was as Corwyn said. All five cards bore the green leaf suit: a king, queen, prince, priest, and a jester.

Corwyn was a young, clean-faced, slender man of Telborian descent. He was a traveling chronicler, entertainer, and mild adventurer among other pursuits. He had worked up quite a reputation for himself in the Midlands over his short career for his exploits and tales. In fact, one of the reasons The Phoenix had docked at Elandor was because the bard had requested to join the expedition, having received a rather strong recommendation by a good gnomish friend who often helped promote him and his shows. It seemed that this same gnomish friend happened to have a rather large share invested in this venture as well.

The bard's reddish-blonde hair was kept short about his fair face, blue-green eyes scanning the tipsy halfling who smelled of sour wine that was sweated out from his pores. Corwyn's dress was a pair of simple leather shoes; breeches and a cream-colored linen shirt completed his garb, a coin purse dangling from his side.

"Hmph," the halfling slumped back down into his maple plank chair with a sigh, "jester's wild…why does it have to be jester's wild?"

Those around Charles laughed in response to the halfling's lament. He hadn't yet won a hand, not uncommon, since during their infrequent games since leaving Breanna, Charles rarely broke even and usually lost. Even more amusing was the fact that before they had started playing their first game over six months ago, the halfling had boasted that he never lost in cards – that he was the best player there ever could be found. His empty pool of coppers, which had shimmered with the tiny man's arrogance before the games started, would seem to have quickly revealed otherwise.

"So now I'm out of coin." Charles flung his cards into the center of the table near the small mound of copper, as did the others while Corwyn moved the pile of glittery gain toward himself. It was added to the bard's own modest pile before him which, even with the newest addition, was about average with all those gathered around him, save Charles.

"I'm surprised you've kept what you had so long, considering the poor playing you've been doing since I let you on board," Hirim smirked.

"Just a run of sour luck is all," Charles waved the captain's comment away, "I'll be back on top and you'll be my debtor soon enough. I just need one hand to win it all a back…and something valuable to get me one more hand…"

The halfling's eyes darted back and forth to each of the three players at the table. He knew his luck was just ready to turn around – that Saredhel was going to shine on him at last – and he wanted to be ready to rub it in their faces when it did.

"You still got that map, de Frassel." Hirim poked fun at the halfling's loss.

"And it's staying in *my* possession. Thank you very much." Charles removed a slender rolled cigarette from a rectangular, silver carrying case in his shirt's side pocket, tapped it on the table, and placed it in his mouth. Gaining a spark from the dying embers of his previous cigarette that smoldered in an ash and butt-filled tin beside him, he lit the newest one. A sudden burst of a mixed blend of varied plants bloomed over the table.

"Ah," said Charles as he blew out a thin jet of creamy smoke. "halfling-cut tobacco, the best there is."

"One would disagree," Josiah submitted between pipe-clenched teeth.

"So now what are we supposed to do for entertainment?" Charles took another slow drag on his cigarette, the lit end crackling with a reddish-orange glow. "If I can't play cards, how am I supposed to pass this godsforsaken boredom?"

"We have quite a long trip ahead of ourselves here, if your map is to be believed." Josiah removed his pipe from his lips with his right hand, which held it as he spoke.

"You certainly believed it enough to take on this venture," the halfling chased down his words with a swig of wine from an open bottle beside his chair. Finding the bottle empty after his indulgence, he returned it to the floor beside him, crestfallen.

"Hey now, try to ration yourself a bit more." Hirim started to shuffle the cards for another game. "I don't have enough booze to keep you going, if that's what you're seeking."

"Indeed, Mr. de Frassel, it would seem that your indulgence of the juice of the vine has been quite excessive since we left port in Breanna."

The gnome adjusted some fallen locks of his white hair; the longer strands, though thinning, had cascaded down his crown. They were touching his neatly trimmed, but still thick and bushy sideburns that descended toward the back of his lower jaw.

Corwyn (from past dealings with his gnomish promoter and those whom he worked through) and now the entire crew of The Phoenix, since they had traveled with him, knew that gnomes had a strange habit of referring to everyone by Mr., Mrs., or Ms., as a prefix to their last name. Only those with whom they were intimate, such as close friends and family, did they address by their first name. Otherwise they even referred to people as "sir" or "madam" and spoke in a rather elegant, if not verbally robust term of conversation, when compared to their Telborian counterparts, whose language they shared with slight modifications.

Legends claimed that the gnomes became such successful traders and businessmen they forgot their own native language by excessive use of Telborous, the lingua franca of Tralodren, or at least a good portion of the world. None knew for sure, but it did make a good story and seemed to fit their nature.

"Well, I have to do something around here to keep myself entertained if I can't gamble anymore," the halfling snorted in despair.

"Why not help the crew?" Hirim asked sardonically, knowing full well the response.

"Pah," the halfling snorted again. "Work like a dog with common men? You have got to be *joking*, Hirim.

"Now, had your superstitious sailors allowed me to take aboard *all* of my cargo, I might not be so apt to cause complaint."

"Mr. de Frassel," Josiah addressed the halfling in a tone of speech resembling a parental lecture, "you know full well that we at Coggsbury, Elliott, Chesterfield and Company are a moral company and your entourage of fallen persons of the weaker gender is not something with which Coggsbury, Elliott, Chesterfield and Company wish to be associated."

"Blah, blah, blah," Charles used his free hand to form a simple mocking puppet opening and closing its own "mouth" in time with Josiah's words while the halfling simply rolled his eyes in mocking annoyance.

11

This only seemed to raise Josiah's dander, who grew more parental in his mannerisms. "Mr. de Frassel, I trust you are aware that I am the representative of the wonderful company whose bountiful investment in your offer has made this whole venture possible in the first place. I will not be mocked.

"You were aware of the terms and conditions as laid out in your contract, which I might add, you signed quite readily. So I would ask that you at least conduct yourself with a modest amount of tact and decorum whilst we are on this journey."

"Fine." Charles extinguished his cigarette on the small tin dish where it expired with the rest of his spent butts and ash. "Can anyone then lend me some coin for another game?"

Hirim's eyebrow rose. "I thought you said you were a professional gambler." The Celetor now smiled wide. "Seems to me you've done nothing but lose – and quite badly at that – since you got on board. Why should anyone lend you anything?"

"Well, I would have won more if we had that bookworm in here," Charles' lips puffed out in a childish pout, "he'd be a push over to take coin from."

"I'll loan you some coin if it will shut you up for a while." Hirim proceeded to deal out the cards to the players, his smile fading as his card playing expression once again became firmly entrenched over his face.

"Thank you," the halfling bowed his head slightly though there was little to no actual gratitude in the words themselves.

"I'll win it back soon enough anyway," the Celetor chuckled.

The others joined him.

"Oh," Hirim looked the halfling in his bloodshot eyes, "and jester's wild."

"Your humor is quite profound," Charles shook his head as caustic lines etched into his face.

In a smaller room on one of the ship's lower decks, cluttered between chests, scrolls, and stacks of books, sat a Patrious elf named Mathias Onuis. Above him was the soft, dirty orange glow of an oil lantern that swayed ever so subtly from its resting place on a nail hammered into a thick beam overhead.

It was enough to see and even read by surprisingly – for the elf also had supplemented a tapered candle resting in a brass holder on his desk. The flickering illumination revealed the elf to be dressed in a simple gray robe that was of a darker gray than his gray-tinted alabaster skin, but complemented his high-strapped black leather sandals, pale sapphire eyes and short black hair quite nicely.

Mathias had been on board The Phoenix since its departure from Rexatious, where they had first stopped after leaving Breanna. Hired by the venturing gnomish company for his insight into old languages and grasp of ancient history, Mathias had been given the task of deciphering Charles' map. This map was the basis for the trip. The history of the map's arrival into the hands of the gnomes, and how the elf was brought into the matter, was quite interesting.

Charles had approached some gnomes on Breanna about a year ago with a moneymaking idea using the old document. The halfling was convinced that it lead to some kind of treasure and so had tried to entice the gnomes with the dream of great wealth. The gnomes, though, were a practical bunch and instead hired out a skilled translator they knew who was also an expert document crafter (Mathias) to guarantee the map's authenticity – it *was* coming from a halfling after all…

Once the map had been verified as authentic, Mathias was then able to get a few lines off the map that piqued the interest of the gnomes. A few lines of text near an island in the Northlands, which none knew existed before, were translated to read: 'The secret of eternal life here'. Naturally, the gnomes were more than willing to fund and assemble an exploratory venture with such documented motivation. After all, if they could corner the market on a product that would grant eternal youth and life, or in the very least keep folks from getting any older, then they would be rich indeed. Richer than the fabled tales of the gnomish race would even have everyone believe.

So Coggsbury, Elliott, Chesterfield and Company was formed after the three largest contributors of the venture whetted their pallets on the profits they would take in, should such an exploit indeed prove ample reward.

Following that, The Phoenix made it from its port in Breanna to Rexatious, continuing its path toward Talatheal where they picked up Corwyn, who had been asked to come on board in order to chronicle the event.

Coggsbury insisted on the action since he was also Corwyn's biggest promoter and supporter and liked the idea of his bread buttered on both sides. Though the company had hired Josiah Brookshire to represent their interests on the journey, Coggsbury didn't see any harm in safeguarding the safeguard. One could never have too much insurance after all, and Corwyn would no doubt be able to spin some clever tale of the adventure as well, from which Coggsbury would later profit when he was able to fund another tour for his favorite bard.

Besides, Coggsbury didn't like the idea of Charles being left alone with the map. His bold demand to share in the profits by being made a junior partner in the company was bad enough (thus the "company" part of Coggsbury, Elliott, and Chesterfield), but his insistence that he and he alone be keeper of the map and remain sole owner of it, served to be an annoying thorn in the gnomes' flesh. Best to keep an eye on him as well, and two sets of them are better then one where halflings are concerned.

Though Mathias had been with the crew almost since the beginning of the voyage, he didn't take much time to leave his quarters and fraternize with the others. His days were filled with reading and transcribing, recording what he had read, and then trying to pull out any meaning from it that he could. A scholar and scribe by trade, he didn't have that much of a grasp of social skills, nor did he put himself into too many places in where such talents might be needed. Had he known a little better how long this trip would be, or at least seem to be at this point in his journey, and the extra work that that was needed, he would have asked for more money.

As it was he knew now that the fee he asked of the gnomes was very cheap indeed. Now he could see why they had smiled so when he had proposed his offer. They had gotten a very good deal. That was the past, though, and he won't have any hope of claiming that coin until his return, which meant getting back to work and fleshing out more of the map and their eventual destination.

During the journey, Mathias had made great headway translating more of the ancient text on the map as well as compiling an interesting background on the island to which they were traveling. Though it was cobbled from myths and legends – hardly-rock solid proof – the tale emerging was still intriguing and insightful.

Apparently Nordicans had avoided the island for centuries. Only in the last three hundred years did a pair of adventuresome Nordicans make their way to the shores of Troll Island, another locality the Nordicans don't commonly frequent. This is where they found Charles' map. It had been buried in the skeleton of an ancient vessel long since beached, picked clean, and half submerged in the soupy beach like the remains of a decayed whale.

The explorers lost it later, in a game of cards with some fellow seamen who then took it south from there…and so it traveled about for some three-hundred years. That is, if what Charles had said was entirely true. He had declared how he wound up with the same document after winning it in another game of cards. The investors hadn't been able to verify how the halfling came into possession of the map or even its supposed origins. While the background story was a bit dubious, the map was authentic enough, however it came into the halfling's hands. Mathias was convinced of that.

The worn vellum map pointed to an unknown island farther north than Troll Island, making this landmass the most northern of all the Northlands. It was near this unnamed island that the text, which first so enthused the gnomes, was placed. The only problem was that the island didn't seem to exist…at least at first.

While few Midlandic and southern races claimed to have that much of an interest in the Northlands and their inhabitants to document much about these colder, and most say, barbaric lands, some however, managed to keep a splattering of records. Mathias had taken his own volumes with him on the voyage. It was a small sampling of his personal library – mainly a collection of guides and translations of various Nordic texts, as well as other volumes on the geography of the Northlands, and other books and scrolls the scribe thought would be helpful in his studies. Mathias had also been able to track down some Nordic legends supporting the claim to a small icy island being off the shores of Troll Island. He came by this information through a good handful of sources, many of which were located in the Great Library of Rexatious. Further research revealed that Nordicans called this island Sidmudsson's Isle or, in some renderings, Rainer's Island.

From what he had been able to gather so far, the island was small and almost totally covered with ice. None of his books or scrolls spoke of any Nordic sailor making landfall. Always, once sighted, they would sail around the island, steering well clear of its frosty shores. It was really a most interesting mystery. A mystery that Mathias was enjoying trying to unravel, when a rapping at the door brought his head up from the latest volume he'd been searching through for clues.

16

"Mathias?" Corwyn's voice came from the other side of the door. The elf spoke Telborous, as did all on the vessel to one another, since the language was something each shared in common.

"Yes," the elf looked up from his reading, "come in, Corwyn. I thought you were with the others playing cards." Mathias watched the bard enter the room.

"I got tired of winning and Charles' whining wasn't helping any." Corwyn made his way slowly through the doorframe; the interior of the elf's room was filled with all manner of material. It took a moment for the bard's eyes to adjust to the darker room. There were no windows in the rooms below and so the only light came from the dirty glow of the oil lamp and candle beside the elf. Subdued light and the earthy scent of old scrolls and books assailed Corwyn's senses

"Halflings…" Mathias mused dryly.

"I needed some fresh air too. Between those three chimneys I think I know what a smoked pig feels like now." Corwyn moved closer to the scholar, stepping over the precarious literary panorama that set pitfalls everywhere to snare his feet. His vision had sharpened and the aroma of time-seasoned books had started to lessen in intensity. "So have you made any more progress?

"I'm sorry I'm not able to offer up any new insight, but I'm not too well read on my Nordic myths and legends. A lot of the Northlands are still a mystery to me." Corwyn finally came to stand beside the elf, leaning over his shoulder to glance at what he was reading. "That's part of the reason I signed up for this journey – to learn more of the Northlands."

"And to keep an eye on things too, I'm sure." Mathias' face seemed to lighten from its normally serious expression as he looked into Corwyn's visage.

"I'm just helping him out, not *spying* for him, Mathias." Corwyn took some small delight in the increased levity (though still minor in the bard's definition) in the elf's visage. "Waylan Coggsbury can certainly take care of himself."

"No need to convince me of that." Mathias turned back to the book he'd been reading before the bard had entered. "He was the one who signed my agreement for payment. I don't think he'll be out on the street begging anytime soon."

"Did you find anything new yet?" The bard joined the elf's gaze at his book, trying also to change the subject a bit since he knew the matter of his compensation was a sore spot for the elf.

"I don't know that much more than when last we spoke," Mathias turned a page. "I've been able to get a few faint leads here and there, but nothing has panned out as of yet."

"The island is real though, right?" Corwyn looked up from the book at Mathias.

Mathias mimicked Corwyn's action. "Oh yes, the island is certainly real."

"Good." Corwyn did his best to move back a few steps from the elf's simple and squat desk, which the Patrious hunched over most of his waking hours. Somewhere in the room was a bed that the elf uncovered each night to rest his eyes and dream about finding more answers. "I'd hate to be on some wild goose chase or be lost somewhere in the middle of the Northlands."

"That remains to be seen," Mathias turned another page in his book. "The island may be real, but I can't vouch for any of the other things that we're seeking. It really seems more fantasy than reality."

"I thought followers of Dradin believed all things that they recorded." Corwyn spoke true, for he hadn't in all his years and travels met anyone who would believe what he was reading or recording was totally false. Even myths were seen by sages and priests of Dradin as holding some kernel of truth, or as once being true tales that have become misunderstood over time.

"Most do," Mathias confessed, "but I find a hard time in finding any truth to what we're going searching for. Even if there *was* an island and people lived there at one point in time, I doubt that we'd discover what your investor friends are searching for."

"Why not?" Corwyn's question pulled the elf away from his reading to have him look over at the bard. Corwyn was one person with whom the elf had found himself comfortable enough to engage in conversation. The bard was a good listener, and when he asked questions and took up a certain position, Mathias didn't feel like the bard was trying to argue a point to win a debate but to better understand a matter. Indeed, Corwyn might have made a fine sage.

"Because I believe we tend to romanticize history too much and that, over the years, people have tended to put their own take on certain things so as to make a history of their own choosing.

"Now, to be fair," Mathias' tone became very respectful, "the priests of Dradin and his followers have done a very good job at sifting through false history and true tales. The Great Library of Rexatious has been very helpful as well at keeping an accurate record, but what we're dealing with here is fragmented tales and dusty myths and legends."

"Legends that had enough conviction behind them to pull together the investors for this venture and hire you," Corwyn countered. "And you just said that you believe our destination to be real enough."

"Yes, the *destination*, but not necessarily the object we're going there to find," said Mathias. "Think about it for a moment logically, Corwyn. We're talking about the secret for eternal youth being hidden in some frozen island. Don't you think it sounds a bit far fetched?"

Corwyn conceded a bit with a soft sigh. "Yes, it may seem odd and perhaps unreal but what could it *really* be? That's what a true follower of Dradin would ask."

"Would they now?" Mathias' tone had turned a bit sardonic.

"What if..." Corwyn held his hands up to caution the scribe from responding just yet, "what if it really is something that helped to restore youth?"

"Then why has no one gone after it before now, save us?" the elf crossed his arms.

"Because they didn't know where to look and now *we* do." Corwyn replied.

"You have the makings of a good story there," the elf uncrossed his arms and made ready to get back to his work. "But I'll believe it when I see it… *if* I see it."

"Well, I don't want to give up hope just yet," Corwyn looked around the mass of materials that covered a great deal of the floor. "I think you have enough to head us in the right direction. I just hope that we're able to get there without getting lost."

"We won't be. Not if Hirim can keep the course the map conveys. We should reach it just fine."

"Great." Corwyn backed up his steps once more, meandering over the vellum valleys and hardbound mountains with graceful strides. "Say, it's bound to be dinnertime soon. You want to get out and have some food on deck with me?"

"Thank you, but no, I have to keep at this." Mathias returned to his book. "The firmer the factual footing I can create, the better it will be for all of us."

Corwyn managed to make it back to the door without disturbing the contents of the room, then turn around once he had the door itself in hand, using it to steady himself as the vessel shuddered for a moment, which also caused a greater sway with the lantern above the scribe's head for a few heart beats. Corwyn had almost gotten his sea legs, but every so often he'd be reminded he was still new to the ocean. At least the salty sea air was a welcome change from the stale aroma of the elf's room.

"You've been in here since I've been on board. Stay any longer and you'll start to sprout roots. I'll have to call you a potato."

"I'm fine, *really*." Mathias didn't look up from his book, "I was hired to do a job, and I intend to see it through to the end."

"Are you sure you don't need any more help?" asked the bard. "I can come back later and try to narrow the search. Maybe I could clear up some things with what I do know."

"That's okay. It's easier to have just one person in here at a time." Mathias motioned around the cramped chambers, letting the clutter add weight to his words, slightly peering up from the tome as he did so. "Besides, I work better alone."

"You sure?" Corwyn softly persisted.

"I'm sure." The elf's eyes and thoughts returned fully to the book.

"Okay, let me know if you change your mind." Corwyn closed the door behind him.

"I will," Mathias, answered absentmindedly, his attention fully engrossed in the book before him.

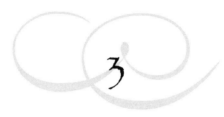

The next night, all of Hirim's guests were invited to a meal to celebrate the commencement of this second part of their voyage. It was a simple affair, with fresher food than they would be eating for the rest of the trip, and a welcome respite before the monotony of life at sea would return. The celebration took place in the room off the captain's private residence, which had been renovated somewhat to allow comfortable seating for all five of Hirim's guests plus himself. The spread was plain but favorable – steaming hot, wooden bowls of stew set before all six of the five occupied seats. Some loaves of bread were also in the center of the table – the freshest among the batch they had just acquired from Elandor.

"I say we start without him," Charles stared down at his bowl with eager eyes, careful not to get ashes from his cigarette into it. He didn't know what was in it, but it didn't smell half bad, and after weeks at sea with nothing even remotely appetizing, he couldn't wait to take his fill.

"Give him just a little more time," Corwyn advised, "I'm sure he'll show."

Corwyn again found himself contending with the incessant smoking of his dining companions, but he thought he could manage for a short while given that both windows in the room were now open. There was enough of a breeze flowing inside to toss about the growing haze and allow some fresh air access – much to the relief of the bard's lungs. The pungent smell of the stew also helped to keep the choking fumes from getting any nearer his nose. He had to admit, the aroma rising from the bowl beneath him half tempted him to side with the halfling. He was a bit hungry himself.

All of them had come to be seated around the table save Mathias. Corwyn had made a strong effort to convince him of the benefits of leaving his room for at least one night and enjoy a change of scenery. The food had been served about ten minutes before and the courtesy of waiting was wearing thin.

"I don't think we should wait forever, though, Mr. Danther," Josiah was trying his best to look relaxed and unaffected by the meal before him, but Corwyn knew the gnome was as hungry as the rest of them. With rationed food and journeys, such as this they were on, the mind tended to take an extra large degree of time mediating upon food and its consumption or lack thereof. The gnome's pipe was his only consolation for the moment and he was taking full advantage of it.

"I'm sure he's just–" Corwyn was interrupted by Mathias' entrance.

"Finally," Charles turned around to watch the scribe make his way to the open high-backed wooden chair beside Corwyn, "you forget the way up here?"

"I just had a few last minute things to attend to," Mathias sat down before his bowl and empty wooden mug.

"Now that we're all here," Hirim bent down to pick up a jug that rested beside him, "I think it's time we had a toast to set this evening off right and incur the continued good graces of Perlosa."

Hirim gently placed the jug down on the table, pulled the cork out of the clay vessel and grinned. "A fine vintage of port that I picked up when I first bought this ship." He proceeded to pour a small amount into his cup. "I've kept it with me to savor at times and thought it fitting that since this is the farthest that The Phoenix has ever sailed, tonight would a proper time to have some."

"Now you're talking," Charles' eyes lit up.

"To savor," Hirim's eyes hammered the point home to the halfling, "not to drink bone dry."

All the men in to room let out a tremendous roar of laughter.

Hirim then rose and proceeded to pour out a small portion of the wine in each diner's mug. When he had finished his stroll around the table, he re-corked the jug, placed it back down beside him, and seated himself once again.

"A toast then," Hirim removed his cigar from his mouth, keeping it in his left hand while he raised his right for the toast, "to fair seas and prosperous ventures."

The others raised their mugs and repeated in unison, "fair seas and prosperous ventures!"

This done, each drank down the swallow of port.

Hirim returned his cigar to his smiling mouth. "Fine stuff, eh?"

"A most well-rounded flavor," Josiah nodded as he took the final pleasing puff from his pipe before placing it beside his meal to cool down.

"I've had better really," the halfling flatly offered his opinion.

"So how long have you had this ship?" Corwyn asked, as the others present ignored the halfling's critique.

"Close to twenty years now." Hirim put out his cigar by pinching it between his thumb and index finger. "Some days it seems longer, others like I only just got it yesterday." He placed his half used stogie beside his wooden spoon.

"Can we *eat* now?" Charles' tone had become an almost caustic whine.

"This would be one of those *long* days," Hirim picked up his wooden spoon at the side of his dish.

Charles had his answer and started to dig into the stew with reckless abandon. He would have swallowed his half spent cigarette too if he hadn't remembered to take it out of his mouth and extinguish it by crumbling it out on the table. He would have used the tin plate he had early in the card game, but it wasn't on the table at the time.

The others, as they did so far and would for most of the voyage to come, tried not to think too much of Charles or even remind themselves that he was there. It may have been rude and a bit cruel, but in so doing they were able to make it through his company fairly well.

"How long have you been a bard?" Hirim asked between bites.

"I've been back in the Midlands now for little over two years but I've been a bard, getting trained and practicing my skills, for the better part of ten years." Corwyn was pleased with the stew; it was hearty with chunks of beef, potato, and carrots and had a mild but pleasing seasoning.

"You have to be trained to tell stories, eh?" Charles wiped his mouth with the back of his hand.

Corwyn swallowed, "Yes, if you want to be good at it, you'll seek out training; not just that but musical training and voice lessons and basic knowledge of myths and legends."

"Pah," the halfling dismissively waved the notion away with the same hand that he had just recently used as a napkin. "Waste of money if you ask me. So that all we going to get to drink tonight, Hirim?"

Hirim bent down to pick up something at the side of his chair and pulled up another ceramic jug. It looked newer and slimmer than the one he had pulled up before, but also by the heft it seemed to carry in the Celetor's hand, told all that it was full.

"There," he placed it on the table near the bread with a heavy thud.

Charles bent over the top of the table in an attempt to struggle for the jug. It was just out of his reach, however.

"Here," Mathias picked up the jug and put it before the halfling's searching hands.

"Aha," the halfling pulled out the cork with his child-like fingers.

"Just remember that it's for *all* of us tonight," Hirim warned the stubbly, sallow-faced man.

Charles looked over to the captain with a petulant gaze. "I know, I know." He proceeded to lift the jug from the table and then after some skillful maneuvering, filled his mug to the brim.

"Is there anything of note that you have discovered in your studies Mr. Oni–"

"Hey," Charles' cry brought all eyes back to him, "what kinda game you playing Hirim? This is *water!*"

"What did you think it would be? *Wine?*" Hirim chuckled.

"Yeah," Charles bluntly replied.

"Not tonight." Hirim reached out for a hunk of bread and tore off a piece, returning what was left of the loaf to the table. "For one night, you can be sober."

Charles' face contorted into a scowl but he said nothing else, merely took to finishing his stew.

"As I was saying," Josiah started his previous chain of thought, "have you found anything of note in your studies thus far, Mr. Onius?"

"Not anything more than I've already told you." Mathias took a piece of bread for himself.

"I for one am most intrigued by the notion of this venture," Josiah sat back a moment to dwell in the thought he unleashed upon the group. "Think about what could be at stake, and your mind does indeed travel far in the field of speculation."

"Immortality," Josiah took the jug of water from the grumbling halfling and filled his mug as he spoke. "What wonders one could work and see and even accomplish, I dare say, if one could indeed not have to worry about his best years slipping away from him."

"Do you want to know what *I'd* do with immortality?" Charles butted into the discussion, his former grumbling abated.

"No." Hirim took the jug as Josiah offered it to him.

"And why not?" Charles had finished his stew now and was reaching for some bread of his own.

"Because I'm trying to enjoy my meal," returned the captain.

Charles had managed to secure his own loaf and was angrily ripping it about as he spoke. "I sense a real fear of imagination here. I bet you couldn't think of *half* as many things to do with immortality as me."

"Let's just take your word for it," Hirim shuffled the challenge under his concern, passing the jug over to Corwyn who took it and filled his own mug.

"I'm sure it would be something in keeping with your character," Corwyn tried to be as tactful as he could to distill the hostilities growing between the table guests.

Charles stopped for a moment, letting the crust of the bread he'd been gnawing on like a dog with a bone rest in his mouth. He wasn't sure what to make of what was being said. Was it a compliment or an insult? He hadn't gotten to know the bard that well since he came on board, and was unsure of just how to read him. Finally the halfling decided that he must have been paid a compliment because no one was laughing at the bard's words. That had to be a sign of something in his favor then.

"Yes, it would," Charles answered without the courtesy of removing the hunk of bread from his mouth.

This brought a round of laughter from the others to which Charles snarled. He had come to loathe being the butt of the humor in these encounters. Although, he like others of his race, had come to accept it as the fate of all truly misunderstood, enlightened people who lived in a barbarous land with savages around every tree. It was still a bit irksome since he had no real place to hide from it save his personal quarters – and he was already stir crazy from staring at those four walls all the way from Rexatious to Talatheal.

"So did you learn any good tales in your training?" Hirim asked Corwyn.

"Yes, many in fact," the bard handed the jug to Mathias.

"Then why not share some with us tonight, something that might fit with our current adventure."

Corwyn nodded. "I think I have a few tales that might just fit that request…"

And so Corwyn started to spin a tale that ran into another and then another as the hours grew late and the company departed for their cabins to rest. For tomorrow would be another day of travel, and home to the same scenery for several weeks until they made their way into the colder waters of the Northlands.

Weeks later, The Phoenix was still at sea and Charles was growing stir crazy…and the crew was growing crazy from Charles. Occasionally Corwyn would pull out his worn cherry wood lute and strum a few songs, which would distract the halfling for a spell.

With such encouragement, Charles frolicked while singing his bawdy halfling melodies, which Corwyn reluctantly did his best to play as per the diminutive man's requests. This would only last for a few short hours as Corwyn couldn't stomach the constant barrage of profane songs without getting sick of the halfling's company. Not to mention the short fellow's span of focused attention to one matter was compressed to say the least. It was almost as if Charles was a child when it came to keeping his attention focused on one thing before declaring his boredom to all present.

So it was that he was soon bored again and growing more bored with each passing day. He made sure to let every crewman know of his increasing boredom too. After all, they had a responsibility to keep the halfling entertained. He was the junior partner of this expedition and they were working for him, weren't they? Moreso, Charles was running low on wine (he would easily drink what he had been rationed for the day) and he was down to a few fat handfuls of cigarettes. He had smoked so many already that he now had to ration these as well… and he was not too thrilled about this development either.

The constant complaints of the shortage of drink and cigarettes, compounded with Charles' rants and groans, were wearing thin on all. One crewmen, a Napowese sailor well known by all the crew for his calm, controlled nature, nearly got into a fight with the halfling as Charles' whining continued. Only when the first mate, a strong-bodied Napowese named Chang, intervened by holding back the other sailor, was the halfling saved from being gutted with the other's knife.

Hirim had reached the point of sending the halfling off in one of the rowboats and have him fend for himself, but was held back by Josiah. The gnome had rebuked such pleasant fancies by touting the banner of contractual obligations, which was starting to drive Hirim mad at how often it had to be repeated to stay his hand from other similar actions. Even with the tension, all on board had so far managed to put up with the halfling's most colorful antics before the wine rationing, antics such as running around the upper deck stark naked and drunk claiming to be "the wind of fortune"; "enlightening" the crew as to why the halfling culture was so great and worthy of world dominance and why they were so inferior and weak before it; and later even trying to light his own gaseous emissions – which actually proved quite dangerous when a flame took hold of some nearby rigging.

While the others dreaded the daily incidents of their shorter companion under restrained stress, Mathias had been able to update them more to what he had discovered on the map, along with its possible origins and nature of the island itself. As they neared the Northlands, it would be crucial they know which way to go in order to make sure that they didn't end up in The Crown of the World and worse yet, sail onto the other side of the globe where there was nothing but an empty, watery expanse.

Once every few days the scribe would brief the group as to his findings. Some days were more fruitful than others. Today was a day of slim offerings. The elf was getting low on notes and tomes and was feeling the pressure now to deliver his answers to the others gathered around the table in the room off the captain's quarters.

"That's it?" Charles questioned. His face was twisted with a vine of smooth, white smoke as he clenched a half spent cigarette in his teeth (he'd been trying to make it last as long as he could that morning). Josiah had refrained from using his pipe, as he wanted to set a better example for the halfling who seemed to be suffering too much over the rationing of his addiction.

"That's all I have been able to discover in the last few days, yes." Mathias continued, feeling the weight on his back grow heavier from the unspoken disappointment hanging about the room.

"Well, I better get some big pay off here for being put through this dreadfully awful trip. Had I had been allowed to take on my entourage, I wouldn't be as bored as I am now. And I dare say captain, your crew, you, and the rest of you would have benefited as well," the halfling unleashed a nasally chuckle. "Course getting to live forever might not be a bad trade off too, should we find what we're looking for."

"You have already been compensated for the map you have provided to make this venture in the first place, Mr. de Frassel," Josiah bristled beneath his calm and dignified demeanor, "and, I would like to stress that you are indeed looking at a healthy compensation for your investment in any shared profits Coggsbury, Elliott, Chesterfield and Company will experience."

"It's not that bad, gentlemen," Corwyn voiced some optimism.

The others all turned to him as the bard pulled the map closer to himself on the table, turning it so that the others could see it better as he spoke. He had been learning a new part of the puzzle from the frequent updates from Mathias and snippets of conversations he'd had with the elf over the past weeks at sea.

"Now we already know, from what Mathias has told us, that the place is off Troll Island. We also know that the Nordicans supposedly avoided it for unknown reasons, which would mean, if true, that it has probably not been disturbed since this map was created.

"So that means whatever is there probably hasn't been touched in centuries," the bard looked over to the stubble-faced halfling, "so your profits, Charles, and all those involved, are more than secure."

"I still need some bearings to go on." Hirim jabbed a finger at the drawing of Troll Island on the map. "I can't trust this map to be totally accurate and I don't want to end up getting lost in the Northlands or going over The Crown of the World."

"I believe, Mr. Koofehi, that we all share such a sentiment," said the gnome.

"Right," Corwyn looked over the map once more. "I'm more interested in trying to figure out what this island is supposed to have on it. Mathias has almost exhausted his books and scrolls and has yet to come across anything to help us along, save vague rumors that offer nothing in the way of additional clues."

"We can just as easily find out what is on the island when we get there," Charles chided the bard as one would a dumb child.

"I don't think that would be wise, really. What if there is something there we should be aware of? I mean, this map says it holds the key to eternal life or some such thing," Corwyn raised his gaze, "if that's true, won't such a thing be guarded or protected in some way? *I* would guard something like that if it were *me*."

"So what are you proposing, Mr. Danther?" Josiah was studying the bard now, as were the rest in the room.

Corwyn turned toward the gnome beside him. "I think we should stop off at one of the Valkorian Islands to try and gather some more information before we get to the island. Perhaps we could even get better bearings from the locals."

Hirim stroked his mustache in thought; Charles took a long drag; Mathias was silent; and Josiah stared down at the map.

After a moment, Hirim spoke, "That does make sense. How about it, Josiah? You think the company would be willing to take a little detour?"

"Speaking as its representative, I can say that while the merits of the idea might be sound enough, we would open ourselves up to the possibility of losing our unique claim on the find." The gnome was about to fish out his pipe when he stopped his hand in mid-movement, mindful of the halfling's eyes on him. Josiah wanted to be known as the more disciplined between them.

"We would be risking not only our claim on what we are seeking, but open ourselves up to the possible hostilities of the Nordicans." Josiah looked up at Mathias first and then gazed across the rest of the table as he finished speaking. "Having read accounts of their savage nature – even going so far as to attack their own kin for basic supplies – I think it wise to avoid contact with them altogether."

Charles mused as he extinguished the last of his cigarette in the tin dish that had been cleaned out from when last he used it so to better take in more of the halfling's vices. He had been able to make it last longer than he thought; perhaps he wouldn't be out of cigarettes as soon as he had expected. "I hear the Nordicans have lovely maidens – *giants* of women – but I'd be more than happy to climb *that* mountain. Maybe we all could do with some shore leave just for some recreation. Wouldn't even have to tell them what we were after."

"The matter has been decided, Mr. de Frassel," Josiah firmly replied.

"Mathias?" Corwyn's voice directed all to turn the Patrician scribe. "You've been pretty quiet over there. This all seem okay to you? I could help you gather some information from what you still have to look over I suppose, but I'm not as skilled with the Nordic language as you."

"Still," Corwyn sighed, "it's better than nothing if we aren't going to be allowed access to any possibly new information."

"I suppose," the elf's voice was dry and low. "An extra pair of eyes would be helpful. Maybe I missed something."

"How much longer till we get to Troll Island?" Corwyn asked Hirim.

"We're probably about three more weeks out if the weather and winds hold," he replied as he looked down at a series of maps – the halfling's among them – scattered around the top of the table.

"Three weeks?" Charles whined. "I'm going to be stuck here for *three more weeks*?"

"Believe me, we feel the same way," Hirim muttered to the halfling.

"Hey, you all haven't been the best of shipmates, either," the halfling snipped.

"That's the longest it could take, Charles," the bard tried his best to calm the situation with his words, "it could be much faster than that too."

"If we had a priest of Endarien or Perlosa on board it would be," said Hirim, "we don't though so we'll just have to rely upon both gods' favor without a priest to call their blessings our way. So far they have been more than gracious since we left Rexatious."

"I think I can speak for all, Mr. Koofehi, when I say I look forward to a safe and rapid final trek to our destination. Mr. Onuis, I expect both you and Mr. Danther to be able to come up with a little bit more from the tomes you still have to go through. Any small fraction of insight could be of great benefit if it provides a better picture of what this island is all about. I'm sure, with the added help the process will go much better, as I have faith and confidence in both of your abilities."

"Don't you want anything from me, gnome?" Charles smiled with sarcastic delight. He already knew the answer but just wanted to entertain himself by pestering the gnome.

"To be honest, Mr. de Frassel, if you could find something to safely contain yourself and hold your interest, I would be very supportive of such an endeavor." Josiah looked toward the halfling with a dry expression.

"I see." The halfling studied the gnome with an amused eye.

"I am told that reading is quite the most powerful of pastimes one can undertake," Josiah continued.

"*Reading*?" Charles' face and head slouched forward off his shoulders.

"Yes, reading. Of course, someone of your…immense appetites might find it better still to write," Josiah was as congenial as he could be.

"Write what?" Charles was interested now in both the idea and to hear what the gnome might say next.

"Well, perhaps a log of the journey thus far," Josiah rubbed his chin in thought.

"I thought the Telborian was doing that," Charles nodded over to Corwyn who was raising from his seat alongside the others around the table.

"He is…" Josiah raised himself from the table as well now; Charles following suit, "but maybe yours can be from another point of view, or you could even write a story." The others were now leaving the captain's room one by one as the two diminutive figures conversed.

"Write a story, eh?" The halfling's face entertained an odd humor, which twisted up the side of his face in a lopsided grin. "That would be something, wouldn't it?"

"It certainly could be. I myself know of no modern day halfling writers. Perhaps you might be the first one to gain the world's attention." Josiah himself now stood up and made his way out of the meeting room.

"Well, you don't get out much, Josiah," Charles leapt down from the chair to follow the gnome.

"Hmph. That may be. Why, with what your mind can come up with I am sure you will find the weeks just passing by like flocks of birds."

"Ah, why not write? I mean it's about time true culture and proper tales were put into the public square, right? And who better to do so than the most cultured race in the world. It's about time halflings reclaimed this portion of life too."

The two left the empty room and stepped into the new day beyond. Charles followed Josiah, whose own face was a mix of joy and a small amount of squeamishness.

"I even have a title: 'Charles the Great and The Ship of Fools'." Charles chest now stuck out in pride for the work he had yet to create.

"Oh my… that is… certainly *boldly* original, Mr. de Frassel," Josiah fumbled over his tongue.

"Yes it is, isn't it?" Charles nodded in obvious pleasure. "Now I just need a plot…"

" So we know what this means then…for the most part," Corwyn was back in Mathais' room looking over the map resting on his lap, "but what about these things?" He was seated at the bed that had been cleared off for the two of them to work. He had learned to get used to the smell of old books and scrolls, but had added another oil lamp, hanging a few beams over, closer to where he sat. The extra light did much to help in his searching.

"What things?" Mathias looked over from where he sat at his desk with a pile of books and scrolls wrapped about his feet and a few good-sized volumes on the desk.

"These black spots?" Corwyn turned the map to face the elf so he could get a better idea. "Here," Corwyn's fingers pointed to a small section toward the top right of the map.

"I just assumed those were ink spots," said the elf, "or stains. I don't see or have read anything yet that would lead me to think otherwise."

Corwyn turned the map back around to see it once again, "Just a thought."

"I hope this isn't too inconvenient for you," the bard took to studying the map again as he spoke. "I didn't want to impose, even if Hirim said–"

"No," Mathias cut the bard's thought off, "it was needed. Hirim was right for having us work together. I'm not going to get all the answers before we need them; that's apparent now. So it's a good thing you're willing to help as you have been this last week."

Corwyn didn't like the defeated tone he heard in the elf's voice and felt partially to blame for it. In a way he was muscling in on the scribe's domain and probably making him feel even less useful, since Corwyn was more or less causing him to second guess everything. Not to mention that Mathias was helping to tutor him in the Nordic language so Corwyn could be a better help to the scribe.

"I know this can't be that much of a joy for you, Mathias, and I know I'm probably slowing you down more than I'm helping. I don't want to get in your way or impede you in anyway. I already do that enough by having you help me read these documents."

"Yes and no," Mathias replied, "in helping you I help myself by going over the things once more and making sure they've been combed through for any hints and leads."

"Have you changed your mind yet?" Corwyn's curiosity spilled into his words.

"About what?" Mathias was caught off guard by the bard's question.

"About the truth of what we're looking for," said Corwyn. "When I first came on board you said you didn't think that it existed."

"And, to be honest, I still don't believe it to be something real," Mathias turned back to studying at his desk. "A nice allegory or story perhaps, but nothing real."

"But it has to be based on something – some kernel of truth," Corwyn persisted.

"Ever the romantic, eh?" Mathias turned a page of the book he was studying. He was getting pretty close to the end of this one and still hadn't found anything noteworthy.

"I'd like to think I'm more of an optimist," Corwyn stood up from the bed to stretch. He'd been hard at work assisting Mathias as best he could for hours now and needed to move around a bit. "So then why are you on this ship if you don't think what we're seeking is even real?"

Mathias looked over his shoulder at the bard, "I needed the money."

Corwyn nodded in understanding.

"I'm a bit of a practical man myself, I guess," Mathias confessed. "Though it isn't that great an amount of pay, it is still some coin and at the time I needed it."

"So you're more *mercenary* than *scribe* it would seem," Corwyn joshed Mathias with a lopsided grin.

"Perhaps," Mathias returned to his studies, "but then that would put me in good company since all here are doing this for the money and the hope of greater rewards still to come."

"Not all of us are," Corwyn corrected the elf hoping that his ribbing wasn't taken the wrong way. "I'm not here to turn a profit, but I am curious to see just what might await us on that island."

"Probably nothing." Mathias had started to grow tired of this speculation of what could be or must be hidden away and awaiting them. He just wanted to read his books and scrolls and do what he was hired to do.

"So you really think nothing is there?" Corwyn wouldn't let the scribe flee into his studies so easily.

Mathias kept his eyes on the text before him as he replied. "I think something might very well be there, but it won't be the secret to eternal youth or life or anything like that. That sort of thing is impossible."

Corwyn's face showed the uncertainty he felt at the scribe's words. It was almost too amazing to believe. "But we live in a world where wizards and priests and all sorts of creatures and things hidden and yet to be discovered from the dawn of time reside. The gods have made many strange and wonderful things. The stories of the Ancients and the Titans before them speak about a whole host of wonders they took part in, created, and used. How can you think nothing will be there? There *has* to be something, maybe even the very thing we're seeking."

"Spoken like a bard," Mathias looked over again at Corwyn.

Though it was flatly stated, Corwyn didn't take the comment as anything spiteful but rather a compliment.

"I just don't see the world like you do, Corwyn. You live in a place of pleasant fiction and fantasies. I do believe in the gods and know about priests and wizards and the powers they have, but that doesn't mean that everything that has been spoken or written down over the years is real or true.

"If you can show me something – something tangible, then I'll believe it, but if you ask me to take too great a leap of faith then I just can't do it. I know the gods are real, for I see the power of their priests. I know the wizards have power as well for I've seen that too. However, there is no real documented proof or evidence for what we seek. We only have some old tales, legends, and myths to go on. That's all. No trusted eyewitness accounts, no documented evidence of what we seek, beyond proof that the island exists. Nothing."

Corwyn stood there for a moment, letting the words of the scribe penetrate his thinking. He could see the scribe's position and was in truth, sorry that the two of them had this difference of opinion on the matter, but wasn't going to let it come between them in trying to figure out what it was they were seeking. He also knew that it was pointless to carry the conversation any further without risking some offense or argument that wouldn't be productive for any of them.

"Then I guess I'll just have to be the optimist for both of us." The bard made his way over to a book on top a pile beside the elf. "Now what else can I help you with?"

Mathias pulled out a piece of parchment. "If you can verify these dates I've found in those old reference documents and then…"

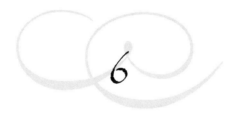

The Phoenix skirted the cold and empty coasts of Troll Island. In these northern waters, the pale, lifeless waves were tipped with frost. The temperature had changed greatly in just the past few days as they crossed into the Sea of Glass, taking on a colder snap than what many had expected; it would only grow colder still as they came closer to their destination. It was just reaching spring in the Northlands, but the chill of the past winter wouldn't let go of the lands just yet and one more blustery wind was sure to come with the final snowstorm of the season.

The weather would hold for only a while longer until the harsher winds would pick up in the weeks to come, one season forcing out another. This gave the crew the needed window to locate their hidden mystery, time to discover it and start back before the two seasons clashed, making their return trip a bit more difficult.

Hirim didn't want to sail too close to the island and so kept his distance. He thought it wise to heed the old Nordic sailors who thought it best to steer as clear from the Troll-infested land as they could. The frigate remained well enough away from the island. It was just close enough to see in the partially hidden, melted bronze sun, but not in striking distance of anyone or thing that might make their lair close to the shore or shallow waters near its thick, pine-forested coast.

The pace was slow going, the winds weak and conflicting the further north they went; small flurries of snow dusted the crew and deck in fluffy frenzies of flakes. It was soon cold enough to see small chunks of ice bobbing up and down in the water beside them. They were reaching the fabled Crown of the World – the very place where it was said one could look to one side of himself and see the endless of expanse of water that was said to dominate the other half of Tralodren,

With the frosted air and water, The Phoenix creaked and groaned more in protest of the climate. It seemed the colder it grew, even the weakest of sounds seemed to grow in volume. Whispers carried further, the clamor on deck was all the louder, and every movement of the ship – from the flapping of the sails, the creaking of timber – even the movement of the rigging – seemed to be greatly amplified from even a week before.

All the crew and guests had donned winter weather garb to stem off the harsh elements: fur-lined coats, boots, thick woolen tunics, mittens, and padded leather pants. All had also taken to doing what they could to keep out of the wind; this proved hard to do as it seemed to come at them from some new angle every few minutes or so in this chaotic mesh of seasonal disputes. It didn't take long for red noses and checks to bloom amid the crewman and even the passengers. Facial hair was soon matted with hoarfrost and dripping mucus quickly trickled out from frigid noses, adding to chapped nostrils and lips.

The crew kept themselves busy to stem off the nipping wolves of ice that frolicked in the open air. Many had to continually work their fingers, keeping the digits fluid enough to be able to keep up their work lest they find themselves with numb hands of ice instead of flesh.

None of the crew spoke, saving their energy for keeping warm and sucking back the runny rivers of snot that never seemed to slow in its flow. A focus on duty held them together as well as the commands of their captain and his lieutenant.

They had almost reached the end of the known world, skating just below the line of denotation dividing the Northlands from what lay beyond: the farthest expanse of water that anyone could ever conceive. Hirim looked over the waves with his spy glass, orange woolen scarf flapping in the light breeze from around his neck.

"I don't see anything yet," his voice was grim.

"My calculations *have* to be correct," Mathias stood beside him, fur-lined hood drawn tight about his face, map in mitten-covered hand as he made triple sure of his work. "Corwyn and I went over this map with a fine toothed comb to be totally sure."

"Well I don't see anything," Hirim passed over the rocky outline of Troll Island with his spyglass. He only spied tall, dark pines and mountains creating a fence impenetrable to the naked eye. Nothing that matched anything on the map so as to give him a reference point to where this hidden island was suppose to be located.

"It should be just two leagues north of Troll Island…" Mathias continued.

"Well, we've gone *seven*," the captain collapsed the spyglass as he turned to look down at the elf.

"Let me see that again," the Celetor took the map from the elf's hands with a rough tug.

"Hey, be careful with that now," Charles whined in-between shivers. He'd shoved both mitten-covered hands under his armpits and was focusing all his energy on just trying to stay warm. He was cold – almost frozen solid – but wouldn't dare leave the map out of his sight. No, he'd tough it out as best he could. With the limitation on his drink and cigarettes that would have helped him through this experience, he found it even more challenging to keep warm. In this dedicated behavior to defending himself from the cold, he had managed to give the crew a small respite from his more usually disruptive behavior. The crew, however, had little time to enjoy it for they were constantly at work to clean the snow off the deck and keep the rigging free from any ice that might be forming. It was a welcome respite from the halfling's complaining nonetheless.

"Are you sure you calculated correctly?" Josiah huffed on his pipe beside them on the upper forecastle where he, Charles, Corwyn, and Mathias were all nestled closely together like chicks for warmth.

"Positive," Mathias turned to Josiah, "I've done the work ten times now…it's all come up the same."

"Corwyn can verify my efforts."

"He's right," Corwyn defended Mathias, "it should be here."

"Hmph," Josiah let out a fat puff of smoke.

"Well *this* is exciting," Charles grinned sardonically through some infrequent shivers.

"You're just lucky we haven't tossed you overboard yet," Hirim spat at the halfling.

"Well it's about as useful as an empty cask of wine. We don't even know where we're going," the halfling cussed from chapped lips.

"Might I see the map again?" Corwyn addressed the captain. "I don't see how, but we must have missed something. Maybe I can find it."

"Why not?" He handed it over to the bard, resigned to their fate. "Not much good it is doing us now."

"There's not much more to see here either." Hirim leaned over the railing of the forecastle, pondering over the frosty water.

Meanwhile, Corwyn devoured the map with his eyes. Though he had looked over the map already for many an hour with Mathias, as he had been advised to do both by Hirim and Josiah, he tried one last time, hoping to find something that he had overlooked, perhaps misinterpreted... He saw the old inked outlines of the Northlands: Baton, Troll Island, Frigia, and Valkoria; the waves around them and the island off the coast of Troll Island...off the coast and near some other specks on top of the map...

"Mathias, did you ever make any sense of these specks up here?" The bard's eyes looked up from his searching.

"What specks?" the elf moved closer to the bard.

"These here, the ones I asked you about but we couldn't seem to make heads or tails of," Corwyn pointed out a dusting of dark dots toward the top end of the map, a good distance from Troll Island, but still something to consider nonetheless. The three others were now intently watching the discussion between the Telborian and Patrious with mild interest.

"I just thought they were ink splatters...they aren't labeled nor could I find reference to them in any of the books or scrolls." Mathias shrugged. "Why, do you think they're important?"

"I didn't think so at the time but now I think they're something *very* important," the bard nodded.

"Look here," Corwyn pointed to the mysterious island they were trying to discover, "the map has it listed as being no more than two leagues from Troll Island, right?"

"Correct," Mathias' face was unemotional. They had gone over all this so many times it was just cut and dry rehashes of old conversations.

"But what if the island was there when the map was made but now has drifted off?" The bard took in the face of the scribe who seemed lost now to the suggestion.

"Drifted off?" Mathias shook his head, "Now you're just wasting time."

"No, I'm not. Think about it a moment." Corwyn lowered the map so that it rested at his side as they spoke.

"I've never heard of an island just floating away on its own," Hirim added his thoughts to the conversation.

"It could be magical," Josiah countered, "for all we know the whole thing could be a magical island. If it holds eternal life on it then it probably would have some type of magic to it."

"*Magic*?" Mathias addressed the gnome with doubt in his voice. "Now don't go start telling some bard's tale as well…"

"Not magic," Corwyn stated, "but a large piece of ice and debris."

"You haven't been drinking, have you?" Charles frowned.

Corwyn ignored the halfling, as did everyone else.

"Listen, I read a few old sagas from Mathias' books that claimed large blocks of ice float around the water toward the top of The Crown of the World before they disappear over onto the other side of Tralodren. A similar tale was even mentioned in Argos when I was being trained. It was one of the few tales the college verified as truthful from the Northlands."

"So?" Charles thinly parted his lips to let out a frustrated sigh.

Corwyn continued. "If the island isn't here then it must be something like those ice chunks and floated away."

"Either that or he read the map wrong," Charles glared up at Mathias.

"Or there never may have been an island in the first place," said Josiah. "We have to come to that possibility of thinking as well gentlemen, should we understand the nature of this venture in full. There might never have been an island at all and this whole expedition might have been conducted in vain."

All fell silent for a moment, letting the gravity of the gnome's words hit them full in the head and then travel down into their heart and gut. None wanted it to be true, but pragmatism was of some virtue and powerful in the face of this present discouragement.

"I don't think your employers would put so much effort and money into this enterprise if they didn't believe, after they had checked it out on their own, that there was a very tangible possibility the island was real." Corwyn's words brightened the mood some, but not by much.

"It may not be *here,*" Corwyn peered at Josiah's face, "but what's the harm in looking just a little further? Let's just look a little ways ahead, till we get to these ice flows and then see if there is anything there.

"If we don't find anything, then we could turn around. Why not be thorough for your employers in this matter?" the bard pressed the gnome.

Josiah puffed on his pipe for a moment, holding the smoke inside in an attempt to warm up his insides, while he thought for a few heartbeats, before letting it out once more with this answer, "Why not indeed, Mr. Danther."

"I'm still not going over to the other side of the world chasing after floating ice chunks," Hirim firmly stated.

"Not at all, Captain. Simply in their direction; no further." Josiah eased Hirim's disposition, "I have no desire myself to see such a spectacle as the other side of the world. I may have an entrepreneurial soul, but I am no fool."

Hirim huffed as he made his way down the forecastle toward the upper deck, shouting orders to his crew to take their course further north. Josiah looked up at the bard as the captain did so.

"It still might not exist," the mustached Celetor grew calm again.

"Where's your sense of optimism?" Corwyn smiled and turned to look out over the water.

"So then how come I never made the connection you just did?" Mathias joined the bard in looking out toward the water.

"I'm sure you would have in time," Corwyn handed the map back to the elf.

"Perhaps," the scribe sighed, "but I just can't shake the feeling that you saved this whole expedition and you weren't even paid to do it. I should have seen what you did. Even with all my books and learning I was blind."

Corwyn turned back to the elf with a soft expression, "It was just a suggestion. I could be wrong. There could be nothing there but snow and ice."

Mathias absently nodded as Corwyn returned to his gazing.

"So what was the tale they told you in Argos?" Mathias asked.

"It was a tale of a giant slayer, Erik the Tall. It's a saga about how he travels to the far north to seek out his archenemy, the Jotun named Latham Life-taker. It's not that popular anymore and wasn't widely sung by the skalds I guess, either."

"Well, if this proves true, then..." the elf let his thoughts finish the sentence for him.

"Only one way to find out," Josiah closed his mouth over his pipe for a good long smoke; his words and stare upon both the bard and scribe as he came to stand closer to them silenced them for a while. A silence in which everyone pondered the coming future, huddled in their clothing to stay as far from the cold as they could.

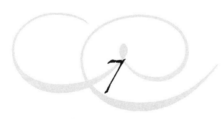

A few hours later, the lone frigate plowed along the slushy waters surrounding the last known bastion of reality before everything turned and shifted to the other side of Tralodren – a place where those who were foolish enough to venture didn't often come back and many saner men avoided at all costs.

The Northlands were no longer in sight. Only small blocks of ice and half frozen waves greeted them. Colder than any could think possible, the climate was beyond frigid – beyond freezing – something like marrow-cracking numbness that hung low and thick over everything. Even the soft breeze of before had become honed razors, dashing exposed skin with its cruel kisses.

The Phoenix creaked and groaned even more under this extreme weather. If before it had sounded like an old man, now it had taken on the groans and wails of childbirth. The crew had slowed to little more than turtles as their bundled frames did their best to keep up with the needs of the ship as they fought the numbness that was slowing falling upon them, trying to keep from freezing solid. Hirim wasn't pleased and often cursed as he paced the upper deck. His black mustache had turned a hoary collection of frost, speckled with small lines of chilled snot – like melted candle wax over the facial hair.

Charles had taken to bed to hide from the cold, his map with him, while Mathias stood near Corwyn on the stern. Both were tightly wrapped in their coats as they studied the horizon about them, looking for anything useful. Josiah paced the stern near them, his pipe ever smoldering. With Charles below deck he could now be as liberal with his own habit as he wished. He claimed it was one of the few things he could do, apart from consuming spirits, to keep his insides from icing over. Since everyone had to stick to his rations of spirits, which they all had little of thanks in part to the halfling's gluttony, he had no other options left.

So far neither they nor the crew had found anything. A few larger collections of ice, but nothing matching the size of the island for which they were looking. The further they sailed, though, the greater the chunks of ice became, some even starting to tower upward like small hills, and in the distance they could see others that looked like mountains coming into view.

Hirim placed the cold lens of his spyglass to his eye once more and took in the spectacle of ice, sky, and water, which now seemed to merge into one blurry hue. The mountains of ice leapt toward him – imposing giants of silent nothingness – like solid breath spent from the lungs of some great beast. He could find nothing of note amid their cold crags, however, and was growing more restless by the minute. He didn't want to risk the ire of either god or luck by trying to go too much farther than he had already dared to go.

Hirim's manner was tense and his crew ever alert; they had discovered that oftentimes more of these large chunks of ice dwelled beneath the waves than above. Get too close to one of them or even try to steer a safe distance around another and you may end up running around or gouging the hull of your vessel instead. Jagged teeth, these chunks of ice were motionless in their pointless vigil – watchmen in a realm of desolation.

Hirim's eyes suddenly narrowed.

"What did you say the island looked like again?" Hirim shouted back from his forward position.

"The legends just spoke about a palace being built there, hollowed into the rock of a nearby mountain," Mathias shouted back.

"I think I see something," Hirim hollered.

"Take us hard to port and then steady on 'til I tell you otherwise," Hirim bellowed the order below.

"Aye, Captain," came one crewman's raspy reply. The other crewmen then scattered about to enact the command; the wheelman huffing out steamy blasts as he fought for mastery of the wheel, directing the ship to its new destination.

"I think I may have sighted your island," the captain turned toward the others.

8

The sun was already slouching in the slate gray sky when the frigate drew close to the large, floating isle of ice. All on board were silent as the white island drifted closer to them like a giant buoy. Around it were a few smaller, bobbing fragments of frozen water, icy white and topped with crusty snow. The ship itself was getting another light dusting of thin flakes in the crisp air, forcing all on board deeper inside their warm coverings, shivering only when a lone wind happened upon naked flesh. It seemed to those onboard that the cold had stopped getting colder. Perhaps they'd finally come to a place of tolerance to the chilled air.

The water had turned thicker now as well; the soupy slush from the previous hour transmuted into harder, dough-like clay; as Hirim gave the command to look for a safe spot to lay anchor around what they believed was Rainer's Island. When the crew had found an acceptable spot it did so, dropping the massive weight of the anchor where it hit a piece of ice underneath the waves with an echoing thud on its journey to the depths of the liquid ice.

None knew what to make of the island itself. Few had even thought such a thing could exist and others didn't care as long as they didn't have to venture onto it. Most of the crew wanted to keep as far from it as possible. Many thought it to be an ill omen, for who'd ever heard of a moving island? They were already close to The Crown of the World, and had risked more than their fair share; why risk anymore? While the crew muttered to itself, they knew that some of them would be required to make landfall. Each just prayed that it wouldn't be them that were joining the passengers in the expedition. In the end, however, each also knew that if Hirim ordered them to, they would make landfall anyway. They had faith that Hirim wouldn't lead them into anything too dangerous.

The island was pure snow and ice. Jagged peaks of the stuff sprung out and around it like faux mountains; more made up an empty "beach" of sorts, which slid further inland. The frozen mass of the island was larger than what they expected, perhaps even a little over a mile in both directions. Surely, it was worthy of the denotation as an island by those who had found it centuries ago. Even from the beach of powdery-looking dandruff, a large, lone structure jutted out of the landscape alongside an icy, snow-swathed mountain in what appeared to be the center of the isle.

This structure was white, like everything else, half covered by snow and caked with ice in spots but it certainly had the look of something man-made – something that didn't seem to fit into its natural setting. All eyes on the deck were drawn to this structure, nestled behind curtains of low riding hills and broken, frozen mountains of ice.

"I think we may have found our destination, gentlemen," Josiah smiled with chapped lips. "Can you make anything out of it, Captain?"

Hirim was with them on top the forecastle once more, spyglass in hand as he surveyed the landmass before him. "It looks like it's a citadel or tower of some kind. A bit covered in snow and ice here and there, but still standing. The building is about halfway into the island itself–"

"But through ice and snow the whole way." Charles, who had recently somewhat reluctantly rejoined the others when news of a possible discovery had come to his hammock, grumbled.

"No one said you had to come along," Hirim condensed the spyglass with a slap.

"And miss out on the *money*?" Charles looked up at the captain with a huff. "Hah!"

"Well," Josiah rubbed his cold-reddened chin with his mittened hand, "Coggsbury, Elliott, Chesterfield and Company certainly is prudent and wise in its investment, but we did not see this particular predicament of reaching said citadel coming to pass.

"We have some gear that should allow for safe snow travel, but nothing that will allow us to get near that structure in any record amount of time. Moreso, I fear that though we might be able to traverse snow with a steady step, climbing those hills and sharp peaks would be quite hazardous indeed."

"Not to mention what might happen if we get caught in that ice heap when the sun goes down," Mathias shivered involuntarily as he thought of being caught in even colder climate than what they now endured.

"We'll just have to improvise then," Corwyn's optimism seemed to warm the air between all gathered. "Hirim has found us the safest spot to lay anchor, so we'll have to work with what we've got. Maybe we can convert the landing boats into some kind of sled."

Hirim nodded his head slightly in thought. "Interesting idea. It might be possible."

"I'll see what we've got in cargo to work with and then what we can come up with. I'm sure we can work something out that can help us get there faster and with low risk – before the sun sets." The bard ran off to the upper deck en route to the lower holds of the ship; optimism and excitement of the upcoming adventure taking some of the chill away from his person.

"You probably should get what books and scrolls you'll need too, Mr. Onuis," Josiah turned to the scribe after the bard's departure. "I trust we will still have some quandaries of mental obscurity and challenge which only your muscular mind will help solve."

The gnome then inhaled deeply from his pipe, flushing out the smoke which followed through his nostrils.

Mathias nodded, "I'll get a working collection together. With my notes and what I've read so far, I think we should be okay for anything we might encounter."

He then left for his cabin, happy again to be away from the flesh-chapping wind and to have something to do besides scan the frozen waves for hidden islands.

Josiah blew out another thick cloud of scented smoke as he turned to take in the others gathered around him. "I would imagine the rest of us should make ready for this adventure now as best we can."

"I was *born* ready, Josiah," Charles smiled with his own chapped, torn lips – thin lines of red leaking out from underneath, adding another touch of color to his yellowed teeth. "Just get me on that island and near that secret of eternal life–"

"Now, Mr. de Frassel, you know that we have to follow protocol. We must be cautious and not rush into something that might indeed prove very dangerous – not just for the individual, but for *all* involved." The gnome had taken on his fatherly tone once more as he looked toward the halfling.

"I would much prefer if you were to defer to the captain, Mr. Danther, or Mr. Onuis before you lurch ahead like some wild animal, half crazed with hunger upon catching sight of some new prey."

Charles looked into the face of the gnome for a moment, his face awash with stoic silence, then finally spoke. "You talk a lot, you know that?"

A short time later the crew and guests were getting their final preparations underway to disembark. Corwyn and some of the crew had come up with something ingenious for travel that should work quite nicely on land. The two smaller boats on board The Phoenix, which they used for making landfall like they were about to do now, had been converted into a type of rough sled without degrading much of the structural integrity of the smaller vessels to keep them seaworthy. The innovation was simple enough to make and yet sturdy enough to withhold the possible pounding they were going to endure.

Amazingly, the skilled hands of the sailors had been able to put these modifications together in no more than an hour – a record if ever there was one for such a deed. As these were made ready, other matters were attended to in readiness for their exploratory landfall.

Part of these preparations involved each grabbing a weapon of some kind; cutlasses for the crewman, a mace for Josiah, and daggers for Mathias and Charles. Not that the last three were skilled in the used of such weapons, but when it came to self-defense, each felt safer having a weapon, should the worst befall them.

"You're not carrying a weapon?" Mathias had managed to bundle what he thought he would need into a small chest and was making his way back to the upper deck when he bumped into Corwyn and saw that he hadn't strapped on any type of self-defense.

"No." Corwyn saw the dagger sheath that had been girdled about the scribe's waist and paid it only fleeting interest.

"Aren't you afraid of being unprepared in case of danger?" the elf climbed the stairs with the bard. The small chest was a bit more than the scribe was used to carrying and caused him to huff out white gusts with every other step.

"Not really. It's my opinion that whatever you prepare for is what you tend to end up with."

"Oh," Mathias reached the top of the deck first, "I see."

Both of them made their way to the others who were dividing up the crew and making final plans as to what they were about to do during their rapidly approaching disembarkment.

"I guess I believe in being a bit more cautious than that," Mathias' breathing had returned slightly to normal, though he was still a bit winded from his climb up the stairs, "I'm not one to be as free form in my ways as you bards have a reputation for being." The elf gave the bard a soft smile, which tried to hide his disagreement with Corwyn's opinion.

"And that's fine," Corwyn smiled back. "The world would be a pretty boring place if everyone was like me."

10

As the crew of the Phoenix completed its preparations and made ready to make landfall, a set of eyes held them fast. This stare came from inside the rougher section of the island, where the beach was overshadowed by large, jagged sections of ice that looked like cresting waves frozen solid in mid-ascent. Near a patch of smooth ice, now bashed open to allow access to the frigid waters beneath, a white bear took in the shape of the ship and the men on board.

Its blood-covered muzzle wrinkled a bit as it sniffed the air. Under its gore-splattered chest and stomach was the carcass of a seal, whose contents had been eviscerated and skewed across the colorless ice by bloody paws.

The bear licked at its muzzle, clearing off some of the clotting blood, then abandoned the seal as it kept its gaze focused on the ship a good distance from the creature. The activity of the ship's crew sparked its interest, making it aware of some thoughts and understandings that it hadn't experienced for quite some time. Rising up, it began a cautious lumbering to a rather good-sized dune of ice and hardened, powdery snow that did much to conceal the bear's shape. Here the bear could get a better view of the activity around the ship without being seen as easily as it might have been before.

The longer it spied on the ship the more a glimmer in its eyes took over. Faint at first, it seemed to reflect a type of understanding not common among the beasts of nature, something more akin to the ken of mortalkind.

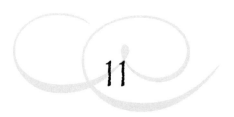

"Are you sure this will work?" Charles took a precarious step into the back of one of the modified rowboats that had been brought ashore. It had sailed the icy water just fine but it had yet to be proven in the new terrain it was altered to traverse.

"Shut up and get in!" Hirim snapped. The cold had grown fiercer off the vessel and was making him even less in the mood for the halfling's whines.

A crew of twenty men, assorted at random and lead by two of Hirim's lieutenants, accompanied the five adventurers who now clamored about the modified rowboats that were being used as makeshift sleds. In one of these boats sat Josiah, now joined by Charles – who had complied with the captain's orders – both of whose small stature hindered them from treading into the deeper snow. They had made landfall on the snowy beach, sinking down to just below their knees in white, powdery drifts. There was great concern for them possibly being swallowed whole by the white island with simply a misstep, or tumbling into a deep snow drift or hidden chasm. Not to mention that their shorter strides would make the trek even longer, should they be allowed to travel on their own.

In the other modified boat were the assorted tomes and scrolls Mathias thought he might need once they got to the citadel. Mathias himself stood beside the modified vessel, shivering. The elf hoped that he didn't need to be here any longer than what was required. The cold was much more than he thought he could bear if the hours turned into days on this forsaken isle. Already he could barely feel his fingers and toes.

"Get those shoes on, men," one of the lieutenants snapped. He was a middle-aged Celetor of a darker complexion than Hirim. Upon the order, all the men put on the snowshoes that had been provided them by their patrons, which would allow them to better stay above the deep drifts and hungry sink holes that called out for unwary feet and victims in such terrain as what was now before them.

Hirim had made a small fuss with Corwyn ashore when he saw the bard still didn't carry a weapon, but Corwyn assured him he would be just fine without one – citing that he won't be in any danger and if he ever was, he'd find a way out of it besides combat. Hirim simply raised a lone eyebrow in confusion and turned away muttering something about Olthoans (followers of Olthon the goddess of peace and prosperity) under his breath. Hirim was too cold to argue. If Corwyn wanted to be so foolish then he'd let him. 'Fools suffer for their poor choices' Hirim's mother had always told him and so he'd leave the bard to his fate.

"Just sit down and relax," Corwyn now looked back at the halfling as the bard finished attaching the last snowshoe to his own fur-lined boats. "If this works, we'll be there in no time and both you and Josiah will be dry and safe."

"And if it doesn't we'll be stuck on this chunk of ice to freeze to death," Charles grumbled, peering over to his traveling companion beside him.

Josiah took no other action other than to savor his smoking pipe, eyes and thoughts focused before him. The gnome's mind was already busy pondering what lay ahead and the next step beyond that.

"And the world will not be too troubled over the loss of one halfling," Hirim replied in a sarcastic statement.

Charles's face soured at the comment.

"If you're not careful, your face might freeze that way," the captain chortled.

"Shut up and get this thing moving," Charles grumbled, "I'm already colder than Perlosa's icy mounds."

"Say, you don't have any of more pipe weed to share, do you?" The halfling suddenly turned toward Josiah, offering a smile that bordered on the sickeningly sweet.

"It seems to me, Mr. de Frassel," the gnome eyed him once then huffed out a fat puff straight into his face before looking ahead once again, "that you have ample supply of your own tobacco products, which are rationed now, as are mine."

"Fine," the halfling's smile melted like ice in a fire as he turned to look out over the pale white expanse once more, responded as would a frustrated child.

Upon Hirim's orders, five crewmen took charge of each vessel, pulling them along the snowy landscape while the other fifteen and the leaders of the expedition did their best to forge a safe pathway before them, trading off the work in shifts to keep all from getting fatigued. The crewmen used fifteen-foot poles to judge the ice and snow, prodding them and tramping down any drifts that might have stood against them. They managed to make some good time until they encountered the hilly region that surrounded the citadel, which they could now see as they drew closer, resting at the center of a crater-like valley rising up with the long, stalagmite-like ice mountain in its center.

All kept their words to a minimum. This only added to the unsettling quiet upon the place. It seemed as if the very ice and snow around them were soaking up any sound they could, creating an odd sensation of stillness and peace for to the explorers. The sun was proving to be a minor challenge, however, in that its reflection off the seemingly endless stretch of white ice and snow threw up a bright shimmer all around that caused them, at times. to have to squint in order to see beyond the sometimes brilliant glare.

The battle to get up the hill was harder than they had thought; the ones pulling the modified boats hardest hit of all as they strained their legs and backs to not only stay above the ice-coated, hard-packed snow, which creaked and cracked beneath their tread-like tired hinges, but to keep themselves upright as well. Even so, this was by far the easiest path to the center of the cold, white isle; the other spots of the island were too jagged and seemingly impassable.

No matter the sluggish ascent, they still had the light with them (even though it fought them too at times). Their location near The Crown of the World would assure a a few more hours of daylight, but wouldn't hold back the night forever. With the extra daylight and persistence, they had managed to get to the top of a hill and from there took a brief rest from their accomplishment. While they rested, the sun sunk into the sky – falling faster with each passing moment – bleeding orange light all over the horizon as it did so. What favor they had incurred from Rheminas was now fading.

The firn in which they now stood had swelled into a white foundation from which the company of men peered down onto the landscape. Below them rested the low, hoary valley, stained a tarnished gold and silver by the sun's fading fire. From their new vantage point, the expedition could see all around the circular depression. Around them small drifts of snow gave rise to pregnant hills and then jagged cliffs of ice that encircled the low lying tract of land in a hedge of wintry design. Indeed, it seemed to some that the whole circle around the citadel was almost planned, as if it had some purpose that went beyond the natural. Such thoughts, though, went unspoken and were quickly erased when all drew their eyes toward the ice mountain in the center of the valley and the citadel attached to it. If anything of importance were to be found, that's where it would be.

Sharp spears of ice shot heavenward amid the white marble spikes that dared to stab at the sky. Angled slabs of silver joined them and buttressed up the white marble walls. Together they drew up a shape akin to a gnomish cathedral anchored to the lone rising mound of ice beneath, which itself seemed like some archaic set of worn fangs. The citadel, if indeed it was truly a citadel, was of solid stone, allowing for no windows or openings of any kind. Thick icicles, the size of men, plunged down from buttresses and near the overhangs of the sloped roof; a snow-capped peaked central roof some two-hundred or more feet from the empty snow-smothered ground.

"That's it?" Charles snorted from under his hood. "The secret to eternal life lies in *there*?"

"It looks deserted," said a crewman.

"Aye, and riddled with snow and ice," Hirim nodded, his mustache sporting a few new small icicles he'd grown since he'd cleaned out what had gathered before making landfall. "Can anything of value still be in there, you think?"

"Only one way to find out," Corwyn climbed into one of the boats.

"I must concur with, Mr. Danther," Josiah took his pipe out from his mouth to speak, the first time he had done so since they'd started the trek inland, "we have not traveled this far to squelch the investment of Coggsbury, Elliott, Chesterfield and Company. If indeed what we seek is inside, then we have almost completed our mission and shall be quite handsomely rewarded."

Seeing how no one sought to argue with the gnome, the bard took action.

"Get in, Mathias," Corwyn spoke to the scribe who had taken of late to shivering beside the modified boat where the bard now sat.

"I'm not so sure this is such a good idea," Mathias' face became a little lighter than what its pale shade had already been. "After all, I mean it's already dangerous now. Why not just trek down to the valley on foot? Why add to the peril with this makeshift sled?"

"If we climbed down it would take far longer and be far more dangerous still." Corwyn tied a rope snugly about his waist and then fixed it to a small iron loop which he and a few crewmen had affixed to the inside base of the boat. "We'd even lose what daylight we have left. This way we will get there faster and with minimal danger when compared with the other option of walking down to the citadel."

Mathias remained still and shivering as he watched Hirim and the rest of the crew get into their respective seats on one of the two boats. He soon was the only one outside a boat.

"Come on already," Charles shouted, "I'm so cold I could piss ice."

"Just hop in and close your eyes," Corwyn motioned the hesitant scribe forward. "It's already getting dark and I don't want to get any colder if I can help it."

Mathias slowly walked over the bow lip of the boat and stepped inside, one leg at a time testing to make sure it was sturdy, then took a seat next to a Napowese sailor who said nothing, only handed the scribe a rope. He, like the rest of the crew, was cold and shivering but had taken to silence as it was hard to talk with the flesh of their faces being so cold. In truth, they had little to say anyway and focused instead on keeping alive and keeping warm. They knew they'd be called into action quite soon and so saved their energy for then.

"If I die then it's the bard's fault," Mathias sighed a steamy cloud as he tied it about his waist then bent over to run it around a metal loop that had a few more ropes anchored to it.

"Everyone set and tied in?" Hirim asked from the other boat.

When the captain was confident that all were, he continued, "All right then, heave off lads." He addressed two stalwart Telborians, connected to their boats with rope belts, as they bent down low and began to shove the boar off the frozen hill. Within moments, each boat was moving to the edge and then off the edge. The Telborians, pushing the boats quickly, leapt inside the spot allowed them at the rear of the boats as the vessels slid over the lip of the hill and then down into the valley below. At first the modified boats were slow, but they quickly picked up speed, skiing down the slope at an ever-increasing rate. The two Telborians who had jumped into the back were now were using oars as makeshift rudders to steer the vessels as best they could, keeping it on as much of a straight path as possible, avoiding any spur of ice or troublesome area that might rise up before them.

Everyone else on board did their best to attach their white knuckled grips to anything solid or seemingly solid and prayed to make it through alive.

At the top of the same hill where the others had begun their sled ride down to the center of the island a few moments before, the lone white bear who had watched the arrival of The Phoenix and followed their progress, now halted to study their tracks and sniff about the trampled snow. After the bear was satisfied with its investigation, it sauntered over to the lip of the hill and peered down at the rapidly descending boats in silent observance. It tilted its head in a curious manner for a moment, as if pondering a deep thought, then pushed some snow over the crest of the hill with its red splattered paw; breaking the hard, dry stuff that creaked in protest as it did so.

For a moment more it stood there – silent as the landscape – as if pondering something profound, something beyond the inkling of its baser mind. Then it turned around and slowly backed down the hill with its large rump until it too began to slide over the hill and down to the citadel.

The makeshift sleds continued to speed down the hill as the two crewmen attempted to ferry their course. Icy rocks bumped them to and fro in their rapid descent as the wind sliced into everyone's skin like cold razors, tearing the tears from their eyes before they could even fall or freeze. All held their breath. Struggling with their stomachs in their throats as they jostled around the smaller bumps and lumps of the hill, growing ever closer to the icy citadel rapidly rising up before them. It was then, as the ice-covered structure grew closer, that the stalagmite-like ice mountain it was built into grew more gigantic in their sight like some approaching giant.

"So how do we stop these things again?" Hirim asked Corwyn, who had seated himself beside the strong Celetor, over the rush of wind.

Corwyn's was emotionless as he thought.

That *was* a good question…and he did have a *good* answer, just not one that the captain might want to hear. He didn't want to share that part of his plan until the boats were on the beach, in case Hirim would object. Thankfully, the question never came up so the bard didn't have to share it lest the others might take a second thought to traveling in the makeshift sleds. Corwyn knew these boats were the only way to get to the citadel quickly and safely… if not for the whole stopping part of the vessels. Oh well, it was too late to change that now, wasn't it?

"Snow." The bard's answer was barely audible over the noise of the ride.

"Snow?" Hirim's dark, cold chapped face was covered in confusion. "I don't–"

The ice mountain and the small snow mounds around it were getting closer – too close – and the boats hadn't shown any signs of slowing down.

"Somebody stop this damned thing before we crash," Charles shouted over the sound of their descent.

Hirim turned his attention from Corwyn back to the scene before him and his eyes went wide. The citadel had sprung up like some icy spider ready to crush them and the vessels had yet to diminish in speed.

"Slow us down! Slow us down!" Hirim shouted orders to the two helmsmen.

They tried as best they could, but they could only create so much drag with their oars on the brittle snow and stubborn, clumpy ice. The surface of the hill they were descending was rapidly growing more level – bottoming out as they came to the center of the crater. While this did some good in stilling them, their momentum still persisted.

They had gotten so close now to the citadel that they could see that it was crafted from large white marble blocks as cold and lifeless as the snow around it. The silver filet work and overlaid buttresses, which peeked out from the frosting covering most of it, shimmered pure white in the remaining light. The blocks were seemingly fresh and unaltered by the passage of years. At first impression, Corwyn thought it looked like a mausoleum of some kind – a lone burial plot on this forsaken and drifting island of ice.

"I'm too young to die," Mathias clenched his eyes shut and clamped a white-knuckled hand on the rope about his waist.

"I do not believe that any of us shall die, Mr. Onuis," Josiah remarked, though his voice held the hint of a slightly agitated air.

"Shut up yah over-stuffed bureaucrat!" de Frassel did his best to grasp onto the rope about his own waist, face even sicklier than usual. "If anyone shouldn't die here it's *me*. I've too much to offer to the world."

The boats were slowing down some now, the oars digging deep rifts in the snow as if they were plows in fertile soil, sending rooster tails of powdery white spray behind them. However, they still continued to skate up to the entrance of the citadel at a speed where a simple bump with the structure would possibly do harm to them and the boats as well.

"Snow." Corwyn's advice was a bit louder as he motioned with his free hand, his other holding the rope about his waist. He pointed to a pile of white powder near the base of the citadel, a few yards from the structure itself. "Steer toward the snow!" the bard raised his voice to just above a shout.

The two crewmen working their oars wasted little time in doing what the bard decreed. Muscles straining and grunting curses beneath their breath, they managed to veer the course of the boats toward the bank as the land finally grew level at the bottom of the depression. The two boats slid closer to the banks and then into them. First one boat, then the other sheathed itself beside the first in the cold, diamond dust, spraying the air all about them in a cloud of fine powder.

For a moment no one said anything. Each sat still – comical sculptures dotting the icy landscape. The first few feet of the converted boats, and the crewman seated there, slammed into the snow bank; they emerged looking like living snowmen, spitting and sputtering and shaking the snow from their frames. The others seated farther back weren't so coated but still were dusted with the cold crystals, which they took pains to remove from their face and clear out from between their garments in a relatively quick fashion.

"Great." Charles shook snow out of his hood and then moved on to clearing up his head. His face was splattered with snow, his eyes peering out from behind white cheeks and frosted eyebrows. "Just great, as if I wasn't cold enough."

"Are we dead?" Mathias dared to open up one of his previously scrunched up eyes. His mittened hands still clung tightly to the rope about his waist. He'd been just lightly dusted, as he sat toward the rear; his face sparkled with the shimmering spray of flakes.

"No." Josiah had taken a grooming brush from an inside pocket and was busy cleaning himself up. "We seem to be all right and whole, Mr. Onuis...at least as far as I can tell."

"Everyone okay?" Hirim climbed out of his seat, shaking snow from his person as he did so. The crew now became active, clearing out the boats and themselves like ants emerging from a disrupted hill. This time they allowed for a few muttered curses and complaints as they took to their tasks.

"How we stand, Chang?" Hirim asked his other lieutenant as he finished cleaning himself off by rubbing his mustache between his thumb and index finger; pulling out some of the annoying icicles that had still clung to the black hairs.

"They're solid enough, Captain," Chang answered back. The others busied themselves pulling the vessels out and having a good look over the riggings and wooden planks of the boats as they were recovered from the snow.

"That worked better than I thought," Corwyn smiled. He had gotten out of the boat and had been able to free himself from the larger dump of snow that had fallen upon him. He even looked happy, much to the chagrin of his companions.

"Yeah," Charles stepped out of his boat with a scowl, "*real fun.*"

"I wish you would have told us about this first." Mathias fiddled with his rope belt; cold, desperate hands struggling free of the thing like it were a viper encircling him, seeking to get out of the boat all together.

"Ah, it wasn't that bad," said Corwyn.

"Speak for yourself," the scribe finally managed to untie the knot with his frozen, mitten-covered fingers.

"We made it here in one piece though," Hirim's tone was gruff and businesslike. "Now we need to get inside this thing before it gets dark. I don't think it would be too wise to freeze out here when night comes. We're already cold enough from that snow."

"So I propose that our attention be directed at this citadel, gentlemen." Josiah joined them in a rough circle as the crewmen stayed warm with the task of clearing out the boats.

"That would be Mathias' territory," Charles looked up at the gray-hued elf.

Mathias turned his head toward the white marble building with a silent, contemplative face. He was looking at the most bizarre thing he had ever seen – a piece of apparently ancient architecture in the middle of nowhere. The outer walls were smooth and clean. Silver accents could be seen through the frost, ice, and snow, and appeared to outline the spear-tipped roof on each of the four corners which worked out in a peculiar display of silent majesty. There was something else about the structure, something that seemed faintly compelling but compelling nonetheless – he felt both attracted to and repulsed by it at the same time…

"Mathias?" Charles snapped his fingers.

"Wha–" Mathias was brought back to his senses by the halfling's obnoxious action.

"How do we get inside?" Hirim asked.

The others then followed behind the elf as he moved closer to the building, shifting restlessly from foot to foot in a small dance to keep warm. The crew had just about finished up cleaning and inspecting the boats, and some were joining their captain when the lone white bear slid down a fair distance from them to then hunker down into the snow. No one heard it or saw it as it laid its body as low to the ground as possible, blending in with the few snow drifted mounds around it, while its dark, unnaturally intelligent eyes watched them with growing interest.

14

The front of the citadel was partially covered with a snowdrift, the rest being merged with the ice of the towering mountain near it. Just at the end of the snowdrift, a faint outline came to the scribe's eye.

"Something's here." Mathias moved to trace it gently as best he could with his mitten-covered hand.

Corwyn joined him in clearing away the crusted snow that covered the discovery, scooping it away with their hands and feet. After a few moments of such efforts, they had cleared away what looked like a white stone door, which had a single line of runic text carved deep into its surface about one third of the way down from its rounded top.

"What's that?" Hirim pointed to the text from over their shoulders.

"Looks like the Nordic tongue." Corwyn stepped back, mirroring Mathias, who was already engrossed with the sight before him.

"Seems to be an older dialect though," Mathias added.

"Can you read it?" Josiah had come to stand beside the two men. He was amazed that anyone could read the strange chiseled depression in the rock that looked far more decorative than literary.

"I think I can." Mathias stared at the text in heavy concentration.

By this time, the rest of the crew had managed to join the others to form a semicircle around the discovered doorway; their breath formed a constant misty sea around them as they too now danced from foot to foot to keep from freezing solid. The light was fading and the cold around them was increasing. Soon they'd be in the dark, under the twinkling stars, which were just as frigid as the powdered diamond dust around them.

"'Eternal Life…'" the scribe trailed off.

"A promising start," Josiah mused under his breath as he stuffed his pipe with some tobacco – a fair deal less than he normally would now that he had to ration it – and made ready to set it alight.

"'Eternal life, for all who dwell inside these mundane walls,'" Mathias continued his translation.

"Are you sure?" Josiah struck a small chunk of flint on a scrap of steel for a spark above his pipe, which he clenched in his teeth. "I do not mean to doubt your talents, Mr. Onuis, but I want to be sure we have the right information before we proceed further." The spark had caught alight, falling into the bowl of the gnome's pipe, allowing him to puff out a few breaths of smoke once again. "Safety is of the utmost concern here now."

"Yeah, he's got it right, I think." Corwyn could see some sense in the runic text before him. "From what I've learned so far from the books and Mathias, that's what it says."

"So we get eternal life if we *live* inside this place?" Charles tried to reason aloud the cryptic phrase. He wasn't that thrilled things were taking so long, but he could perhaps distract himself from the cold by trying to help solve the mystery.

"I do not think that is the case, Mr. de Frassel, but the potential of their being the secret for eternal life certainly would seem to reside therein." Josiah let out a puff, "If I understand the basic idea here."

"So how do we get in then?" Hirim's voice had become more weighed with frustration. "I have men here who I don't want to freeze solid when the last of this light leaves and the cold gets colder still."

"Hmm. Yes, if you could find a way inside then, gentlemen, I would join our good captain in cheering on such an action." Josiah seemed content now to cradle his pipe in one hand and watch them while he smoked.

Mathias looked at the door, which appeared to be solid without any type of handle or lock of any kind. How *did* it open? He racked his brain for any method, pouring over the library in his head for options, riddles, magical locks, ancient preferences for locking and opening doors, but nothing came to light.

"I can't figure it out. I don't see any lock or even a handle," said the scribe with his own amount of aggravation.

"Well, I can fix that." Hirim drew his sword and took a step forward, before the gnome's hand reached up and wrapped around the Celetor's meaty wrist.

"Hold, Hirim. It would be very foolish indeed to attack the door. I doubt that its creators would have envisioned such a method of entry. There is a proper and safe way here to get inside and we must be diligent in discovering its existence."

"So in the meantime we all freeze out here in the dark?" Hirim's tone was less than pleasant.

"Hardly," Josiah continued, "I have the utmost faith in the talents of Mr. Onuis, and with the combined talents of Mr. Danther, the answer will present itself before the sun should sink any lower in the heavens."

The Celetor huffed his displeasure with this counsel, spilling out a thick white cloud from his lips. However, he halted nonetheless. "Hurry it up then," Hirim sheathed his weapon with another small huff.

"No pressure," Corwyn peered over to the elf with a lost expression. Mathias had a troubled brow and nervous eyes.

"No, none at all," the elf's reply was drier than the pages he loved to read.

The embers of daylight had nearly gone out and still Corwyn and Mathias hadn't managed to solve the entrance's mystery. The crew had finished their tasks with the boats and now the whole collection of men stood idly about the semicircle, mitten-covered hands shoved even deeper under their armpits; feet shifting more rapidly from one to the other amid white clouds of breath. All eyes were trained on Mathias and Corwyn, who pressed their faces up close to the runic designs, their fur-wrapped digits brushing more fine particles of snow away.

Josiah had nearly finished puffing on his pipe, Charles envying him nearby, when Mathias touched one of the runes. Though he had touched the runes before, this time there came a faint blue illumination and a soft humming sound – and then nothing.

"What did you do?" Corwyn turned to the scribe.

"Nothing, I just touched a rune and then–"

"*What* rune?" Corwyn interrupted.

"*This* one," Mathias held his hand above the rune for the letter "r" inside the first word of the text: Eternal.

Corwyn pulled off his mitten and pushed the rune. The faint hum returned as the rune glowed a soft icy blue, and then all went quiet.

"Found something, finally?" Hirim moved closer. He'd been glad to get some progress, having had his lips sealed and tongue locked in his jaw for longer than what seemed possible as he waited for some hopeful event to appear.

"I think so," Corwyn put his mitten back on his hand; it was already almost impossible to move from the cold.

"You don't think you can hurry this discovery up some, do you?" Charles grumbled, shifting his body from foot to foot in a pathetic dance to stay warm.

"I might have one idea, yes," the bard nodded slightly. A small epiphany was upon him. "What was the island's name again?" The Telborian turned to the elf, who merely stared at him in wonder as he spoke. "You said it had two names, right? What where they? Who was this island named for?"

"Rainer and Sidmudsson," Mathias answered.

"Okay, give me a moment here," Corwyn turned back to the door, his eyes feverishly playing about the runic text.

"Mr. Danther, the hour does indeed grow late and I would encourage whatever discovery you may have found be done so in a manner that is most expedient, as to ensure our own continued existence." The gnome's genteel nature was starting to wear thin at the growing specter of greater cold and a perceived lack of progress.

"Don't worry, Josiah," the bard answered without turning from his study, "if I'm right about this then we won't have to be outside much longer."

Corwyn turned to the scribe once more. "Might want to stand back; I don't know what might happen."

Mathias took a few steps back, as did the others, who searched about with nervous eyes – uncertain of just what might happen next.

"Okay." The bard removed his right mitten again. The cold snapped at the exposed fingers instantly, turning knuckles and muscles to stiff, stony digits. He'd have to make this fast if he wanted to still have them whole and functional. "Here goes."

"R." The bard spoke aloud as he pressed the runic letter in ETERNAL again.

The light and noise returned.

"A." He pressed the runic 'a' in the same word.

The light on the runes grew a bit brighter and the humming grew more pronounced.

"I-N-E-R." Corwyn pressed more runes as they lined up in the text, both increasing the glow and the hum, which was now as loud as a relaxed conversational tone in a crowded dining hall.

"S-I-D-M-U-D-S-S-O-N". The bard punched out the last name then donned his mitten once more.

The light from the runes he had selected blazed a soft powder blue and the humming had become higher pitched and more pronounced. Everyone had to shout over the noise to hear another, which is just what Corwyn did.

"That did it," Corwyn shouted.

Mathias turned to Corwyn with wide, wondering eyes. "What did you do?"

"It was just a hunch, but I thought it might work to spell out his name…the letters all matched up so…"

"But what now?" Hirim's voice boomed over the hum.

"I don't know, to be honest," Corwyn made an effort to back up a few steps. "I suppose we just wait and see." This did far from inspire those around him. A handful of the crew took a few steps further away from the door and grumbled under their breath about freezing to death.

None of them had to wait long, for the ground shuddered and then the door begin to rise upward like a portcullis, light spilling into its dark interior. When it was finished, all stared in wide-eyed wonder at the pitch black opening before them. The increasing cold, though, did much to limit their silent wonder.

"Get some torches ready," Hirim's snapped command gathered everyone back to their senses. They immediately complied, happy to do something other than fidget away the minutes and increasing chill.

"I'll need my chest as well," Mathias added and then made his way toward the sled to retrieve it.

"Well done, Mr. Danther," the gnome clapped his hand upon the upper back of the bard – as high as his gnomish arms could reach, "well done, indeed."

"That's just getting inside," the bard returned, "let's hope things are a little easier on the other side of this doorway."

Josiah, Hirim, Charles, Mathias, Chang, and ten crewmen dared to enter the dark portal of the icy citadel. Five of the crewmen stood in front and five stood behind. All had their weapons drawn, all wearing tense frames over nervous eyes. The other fifteen from their party were told to stay beside the door and watch the sled/boats and entrance in case something unexpected should happen. For none knew for certain how long the doorway they had discovered would remain open. Marcus, Hirim's Celetor lieutenant, oversaw these men. Needless to say, none in this party were happy with the prospect of staying out in the cold for any greater span of time, but did as they were ordered – taking turns standing in the doorway to stave off a bit of the cold.

Inside, Corwyn held aloft a torch, the other three torches being carried by the crewmen scattered amongst the group.

"I still think it madness you wear no armor," Hirim addressed the bard as his head turned about the darkness inside the icy citadel. "If you aren't going to carry any weapons, than you should at least wear *armor*."

"Slows me down," the bard's reply was polite but dismissive. "Besides, you haven't seen me wield a weapon." Corwyn lifted the torch higher to try and illuminate the ceiling that towered higher and higher above him until his light could fight back the darkness no longer. "I'd be more help to any would-be attacker than a hindrance."

"So you *are* an Olthoan." Charles curled his upper lip. He couldn't see much from his vantage point since he'd taken to be more in the midst of the taller bodies of the group. Instead he had to rely on his ears rather than his eyes to keep him informed of things.

"No, though, I like some of what her followers are about." Corwyn grew disappointed at being unable to really see anything with the torchlight. "We're going to need more torches." The whole chamber was too large and dark to see any great distance before them.

Hirim turned to a nearby crewman, this one of Telborian descent. "Go and get five more men with torches. Keep the rest of them guarding the entrance and the boats, they can watch from the doorway so they don't have to freeze."

"Yes, Captain," the other responded and then was swallowed by the darkening sky. Just outside the doorway the whole group of them still stood within dashing distance of the opening – letting the nearly dead sun shimmer through the rectangular opening to reveal what it could. This dim light wasn't the least bit helpful, however.

"So what now?" Charles was becoming a bit restless and bored with the lack of any progress. He was disappointed too that what they sought wasn't the first thing to greet them upon entering. "I mean we're inside, so where is this great treasure? Where is the secret to eternal life? There isn't anything but a big, dark, empty room."

"Patience, Mr. de Frassel," Josiah calmed the halfling with a cautious hand. He too was in the midst of the others, cocooned by taller trees in this moving forest of flesh. "When one is in the field of endeavor one does not heedlessly rush headlong into such matters. We have no idea what to expect to any of our persons or just what this secret may be – even what it might look like."

"I'm going to need some more light to read my texts," Mathias commented. Beside him was a crewman who carried the scribe's chest in his arms as well as his own blade, which he managed to hold in his hand in addition to the chest quite well. Both Mathias and the sailor felt a bit better knowing that he could be ready with cutlass in hand should anything require swift action.

"Who builds such a large place without any windows anyway?" The elf brought a scroll he currently had in his face closer to his eyes.

"Maybe they wanted to stay warm." Corwyn took a step closer to the stone wall at his right, as revealed to him by the torchlight. It was solid white marble, as on the outside of the building, and plain. And it was warmer inside than out, save what cold was creeping in from the open door.

The wind was shut out, and though dark, it helped hold some of the bitter sting of the cold from outside away… though not by much. Craning his head, he got the sensation that the walls of this room traveled for a long distance above him. It was probably twenty, maybe twenty-five feet if he had to guess.

What was this place for?

"Well, you know what I'm going to do with eternal life once we find the secret?" Charles' face took on a more puckish nature than usual. He decided to make his way out from among the others to get a better idea of what was going on; Josiah following his lead.

"Nope, still don't want to know," Hirim scanned the room with his eyes and torch. "It's scary enough for me to imagine you even living longer than you already have."

Charles sneered as the captain's comments drew a chuckle from the crewmen.

Five more crewmen entered the large, dark room bearing additional torches. By aid of the extra light, all could see that the room in which they now stood was more of an entrance chamber. A cold, empty and featureless entrance chamber, whose blue-veined, white marble walls did indeed climb for twenty feet until they met a ceiling of similar substance. The hall itself ran for about thirty feet before it faded back into dim, flickering shadow; it too was large and empty. No friezes, no candelabras, censures or any source of light in the least.

"This is odd," Corwyn stated in a hush tone.

"You're telling me," Hirim added with similar wonder.

"Why have no light source at all?" Josiah spun his head about the walls and ceilings searching for an answer to his pondering.

Unconsciously, all of them nestled together closer than before, the closeness of the light burning like a miniature sun in the frozen darkness around them.

"Who *was* this Rainer anyway?" Corwyn moved further along the wall, cautious of his footfalls, lest even the echoes in the frosted air be cause for some grave misdeed – the whole chamber was starting to make him and the others a bit superstitious. "I didn't find anything on him when I searched in a few of your books."

"I wasn't really able to figure that out," Mathias moved closer to the bard as he spoke, scroll now at his side. "I was just able to gleam that he was a Nordic warrior of some repute back in the early days of the Shadow Years, even before the Imperial Wars."

"Really?" the bard's eyebrow rose.

"He had some sort of dispute…they don't say much in the text but some skald scrolls speak of a curse or him being cursed." The elven scribe pulled the scroll he'd been previously studying back up to his face. The light was terrible for reading.

"We're in a *cursed* man's house?" Charles' eyes became wide. "You didn't say anything of this before. That can't bode well."

"I agree," Hirim also was slow in his walk, keeping his feet away from anything that looked strange to him – fearful of a trap or worse. Course, the fact that everything was so sparse about him and strange in its own way, as most new places and things are to the first time visitor, didn't help him any.

"I just found this out a short while ago and didn't have time to share it with you until now," the scribe's voice was calm as he continued to scan over his document. "I brought the rest of that volume in the chest should we need it further."

"Anything that has curses in it I'm not about to be involved in. What's going on here, Josiah?" Hirim's gruff reply murmured down the darker sections of the chamber in soft echo, which made the crewman jump a bit.

"Be at peace, Captain," Josiah clutched his own torch tighter; he had put his pipe away. Best to conserve what remained by focusing on the matter at hand. "We are in no danger, I assure you. Coggsbury, Elliott, Chesterfield and Company does not subscribe to ventures of excessive risk with little reward, and it certainly does not give credence to the notion of *curses* either."

"I don't care what your company thinks or believes; I have enough sense to stay clear of any curses on man or possessions or abode. I'll not risk my crew or self to being exposed to some curse in the name of profit."

Hirim stopped.

His crew did as well. For a moment, the whole artificial sun halted – none wanting to go forward unless the other did; each only having enough courage to venture into the unknown with numbers greater than themselves.

"A lot of old texts say that sort of thing," Mathias had let the scroll rest in his hand beside him as he addressed Hirim's concern with a disbelieving smile. It was the type of expression one wore when another doesn't believe that an adult still believes in childish things they should have outgrown years ago.

"It was their way of saying he didn't have good luck or 'don't touch my things after I'm gone'. Most of the writers took a lot of artistic liberty in crafting such tales anyway. It takes a lot of reference sources and some common sense to even peel back the layers of legend and myth to get to more of the truth behind most tales."

"So is this curse real or false then?" Charles' voice shot up from the elf's waist. He was happy to have something new to talk about again but wished he could occupy his mind with something less worrisome than the matter of a "curse".

"I think it safe to assume that the information we have is not from any source tied to Rainer; that is to say, he didn't have any people to tell the tale in his own words, so we only have the story by those who opposed him.

"Now as to the curse, the Nordicans did and still do raid one another from time to time, wars break out, feuds, etc. It's probably just a general sort of thing like 'curse that thief' or some such thing. No one really believes that you are actually cursing that person in any way – unless one is a wizard or perhaps a priest…" Mathias then lowered his scroll to address the others, "which I'm certain he was not." All present gave a silent sigh of relief at the elf's proclamation. "The only other textual support I got for the tale was that he left wherever it was he had been and was never seen again."

"That's not very helpful," Hirim's hoary mustache drooped with his countenance.

"So maybe he *was* a wizard," Charles thought aloud.

"He wasn't a wizard," Matthias firmly assured the halfling. "Wizards didn't appear until several thousands of years *after* the time Rainer was reported to exist."

76

"It might have been better if I had gotten a chance to talk with some Nordicans…" The elf's words trailed off into the room.

"Mathias is right, though, there wasn't much text at all about this Rainer," Corwyn lent what support he could to the scribe, "at least from the text I studied on the ship." The bard turned toward the scribe. "Unless that last book you have has any more helpful information."

Mathias nodded slowly. "It might be helpful, but it's pretty sparse on details about Rainer or this place–"

"Well, can we move one way or the other?" Charles' biting tone attacked all who heard it. "I'm freezing here just standing still – even amid this forest of crotches and legs."

Josiah turned an eye up to Hirim to see that both had made the same decision and at the same time too.

"Fine," Hirim grunted, "let's keep moving. We'll survive the night better in here than out there." He turned to Chang. "Make sure the others are inside until we get back. Have them take turns outside so they don't freeze to death or catch too great a cold out there."

The sailor nodded and made his way back to the entrance, torch bouncing in the spacious darkness along the way like a firefly in the night. Once the crewman had left, Hirim resumed his pace, the others following. They came to the end of the large empty entrance hall in hushed silence. Only their steaming breath made any movement as they all stopped before the open and empty dark portal before them.

"What now?" Charles snorted in frustration. He could see next to nothing from his vantage point.

"Where are we going anyway?" Hirim turned to Corwyn and Mathias in mild frustration.

"Inside," Corwyn answered.

Hirim's face showed that the answer didn't rest well with him at all.

"So I gathered, bard. Where to after that, though? Do any of you know that much or are we to wander this accursed place in circles?"

"We just have to take it as it comes, Hirim." Corwyn thrust his touch before him, disturbing some of the swimming pitch that made its home in the portal. "If we keep up a good pace, it shouldn't take us too long to look around."

"Then you may go first," the muscular captain motioned for the bard to precede him into the opening with a sarcastic smile on his chapped lips.

Outside the citadel the sun had finally disappeared among the white, craggy peaks of ice. A cold, gray sky had dominated much of the former blue canopy, dimming it to a deep, smoky sapphire; growing deeper in hue with each passing moment. Under this twilight sky, the ten crewmen left behind to watch the doorway huddled against the walls of the citadel, keeping watch over the boats and peering back into the black opening where the captain and fellow mates had entered a little while ago – each hoping they wouldn't be that long in returning. None doubted their captain or looked to speak ill of him, for they had known him for far to long. Marcus, his lieutenant, was a good man too, in many ways a younger version of the captain; for both their sakes each crewman stood their ground. They knew that Hirim would return and do so soon, for he had no more love of staying here after dark than they did.

Snot, made loose from the cold, had stopped dripping from their noses and instead slid down mucus colored icicles and coated the inside of their throats for those who could suck it down and stomach the growing pool in their guts. The few with facial hair – bushy mustaches mostly – had frozen breath draped upon the dark strands of hair like iron curtains, pulling the furry mass downward and straining the skin on their upper lip from the added weight, almost pinching it. This would be painful if their exposed flesh hadn't gone a bit numb from the elements – even the bits of flesh bundled tight beneath fur bindings had grown to be like solid ice.

To fight off this creeping sensation of chilled numbness, pulsating deeper into their marrow with each heartbeat, they huddled together a few feet from the open doorway. Prancing about as they had done before outside the citadel had ceased to work its warming wonders. It would get colder yet, but no one had brought firewood. They thought they wouldn't need it. Foolish indeed and the worst preplanning they had ever done while in service on The Phoenix. They had thought they would be back well before nightfall. So instead, they hobbled about each other, looking into the bleak scenery before them, hoping they would leave here as soon as possible.

Each was too absorbed in staying warm to take notice of the large white bear, which had waited for this moment, now edging closer to them. None of them heard the soft crunch of snow beneath its heavy step or knew that a set of red rimmed, black eyes watched their every move and waited…waited for the most opportune moment to strike.

When it saw Chang run out of the door into the cold it knew its time had come. While the other sailors turned their back on their unknown threat, the white bear leapt forward to charge with a deep bellow. Upon hearing the noise, the sailors turned toward the creature. Seeing the danger, they tried to move as best they could to defend themselves, but their frigid frames were worse than lethargic, and the approaching doom much faster than anything they could prepare against.

Beefy, fur-covered paws slashed two crewmen's abdomens before any could react. Their spilled guts now soaking in the steaming, cooling warmth of their lifeblood as it ran down their legs and into the thirsty snow below. Both of the wounded men fell to their knees even as the bear's jaws found the throat of the third crewman, puncturing the very scream in his throat as the creature snapped him down to the red snow and gorged its fiendish hunger.

The eight that remained, along with Chang and Marcus, had drawn their cutlasses, screaming at the top of their lungs as they engaged the bear. Each swung their blade, half mad and grief-stricken by what they had just seen: their fellow comrades killed in such a horrible manner.

Their attacks were useless, however.

"Strike harder!" Marcus shouted. "Bring it down!"

It didn't matter where the blade connected on the blood-splattered bear's massive hide, they all met up with rock-like resistance or simply slid off before they could even split a hair, let alone gain a small footing inside the fleshy covering. This didn't deter them in the least, however, as each kept on swinging.

The cold, and now a subtle senseless fury, had crept in and they could do nothing but try and hack at the beast in futile vanity. Through it all, the white bear lapped up the warm blood of its victim, even going so far as to shake the man's neck between his jaws back and forth like a rag doll to try and squeeze out even more scarlet drops it may have missed, as the ineffective sword strikes continued.

When it had finished its gorging, it raised itself up on its hind legs and thundered toward the remaining crewmen. The bear stood a good eight feet tall, and the eight crewmen backed up toward the wall, bracing themselves against their unavoidable fate. Relentless and stubborn to the last, they jabbed and sliced, swung and hacked away with their cold, useless steel. At least they would be able to claim that they had gone to Mortis, the realm of Asorlok, fighting. Four strong swipes and a bone-crunching bite laid low over half the crewmen in mere moments.

The three who remained, Marcus among the trio, ran about the bear now as it stood, ringing it with their cutlasses. Gore, was splattered all over the bear in a sickly crimson display. The homicidal animal seemed to grin, as if it was toying with them – almost as if it had an intellect higher than that of a normal animal…almost like it enjoyed all this and took it as a form of sport.

The crewmen let out one final yell each and then were no more.

Three strong swipes washed all into silence.

The crewman's blades fell beside them, dropped from dead hands as their dying bodies slowly skidded down the white marble wall and landscape to the snow below. A wide swath of red followed their descent down the walls and pooled in the once pristine white snow. The last sounds and sights each would recall would be the bestial growl of their attacker draw near, the feel of its hot breath pounding against their face and neck, then a rich and wet crunching sound – like a limb being snapped off a tree mired in mud.

When the bear had finished its ravenous dining, which took it a little ways further into the starry night, it turned its bloody muzzle toward the open doorway. Lifting its head, it sniffed for a moment then bellowed a low, delightful growl. Leaving the cooling, shredded, and mostly bloodless bodies of its prey behind, it shambled over to the open portal and into the citadel itself. Once inside, the portal closed behind the animal with a slow grinding descent.

"I think we might be here a little while longer than I first thought," Corwyn held his torch close to a smooth wall beside him. The white marble surface was covered in a deep relief that rose from floor to ceiling. The chiseled forms were smooth like living flesh and told a tale with runic script and a linear progression of images that was at once both confusing and compelling.

Corwyn had led them through the doorway into a smaller, but still quite large hall. The ceiling was much lower here, about ten feet if he had to guess, and more rectangular in shape. Carved of white marble, same as the larger room from whence they'd come, the room was lined with a solid stone relief that stretched around all the walls toward the far end of the hall where another stone door frame, this one blocked with a wooden door, stared back at them.

The bard guessed that the hall stretched for about forty feet, maybe a little bit over or under. The others had been able to spread out a bit with their torches to illuminate various parts of the room more clearly; all of it was draped in a dim, dingy yellow-hued light.

"This could be very important," Corwyn stared at the runic text and images before him. "Do you have anything to help make sense of this all, Mathias?"

"What's it say?" Hirim too had found a section of wall that caught his eye, this section showing what appeared to be some Nordicans killing another by running their spears through him; piercing him through like a pig on the spit.

"I'm not sure yet." The scribe was busy looking at his own section of the wall, torch in one hand, the fingers of his other mitten-covered hand tracing the outline of the runes with his wooden chest resting open at his feet. The image he had before his eyes showed a large number of white bears savagely attacking a group of humans who appeared to be of Nordic descent. The brutal nature of the attack was gruesome in its portrayal – the stone relief was detailed with flailing limbs, severed appendages, and internal organs spilling out from inside the many victims. Moreso, there appeared to be a person directing them to attack their victims…though Mathias wasn't totally sure, but that is how it seemed to be conveyed in the carved image.

"It's the old Nordic tongue, of course, but these phrases are very archaic, almost cryptic."

"Anything about the mention of eternal life?" Josiah's was looking half heartedly at a series of images beside him with a mild form of disgust. He didn't have much love for this chamber at all, that much was certain.

"Yeah, where is it?" Charles whined. Like Josiah, he had only a faint interest in the images, his shorter stature probably adding a bit to this disinterest.

Mathias keep his attention on the frieze as he gave his reply, "Nothing yet, but–"

There came a heavy thud from behind them. It echoed with a slight clap and stilled all communication in the dimly lit hall. Not even breath was expelled from those gathered.

"What was that?" Charles finally asked in a tone that was uncharacteristically meek.

"Sounded like the stone door at the entrance." Corwyn turned toward the black opening where they had entered the room.

"We're *trapped*!" The halfling's eyes grew wide as a flush of fear overcame his forehead, neck, and stomach. "By all the gods, we're trapped and now we're going to *die* in this accursed place!"

"Shut up!" Hirim growled. "Get a hold of yourself." The Celetor then turned to a nearby Patrious crewman, who held a torch and carried a concerned visage about his gray-tinted face.

"Take three men with you and check it out. It could just be Chang getting back in and he might have tripped the door or something."

Two rough-faced Telborians joined the Patrious; all three, with cutlasses drawn. made their way into the doorframe.

"Just check things out, no heroics. If there's something here then we can't afford to face it in low numbers. Just check it out and get back here as soon as you can." The captain motioned with his head toward the doorway to speed his men along.

"Aye sir," the Patrious nodded then all three merged into the inky opening of the entrance hall.

"Brave man sending his crewmen to fight for him," the halfling mocked Hirim. Even when fearful, the short man's snide remarks could still compel another to give him a swift punch in the face.

"Feel free to attend them, halfling." Hirim turned back to the wall he had been studying before with a sneer.

"Please gentlemen, let us strive to keep a civil tongue about ourselves. This is hardly the time or place where strife and dissension should be entertained," Josiah's words soothed some of the tension, although pockets of it still simmered. "I recommend that we use the time given us, while we await the return of those brave men, to make sense of this great work of art before us."

Neither Hirim, Charles, nor the others responded to the gnome's plea; they only stared at the wall before them. Some of the crewmen who remained, however, silently peered into the dark portal into which their friends had disappeared. Each wondered their fate and petitioned the goddess of the waves to aid them, to protect them from danger – for the land of frost and snow was also her domain. Each also silently dreaded the thought that, just as their fellow crewmen had left them to embrace certain danger, so too might they soon enough...

The thought was less then comforting and if it had been a bit warmer, they might actually have broken out in a concerned sweat over the matter. As it was, they simply shivered beneath their heavy, fur-lined garments.

"I might have something," Mathias' voice caused everyone present to jump.

"What is it, Mr. Onuis," Josiah walked toward the elf, puffing on his pipe as he went.

"It's a line from what looks like a ballad." The elf directed the gnome to the line of text on the wall where he'd been standing. "Seems to be talking about this place, it reads: 'Pale is his flesh yet paler still his keep'."

"Okay." Charles resumed shifting from foot to foot in a desperate effort to keep warm. "That almost makes sense."

"Captain," a younger, torch-bearing Celetor on the opposite end of the room called out, drawing all eyes to him, "I think I've found something too."

All moved to gather around the crewman, eager to see what he might have discovered. The combined light did much to showcase the unusual image, which was larger than those around it. The image revealed was of a Nordic man, taller and more regal than the others portrayed who were bowing around him in a circle.

The larger Nordican in the center was young, not even having a beard or mustache (that many of his race at that time looked to as a sign of manhood) and dressed in a common tunic and breeches. He was holding up what looked like a skull and had the expression of a haunted figure; his eyes, even in the relief, looked forlorn yet sinister all at once. Under the image was more runic text, this text longer and larger than the other runes around it.

"What does it say?" Josiah soaked in the rising level of nervous anticipation of the room with all the rest. He was right in front and close to the Celetoric sailor who had made the discovery.

Mathias and Corwyn drew closer.

"'Rainer Sidmudsson.'" Corwyn pointed at the fat line of text. "I got that much out of it."

"'To him has been given the secret of eternal life,'" Mathias translated the smaller sized runes under it.

"Finally," the halfling slapped two mittened hands together with a grin, still unable to see much of anything save a tangle of legs from his vantage point behind the clump of bodies that had come to nestle together before the wall. "We're getting somewhere."

17

The three crewmen Hirim had sent to investigate the whereabouts of the recent noise walked with soft and careful steps through the darkness. Their torches allowed some light, but it wasn't enough to pierce all the gloom about them that nibbled away at the luminous aura in which they resided; trying to snatch them away fully into its grasp. Without the failing sunlight from the entrance, they were unable to make they were unable to successfully navigate the room by sight, having to rely on memory and guess work to make it through. It was a bit more like a blind, drunken stumble more than a confident progression, but they were brave men and so persisted. It was, after all, probably just as their captain had said; Chang and the others probably had stepped inside from the cold and they just hit a wrong rune or leaned on a wall or something – as simple as that – and triggered the door to close. It was certainly feasible, given that each would probably be half numb with the cold from outside, and unable to feel anything if they should brush up against it in the first place. Hopefully, they'd be able to figure out how to undo what they did…though none of the sailors knew how to read the Nordic runes.

"Chang?" one of the Telborians asked of the darkness.

The room swallowed his question whole.

"Chang?" he tried again.

Nothing returned to him.

All three felt the hair on the back of their necks bristle, the bile in their stomachs turn, and hearts pick up their pace. Each held their cutlass a bit higher as they made their way toward the door. Slowly and seemingly eternal in progression, they trod on until they caught sight of the stone door in the outskirts of torchlight. When closed it nearly blended in with the rest of the wall so that one would never have known it was there, had they not known what to look for in the first place. And, unlike the front side of the door, it was bare: no runes or markings could be seen anywhere on its surface.

"What was *that*?" One of the Telborians turned his head.

"What?" The other then turned his head.

"I could have sworn I saw something." The other made a quick survey of the darkness.

"Chang?" the elf called out. "Gregory…Fin…Abelard… Russel…Axel?" He motioned his torch around about him, circling himself and the others to extend the light by a few feet. "Anyone?" The increased light, however, did little to show anything but empty space and darkness beyond.

"Think they're trapped outside?" The elf dared a cautious look toward the closed stone door, viewing it as if it were a lion ready to pounce.

One of the Telborians walked to the door and pressed upon on it, then put his ear to it, not bothering to remove the hood of his coat to do so. "If they are then we can't get to 'em."

"They have to be if they aren't in here. They wouldn't go anywhere else or be anywhere else. They can either be out there or in here," the Patrious replied.

"So what now?" asked the other sailor gloomily, "we could wait until they opened the door again I suppose…"

"Do you think they know how?" The Patrious looked sullenly at the Telborian. "Do any of those guys even now *how* to spell?"

"Marcus would…" the other Telborian shifted in his feet as he peered about the shadows of the large chamber, "…so would Chang. Where is he anyway?"

The elf interrupted any further thought with a brisk turn on his heel so that he faced opposite the door. "We need to go back to the captain and tell him what we found. Not a whole lot we can do here right now anyway."

"All right," the others relented; secretly glad to be leaving this place as fast as they could even amid the knowledge that they were trapped in this place. "But what about Chang?"

"He isn't here and so I can only assume he's outside the door, probably working on it now to open, if Perlosa's looking to be kind tonight." The elf started to walk back the way he'd come, the first Telborian falling in beside him. "There's not much we can do here now, if anything."

The lagging Telborian nodded solemnly and then followed behind the other two sailors. They turned back the way they came, moving just as slowly as they had before, but with a heightened sense of urgency to be out of the chamber now so that they would not risk anything attacking them from behind. Though they all had established that the chamber was empty and they had nothing to fear, none were taking their chances. The whole citadel itself was something that didn't sit well with them in the least, and it was wearing on them more and more the longer they stayed inside.

Though none wanted to admit it out loud, each was also entertaining the idea of being trapped in here. With no windows and no doors to speak of so far, save the one that closed and seemingly locked them in, they very well could be trapped here until they died from the cold, starvation or worse…

Above them, the bulky white bear looked down from the ceiling. Its whole frame sat on the ceiling as if it were the floor and gravity simply was reversed. Red glowing eyes beamed out from the swimming, swarthy air that cloaked it from sight. It watched the three crewmen wander under it to the door and then move back the way they had come. When the bear was sure they were gone, it waddled toward the adjoining wall, and then climbed down the smooth surface with an eerie, graceful silence that would have driven anyone mad had they witnessed it. The bear reached the floor a moment later and then turned in the direction the crewmen had followed, its gait slow and measured and quiet as the grave.

18

" So the secret is here then, but where?" Josiah took a deep draft of his pipe, which he had taken to kindling once again, to aid in pondering and keeping the chill at bay.

"Or it could have been here too, but now isn't around for anyone to benefit from." The bard moved to the left of the drawing beside the previous image of Rainer to study some more of the friezes. These were more simple and crude compared with those around it. The bodies were of men and women who were adorned in animal hide garments and bone jewelry. They looked to be huddled around a fire for warmth amid a cold and snowy landscape, all hinted at in the artwork.

Runic text was sparse in this section of the relief, but Corwyn could discern the word "Perlosa" amid the runes for what seemed to be "curse." The words were close together but also far enough apart to be unrelated as well. Archaic Nordic runes were hard to totally understand, he was learning, and on this section of the wall, with the various splashes of scenes that all tied together in a larger way, it was even harder to make sense of it all.

"This might not be anything, but I read Perlosa and curse from this image," Corwyn shared his discovery.

"*Curse?*" Hirim and Charles spoke at the same time.

"A *figurative* curse, though, right? That's what the elf said," Charles waved his previous concern away as if it were the foolish demand of a child.

"I didn't say it was cursed, just that the word shows up here," Corwyn clarified his remark by pointing out the text on the wall beside him.

"You're right, Charles, the ancient and present day Nordicans were very into curses and luck," Mathias added as he joined Corwyn in peering at the next section of the relief. "Remember what I told you all on the boat about these things? It's probably just as simple as that."

"Probably," Corwyn echoed, though not with the same air of confidence as Mathias.

"It looks like no one's been here for a long time. So if this secret hasn't been disturbed, it must be here somewhere." Charles walked out a little ways and made his way to another closed doorway opposite through which they entered. "And if it isn't in here then it must be through that door." Greed had found some kindling to spark in the halfling's belly and was swiftly rebuking the chilly winds of fearful uncertainly from his person.

"Mr. de Frassel, I would think to embrace such a reckless attitude toward this venture would be very detrimental to say the least. Let us progress along this discovery together," Josiah took a step in the halfling's direction. "After all, we are not totally sure what it is we are looking for. It could be a scroll or relief on a wall or something else altogether."

"Well, we're not getting anywhere if we don't see what we have in the rest of this place, now are we?" Charles voice and expression were now dripping with sarcasm.

"I don't think—" Josiah started.

"Captain," the returning elf, flanked by his Telborian crewmates sent to investigate the noise, interrupted the gnome.

"What is it?" Hirim's face grew grave when he saw the answer reflected in the eyes of his men. "Where's Chang?"

"Nobody's there. They must be trapped outside. The door's closed too and doesn't seem to be able to be opened either."

"Wonderful," Charles grumbled beneath his breath.

"How did it close?" another crewman, this one a young Napowese near Corwyn, asked with a panicked voice.

"Who knows?" Corwyn turned from his study of the wall to address the sailor and others. "Maybe it was only to remain open for so long – keeping out the cold or something."

"Or keeping others in," Mathias' face had gone a bit paler than his normal shade; he looked down at a scroll he was trying to read by the torch carried in his other hand.

"Friends," Josiah had begun to sound more like a statesman than a company spokesman, "let us not dwell upon such a negative prospect, but rather search out and lay hold of the positive aspects. If we explore more of this citadel than we shall not only increase our odds of getting out of it, but of finding what we seek as well,"

"Such cheery optimism," Charles turned to continue his advance toward the closed wooden door. "So let's get moving then before we suffocate or freeze or something worse. Course the best thing is I'll outlive you all if we do die from lack of air, 'cause you're all such gangly giants and my perfect size has reduced my chance of suffocating by at least half."

"Thank the gods for small favors," these sardonic words came from Hirim.

"He's right," said Corwyn, "we have to keep moving – at least try to find something or a way out of here. If we can't find what we came here for, then this whole trip's a waste of time."

"Not to mention our lives," Mathias glumly added as he kept his eyes focused on the document in hand. "I still would like to study more of this text." The scribe then turned to Josiah. "I think there is a lot of information we can glean from it."

"No doubt, Mr. Onuis, no doubt. However, we probably should stay in numbers – not leaving ourselves alone or splintering up our forces – lest something like that door incident should splinter us, lessening our effeciveness and compromising the security we have in our present larger body."

"Okay," Mathias sighed, "but we should come back here soon to see what else can be found." Mathias packed up the scroll and closed the chest, which rested at his feet, then nodded to a nearby sturdy Celetor to pick it up and take it along. Happy to have something to momentarily occupy himself with, other than his possible impending death, the Celetor rapidly complied.

"We will, I am sure, Mr. Onuis. Let's just get the lay of the area first, if you will," the small gnome grinned a reassuring smile at the elf then joined the others as they made their way toward the old wooden door. It was frozen solid, giving it the semblance of ice cleverly carved to appear as wood. Corwyn pushed it inward with a small grunt. The wooden object didn't have a handle or lock of any kind, but fanciful, archaic hinges made of silver that unleashed a high pitched squeal as they grated and moaned – as if they were being tortured – as the door slowly swung inward.

All were silent as they shined a few torches inside the dark doorway. Behind the fleeing shadows was what appeared to be a large room – this one dangling with iron chains, some of which had cuffs attached to them.

"This can't be good." Charles stuck his head in from around a narrow gap between a pair of legs and the door jam.

Corwyn took a step inside and raised his torch higher. The chains ascended with his gaze to attach themselves to another high ceiling some fifteen feet above them.

The bard moved a little further into the room, which was proving to be somewhat larger than the one they had left.

"How is *this* part of eternal life?" Hirim slid a chilled chain from before him with the blade of his sword as if it were some sort of dangling vine.

The more torches that were brought to bear, the more the room revealed its secrets – and they were ghastly ones at that. While the room had a tall ceiling, the rest of it was leaner, about twelve feet in width and fifteen or sixteen feet in length. The floor was made of fieldstone, tightened and packed together around circular depressions that held a tarnished silver basin underneath each collection of chains. All in all, the room held five such basins. Corwyn drew closer to one such basin and bent down to look at it more closely. His torch revealed that its lip was encircled in runes. The rest of it was murky, the inside bottom of the container darker than the rest of the basin.

"There's some writing here. Mathias, can you help me decipher it?" The bard stood up and looked at the scribe who was peering with great dismay at the collection of chains sitting over another basin a few feet from Corwyn.

"Huh? Certainly." The elf came toward the bard and bent down to peer over the basin itself, careful not to touch the basin as he used a torch to make some sense of the ancient Nordic runes. "These seem older than those on the door and relief wall."

"So what does *that* mean?" Hirim turned to them, having been looking at the clear and empty marble walls that framed the room.

"It means that they were either written using an older script or were made in a time before the runes on the door were carved," the scribe squinted his eyes as he continued his studies.

"I understand that we have not been able to date the map specifically, only claiming a pocket of years in which to hedge it, so what does this discovery add to the chronological placement of this place and prize?" Josiah leaned over the bard and scribe as they worked. His smaller stature didn't allow him to see or do much more then catch a glimpse of the tarnished silver between them.

"It means," said Corwyn, "that these basins are probably older than the text on the walls we just passed. And that was already older than most runic script Mathias has on record."

"Brilliant," Charles snorted. "I always found exploration and scholarship to be such *invigorating* subjects."

"We don't know what we are looking for here, Charles, and that is slowing us down." Corwyn stood up, causing the gnome to bounce back a bit from his position behind the bard.

"I can't make any sense of them – they're too old for me – so it looks like Mathias has to struggle with them for a bit. If you want to make yourself useful, then feel free to explore this room a bit. See if there are any more doors or help figure out what these basins were for," the bard advised.

"That's easy enough," the halfling's smile was ostentatious bordering on haughty, "they're there to collect blood."

The room went silent.

All eyes swung to the basin over which Mathias stood, he too stopping his work, wide-eyed at the revelation of the halfling's words.

"*What?*" Hirim spun around to stare down at the halfling.

"At first I thought it was some kind of pleasure apparatus, you know, to really get someone into the experience more so than before, but after a while it just dawned on me – looks like when you gut a deer. You string it up, and clean out the guts and let it bleed clean."

"So then you are saying that this place is for what? Killing deer?" Josiah had turned to the halfling now with concerned eyes, trying to keep his upper lip as stiff as he could.

"Could be. Course, where are they going to find deer here, huh?" the small man's yellow-toothed grin didn't encourage anyone.

"Captain," one of the crewmen started but was hushed by Hirim's hand.

"Hold your ground. We'll be out of here soon." He tried to put on his sternest face to convince his men, as well as himself, of his statement's validity.

"Well, it wasn't deer, that's for sure." Mathias moved his torch around the basin as he himself stepped around it like a squatting ape. "At least part of what I can read here says that they were 'to collect the tribute fitting their king'."

"Gold?" Hirim wondered aloud.

"More likely a torture chamber for people who didn't agree with him; I assume it mentions Rainer?" The bard made his way to a nearby empty wall beside Hirim where he stroked it with his fur wrapped hand in investigation.

"Yes, but it only calls him the 'son of Sidmund,'" said Mathias.

"Who would torture people way out here, I wonder?" Josiah rubbed his muttonchops. "For that matter, who would build a place so bizarre to inhabit a floating piece of ice? This is a very odd thing indeed."

"Captain, there's a strange marking here on this wall," this same crewman's voice that had spoken just a moment before, drew their attention to his location.

"Let me see." Corwyn hurried to the spot near the far end of the room with his spitting torch, opposite the door through which they had come in.

"Anything else, Mr. Onuis?" Josiah had started to pace a bit around the spot, more so to keep warm, but also to help his mind think upon the matter at hand.

"Just something else here that I can't quite get figured out; it says that 'the eternal king's empire shall never be extinguished'." Mathias stood up. "That's about all I can make sense of without having more time to study it."

"Eternal king, eh?" Charles devilishly mused aloud. "I like the sound of that."

"But nothing about eternal life?" the gnome's face was now troubled.

"Nothing," Mathias repeated.

Josiah sighed. "I really do wish we had more time and a better idea of what we are searching for. This indeed is a mystery that I am finding very difficult to unravel. I had thought that once we arrived, the object of our quest would become evident."

"This might prove interesting," Corwyn's voice drew all to his position further into the dimly lit room, near a wall that had a large

CHAD CORRIE

crescent moon relief carved into it. The raised relief was close to four feet wide and covered with silver. On the moon itself was a small series of scratches that the others could not see from their distance, but were plainly visible to the bard where he stood.

"What is *that*?" Mathias moved toward Corwyn.

"A last will and testament." Corwyn ran his fur-covered fingers over the text. "The runes are in the same manner as the basins, but the first part of the text is more modern and from what I can understand, they claim the runes that follow them are the final will and testament of 'the Great Rainer, the Eternal King'."

"What do you make of it, Mathias?" Corwyn motioned the elf to stand beside him. Once there, Mathias studied the tight block of runes arranged on the plain white marble portion of the moon in a one foot by one foot block. The runes were smaller and carved deeper into the stones, but still readable to his trained eye in most places.

"Seems to be a bestowing of blessings and curses upon various people…" Mathias translated.

"Curses again," Charles frowned.

"Standard Nordic practice," Mathias dryly rebutted any rising fear without moving from his location, "as I have said before."

"Still not comforting," the halfling muttered into his second chin.

"'He curses those that would defile his stronghold and who come to seek his harm…and…blesses those with whom he highly favors with life eternal.'"

"*That's* more like it," Charles' demeanor instantly perked up.

"I don't understand," Hirim asked, "so this king – this *Rainer* – has eternal life in his possession and gives it to people he likes?"

"Sounds that way," Mathias answered.

"But what *is* it, I wonder?" Corwyn tried to get something more out of the text but just met with more frustration and confusion. "Does it say anything about how he did this or who he favored? We don't know if it was an elixir, a spell, or something else – like a poetic metaphor."

96

"It better not be a poetic metaphor for all I've had to suffer through," Charles wiped some fresh snot from his nose with an already snot smeared mitten.

"I'm still looking…" Mathias continued to concentrate on the text, "it just follows up with a litany of how he wants his empire to be divided should he meet with death–"

"Wait a minute," Josiah butted in as he had joined the others by the crescent moon relief. He had also come to put away his pipe for what he thought would be the rest of his stay here lest he over indulge and use up what he had rationed. "How can the 'eternal king' *die*? I thought you said he was *immortal*."

"That's just one interpretation," the scribe turned around and looked down at the gnome, "runes can be read in many different ways at times – the same symbol being read as something else with the same expressive thought – like a synonym of sorts.

"The rune that they have for eternal here, if I'm reading it right, could be read as eternal, everlasting, even undying, as well as immortal."

"So it means the *same* thing?" Hirim took in the gray face of the elf, trying to get a clear understanding of what he was presenting.

"For the most part…they're just synonyms, but one could interpret them to mean slightly different things," said Mathias. "In this case I think we can all agree that they mean that what we seek is here and that Rainer was somehow tied to it."

"So where is he?" Hirim looked around the room once more. "We haven't seen anything but this torture chamber and that image-covered hall."

"True, but this is a big place and there's got to be more rooms…somewhere." Corwyn motioned around the chamber to emphasize his words.

"Well, you better find them soon." The halfling moved over and reached up to touch the silver moon himself with his pudgy, frozen, snot glob-covered, mitten. "I don't want to spend my last hours of life here with you. If you're going to die, you should go to

Mortis in bed with a smile on your lips and four very tired women beside you."

"More halfling wisdom?" Corwyn raised an eyebrow.

"Common sense." Charles sucked more loose mucus back into his nose with a slurping snort.

Corwyn was about to say more when he heard a soft click where Charles' hand had been. The halfling heard it too and turned his face toward the bard's, mirroring the same wide-eyed wonder. Corwyn touched the same spot as Charles had on the silver moon and again heard the faint click. "I think we've found something."

"*I've* found something," Charles corrected the bard, trying to stick out his chest but only succeeding in making his gut swell to even greater proportions.

Corwyn pushed a little bit harder and felt the silver crescent give way, as if it was loosed from its ties to the wall. It seemed to wobble a little toward the right now as well. Cautiously, the bard moved it toward the right and found more writing on the stone underneath. He pushed more of the silver moon higher toward the right until it stopped at one hundred eighty degrees where it had been before, another faint click that served to lock it in place. What the silver crescent had covered was a small chuck of runic text that appeared to be in the same archaic manner of the exposed block on the left side of the relief.

"What does it say, Mr. Onuis?" Josiah anxiously awaited a reply.

Mathias feverishly poured over the symbols, tracing the lines with his finger. "It seems to be a poem. It's a bit rustic and my translation isn't totally correct with all of it, but what I can read right now says:

"'He who seeks eternity is brave indeed'…ah…'the sun is not his ally, for it burns the days away. To him who breaks the'… no, that should be through. 'To him who breaks *through* the barrier, a new world shall be his.

"'For Rainer, son of Sidmund, favors the brave, and those who seek to cast off their former life in favor of the undying must seek him out'… umm, 'the King of Eternity…'" Mathias stopped. "It goes on like this for a little bit more…more titles and exalting the greatness of Rainer…but nothing else about eternal life."

"Only that Rainer is the one who has to be sought to gain it, I suppose." Corwyn looked toward the rude, rustic scratching in the stone. They seemed almost barbaric when compared to the ones engraved on the silver moon above them and he had no hope of making heads or tails of them.

"Why hide this under the silver moon, though?" Hirim wondered aloud. "What is there to protect in this poem?"

"A secret?" Josiah mused.

"This Rainer guy is a Nordican, right?" Charles asked.

"Yes, from what we can tell," Mathias humored the beginning of the halfling's reasoning process, though some part of him warned against doing so.

"Don't they worship Perlosa?" Charles continued.

"Most pay her some form of respect as the goddess of both the icy wastes and sea," Corwyn added. "But this moon isn't her symbol – at least from how it appears today. It could be a sign of their devotion, however."

"Why would one place a token sign of adoration and worship of Perlosa within a torture chamber?" Josiah rubbed his chapped chin, trying to bring warm blood to the surface of the frozen flesh. "The two, to me, do not seem to mix well at all, I am afraid."

"This whole place doesn't seem to mix well at all," Hirim agreed, "and I'll be happy to be rid of it when I can see daylight shining through some chink or cracked door leading out of here."

"That is another thing." Josiah turned about to get a better view of the solemn crewmen and unnerving room. "Where is the light source in this structure? There are no windows anywhere, which I can argue might be excluded to keep out the cold, but it would stand to reason to have set up some conveyance of illumination."

"Yeah, I wondered that myself." Corwyn traced some of the formerly hidden text with his fingers. "Well, this doesn't seem to trigger any door like it did at the first door we encountered.

"There's got to be another doorway here somewhere – some passage or something to get us deeper inside and help us find a way out. The place outside was too large to just contain the past few rooms we've seen." Corwyn spun around to face the entranceway.

"So where are they?" Charles had started to shift his weight from foot to foot again as more of the warmth from earlier was waning, and the dark, deadly chill of night – indeed the chill inside the black bowels of the maddening citadel itself – were sinking their teeth deeper into everyone's flesh.

"Somewhere here, just start looking. Maybe it's a wall, or something we missed," the bard stated. "Let's just start searching everything and anything…but carefully. We don't know what could be here too. This place could have some deadly surprises in it, even after all these years."

The crewmen and the others broke up into groups and began to study the walls, floor, and even the chains and basins themselves, albeit with a healthy dose of moderated excitement and extra doses of precaution. Corwyn and Mathias stayed at the moon carving to try and garner more if any lost secrets that may have been there. Together they started to share some texts from Mathias' chest, hoping to gain a new clue from them. None in the room noticed the blood red eyes that peered at them from the top of the wooden doorframe at the room's entrance.

The blood-splattered white bear leered at them from above the doorframe from where it hung, more like a bat, clinging in a most eerie and unnatural manner. The animal's eyes, which should have been much more subdued, were instead devious in their reflection with something of a keen mind shown through them – a mind that had plans of its own for those it watched.

While the others looked and thought, Corwyn made a discovery of his own. He had taken a fair sized tome from Mathias' chest and opened it to search out any possible answers to their current situation. As he turned toward the back portion of the book, a stray page jutted out and then came loose from the others. Corwyn gingerly pulled the parchment out from the other pages.

It had been folded over and had the look of being placed in between those pages for some time. Closing the book and placing it back with the others in the chest beside him, the bard gingerly opened the heavily creased page. He discovered that there, on that page, was an epic poem, a saga – at least in part – of Rainer Sidmudsson. The text was also oddly written in a more modern styling of the Nordican tongue, which aided him greatly in making the translation into his own understanding.

"'Hail to the slayer of Jotun, the savior of his kind,'" Corwyn whispered to himself as he read over the text. "'Him who was cursed for the sake of saving many. The White Prince, the Crimson Lord blessed with a curse and cursed to be a blessing.'"

Corwyn stopped himself and looked up at the runic text before him as he thought these strange lines over. Poetic or not, they were certainly odd comments to ponder. Looking around to see the others still fruitlessly examining the room for clues, he turned back to the folded parchment.

"'Son of Sidmund, great chief now gone,'" Corwyn continued to whisper to himself. "'Son of the tribe now faded away. Hail to Rainer who stared down the goddess and yet lived. Hail to Rainer who forged his own tribe from the ashes of the old.'"

"What are you reading?" Mathias' question jarred the bard from his thoughts.

"Something I found in one of your books." Corwyn looked over to the scribe from atop the page. "It's a saga of some kind – about Rainer."

"Really?" Mathias seemed more than a little surprised. "That's a little fortuitous. Anything useful?"

"Nothing yet," Corwyn continued to scan the page.

"You can read it?" Mathias was impressed.

"It's written in a more modern style so I can make most of it out. Not that I can make much sense of it, mind you, but I've learned a fair amount on our voyage." Corwyn lowered the page from his gaze. "You have anything?"

Mathias shook his head. "I'm beginning to think that we've reached a dead end. I don't know where to go next and the resources I brought along aren't proving to be that helpful."

"We should be trying to find a way out of here if you ask me," the elf sighed. "There won't be any point in looking around for this secret of eternal life if we don't have a way out of this tomb."

"We'll find a way," Corwyn rested his hand upon the Patrious' shoulder, "don't lose hope just yet."

Mathias only nodded then turned back to his tome. Corwyn returned to his saga…

The white bear slid down from his vantage point with amazing grace and supernatural skill. Keeping clear of the doorframe so none would see his descent, it proceeded to tread down the wall onto the floor in utter silence. After a few moments, it made its way toward a spattering of carved reliefs; this section was lined with a selection of people getting beheaded and run through with swords.

It was here where the bear stopped for a moment and sniffed. After it was satisfied, a soft nudge with its blood-caked nose pushed in one of the severed heads that rested on the ground next to its owner's dying body. Doing so caused a faint click followed by a large thud behind the carving and then a grinding, scrapping sound as marble rubbed against marble to reveal a secret door amid the chaotic stone mural.

Waiting for the doorway to completely open, the bear tilted his head for a moment, let out a snort, then shuffled inside the gloom with silent steps. Within moments it had vanished into the darkness beyond the hidden door.

20

" N othing," the halfling cursed. "This whole gods-cursed room is a waste of my time."

More time had passed since Mathias' and Corwyn's talk, too much it seemed to the others; days instead of hours, but the frustration upon finding nothing was real enough.

"Let's just calm down." Corwyn looked up from the silver half-moon he was examining. He had finished reading the saga a short while ago and returned it to approximately where he'd found it in the book. It hadn't been of that much help after all. For a few more stanzas it declared the wonder of the great White Prince of the North and his empire of ice he had made to spread over the Southern Lands. It also referred to him as The Crimson Lord of Night who reigned supreme from his citadel, killing all who opposed him.

Then it just stopped.

"There has got to be an answer here–" the bard started.

"To the Abyss with your patience." Charles stomped his way toward the hanging chains and tarnished silver bowls. "We're all going to die here unless we start making some progress."

"A modest degree of self-control would indeed be most advisable in such a situation as this–" Josiah turned his attention from a nearby wall to reprimand the vertically challenged halfling.

"Shut up!" the halfling spat back.

Before anyone could say anything else, their came a noise similar to the low grinding sound they had heard earlier of the entrance door closing. All conversation and exploration of the room stopped. Everyone turned and listened to the heavy thud and grinding echo from the chamber behind them.

"What was that?" Hirim looked at the wooden doorway, as did all the rest in the room, from whence they came.

"Something from the other room," Mathias' wide eyes were focused on the doorway of darkness.

"You don't think the door has opened back up again, do you?" Charles' face began to take some cheer. "Maybe they got it open."

"Hope springs eternal." Josiah did his best to not get his hopes up too high just yet.

"Do you really think it could be the others, Captain?" an unsettled crewman asked Hirim.

"I don't know," Hirim's own nervous face was hard to hide behind his large mustache, "but we need to check it out."

"You didn't do anything to cause that, did you?" Mathias peered over to Corwyn.

"Nothing…that I know of anyway," the bard replied in a similarly confused state that had descended upon the rest of those gathered.

"Well then, someone should make an inquiry as to the nature of said sound." Josiah looked toward Hirim, his demeanor the subtle pressure of diplomatic urging.

"You volunteering?" Hirim reflected the gnome's gaze.

"I would be able to do so, yes, but only with a handful of others to help safeguard the representative interests of Coggsbury, Elliott, Chesterfield and Company." Josiah returned the captain's gaze with equal weight.

"Maybe we could *all* go." Corwyn made his way to the door. "I doubt we'll find much more in here anyway." Corwyn noticed the faces of many of the crewmen cheer a bit at the suggestion.

"Fine," Hirim's lips disappeared into his mustache, "come on then."

Hirim made his way toward the sound. He motioned his crew forward with his sword as he did so. "We'll make sense of this yet, men."

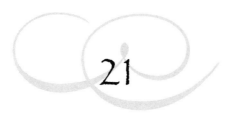

21

"Where did *this* come from?" Charles traced the smooth, seamless outline of the secret doorway opened by the white bear, now visible amid the stone reliefs in the other room, with his mitten.

"Don't touch it!" Josiah slapped the halfling's hand. "We do not know what this is about and I would strongly advise keeping your hands away from *anything* – only touching what we must."

Charles curled his lip at the defensive measure.

"How this got here, though, is still a good question." Corwyn pushed his torch inside the gloom but to little avail. The darkness was too thick to see much of anything save the beginnings of a white marble hallway.

"More importantly, where does it lead?" The halfling began to take a step toward the blackness, content on moving right inside when Hirim's strong hand grasped his shoulder and held him fast.

"No you don't, little man." The captain reeled Charles back. "You're staying right here until we can all go together. I'm not letting you out of my sight."

"I never knew you *cared* so," Charles turned back toward Hirim with the sweetest sarcasm he could muster.

Hirim only huffed out a puff of gossamer breath.

"Well, let's get moving here. The sooner we find what we're after the sooner we can leave and get *rich*. Then the sooner I can warm up in a bed full of well-endowed and nubile young maidens," the halfling chuckled to himself.

Josiah shook his head in silent disdain and mild disgust toward the halfling's comments, while the others ignored the rotund, balding little man as best they could.

"So you think we should go inside all at once?" Hirim had to admit it was getting easier for him to ignore Charles all the time.

"What if it's like the entrance door and closes?" Mathias kept his distance from the opening. "Should some of us stay outside to get it open again?"

"How did it open in the first place?" Corwyn countered the elf's fear.

They then drew silent.

How *did* it open?

"Is that really the question here, my friends, or is it rather why are we not pursuing this fortuitous occurrence instead? If indeed Providence has taken a moment to shower us with her favor, then we should so embrace the gift as to make full use of it while we have the chance." Josiah's voice rolled in an even march across and around the relief covered room.

"If that is how you feel, then you can lead us," Hirim bowed forward and extended his hand in an inviting gesture to the gnome to do just that.

"Very well," the gnome sighed, "if that is what is needed to be done to keep things moving along, then I will do just that. It seems harmless enough, but we will not be able to determine that without further study and that would mean going inside, and since we are not open to making progress in any other place here at the moment then this is the only real option left." Josiah shined his torch before him as he took a step into the blackness, which parted before him to reveal a white marble staircase a bit further inside the hall. "It seems we have a set of stairs to climb, gentlemen."

22

A t the top of those stairs, behind a large oak door that the white bear had shoved aside with a beefy shoulder, laid a splendid room wrapped in blackness. With a low, muzzled growl, which the animal let out upon reaching deeper into the room's depths, a ring of sconces lining the walls of the circular chamber, came alight. The glow they produced was like stars; only giving off a faint shimmering brilliance birthed from supernatural means, for they had no flame within them, bringing forth only a cold white glare. Windowless like the rest of the citadel, it was by this illumination alone the bear made its way into the chamber.

The cold light was enough to reveal the confines of the room to the naked eye. It was spacious and lovely, a chamber that seemed more a mausoleum or some seat of regal power than simple room amid the citadel. Round all about, it rose to a domed ceiling, the distance of top to bottom and side to side being an equal measure of fifty feet from the center of the chamber – creating a strange span of nearly spherical dimensions.

At the center of the room was a white marble altar. It stood on top a dais made of the same stone, standing the height of a man off the floor. The altar was plain save for a simple silver chalice that stood alone in the middle of the white, rectangular block. Around the dais were eight granite slabs hewn to resemble beds; pillows of stone rising up to cushion the head of their user; accompanied by immobile sheets carved for ready use. All of these beds rose up about three feet from the stone ground and all but one of the slabs were empty.

On one slab opposing the doorway, rested the shape of a woman carved entirely of ice. Hands folded over her full breasts, long hair pooling under her head and down the stone pillow, the sculpted figure was a fair semblance of the female form. Though it bore a reasonable resemblance to a human woman, it was far from attractive. Indeed, where the shape allowed the viewer to recognize that the sculpture was feminine, the rest of the body was a disservice to the pleasant physical graces of the fairer sex. Under the plain white dress that covered up much of the sculpture's crystalline frame, her features were sharp and cold – almost feral in nature. Her cheek bones rose to near spear points and her closed eyes had sunken in some and grown more savage in appearance.

Her crossed arms showcased hands that appeared bone-like; as if they might be some type of talon or claw rather than slender, appealing digits. The body itself, though lean and muscular, was still in possession of curves and two mounds of flesh on top her chest – these all seemed to play false with the sculpture though. The normal feminine form, as found in other works of art, seemed here instead to simply be a veneer for some type of animal – a wolf or bobcat over which the female mantle uneasily rested. By aid of a white linen gown that covered the sculpted figure, the illusion of feminine allure held a bit longer…but it was a tenuous grip.

It was to this statue that the bear traveled and upon reaching the destination, sniffed about the icy woman's face and hands. When it had contented itself by this olfactory investigation it then reared itself upon its hind legs and proceeded to vomit up all the blood lapped up from the slain victims. Teetering from one foot to the other as the bear walked down the whole length of the sculpture, it made sure to cover all of it with the steaming red gel that slowly congealed on top the white dress and transparent shape that formed the coldly-fashioned woman. When it finished, the bear plopped itself down like a pat of melted butter hitting a hot pan at the foot of the stone bed. From here the bear merely peered at its work in silent expectation.

The wait wasn't long.

As the faint echoes of those traveling up the hidden staircase reached the bear, the statue started to move. First her eyes flung wide; semi-milky things that stared up at the domed ceiling, much of which was masked with shadows and darkness. Then her mouth fell open, her narrow lips parting for a transparent tongue that lapped up what blood it could around its lips and mouth with stiff, choppy movements. Her whole gore-splattered frame was still more solid than supple, made more evident by her jerky attempt to sit up from the bed.

Blood dangled from the tangled, still semi-solid, clear strands of hair which, like her eyes, had taken on a more milky quality and were more fluid than they had been before. With purposed effort she pulled her right hand before her and flexed the fingers; the bony claw cracked and popped like icicles falling from a roof. She repeated the same effort with her left hand.

A slow scan revealed the rest of the room. Her eyes stopped when she saw the white bear obediently seated at the end of her stone bed. Taking her right hand, she made an effort to scoop up some of the now-rubbery blood from her red-stained attire, cupping it to her lips where she ravenously slurped it down.

When she had finished, she cocked her head to one side, listening to the gathering noise on the stairs as the others drew closer to her location. A haunting, wide grin shot across her still partially transparent, blood-splattered face. The grin did little to add any charm to the visage but instead deepened its repugnant nature, as sharp teeth barbed from her jaw like daggers amid the still, crystalline visage.

"How much farther?" Charles groaned from the middle of the procession climbing the tall flight of stairs. He was nestled between Corwyn and Hirim, who where themselves toward the front of the group – other crewmen lagging behind them with Mathias and with a few up near the gnome. All who had a weapon with them had made it ready.

"Afraid you'll break a sweat?" Hirim and his crew chuckled.

They'd been walking for a little over ten minutes and while it would have taken them less time to ascend the steps, they were still led by Josiah, whose smaller frame and cautious nature slowed the process for all.

"No, afraid I'll die of old age before this gnome gets to the top," Charles let loose his caustic barb.

"Patience, Mr. de Frassel. That is how the day is won," Josiah's calm, though strained, polite voice returned from the front of the line.

"Well the longer I wait, the closer to becoming an ice sculpture I get," the halfling retorted to the gnome.

"Shh." Corwyn turned back toward the halfling. "I think I hear something."

All fell silent upon the bard's words and stopped; each straining their ears and imaginations at what even the slightest sound could be. When they had been stilled for a while and nothing came to their hearing, they collectively let out the breath they had been holding back since the bard's statement.

"Nothing." Hirim echoed everyone's thoughts.

"Can we keep moving then before I freeze to this stair?" Charles whined then wiped another stream of fresh snot away with his mitten.

Again they continued their climb. It wasn't that much longer until they had made their way up to the top of the steps and the aged oak door yet a little further.

The door was unadorned, only aged and stiff from the cold where it had stood for countless years and would stand for countless more, given the way the cold seemed to keep it intact. Each was cautious as they neared the door, studying it in their own way. None wanted to touch it or get too close to it lest it looked like a commitment to enter into the opening.

"So we go in?" Corwyn asked after the others had finished their examination and moved to pool around the opening.

"Certainly, Mr. Danther. We must be getting close to something. I can feel it in my bones," Josiah stood tall and brought what gusto he could to his words – the bureaucratic nature of the gnome shining through once again.

"That's probably the cold gnawing away at your marrow," the halfling mumbled.

A sharp intake of breath echoed around the bard as he placed his hand to the door to push it all the way open. Silently the opening widened before them, allowing a flickering light to dash out at them like silvery dust, or the moon upon the crystals of snow at night.

"*This* looks promising," Charles weaseled up between a pair of legs and the sliver between them and the doorway.

"Indeed," Josiah replied.

Corwyn lead the way inside the room, flanked by two crewmen and followed by Hirim and the rest – Charles being last in the procession, joined by a set of remaining crewman.

All were uneasy at what they saw.

"How come there's light in here?" Hirim's head studied the room with a wide panoramic sweep of his head.

"This feels odd somehow." Josiah peered toward the wall on his left, taking in painted images pulled from the darkness by the cold light above them. The fresco contained a battle between what looked to be priests of Asorlok clashing arms against a collection of wild Nordicans.

"You're telling me," Charles then stepped into the room. "This whole place feels like a crypt."

At that, a pervading silence hovered over the company as the halfling's words seeped deep into their minds. None wanted to have such grim imagery playing about their head that particular moment, but couldn't help but agree with the halfling.

"Do you think this would be where it is?" Corwyn broke the silence, putting his hand to the shoulder of Josiah.

"Huh?" The gnome shook his head from a daze upon the gesture. His thoughts were still focused on the fresco, which stretched across the chamber's walls like an unrolled scroll.

"Do you think what we're looking for is in here?" the bard repeated.

"It's a better chance than where we were before," Josiah studied more of the room.

"What about it, Mathias?" Corwyn looked over to the elf, who was staring at another fresco.

"This whole place could be filled with secret rooms like this one." Mathias' comment revealed his mind was more on his observations than the conversation. "It's a very large place after all and we don't know exactly what we're looking for."

"Start searching then," Hirim motioned for the crew to spread out. "You stay here and watch the door," he stopped four sailors, the ones who had followed behind Charles, from leaving the doorway. "If you hear anything from downstairs – like that door trapping us up here – you let us know."

"Aye, sir." One of their band, this one a Celetor with a cutlass in one hand and sputtering torch in the other, turned into a watchful guard upon his charge. Meanwhile, Corwyn and Mathias made their way to the altar, climbing up the dais and wading around the stone slabs with care. Once they reached the top each took a turn looking at the silver chalice; studying it without touching it as best they could in the starry light accented by Corwyn's torch.

"What do you think?" Mathias asked the bard after both had given the chalice a cursory glance.

"I think I'm not sure I want to touch it," Corwyn replied.

"Me either," said Mathias, "but what could it be used for? Ceremonial?"

"Could be…" Corwyn joined the elf's contemplation.

"You don't think that the chalice is what we're looking for, do you?" Mathias drew a bit closer to the silver cup but was stopped by Corwyn's hand holding him back from any further progress.

"Look there," the bard motioned to a faint scratching of runes on the altar itself beside the chalice, "what do they say?"

The scribe squinted his eyes a bit as he read. "Ah…'Hail… Hail the Eternal King.'"

"Looks like there's a lid here of some sort," Corwyn held his finger above the altar and traced out a square where a faint line disrupted the uniformity of the surface.

The others in the chamber wandered about the walls silently, mindful to watch their step and be prepared for anything in this room, which seemed more unnatural to them than anywhere else in the citadel they had thus far encountered. Some crewmen studied the plainly designed sconces, others ventured up toward the altar to see what they could find. They stopped to look at the undecorated granite slabs that had been made to resemble common beds, encircling the dais and the altar. Still others were intrigued by the frescoes on the walls.

Josiah was one such person so intrigued and he looked closer at the painted images he'd seen from the door. Standing beside the fresco, he proceeded to carefully walk around the chambers so as to follow the progression of the unfolding visual story. So far he had seen some Asorlins fight some Nordicans. Judging by their attire, it seemed to have been from some distant time ago. This flowed into the next image of the priests of Asorlok running some of these Nordicans through with gold-tipped spears. The spears jutted up their chests and out their backs with a violent shower of crimson gore.

Following this attack, the Nordicans slaughtered the priests with their bare hands, some even being so feral in combat as to gnaw into the priests' necks like a wolf taking down its prey. Josiah shivered at the image not for its graphic nature, for he had seen depiction of violence before, but because of some other hidden meaning that he didn't yet fully comprehend. This shadowy recollection hid behind the more orderly halls of his intellect, scurrying away from any attempt to wrangle it out into the light.

"I think we found something," Mathias' words drew all toward the altar.

"Me too," came the words of the Telborian crewman who stared down at the blood-splattered granite slab, torch in one hand, cutlass in the other, but both eyes wide with fright.

"What is it, Mr. Onuis?" Josiah joined the others who had beat him to the dais to take in the sight of Mathias and Corwyn peering into a hole in the altar. Together, they had observed a square in the altar, and discovered it to be a lid to a pocket inside the altar itself.

"I think you might want to see for yourself," Mathias' tone was far from optimistic.

"Well then," Josiah made his way up the dais and toward the altar, parting people before him all the way, "let us just see, shall we?"

Both Mathias and Corwyn stepped aside from the altar to allow the gnome room to get up close then crane his neck down into the opening.

"My word," Josiah's face went white then stern as his upper lip became more solid than steel and his eyes just as resolute. "Dear me, gentlemen, this a peculiar quandary. Is *this* the object which we seek?"

"What?" Charles wormed his way through some legs but was unable to get to the top. "Let me see."

"What about *this* then?" Hirim's deep voice came from in front of them where a few of his crewmen had gathered around a granite slap covered in a dried and partially frozen layer of blood. The discovery, lined with a ring of blazing torches, did little to create a feeling of good will. Instead, Corwyn noticed each crewman now held his cutlass in a deathlike grasp; each's eyes darting about like a bee in a bouquet with a racing heart and quick, feverish breath.

"This is bad luck, Captain. It's the curse, the curse that the elf was talking about before," an old salt Telborian's voice cracked.

"Nonsense," Hirim's reply was as mellow as he could keep it despite his own concerns. "It's blood – and fresh at that; something is in here with us lads. Maybe even the same person who closed that door on us. It's no curse, but a real enough threat that befalls us – one that bleeds."

"Comforting," Charles' sarcasm fluttered from his lips with a puff of smoke from a freshly lit cigarette. He had tried the limits of his willpower for the day and with the added stress of this discovery, he needed his addiction to calm him more than ever.

"I think we should be going, Josiah," Corwyn turned to the gnome. "We should really find a way out of here and then come back once we–"

"You are giving up *now*?" Josiah shook his head in solemn disappointment. "Mr. Danther, I may be a meek man in many things, but I have not been known to leave an obligation undone. We came here to find the secrets of eternal life or some such boon as related to it from this map, and we have yet to find it.

"As the representative of Coggsbury, Elliott, Chesterfield and Company I believe we soldier on. Keep our wits about us and we'll get out of this safe and sound."

"There's blood here, Josiah." Hirim jabbed his cutlass at the granite slap for added emphasis. "I don't know where it came from, but it's fresh, and I don't want to add to it or have any of my crew add to it either."

"So what are you saying, Mr. Koofehi?" Josiah's eyes had taken on a bit more resolve than when Hirim had last spoken to the gnome.

"I'm saying we leave. There's nothing here. This was a failed venture," the Celetor was blunt.

The gnome set his torch on the altar. "If we *do* find a way out of here, and we will, rest assured, there is no guarantee we will be able to find our way back inside. We have only now found a chalice in this apparently sacred room and..." Josiah released a small grunt as he shoved his dainty, mittened hands into the stone pocket and dug out its contents.

"Josiah–" Corwyn started.

"Don't–" Mathias added.

"...this skull." The gnome had pulled free an aged human skull from inside the altar. It was missing its lower jaw, but was otherwise whole. Dry and clean, it was like some gruesome trophy amid the gnome's uplifted hands.

Before anyone could do anymore, the roar of some animal, blended with the surprised screams and shouts from behind those gathered around the altar, filled the chamber. All turned to see a large white bear, blood splattered about its face, chest and claws, rapidly charging down from the wall above the doorway like some bulbous spider. The crewman standing guard at the door could do nothing but scream in fright – the beast was upon them before they could do more. Meaty claws, already bloodstained from previous battles, slashed into one of the Napowese crewmen before he could even raise his weapon in defense. He fell to his knees in a crescendo of agony, clutching the contents of his abdomen as they spilled out between his red fingers.

"To arms men! To arms!" Hirim's shout bellowed all around. He didn't need to tell his crew what to do, they already had lunged into the fray, coming to the aid of their fellows – blood boiling hot for revenge.

Some of them dropped their torches to the ground so as to be able to better fight this threat, others who had held them gripped them all the more to aid them in the violence to come.

Those nearest the strange bear then struck.

Two Telborian's with a hearty heft slashed home their blades only to have them hit up against something that felt like stone rather than living flesh. Undaunted and fueled with the fire of life and death combat, each struck once more before the bear was full upon; having climbed down the wall from which he first attacked the Napowese, to stand before them on his hind legs. The crewmen's additional attacks were worthless. With each ineffective blow, the bear seemed to roar out in mock victory.

"It's not *natural*, Captain!" one of the combatants shouted in fear. "We can't cut into its hide with our blades."

The others had joined the fray now, though kept a brief distance to steer clear of the swings of the beast. A downward strike of one paw plowed the leathery skin of one of the Telborians along his neck and face, the force behind the assault pulling him to the floor with a stream of curses.

The other Telborian near him dared one last strike, this time a sharp lunge of his cutlass into the bear's chest. Though he drove it true to its mark with all the force he could muster, shouting his defiance to further give him aid, the point of the blade halted when it touched the bear's flabby, furred skin. The sudden loss of momentum caused the sailor to trip on his own feet and tumble backwards, dropping his weapon as he tried to right himself. The last thing he saw was an ivory mountain of fur topple down upon him.

Those gathered around the altar could do nothing but watch. Josiah, still holding the skull in his hands, became drawn to it once more as his mind raced for options of escape in such a perilous situation. The only way in or out blocked by bloody and seemingly pointless combat – he was trapped… or was he? He still had the skull. But, what good was it? It was just old bone, it couldn't save him now. Why even keep it locked up in an altar in the first place? What value did it have to be placed away so?

Josiah rapidly mused on these and other thoughts, doing his best to turn the screams of the dying from his mind as he directed the skull to face his gaze. Empty eye sockets looked back at him. For a moment, he could imagine what his own skull would look like years from now after this whole encounter had ended…but he pushed such grim musings from his mind. For now he needed to concentrate and delve deep into the pool of his intellect for an answer.

The skull was a brownish, almost parchment shade of bone. Dry and cold, it was clearly human…a human who had once possessed some rather odd teeth the gnome noticed after careful inspection. Josiah saw that the teeth he had first assumed were normal like all mortals were in fact sharp fangs, more in keeping with the maw of a wolf or some other large predator. The largest of these fangs were two large incisors, which drew themselves lower than the rest and focused the worried eye of the gnome heavily upon them.

It was as he focused his mind closer on the skull that he thought to see two red pinpricks of light from deep inside the empty sockets. These sinister dots made the skull look more alive;

a frightful shadow of life that was far from natural. The longer he peered into the skull's sockets, the more uneasy the gnome became. Soon he could hear the sound of faint screams mixing amid the growling and snarling of wolves. He could smell fresh blood, hear the rending of limbs, and a slew of guttural orders being bellowed out by a Nordic tongue…

All these things came to Josiah in faint echoes that grew more intense the longer he held the skull. Soon, the din overshadowed the activity around him, bringing him into a place where he never wanted to be again…

In horror, he dropped the skull to the floor where it hit the ground with a soft, hollow clunk. Instantly, he was back to his senses and the danger around him – though his face was far paler than it had been before and his eyes were wide and panicked.

While Josiah had been having his experience with the skull, Corwyn and Mathias were making to leave the dais when from out of the darkness of the ceiling a pale, blood-splattered woman leapt down before them. Wild-eyed with disheveled white hair that looked like a clumsy bundle of hay falling apart; she gave the two men a dreadful start. The fear only rose into their hearts when she smiled.

It was then that they saw her teeth… her razor-edged, fanged teeth and larger incisors pressing down from above her jaw amid them. Flesh that was so white it could have been marble rather than skin made up her body. Indeed, both men didn't know if they were facing some kind of animated statue, as some tales have said wizards had created in the past to guard certain treasures, or some kind of new threat entirely. Most of the woman that wasn't a cold, lifeless white was splattered red with what appeared to be fresh, though now clotting and, in some cases, partially frozen blood.

"What now?" Mathias was barely able to get out beyond the struggled whisper that escaped his mouth.

"I don't know," the bard shivered, but held his ground.

Suddenly, the temperature in the room plummeted, colder than what any of them had ever experienced, as if the entire room had been flung into the depths of the floating ice isle. The bard felt as if he was about to freeze solid when he caught another good look at the woman before him. It was then that he saw her eyes blink and behind them a faint circle of blue beginning to emerge for irises on the blank orbs. Looking lower, Corwyn saw her opaline tongue pointing and luridly jabbing at them between her pale lips and jagged teeth.

Josiah, who had just come out of his experience with the skull, now looked to the woman. Upon sight of her his flesh grew paler still. "Ah…I think we should be leaving now, gentlemen," Josiah's voice was the weakest any of them had ever heard.

Josiah started forward and accidentally kicked the skull with his foot so that it rolled into Corwyn's boot. The bard dared a look down at the object and made a move to retrieve it, watching the strange woman with leery eyes as he did so. As the bard picked up the skull, the woman's eyes plunged their cool hatred with full force into the Telborian. Scrutinizing his movements, she glared and snarled as Corwyn turned the skull around to face him. Like the gnome before him, Corwyn saw the pin pricks of light. Corwyn thought it was a trick of his torch, but this time he felt his mind go deeper into the place Josiah had only inhabited in a shadowy way…

Suddenly the whole chamber was gone. In its place was an older village of Nordic make. The village was empty and Corwyn was in the middle of it, but somehow knew that he wasn't really there too. It was as if he was in a waking dream. Dirt roads and a handful of longhouses built of rough hewn logs squatted between the walls. It was a simple rustic village, like many Nordic villages, only this one had the chieftain's house and served as the capital of the whole tribal landscape. How Corwyn knew all this was beyond him. He seemed to be part of a play that was revolving around his person regardless of how he felt or thought or did for that matter.

Corwyn didn't know what to think – what to do when faced with such a situation. It felt so unnatural, so haunted with the workings of some kind of supernatural quality that he didn't know where to start.

This didn't make sense to him at all.

If he had been transported to a new locality, and he supposed it could be very possible given that what they were seeking on this quest was probably guarded by spells or faith-filled prayers of some type, then where was he? Furthermore, why was this village he'd come to be in abandoned? And of course, how long ago was that? How did a whole community just disappear? The livestock? Pets?

No, the bard wanted to be done with this place as soon as possible. He had seen some sights in his young life thus far, but this was by far the most unsettling. Best to be quick here and be done with it…but how to leave a place he had no hand in traveling to in the first place?

"Hello?" Corwyn shouted in Telborous.

He tried again with what he had learned of the Nordic tongue.

Still nothing.

Gingerly, he walked onward, drawing closer to a stone well built in the center of the village. Corwyn moved forward, scanning everything in sight while attempting to stay focused. He chanced a peek into the well when he reached it and found nothing save water and a wooden bucket floating halfway down the stone shaft, attached with a simple rope to the crank above.

Suddenly, the bard jolted when he heard a low clamoring of voices off in the distance. Frantically he searched around the sparse area only to find nothing. Uneasy, but unable to do much about it, he continued moving about the village, which consisted of only about seven longhouses.

Besides this he spotted the largest longhouse. The bard knew a chieftain or leader of some sort would probably make his home there, given its large and more ornate nature, and the two poles with a long toothed feline-like skull perched on each. Looking beyond, his eyes stopped when he found what seemed to be a tavern.

Corwyn walked over to the simple rectangular building. A bull's skull adorned the overhang, from which dangled a sign on a wrought iron chain, carved in runic text. With his limited studying with Mathias and his previously scattered knowledge, the word came to him quite quickly: *Mead Hall.*

Corwyn walked up the roughly-hewn, well-worn stone pavement outside the entranceway, pushing the thick iron reinforced wood door aside. Soured air smelling of sweaty bodies and alcohol came at the bard with a stale slap and grating squeak. Inside it was dank and dark, with very little light at all streaming in from anywhere save a few cracks in the walls and the doorway itself.

The bard was rebuked from going any further, however, by a wild looking woman who stepped out from the darkness before him. Garbed in tattered furs and snarling like a lunatic, the bard noticed her sharp teeth and unnatural cold white pallor almost instantly. This wasn't the same woman who he'd faced just moments before, but of similar relation. Her disheveled blonde hair was so light as to be almost white and her hands were bloody claws.

Corwyn wasted little time running from the sight only to charge into a collection of ten similar figures – men and women who shared similar dress and appearance to the first woman Corwyn had encountered. All made an attempt to get closer to Corwyn, clawing and lunging forward with snarls and hungry growls. Inhuman creatures encased in human flesh, the bard didn't know what to make of them or what was happening to him, only that he wanted to be free from this place as badly as he'd ever wanted anything in his life.

He did his best to stand clear of their attacks, but they were drawing closer and had encircled him. Any hope of escape was impossible now. Yet, even as this reality continued, the din of battle from the chamber he'd recently left echoed once again in his ears. Even as these familiar, grim sounds came back to him, the bard saw the circle around him part to allow a tall, strong Nordican step between them and toward Corwyn. He was the most bestial of all of them, clear blue eyes gleaming with an animalistic fury. Sharp features molded over his pale white flesh like jagged contours of chiseled stone.

This new figure, whom Corwyn took to be their leader by the way the others carried themselves around him, bore identical traits to the woman in the marble chamber. Even his long white hair and sharp teeth, which he bore in a smile, seemed to be a duplicate of the former woman's visage. Dressed in war-ravaged, fur-lined leather armor, the man appeared to be a warrior of some kind, perhaps even a king.

Corwyn couldn't dwell upon this thought much more as the man lunged at him full force, striking Corwyn hard around his shoulders – locking on to them with an iron grip. The bard could do little more than try and move his arms and hands in an attempt to keep the death-dealing jaws snapping at his face and neck far from him. This was almost impossible to do; his attacker's strength was far too great to resist.

The bard felt his arms grow weaker and the feral Nordican's face grow closer and closer. He could feel the impossibly cold breath issue out of his mouth onto his cheeks and neck as he snapped his jaws in rapid succession until finally the jagged teeth found purchase…and then it was over…

26

Suddenly Corwyn was back in the chamber once more. He had dropped his torch to the ground and found that in his hands he held the skull before his face; empty sockets still holding the faint outline of clear blue eyes and chiseled flesh… It was then that it all made sense. The bard shook his head to clear his mind. He couldn't shake free of the knowledge he had gained from that brief vision, and the new insight shook him to the core. Whether it was the added stress of the moment or the glimmering of some short-lived revelation the bard wasn't sure entirely, but everything he had read on the trip, and the things he had seen – even that odd saga he'd discovered, now tied together into a large image he was being made more and more aware of with each pounding heartbeat.

How had he been so blind to the clues?

They had to get out of this place.

"Run," the bard moved as fast as his freezing legs could carry him over the dais and altar and then on top of the very bloody slab where the woman had once lain. No sooner had he done so then she lashed out at Mathias, brazening her hands like claws against him – slicing into the arm of his jacket before he'd managed to pull away from the fiendish woman by skirting around the altar.

Mathias gave out a shrill cry of agony. The attack was as painful as it was swift. The elf didn't take more than a quick glance at the shredded area on his person, however, as he made his way down the steps of the dais behind the altar. When he did look he nearly fainted. His whole right arm was now a deep crimson and throbbed as if it were on fire with every beat of his heart. Fear seized him then like never before and he could do nothing but move slowly backward from the monstrous woman with mechanic steps.

Josiah was now unable to move; he was frozen, both in fright and by the bone-numbing cold that seemed to flow off the grotesque woman in waves. His eyes focused on the coming doom before him like a rabbit cowering before the oncoming wolf.

"Josiah!" The gnome heard Corwyn shout as if from a great distance.

The woman took a step closer. Josiah could smell her then. The salty, metallic scent of blood was heavy upon her. Even cooled, he could detect its sickly perfume on her chilled breath.

"Josiah, run!" The bard's advice came to him again, but it came from some distance now, fading away far behind him… Instead, the gnome held up his hands before his face in some feeble attempt to block the coming attack or at least hide the advancing face of the monstrous woman. Perhaps if he shielded his vision from her face, he might go to Mortis with a better image to comfort his thoughts for eternity.

It was then that Corwyn stepped behind the gnome, skull held before him as if to ward of the monstrous woman. Upon seeing the uplifted skull, the woman hissed. Eyes that were once a swimming milky haze turned solid in rage.

With a rapid movement, the fiendish woman found a temporary opening around the bard. The solid impact of her fist into the gnome's upper chest felt to Josiah more like a meteor impact than simple fisticuffs. The sound of snapping twigs came to the gnome's ears as the wind was knocked out of him and he toppled from the dais, landing on the frigid floor below.

The bloody woman then concentrated her attention upon Corwyn.

While Corwyn and the others faced their attacker, the crewman at the door didn't fare too well against the bear. Three more had fallen by the creature's frenzied, savage attacks. The others gathered about him had ceased the pointless melee and moved back from the blood-splattered mound of ivory fur.

"Pull back! Pull back!" shouted Hirim, "this beast is unnatural. We can't kill it with normal steel."

The Celetor didn't know what to do with the situation. What kind of animal could withstand the bite of steel? This was a doomed effort if ever there was one. Even if they were able to escape this room, they would be trapped in this building to be picked off one by one by the frosty devils that called this accursed place home. And who knew how many other things still lurked in this tower and were even now rushing toward them as they created such noise with their fighting?

It was then that the bear gave a growl of victory. Confident that none would challenge it, the bear began to lap up the spent blood of the slain crewmen. None could do anything but watch the horrific sight before them as they continued their slow backwards retreat toward Hirim. If they wouldn't be leaving through the door, then they would take their stand in tightly packed numbers.

"'Tis a *fiend*, Captain!" a Celetoric sailor belted out upon the sight of the bear lapping up blood.

"Keep your head about you – all of you." Hirim's gruff words yanked a few back from the brink of madness. "We'll get out of this yet if we all keep our wits about us."

No sooner had the captain finished these words than the cold woman attacked. Faster then the human eye could even discern, she leapt from the dais, where she had recently been harassing Corwyn, onto the back of a retreating Patrician crewman. His back turned as it was, he didn't stand much of a chance. The very same moment she landed upon him, her jagged maw was on his neck, ripping it apart even as a scream gurgled up from the bloody mess.

"Gods of Light preserve us," said another sailor as he ran as far as he could from the scene, stopping up against a wall, under a pale, twinkling sconce.

All gathered could do nothing. Fright froze their limbs as the woman guzzled the red ichor from her victim, turning the elf from a gray-tinted flesh to a dull alabaster hue. Within moments she dropped the man to the ground, licking her lips in savage delight. Her body had now changed. It had become more flesh-like, losing the previous stony nature, but still possessing an unnatural white pallor. Her eyes, though, were now solid white with powder blue irises amid them, searching out the scattered, cowering men for her next victim.

28

Josiah released a small moan as Corwyn gently slapped his chapped cheeks. Charles still cowered behind the altar, cigarette long since fallen from his mouth in fright and face bedecked with a myriad of sweat droplets. The halfling wasn't even able to move if he tried due to the paralyzing fright. Mathias had come to regain some of his senses, having now braced himself up against the altar to keep his light head from causing him to pass out. He was focusing too hard on keep himself conscious to hear the gnome sputter awake.

"You okay?" Corwyn asked Josiah. Beside the bard was the skull. Corwyn had placed it at his feet in order to rouse the gnome.

"I am quite well, despite the circumstances, Mr. Danther," Josiah rolled his face over to meet up with the bard's gaze. Corwyn could tell he was lying by the pain he could see outlining the gnome's eyes.

"We have to get out of here," Corwyn shot a quick glance up to the woman harassing Hirim and his men.

"Quite obvious, but how? We are locked away in this place and now we have these two denizens of the pit with which to contend." The gnome struggled with a few grunts to sit upright.

"I don't have that answer, Josiah." Corwyn aided the gnome in gaining an upright position.

"I did not expect you to, Mr. Danther, for I think we are all equally allotted to die here, I am afraid. Too bad it will be quite a gruesome death. I had wished that I would expire at an older age, in my slumber; but such is the wish of all I suppose and not all are so fortunate to have such a wish granted them by the gods."

Josiah watched as Corwyn picked up the skull.

"I would not do that if I were you, Mr. Danther," Josiah cautioned.

"I think it's the only hope we have of getting out of here alive," Corwyn turned the skull over around in his grip, looking at every facet he could as the very short amount of time he had would permit.

"I am uncertain if we even *have* any hope left." the gnome's smile was far from cheerful.

"Hope is *all* we have left," Corwyn focused his eyes to find anything of possible use from the skull.

"Well, at least you will die happy then," Josiah turned to look at Mathias and Charles behind him. The gnome could barely suppress a shudder when he took in the elf's ruined arm.

"I think I have some of the pieces, but the puzzle still isn't making total sense…yet," Corwyn mused aloud.

"What is so important about the chalice and the altar?" the bard continued to pour over the skull and speak to himself. "If we know that we might be able to find a way out of this mess with our lives.

The crewmen had gathered together around their captain; cutlasses out and wild fear mixed with determination filling their veins and molding their faces. All stared ahead at the woman before them. Her cold aura wafted over them like a misty cloud. It was a cold that even their fur-lined garments couldn't defend against.

"If we have to make a final stand here, lads, then let's do it right. Let's die like men." Hirim gave what he hoped would be an inspirational speech to his faithful sailors. He wasn't sure, though, as to whose backbone was straightened by those few sentences, for all had accepted their fate; it was only a matter of heartbeats before it came to pass.

All rested in tense silence.

Only the gory lapping of the bear and the thudding of their own hearts, could be heard amid the frozen air. The woman spoke then, though the words were in the Nordic tongue and flat. Her eyes told of the hunger that fueled and drove her onward – a hunger birthed of unnatural desires and fiendish compulsion.

She smiled and another man died.

It all happened before anyone could react. A tiger-like leap and she was upon a helpless Celetor before he could do little more than wiggle his sword in hand. His weapon fell with a chilling clang as the young man's throat was punctured and torn by the pale woman's ravenous bites.

"Vampires," all around the dais turned to Corwyn as he softly spoke this word aloud.

"Beg pardon?" The fear already about Josiah's face took deeper root as he turned to the bard for clarification.

It had started to make sense. The figure in the vision, the one he saw in lead of the other Nordicans, had been Rainer. He was sure of it now. Just as sure as well that they now were facing vampires. Vampires that were connected to Rainer in some way… the saga…the friezes and the…the chains suspended over those basins…

"*Vampires*?" Charles was equally concerned with his question. The halfling could move somewhat again, but it was a sluggish affair. His brow was now a collection of cold, sweaty streams.

Corwyn had moved toward the top of the dais now, doing his best to ignore the sounds of death about him to try and figure out something – anything – to aid in their escape.

"You sure about those runes?" Corwyn asked the barely conscious Mathias, the bard's finger pointing to where the chalice had once stood. It took a moment for the elf to respond, his eyes having to focus on the bard from a glassy stare, but the words that came were still clear and concise. "Yes…that was the translation."

"Vampires," the bard whispered again and all around him felt even colder than before.

"What?" Some color had returned to Mathias' face. He hadn't heard much of the previous conversation, but now he did with enough mental comprehension to make sense of what the bard was pondering.

"Yeah," Charles had nervously risen now and was making his way to Corwyn's side on leaden feet, "what's this talk about vampires?"

"Indeed." Josiah now stood to his full height, wincing a bit as he did so. "I was lead to believe that their kind were extinct – if they ever existed at all."

"I wasn't quite sure they were real either, since all the old tales I know say they died out a long time ago. But I guess some, or at least *one*, is still alive," Corwyn added.

"Vampires?" Charles repeated; he stared down at the altar.

"Think about it," urged Corwyn. "This bear, the woman...the promise of eternal life for those who came here...the blood-letting room...

"Vampires were said to be eternal but they had to drink the blood of the living. It was part of their curse, the curse of eternal life. *That* is Rainer's legacy and why this place has been shunned and forgotten for so many centuries. He's tied to all the vampires because he *made* all the vampires...he was their *king*."

All around the altar drew silent at the bard's words as he drew himself up to the altar to look it over once more. The answer to their dilemma had to be there. If it wasn't...well he didn't want to think about that.

Finally, Charles looked over at the gnome who joined him and Corwyn onto the dais. "So the secret to eternal life is *vampirism*?"

"So it would appear, Mr. de Frassel," the gnome nodded grimly.

"That really ruins my retirement plans," the halfling turned back to the altar. "I was going to have some really fun times with all the coin I made."

"I think obscene profit is the least of our worries," Corwyn hurriedly studied the carvings on the altar stone he and Mathias had removed.

"How you holding up, Mathias?" The bard shot a quick glance at the elf who was slowing fading from life. Corwyn knew that the scribe was close to death and getting worse with each passing moment. His wound appeared to be a grievous one indeed.

"I'm still here," Mathias was able to force out of his mouth, though his speech was starting to slur and weaken.

"So what do we do?" Charles dared to get closer to the altar – as close as he could with his bulbous stomach and tremendous fear, though his sweating had now lessened a small degree.

"I'm working on that." Corwyn tried to remain calm as he kept up his search of the altar. "This skull and chalice have to be important for some reason. If we can use them–"

"Attack!" Hirim's words echoed in the chamber.

Josiah, Corwyn, Mathias, and Charles all turned toward the rising din of disturbance as each crewman, defiant screams in their throats, surrounded the woman, intending to die fighting if they had to die this day. Corwyn noticed that the woman had changed appearances from when he'd last seen her. Now her skin was more supple, like that of a Nordic woman. Her body had filled out a bit more with curves and smooth lines where once there had been only sharp points.

Still thin, her muscles stayed but they looked more lifelike – more fluid than before. Her eyes were now a brilliant soft powder blue and her hair was like white satin. This was not enough of a change to escape her evil nature, however, for her full lips dribbled blood past her chin and onto her breasts which lay under the gore-splattered, formerly white gown clinging about her body. Furthermore, her hands, though less claw-like, were still cruel, deadly, and gore-splattered, like the sharp teeth in her mouth.

"You better hurry," Charles, returned his attention to Corwyn, "once she's done with them, we're next." Charles dared another short glance over to the others who still fought, rather stupidly the halfling thought, against what must be a vampire, then quickly veered his eyes to the bard and altar.

"You two see if you can bandage Mathias up while I see what I can do here." The bard turned back to the altar. "We're going to have to move fast if we are going to get out of here alive."

Urged on by Hirim, the sailors fought against the vampire. Sword swings did little but slice her thin dress to ribbons, the blades being hindered from marring her fair skin just as with the bear. The vampire, for her part, seemed unconcerned about the chaotic dance surrounding her. Instead, she merely latched her hands and then mouth upon another victim. Telborian blood splattered and sprayed scarlet showers all around the other sailors as she eagerly dined upon his flowing fountain.

Even as the warm blood flowed into her, the whiteness of her hair and eyebrows turned to a light blonde then darkened to a soft but still silken strawberry blonde hue. Her eyes grew darker as well – the powdery blue becoming a deeper shade – till they looked like a smoldering blueberry with a black pupil clearly being seen in their center.

The sailors could do little but fruitlessly roar and swing, growl, slash and stab. Though they could take scant comfort in the tattered rag they were making of the woman's dress, it was all they would allow themselves to do in order to feel that they were doing their best against an insurmountable foe. Dropping the Telborian with one hand, she took a swift step and latched on to another with the other hand, lifting this one off the ground and strangling him with but one womanly, supernaturally strong hand. The sailor dropped his sword in his death throes, with wild desperation unsuccessfully clawing away at the pale wrist and arm that held him tighter than a hangman's noose.

"Let him go," Corwyn's strong voice filled the room.

29

At once both the clamor of senseless sword rustling and even the attacks of the blood-stained woman ceased; all turned their eyes toward the bard. All watched as Corwyn raised the skull over his head from on top the dais with the best card playing face he could muster. He was taking a big gamble with this move, but in truth, nothing else was left to them. He either had to act now or face the slaughter of everyone by the vampire's hands.

The die had been cast.

"Unless you want me to smash this, let him go." The bard's eyes narrowed and mitten-covered hands grew tight about the skull. He could see even from this distance that the vampire's eyes understood what he was saying and that there was even a little bit of fear behind those dark pupils…

The Telborian she held still struggled but his efforts were weaker now. Not satisfied he had her attention yet, Corwyn decided to raise the validity of his threat just a little, lifting the skull backwards as if he made ready to smash it on the ground. The white bear quickly raised its lulling head to let lose a low growl of warning.

Instantly, the vampire dropped the man like a rag doll. Then, like some rapid beast, she bowled down those that stood in her way of the dais and the bard. A swift sprint and she was one step below the bard, her dark blue eyes laced with malice and insatiable hunger.

"So you *do* understand me, then?" Corwyn didn't take his eyes off the woman, keeping them locked with her own to guarantee his own safety. Corwyn knew that if he should flinch for but a moment, he'd be dead. He had grabbed a wolf by the ears now and couldn't let go.

"What are you doing?" Hirim's agitated and confused question reached the bard. He was thankful for the reprieve, as were the sailors, some of whom had gone to aid the recently choked fellow – helping him to his feet.

"This skull is important to them," Corwyn kept his hard face upon the bloody woman…the bloody vampire, "it might be the only bargaining chip we have if we want to live."

"And if it's not?" Charles questioned. Both he and Josiah had managed to stem the flow of Mathias's bleeding with some shredded rags torn from their own and Mathias' dress. The elven scribe seemed to be a bit better for it as well – a faint tint of life still graced his cheeks, but it would be a miracle indeed should he survive the trek back to the boat.

"Then, you get to die," the bard resolutely returned without losing his gaze on the threat before him.

"Geve eat toah mee," the woman's words were slow and thick with the Nordic accent but still discernible. When she spoke it was if she had to recall how to form words; even in moving her mouth she had to momentarily struggle to form the right syllables.

"Not yet," the bard bartered. "First, you have to let us go and then I'll give it to you."

The woman snarled which was echoed by the bear's deep angry bellow.

"Those are my terms," the bard remained defiant.

None dared move or breathe as the vampire made her choice of action.

Finally, when the sands of time had seemed to become frozen, the woman choppily spoke something in an old dialect of the Nordic language. The bear lumbered away from the doorway and the mangled corpses it had so recently been enjoying. Hissing, the woman took a step down on the dais, moving toward Corwyn's left to allow him room to descend. All the while she watched him like a wild beast ready to pounce on its prey in the blink of an eye.

"Are you guys able to walk out of here, Mathias?" Corwyn didn't take his eyes off the woman, though his hand had started to ache and go numb from the lack of blood caused by his tight grip on the skull.

"I think so," came the tired sounding words from the elf. "They did a fair job of binding my wound."

"Josiah, you and Charles are going to have to help Mathias out of here," Corwyn took one step down the dais, his eyes fixed on the vampire at all times. For once the halfling offered up no snide remark at the order, merely obeying it as both he and Josiah moved to either side of the elf to help him down the steps.

"Hirim, get you and your men out of here," the bard addressed the others next.

"What about you?" The captain was bewildered at what was happening. It seemed still a bit too surreal for him to fully grasp.

"I'll be right behind you, but all of you have to get out of here first." Corwyn took another step down the dais.

Hirim nodded grimly. He knew this was the best course of action, and found it an odd thing that the one among them least skilled in aggressive confrontation had come up with the answer. The bard didn't even carry a weapon, but yet had managed to save their lives…at least Hirim hoped he had. If he lived through this he'd dwell on the irony later. They weren't out of this room or citadel nor back on The Phoenix just yet.

"Each one of you take a fallen mate and head down the stairs. If you can, grab one of the torches on the floor as well," Hirim ordered his men. "We'll leave no fellow man here to suffer the indignity these two fiends would entreat upon their corpses."

Acting upon his own words, Hirim bent down into the blood splattered, body-strewn carnage to retrieve the fallen body of a young looking Patrious. He still grasped his cutlass in his dead hand and his pale gray face was frozen in horrible agony. Hiram slung the body over his shoulder. The rest of the crew, most having two live mates for one dead sailor, made their way through the doorway and down the stairs. The last two sailors, having finally restored health to the Telborian nearly strangled to death, gave wide clearance to the dreaded bear that had stepped back from the doorway, watching them escape in frustrated anger.

"Can't you go any faster?" Charles asked Josiah as both huffed and puffed alongside the taller Mathias. They were the last to leave the room save Corwyn who was walking behind them backwards – skull at the ready before him like a shield. The vampire and the fiendish bear coldly watched the progress before them.

"*You* are shorter than *me*, Mr. de Frassel. Any implied lack of quickness on my part should first be examined upon your own diminutive stature and shortened stride." Josiah's face was aglow with the first signs of perspiration.

"Just keep moving." Corwyn followed with the vampire remaining just an arm's width to his right, like a wolf being repelled with a spurting torch. Corwyn had left his own torch where it had fallen. He didn't want any chance of unintentionally dropping this skull, and that required both hands.

"You're going to have to let us outside too – let us out of this place entirely," Corwyn told the vampire as he continued out of the room, lowering the skull to his chest so that he could feel his arms once more, arms numb from the extended position he'd held them.

Another snarl and darkly muttered Nordic words spat out of the woman.

"Good," Corwyn nodded.

Mathias and his aides managed to get him safely from the room and into the stairwell below. Giving as wide a girth as possible to the bear, Corwyn followed their path with care. The bear only watched the bard go by, eyes burning themselves into his spirit.

"I mean what I said, let us go free and you'll get this skull back." The bard backed up past the old oak door and to the top of the stairs; he raced down the flight faster than even he knew was possible. At the foot he met up with Mathias, Josiah, and Charles.

"Keep moving. We're not out of this yet," the bard squeezed by them and into the frieze-covered hallway beyond.

"You don't say?" Charles sarcasm had returned, but it was under his labored breath and newly-sweaty brow.

A massive growl came from the stairs above and carried down the stairwell. All who heard it shivered. Only Corwyn dared look to its source as Mathias, Josiah, and Charles made their way out of the secret passage. The bard saw the vampire and her ursine companion at the top of the stairs and though they held their ground, he decided not to press his good fortune.

"Let's keep it moving," Corwyn repeated.

"Move it gnome!" Charles snarled, "You too, bookworm."

The gnome and elf grunted together and moved forward into the hall, following behind the other crewmen whose sputtering torches were the only sense of a guidepost in the cold gloom that rose to greet them at the bottom of the stairs and relief-carved chamber beyond.

The vampire and the bear followed behind them.

In short order the crew had bunched around the closed entrance; Corwyn beside them, still walking backwards; Mathias and his allies a few feet away, gaining ever closer. It seemed that the farther out of the vampires' presence, the warmer it became, even in the midst of such a frosty place.

"Keep your word," Corwyn's words were soft and expectant, yet his eyes and face still held a serious demeanor as he watched the bear and vampire halt on the last step of the marble stairs.

"Wha–" Hirim spun around as the sound of stone grinding against stone entered into his ears behind him. The door that had allowed them entrance and then trapped them inside, had begun to open seemingly by its own accord. Still night outside, the hoary breeze which blew in upon the door's opening, seemed as welcome as a balmy gust.

"Get moving," Hirim ordered. He didn't mean to waste a single moment at the freedom being offered them.

Corwyn stood his ground, watching behind the others as he waited for the rest to exit, letting Mathias, Josiah, and Charles walk past and finally out of the empty citadel before he started to take a few steps back himself. The vampire and the bear, though, were ever at his heels; their patience more fleeting as the minutes wore on.

"Now, I'm going to just set this down and trust that you will let us go as you have agreed." Corwyn made it toward the doorway where he then slowly bent down and set the skull down upon the cold floor. With two more steps he was outside and away from the skull. The woman and the bear remained still as statues during all this. Only their eyes followed the bard, attending to every detail.

"How we looking out here?" Corwyn didn't turn his head to see for himself. Not yet…he had to be sure of everything first as he backed further away from the citadel.

"I've lost more good men today than I care to say," Hirim's tone was a dirge. He and the others had discovered the grisly killing field where others of his crew had started their journey to Mortis. "We'll give them a decent burial, by Perlosa."

When he felt it was safe to do so, Corwyn turned to view the carnage the bear had wrought upon the five crewman standing watch outside the citadel's walls. Their bodies were now rigid from the cold and even covered with bloody icicles in spots. It was then that the vampire dashed toward the door, blood lust on her lips and mind. Everyone shouted with fright until Corwyn pulled out something from inside his jacket that halted the vampire in her tracks with a blood freezing scream.

"I thought as much," Corwyn held out the lower jawbone of the skull. "In case you didn't keep your word I held on to this. Get back inside and let us leave here in peace; I'll throw this back to the beach when we depart. If you don't let us depart, I break this thing into hundreds of pieces."

The vampire growled in defiance but in the end returned inside the citadel.

The doorway closed behind her.

"Well played, Mr. Danther," Josiah looked up at the bard. Sweat fresh on his face and drunk on adrenaline, he was alive and happy that he'd live to see a new dawn.

"You don't think they'll still attack us, do you?" Mathias' voice was weak but still audible.

"No," Corwyn looked at the jawbone in his hand, "they want this too badly to risk it."

"So now we get to keep the jawbone, huh?" Charles smiled.

"No. I intend to return it, just as I said." Corwyn made his way over to the two makeshift sleds where the crew was already loading up the dead and securing them as best they could for the journey to The Phoenix.

"So we did all this for nothing?" Charles pouted as he helped lead Mathias to one of the boats.

"That depends on how you look at it, I suppose," the bard returned.

"Josiah and Charles – join Mathias in a boat," Hirim broke up the conversation.

"With the *corpses*?" The halfling wrinkled his nose.

"Either get in with a corpse or become one. We're not going to come back for any stragglers. While Corwyn's barter might have given us some time, I don't trust those devils at all and the sooner we leave the better." The captain proceeded to organize the dead into rows, maximizing available space for the return to The Phoenix.

"Agreed," Josiah spoke as he climbed into a nearby vessel that still held some room for his smaller frame.

"So what did we gain?" Charles stepped up and over the boat to sit beside Josiah, Mathias taking a place in the other boat where they had placed him.

"Certainly not what we set out to do, that is for sure," Josiah was rueful.

"I can't help you there." Corwyn bent down to pick up the rope tied to the boat and began to pull it forward along with Hirim and the rest of the living crew who started the long trek uphill; pulling the boats behind them. "I'm just happy to be alive."

"But I wanted to live forever and be filthy rich," Charles almost whined in his sulking. "This whole trip has been a colossal waste and now I have to go back without anything to show for it."

"You didn't really want to live forever, did you?" Corwyn asked the halfling as he pulled the rope with the aid of a few other Telborians up toward the lip of the snowy crater. It wasn't as hard work as the bard thought it would be but knew that after the adrenaline and fear had worn off in the morning, he'd be pretty sore for a while. The soft luminance from the snow and ice, along with the stars, would help give them enough light to see their way back to the boat, he surmised – they should be able to backtrack their trail for the most part.

"Who *wouldn't* want to live forever?" Charles thought the bard's question was the most foolish thing he'd ever heard.

"Not me," Corwyn huffed out a steamy blast of frosted air into the night.

"*Liar*," countered Charles.

"I think having a set span of years is what makes life worth living," The bard huffed as he tugged. "If you have endless time, things begin to lose their meaning; life itself becomes cheaper if it's not allowed to have an end.

"It's the journey along the path from birth to death that's the most wonderful and worthwhile. And every journey has a beginning and an end. If life had no end, then it would cease to be a *true* journey and therefore cease to be worthwhile." Corwyn looked back at the halfling briefly, who only crossed his arms in response.

"Uh-ha." Charles stuck out his chest, not believing a word Corwyn was saying.

"Charles," Corwyn hoped to make some headway with the halfling through some reasoning (though he wasn't too hopeful of much success), "think about what that place was offering for eternal life. She was a *vampire*. She doesn't give life, she takes it. It isn't eternal life she would have given you but eternal death.

"Nothing is worth that curse." All fell silent in agreement with Corwyn's words; the crewmen, Hirim, and the bard pulling the two makeshift sleds onward in the moonlight across the silent, sparkling snow.

The coming of dawn found all back on board The Phoenix. The dead had been made ready for their funeral and would be tossed into the ocean after they had returned to friendlier waters. Those who had been wounded had been treated as well. A sense of order and peace had found its way among the men now too, though all would feel much more peaceful once the frozen island was far behind them.

Corwyn spied over the forecastle of the frigate at the snowy beach a short distance from them with the coming light and slight warmth of the rising dawn. The sky was the color of molten lead and reflected the bard's face in a heavy array of shadowy contemplation.

Josiah had joined him on deck and was taking in the fresh light of the new day with a half interested observance. "I trust this will make for a very interesting story." The gnome, who appeared to be quick to mend over the attack dealt to him by the vampire not more than a few hours ago, peered over the boat and the small stretch of icy water between it to the snowy beach beyond. Hirim had been able to lay anchor fairly close to Rainer's Island, good news to Corwyn since he didn't know how strong his arm would be when it came to the task he now had to honor.

The bard looked at the jawbone in his mitten-covered hand one last time. "Who would have thought that this was what we were searching after?"

"Tragic and ironic," Josiah soberly agreed. "I wish to apologize for my rash actions in the citadel. No doubt it was my disturbing the skull that brought all this harm about."

"I doubt it," Corwyn peered down at the gnome with a weak smile. "Those two devils were probably waiting to jump at us no matter what we did. You picking up the skull probably only sped things up."

"No matter," Josiah was resolute in stature as well as voice, "it was unprofessional of me, to say the least, and certainly put at risk this whole enterprise."

"Was it worth the investment?" the bard's gaze moved back out to the snowy beach.

"There is always an amount of risk in any venture. What was done in this endeavor was nothing new, save in terms of what we found from our efforts.

"It seems a pity too that we didn't get to explore the rest of that citadel. Of the fraction we did manage to navigate in our haste, I am sure we have left many wonderful discoveries behind – historical and perhaps financial in nature."

"And probably more vampires hiding in wait or even traps or some other macabre things better left hidden from view," the bard darkly mused aloud. "I doubt there would be anything of beneficial use for Coggsbury, Elliott, Chesterfield and Company."

"Perhaps you are right," Josiah pulled out his pipe and started to fill it with tobacco. "That matter aside, I would be most interested however, in hearing how you came to the bold decision you did regarding our recent escape. Not even Mr. Onuis could piece together what you did there in the end – and he was the *scholar* on the subject."

Corwyn continued to watch the powdery snow sparkle like diamond dust in the rising light. "I saw something when I picked up the skull. It gave my mind the jarring it needed to put everything together."

"I see." Josiah put the pipe in his mouth and began digging inside his fur-lined jacket with a free hand. "I had an uneasy feeling when I picked it up as well, but did not see any visions attached with its possession."

"It was Rainer's skull. That was why they won't risk harming it." Corwyn turned the jawbone in the light of the rising dawn, lifting it up to the sky for closer examination. "I'm holding the jawbone of whom legends say was the king of the vampires and now I'm about to give it back to them."

"You *are* aware you are under no *real* obligation to do so?" Josiah had found what he had been looking for: a small piece of steel and a chunk of flint. "None of us on this enterprise would think any less of you should you keep it."

"I know," Corwyn brought his gaze back down toward the icy water, "but I gave my word."

"So you did." Josiah took the flint and struck it against the steel, causing a few sparks to fly into the bowl of his pipe. He repeated this a few more times until a small stream of smoke came up from the pipe and then grew into a small, aromatic cloud. Content upon his success, Josiah puffed away as he returned the flint and steel to their previous location.

"Coggsbury, Elliott, Chesterfield and Company don't plan on trying to turn some profit on vampirism, do they?" Corwyn raised his eyebrow as he turned his head toward the gnome.

Josiah mingled a cough with a laugh; smoke spraying everywhere as he did so. "Heavens no. Morality and ethics are cornerstones to any business that wishes to prosper. We will do no such thing as try to gain profit from vampirism.

"This venture has demonstrated that there is nothing of merit to take and we have to count the losses and then move on to other things. Such is the nature of free enterprise."

"Glad to hear it," Corwyn smiled. He then hurled the jawbone over the water and toward the beach beyond. Both Josiah and Corwyn watched it skip over the water for a few feet like an oversized stone before it tumbled into the dry, brittle snow.

"Ready to go home?" Corwyn turned and made his way toward his quarters and away from the cold.

"Never has Breanna looked more attractive than it does right now." The gnome joined Corwyn.

A moment later a deep bellow from Hirim brought the anchor up and set The Phoenix moving away from the floating isle into warmer waters and more pleasant thoughts.

Maiden
Rock

The day was fresh when the young Telborian bard made his ascent of the wild hill known as Maiden Rock. It was the month of Asoria and all was budding and new – spring in the Grifftmacht Hills of Talatheal. Fragrant air, caressed with the fragrance of ripe honeysuckle and fresh-bloomed wild flowers, danced about the rolling mounds of earth.

Corwyn Danther, the famed bard of the Midlands, had come to Maiden Rock to honor his goddess and to gain some rest and much needed perspective. Flushed with the emotional and physical events of his most recent adventure, he'd had little time to refresh himself from the wearing down that often accompanied such excursions. The havoc such trips dealt to emotions, mind, and yes, spirit, were detrimental and even serious if left unchecked for long.

Indeed, Corwyn knew of such a thing happening on various occasions – hardened warriors become raving maniacs for a time; their discipline broken over the need to relieve the stress piled upon them. So it was that Corwyn found it wise to keep himself rested as best he could, and endeavored to relieve the stresses upon his own life in constructive ways. That was why he'd wandered off to the Grifftmacht Hills shortly after The Phoenix had docked once again in Elandor. Though the snowy isle at the Crown of the World was physically far from him, the event was still fresh in the mind.

Looking at Corwyn as he climbed, one would never know the weight he carried on his shoulders. He was a handsome young man. His medium length reddish-blonde hair fluttered about in a soft breeze and highlighted his blue-green eyes amid a clean-shaven, peach-colored face. His garb had been changed from that of a few weeks before to more comfortable traveling gear: brown linen pants, matching leather boots, and a plain cotton shirt with a cordovan suede vest. Over his back he slung his well-used, cherry wood lute; in his right hand he held an equally worn walking stick. Along with these two possessions, he had brought with him a small coin purse, a small sack for food, and a drinking skin, all of which hung from his hard, black leather belt.

With the recent events of his travels on The Phoenix and all the things he had seen in the far north – a dangerous and deadly collection of thoughts echoing about his mind – Corwyn needed some peace and quiet. Maiden Rock was just the place to find it. A hermetic shrine devoted to Causilla, Patroness of Bards, the shrine was said to house a wonderful statue of the goddess, called *The Maiden*, naturally enough. Rumors and legends spoke of the site being frequented – some said guarded – by pleasant spirits and servants of Causilla. A vast majority of these tales spoke of Muses, the chief servants of the goddess on Tralodren, frolicking about as well.

Corwyn was pleased he now had a chance to return. He'd only been able to visit the shrine once before in his younger days and welcomed a return. While he hadn't had the encounters that these various tales proposed should occur to people who visit Maiden Rock on his first trip, he did know that it had a great cluster of perpetually blooming rose bushes. Their scarlet blooms more wonderful than any other flower in the whole of Tralodren. These too were tied to many tales, some speaking of the bushes being formed by blood lost from dying lovers, tears from those mourning for lost love, or even the drops of blood from Causilla herself.

If the bard wasn't certain as to the validity of these tales, Corwyn didn't doubt that the flowers were special, for if they bloomed year round then they could be no natural plant.

For all these tales, though, the site was really a forgotten thing. Most in these hills were dwarves who didn't take to their worship of the goddess that well; Shiril and Drued fulfilling their ecclesiastical needs just fine. Other races who populated the area did what most did in other parts of the Midlands: hailed Asora or the Gods of Light as their deity of choice, letting the single-minded adoration of Causilla fall unto a scant, scattered minority at best (mostly adored by young lovers, newlyweds and romantics at heart). Though most avoided the shrine, it still called out to the faithful to come and rest and forget their woes for a while.

Though dedicated to the goddess of love, arts and beauty, Maiden Rock was far from an easy climb. Sloping wide and fat at the base, it was dotted with low-lying green bushes, still a bit moist from recent rainfall. As these bushes thinned, more rock shards – like pottery pieces – splintered through the grasses. Becoming more dominant, mixing with small pebbles and then harder, larger stones, the ground became more abrasive and steep. While not the tallest of foothills in the area, it was still quite formidable, even with the thin game trail that snaked its way along the rocks and green, which Corwyn now followed.

About one fourth of the way up the hill, the bard noticed that the landscape had become much more brown and less green. Patches of color still caught his eye, though, and stout, stubborn bushes yet held their ground amid jagged overhangs and larger ridges of stone that resembled rough-hewn walls. He figured he'd be just about near the top by late morning if he kept his pace.

He'd traveled here on foot instead of horse or carriage in order to slow down and perceive things from a more relaxed view – to see the world around him and be able to enjoy it a little longer as well. In truth, the hill was not more than a day's walk from the small town of Tolan, which was to the east and a bit south from the hills. A simple yet restful night in the wilds yesterday allowed him even more relaxation and time to think away from the crowds, the music… and from past adventures. Yes, here he was confident that none would bother him save an odd farmer or traveler. It was the perfect plan, the perfect time for reflection. He had made his ascent at dawn after finishing up his last crust of bread and hunk of cheese for breakfast at the hill's foot. An hour later he had found himself at his present location – a bit warm from the climb, but excited to see the top.

The bard took a moment to rest from his progress; the rising angle of the slope was not yet that steep, but was increasing quite quickly now. It was enough of a change to weary him slowly, but not bring him to outright exhaustion. The incline was also just enough to cause him to lean up against a dandelion-speckled sandstone bulge and catch his breath for a moment beneath a clump of buttery honeysuckle.

As he leaned up against the hard surface and let out a small sigh. He felt his mind clear a bit and a small portion of the weight on his shoulders lift away. It was good to be away, but he knew that the world, in time, would claim that attention once more.

He couldn't stay still for long.

Corwyn's spirit was too creative, too infused with the need to get something done, to create or see something new. The bard had learned that if his feet stayed too long in one location restlessness soon followed. All this rest was temporary at best, but he would enjoy it, nonetheless, while it lasted.

The young bard closed his eyes from the rising sun and let it kiss his flesh. More relaxing than a hot bath on the coldest of days, the warmth seeped into his bones and brain. It and the soft fragrance of the nearby honeysuckle was a soothing sensation like some healing balm, drawing out more stress from his marrow and muscles. He could have remained that way for a little bit longer, but he had to be on his way soon enough, and so, after a brief respite, the bard resumed his trek once again.

The sun grew higher in the sky before he stopped again, this time to look at a strange track along the side of the rough and overgrown game trail he was climbing. It was made by a bare foot, a rather large one if the bard could read the track clearly. Corwyn stopped to place his own boot inside the impression and saw that it swallowed his entire foot with room enough to expand around the bard's boot.

Cautiously, the bard surveyed the terrain around him. He had wanted some peace and quiet, but now it seemed that would be disrupted if this track was current enough. He really had no way of knowing. His lore on such matters was sketchy at best, even if he had more evidence from which to draw forth a presumptive conclusion. Content to assume, since he had seen no other footprints on his ascent, that he was safe for now, he sighed and continued his journey onward.

No matter the obstacle, he was still going to see the shrine and that was that. An hour later, when he had nearly reached the last quarter of the hill, he had almost forgotten the whole event. He let himself be distracted by the soft chatter of songbirds perched in the bristly shrubs and spidery, short trees that spotted the greener terrain. The bard smiled at the delicate notes the birds sang; the melodious conversation they seemed to be having with one another. The grass here had started to reclaim lost ground as well – beginning to cover the hard rock once more. If he kept up the pace, he should be at the shrine in moments, finally able to rest and enjoy the remaining day.

And so a few moments later he came to the top of Maiden Rock. The stony surface had almost completely given over to soft, lush grasses and bushes and even a few trees; all with green sprouting leaves and buds. He was just about to clear a shoulder-high, erratic rise of grassy, blooming earth. This rise actually parted in the middle to form a miniature valley of sorts for anyone to travel through in relative ease. It was through this pathway Corwyn continued his trek when, from somewhere ahead, he heard a soft melody being sung in an unfamiliar language.

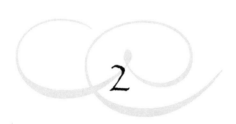

2

Corwyn stopped and slowly moved his face around the exterior of the undulating, swardy mound to where it opened into the top of the hill and shrine beyond. His own face was flush with adrenaline; his back hunched low. It was then that the memory of the footprint returned. A slight pang of fear gripped him as to what might be waiting for him. Though the voice was sweet and pleasant, it still didn't mean that the singer was friendly. His most recent experiences had his imagination running already.

The first thing his eyes found was the shrine.

The main focus was the element-worn granite statue depicting a fair Telborian maiden dressed in an elegant, long sleeved gown and carrying a small lyre in her right hand. It was supposedly an inspired sculpture of Causilla by an artist who was said to have seen her (another legend claimed). It rested on a polished stone mosaic floor of a white painted wooden gazebo. Long locks of hair streamed down the stone maiden's head and splashed around her shoulders and neck, adding to the already natural beauty of the portrayed figure. Even from his current distance, Corwyn was amazed at the detail… he'd forgotten that since his last visit. It even seemed to look lovelier than when he had first seen it, though he was certain that it had been weathered even more by the elements since that time.

The roof of the gazebo was just large enough to cover the statue and a short, flat bench, also made of gray granite, which served as a simple altar in front of the statue. Corwyn knew from his previous visit that pilgrims' offerings of worship were scattered about the top of the altar: faded flowers, tarnished trinkets of luck and various craftsmanship, small lockets, charms, even miniature ceramic figurines representing the ideal mate they sought after, were shuffled amid a myriad of other decaying and dusty things. From where he stood, Corwyn could see that there had not been much traffic of persons here for quite some time, as the trinkets were old and worn and even ruined in some cases – some having toppled around the base of the altar. Around the gazebo were the thick, thorny rose bushes that Corwyn knew would be there, ripe with fat buds and deep crimson blooms. Near the gazebo, however, was the thing which drew the bard's eyes and breath.

Before the shrine sat a woman.

Fair looking, at least from what Corwyn could see of her back as she faced the altar, she continued to sing out her strange lyrical melody a cappella. Upon sight of this maid his mind was placed at ease, for here was not a monster but a woman… at least it would appear that way. Having little desire to trounce through ancient tales and try to label this figure a threat, the bard just assumed it must be a fellow pilgrim or even a bard – perhaps even a priestess. Corwyn braved a move from behind his hiding place to get closer to the shrine. As he did so, the woman stopped her singing and turned to look at the approaching bard.

Corwyn's first thoughts had been correct, she was quite lovely. The woman was probably no older than Corwyn's own twenty-six years. With short white hair, olive skin, and soft brown eyes she seemed a heavenly sight indeed. She was clothed in a long-sleeved, auburn linen gown that hugged her frame in a simple manner – common enough dress with a yellow shawl draped about her shoulders. The garb ruled her out as being a priestess, so she was probably a pilgrim, as he first thought.

She stood up to greet Corwyn, wearing a soft smile that invited him into her presence as if she were sunlight to a flower. The closer he got, Corwyn increasingly liked what he saw. Unlike the case when gaining a closer, more detailed view of a person wherein you can start to see the small imperfections of their visage, this woman had no mortal flaws to reveal. Indeed, she grew lovelier the nearer the bard drew.

Not one to ogle the fairer sex as others of his gender and age might, he couldn't help but become enthralled by this woman. She was just too amazing in appearance to do otherwise. Beneath her dress Corwyn could see she was built like a dancer: tone and supple; her measured, graceful movements matched the euphonic words flowing from her lips.

"Hello." She greeted the bard with a cheerful nod.

"Hi." Corwyn tilted his head back with his own slightly awkward smile. "I didn't know anyone was up here. I thought this was a deserted shrine nowadays. Forgive me for interrupting you."

"You didn't disturb me at all," the woman meant what she said, almost as if she was happy to have been interrupted by the bard.

"That was a lovely song," said Corwyn. "I've never heard anything like it before."

"It's something I composed myself." The woman made her way back down to her previous seat in one fluid motion.

"I didn't recognize the language though."

"You probably won't." This time the woman was seated facing the bard, back to the shrine, and motioned for him to sit across from her by patting the grass with her hand. "It's Syvanese."

"*Syvanese?*" Corwyn stood where he was, not taking the woman up on her invitation. While often able to make fast friends, Corwyn was also weary of putting himself in compromised positions with people about which he knew little. This was especially true of this woman, whose form made his stomach flutter upon sight.

"Come on and sit down already. I *am* tame I assure you." The giggle that followed was like an agilmentic fountain bubbling an alluring call that the bard found himself hard pressed to fight against, let alone resist.

"All right." Corwyn sighed in defeat and took up a seat in the grass as she directed, placing his walking stick beside him.

"You're a bard then?" Corwyn asked after he was seated.

"In a way," the woman smiled softly. "I just love music and art and the many creative gifts with which Causilla has blessed Tralodren."

"Now you sound more like a priestess," Corwyn grinned.

"A priestess?" Again the woman laughed. "No, I'm not a priestess either, just a pilgrim looking for a spot to rest for a while. What about you?" Her light brown eyes drew him into them like a moth to a flame.

Corwyn tried to shake off the effect as best he could by directing the conversation in a new direction. He didn't think he could capably talk about himself while she looked at him with those honey brown eyes. "How do you know Syvanese anyway? It's not that easy of a language to master, let alone learn."

"Hey," the woman feigned a disciplinary glare, "I asked *you* a question first."

"So you did," came the bard's grinning reply. So much for trying to steer clear of self-discussion. "I'm a pilgrim too, I guess."

The woman's gaze focused tighter on Corwyn. "Bard?"

"Yes," Corwyn gave a small nod, "I'm a bard."

"What's your name?" Corwyn could almost swear that the woman's eyes were flirting with him now… Wishful thinking, Corwyn. She was just an outspoken type, the *very* open and outspoken type that wasn't found that often in the world this side of royalty. Don't let your emotions and imagination start playing tricks on you. Don't make this something more than it is: *a simple conversation*.

"What's yours?" Corwyn countered.

"I asked *you* first," she playfully swiped at the bard with the end of her yellow shawl; finely woven, woolen tassels making a very poor scourge against the bard's chest.

"Corwyn Danther."

"Corwyn Danther…" The woman pondered the name like a fine wine on her palette, "I've heard of you I think. What do they say: 'Best bard in the Midlands?'" Her eyes held his tongue captive for a moment. When it finally escaped this grip, it found his mind a bit more distracted – disturbed in its thoughts.

"Something like that," Corwyn grinned again and found himself blushing a bit from the gleeful gaze of the incredibly attentive young woman.

"Modest too, eh? Well how about that? Not too many bards you can find who'd be so humble these days." The woman continued to captivate Corwyn with her lively manner. "So what are you doing out here?"

Corwyn took in a deep breath which seemed to help him focus his mind; bring him back to the task that had brought him here in the first place. "I'm here to pay homage to Causilla."

"At *this* shrine?" She turned toward the small-established structure behind her, almost as if to make sure it was still there and hadn't fallen down into ruin yet while they'd been talking. "Why? Like I said, no one really comes here at all anymore… it's kinda lost its appeal to most. Well, to everyone but ogres who make their way around the hill from time to time."

"*Ogres?*" Corwyn's eyes widened. "That would explain the footprint I saw on the way up here then." The fear that thought generated allowed his mind to pull free of the woman's sticky grip. "Are you sure it's safe with them wandering around?"

"It's fine. Ogres may not be the brightest star in the sky, but they're superstitious and know enough to leave sites and shrines alone and steer far away from them. We'll be fine for quite some time, if not for your entire stay."

"Sounds like you know a lot of things about a lot of things," Corwyn said and then wished he hadn't when he realized just how foolish it sounded.

"Now that," the young woman's face parted wide in a smile, "was almost poetic." The two of them then shared a short laugh at Corwyn's last statement.

"So, you were telling me why you came here..." Again, the woman's eyes found purchase with the bard...but only for a moment.

"Ah, yeah," Corwyn moved out of the woman's gaze and felt more like himself again. The fear of ogres and the burden of the past felt like misty vapors being blown away from his sight. "This place was where I first came when I decided I wanted to be a bard."

"When was that?" The woman's eyes beamed inquisitively. Corwyn was pulled into them again. No matter how hard he tried to move his gaze away, he still slid back into them, drowning in their glimmer. Indeed, it was as if they were honey; sticky pots of dark golden delight that didn't want to let him get away.

"Oh, I was about twelve. I knew I didn't want to be a common laborer shackled to some lord, land or all-consuming vocation, and so decided to see if I could hack it as a bard." Corwyn managed at last to direct his gaze to the ground between them. It took all his effort to do so but away from those eyes he began to think clearly again.

This woman was definitely odd... Her charm and inner spirit shined through almost as a magnificent aura that was at once intoxicating, inviting, and invigorating. It was harder and harder for the bard to resist her addictive splendor. Whereas, before Corwyn once poetically decreed her beauty as something unearthly, he was now almost certain that this woman was something beyond the normal scope of the mortal understanding of what true beauty was. Either wizardry was at work or some other thing, pulling at his head and heart.

Though frightening on one level to the bard, in truth, he welcomed it – invited it even. Something in her conversation spoke to his spirit, a deep kinship that he had heard priests talk about with those who were truly in love – a love as deep as the spirit itself. All this from a woman he'd just met... a woman who continually reminded him to treat her like a person and not a living statue after which to lust.

"So you any good?" she flashed the bard a mischievous grin that pulled his gaze back toward her and out of his myopic ponderings. "What?" Corwyn's head snapped back up as if it were a fish snatched up from the water by a fisherman's line.

"Your *music*? Are you any good?" she clarified.

"I've been told I'm good," the bard countered modestly.

"But *are* you?" The woman's eyelids drooped a bit a she pressed the matter.

Corwyn was speechless. He couldn't go on with what he was feeling. Not if he was going to be honest with himself and this woman. If they were to have any sort of worthwhile communication, he needed to confess this inner turmoil and be done with it – lay it bare and then move on. If Corwyn held it in any longer, he felt he might scream or burst or both.

"You okay?" the woman rested her hand on the bard's shoulder, which felt like a feather fluttering down from heaven.

"I'm sorry, it's just you're so beautiful – I mean that in a good way... I ah... what I meant to say–"

Corwyn was interrupted by the harmonious, free-spirited laughter of the woman, who had to cover her mouth in an attempt to stifle the festosic eruption.

"Silly boy," a few more giggles escaped her lips before the woman grew more serious again. "I understand, no harm done."

"I just had to get that out and done with because I just didn't–" Corwyn persisted.

The woman's hand moved from Corwyn's shoulder to his mouth; her fingers just barely caressing the bard's lips. "Shh. You're sweet." He could smell the aroma of wild flowers and lilacs drifting from her slender fingers. "I like that."

"Not too many men left today who are as innocent and forthright as you," she continued. "Don't worry, I understand and there's no need to explain anything. I'm really interested in your story, though, and would love for you to continue."

The woman crossed her legs in front of her, removing her fragrant finger to allow the bard to continue his tale. "You obviously became a bard, so have you been playing long?"

"Not too many woman like you in the world either," Corwyn shook his head. He tried to free himself of the slight stupor that had enveloped him with the fragrance of her soft touch as she spoke, "No, there aren't," she agreed. "Please, tell me your tale."

Corwyn could see no harm in it, so he started up his life story once more. "I've been at it for about fourteen years now."

"Fourteen?" the woman was impressed. "So you really must be good, or you're just a sucker for punishment."

"I'm sorry," Corwyn looked back down at the ground again. "I'm finding it hard to talk to you. I'm not normally this way with a beautiful woman – I mean I'm not trying to – it–"

The woman's gentle, fragrant hand raised the bard's chin up to eye level again. "I understand, Corwyn. And trust me, I don't think you're trying to *court* me or anything."

Corwyn let out a small sigh.

What was going on here and why didn't he just get up and leave? Why not just come back when she was gone? He didn't know.

"Sorry," Corwyn dared another confrontation with the face of the beautiful young woman. "I guess I'm just a bit tongue tied today. I don't normally have this much trouble speaking to women. You just seem to remind me of the stories of what a Muse is supposed to look like."

"A *Muse*?" The woman giggled softly. "Have you even seen one before?"

"No," Corwyn was in better control now, "but like I said, I've heard a lot of tales, seen some drawings, and I even know that old rhyme they teach in the bardic colleges:

"Thirty-six maidens to inspire and delight,
By goddess' command get up and take flight.
Six to the South to plant seeds in the sand,
Six to the Midlands – fire the hearts of man.
Six more to the North to mix beauty with ice,
Six more to the West to champion virtue ov'r vice.
Six to entertain the gods alone.
Six to stand beside the goddess' throne."

"So then who would I be?" the woman joked.

"Well, I guess one of the six in the Midlands," the bard played along.

"You know, they say that a Muse lives here… well, comes to visit from time to time." The woman's face had grown a bit more serious, but still playful in its nature. "It's one of those old tales I suppose that priests tell to keep people coming to a site. Fun tales that might or might not be true. Course, why a Muse would want to come to this old place…" The woman spun her head about to take in a panorama of the setting. "…well, that is up for debate I guess, huh?"

"I think there is some truth to all legends and that was part of the reason I came here in the first place," Corwyn felt even more in control now as he spoke. "I've heard that story about the Muse being here or even Causilla herself, according to some tales. That was why I came here the first time, to try and see if I was supposed to be a bard – to get Causilla's blessing, talk to a Muse, or get some sort of divine sign that I should be a bard."

"Really?" The woman raised her eyebrows. "So *did* you?"

"No," Corwyn let a drop of regret wash his face. "all that showed up was just me and a few hours of silence 'til I got the feeling that nothing was going to happen and so I left."

"But you became a bard *anyway*?" Those warm brown eyes took delight in the bard as he spoke, drinking in his words like water falling on parched ground.

"I just felt it was something I had to do, something I was gifted at – that I could see myself improving in, with work. I have some friends and family who won't let me give up on my aspiration." Corwyn stopped then and recalled where he was and what was going on around him, what the woman had been doing before he arrived. It was as if time had been frozen up to now but had suddenly melted and flooded down upon him.

"I'm sorry, I talked way too much as it is. I'm sure you want to get back to whatever it was that brought you up here. I suppose I should get some time in as well before it gets dark and I have to head back. I hope I'm not going to interrupt you or anything. I was just going to play a little while, pray and sit here and think. If I'm a disturbance to you–"

"No-no-no. Not at all. I could use the company, actually," the woman pursed her bottom lip with a puff of air to clear away a loose bang.

"All right…" Corwyn was amazed he had let himself get so gabby and shared so much of his life with this stranger. That too was behavior not common to him. "I never did get your name."

"I never gave it," the woman teased.

"So–"

"Play something," she jubilantly insisted.

"What?" Corwyn didn't understand what she meant.

"On your *lute*. Play something on your lute." She motioned to the instrument still slung over the bard's back. "You wanted to know how I learned Syvanese, right? Well I tend to tell tales better with musical accompaniment… and besides… I'd love to hear 'The Famed Bard of the Midlands' play."

"All right, if you insist to have background music for your answers." Corwyn unslung his lute and complied with her request. After a few moments of tightening the strings and getting to a comfortable spot with the instrument resting on his lap, he strummed out a slow, rolling tune the flavor of hearty earth. Simple yet robust, it seemed to strike the most basic chords of life as the notes progressed in their dance. All the while the breath-taking woman closed her eyes and listened.

Swaying with a slow rhythm like a serpent with a charmer, she followed the entire tune until the bard brought it to a respectable end. It was a fair tune executed with skill. Corwyn had learned much in his fourteen years and it showed, even in this simple piece of improvised musical creation. When it was over, the woman's lush lips parted over the field of pearls in her mouth with an expression of absolute delight. "That was *beautiful*, Corwyn," she whispered back with eyes still closed as if she was reliving each note.

"Do you dance?" Suddenly, she stood in a supple motion, catching the bard by surprise.

"I'm not that good really," the bard pushed away the outstretched hands that tried to raise him to his feet.

"Come on, silly," she playfully insisted, "it isn't that hard."

"I thought you were going to tell me *your* story now," Corwyn politely pressed the woman in hopes of avoiding her latest request, holding firm to his seated location.

"I will in time… but if you aren't going to help me out I'll have to dance on my own then." She took her yellow shawl in both hands and pulled it forward, letting the rest cover her back as if she was drying off after taking a bath.

"Now," her eyes playfully commanded the bard "I want something up tempo, something filled with life. I want to do something that I picked up from the Syvani–"

"*Syvani?*" Corwyn looked up at the woman in surprised wonder. "You mean you actually learned this in Arid Land? The Syvani *taught* this to you along with their language?"

Corwyn realized it was a poor question. The woman's charm was so disarming and inviting that he supposed they would teach her anything she wanted to know regardless of any misgivings of her invading their territory. Truly this woman had many tales to tell… and many more charms to unleash….

"Yeah, Syvani with a little bit of my own inclinations and alterations for good measure." She ignored the implications of the bard's question.

"Are you going to play or not?" she stood, arms akimbo before the bard.

And when she looked back at him, Corwyn could do no more than comply with her wishes, as he had all along in this encounter, for her face was so sweet, her eyes so loving, and now her body so amazing he felt himself craving to see it put into further life by dance.

"Fine," he sighed, though he was only half pretending to be upset to do as she had bid.

"So how should I play? An up tempo beat; what's the melody?" The bard fingered his lute trying to catch a chord or two to round out the evolving tune.

"Just follow my lead and you'll get the rest. Free form will be just fine." Corwyn noticed she had placed a set of brass finger cymbals on her right index finger and thumb. Whatever type of dance this was, it would be unique indeed, for only the desert-dwelling Celetors used such instruments.

"Ready?" She took in the bard with those gorgeous, all-consuming eyes once again.

"I suppose," Corwyn gave a sigh.

"Don't be so glum… this will be fun," she flashed him another wide grin. "Trust me."

"You don't have to do this," Corwyn tried to assure her once more of this truth, "I'm more than happy to leave you to yourself. I was just making conversation–"

"But I want to, so please let me do this. I don't get to dance for that many people anymore." And with that the woman clapped her finger cymbals and twirled out her yellow shawl in the beginnings of her dance. Corwyn started with a few chords that he thought might work, balancing them with the rhythm and steps that the woman was beginning to make. This was certainly like nothing he had seen before.

Cha-ching.

She sped up her pace.

Cha-ching. Clap.

Corwyn picked up the chords he needed and felt the music start to flow into him. Inspired by the dance and the woman performing it, he soon found his hands playing music of which he knew very little... almost as if a strange infusion of his spirit were plucking out the chords with self-willed fingers independent from mental decrees.

The pitch intensified, as did the dance.

Cha-ching. Clap. Ching-ching. Clap.

In time, Corwyn wasn't sure he still strummed the chords of his lute or if they strummed themselves. His eyes – and now mind – were focused solely on the graceful woman before him. The bright yellow shawl spun around her lithe frame like fire, the finger cymbals clapping away in time to her calcandic step that punctuated her consciousness-snaring movements. Amazingly, through it all, she still managed to keep her brown eyes focused on the bard, smiling at him as she never broke a sweat from her rapid, fluid actions.

Cha-ching-Clap-ching-ching-Clap-ching-ching-Clap-Clap.

Now his heart followed the rising rhythm.

The whole experience was beyond words.

The bending, twisting, small skips and jumps; twirling fabric, the colors, those bright brown eyes and olive skin... Corwyn was very glad that he could witness this for himself and even more amazed that such a dance could be performed by anyone, for it seemed too intricate, too perfect and refined for even the most gifted of dancers. It was then, at that moment, he became convinced that the woman *was* a manifestation of some higher power. Could it be the legends were more accurate than what he might first have believed? Could he be watching his own *goddess* dance for him?

And then Corwyn stopped playing.

His mind and fingers found difficultly when communicating with each other, causing the agitatic strumming to cease mid-note. He simply couldn't go on. He was too enraptured with it all; battling too many fantastical thoughts and ponderings. His heart pounded in his chest; sweat covered his body in a glistening layer of wet silk. The woman froze mid-movement and looked toward the bard with a playful expression as if she knew the answer to the question she was about to ask.

"Problem?" She rested her hands on her hips again and seemed eager to continue.

Corwyn shook his head to pull himself back from the experience, trying to calm his rapid breath and still his heart.

"Ah… no… er, yes I guess. You're just so amazing – I-I couldn't keep up." The bard blushed and puffed from lungs that felt more like overworked bellows.

The woman released a robust blast of merriment and glided toward the bard with supple steps. Her own body was free from any perspiration and hint of exhaustion. Corwyn silently wagered that she could have gone on dancing as wildly as she had for hours, perhaps even days, without any loss of vitality.

"Well, it's a hard dance to keep up with in truth," she waved the matter away with the delicate wave of her hand. "and you really weren't doing it justice anyway."

"I'm sorry," Corwyn huffed away as he hunched over a bit to try and get his breath as he played with the thought about this woman actually being Causilla. "I just–"

"Shhh," she placed a slender finger again to his lips and he could say no more. Once more the fragrant lilac and wildflower bouquet fluttered into his nostrils. Spellbound, the bard rolled up his eyes to drink in the radiant glamour that was the incredible woman before him. The woman who was *more* than a woman…

"Now," the woman's voice and manner had changed again to something Corwyn was hard pressed to fully define. It was slightly more authoritative, yet still welcoming and charming, "you came here to worship Causilla, well so did I, but in a different way. Give me your hand."

Corwyn compiled in a sleepy, trancelike state.

The woman pulled him up, letting his lute fall off his legs to the ground with a muffled thud.

"What are you doing now?" his words were like syrup in his mouth.

"I don't want to harm you, only enlighten you."

"So you are a priestess?" The bard's eyes opened wide. His mind was becoming fuzzy but his heart and breathing had almost returned to normal.

The woman let another soft smile grace her lips. "I'm a servant of Causilla. Now close your eyes. Go ahead and close them, you can trust me."

"How long do you want me to keep them closed?" Corwyn lowered his eyelids.

"You can open them now," she replied.

W hen Corwyn did so he was speechless. The woman had changed before him in no more than a heartbeat! Gone was the yellow shawl and common dress. Now she stood in an ankle-length, golden silk skirt with sides slit up to mid-thigh. Her top was a white blouse that flowed from the tips of her shoulders to cover her breasts and end at the base of her ribcage, leaving her smooth, muscularly defined, stomach exposed. The top of her sleeves billowed out then banded about her elbows, allowing her forearms to be naked. These white puffs were also sliced open into ribbons of cotton, revealing a shimmering silver fabric under them – a second delightful layer that sparkled in the sunlight.

This wasn't the only change in appearance. The woman's short white hair now seemed to glisten like diamond dust and was spiked in all directions. Her honey eyes still remained inviting and peaceful, but her lips were stained a brilliant red that gleamed like the skin of a dew-drenched apple. Anklets of gold, toe rings on her bare feet, rings, bracelets, earrings and even a diamond nose stud finished off the rest of her transformation. To see her in such a state, when compared to how she had looked just moments before, was beyond amazing and further strengthened the bard's belief as to her true identity.

"Who are you?" Corwyn finally managed to speak through his molasses filled mouth.

"You came here fourteen years ago to gain some perspective on your decision about becoming a bard. Now you have returned to reflect on that and confirm to yourself that you indeed made the right choice. I want to help in that confirmation." The pleasant charm was still there in her voice, but that authority had grown stronger… and there was something more he still couldn't describe – something he felt than emanating off of her.

"I don't understand." Corwyn was at a loss to fully take everything in now. "I told you all this already. If you're a wizardress or some other mystical worker or creature, I don't know what you're playing at but I came here in peace–"

The woman pulled him sharply to her chest. He was pulled right next to her face then, nose touching nose, eye to eye. She was a bit shorter than the bard, but her firm breasts and flower-scented breath stirred his emotions like embers being raked to rouse a flame for some fresh timber.

"Six to the Midlands – fire the heart of man, remember?" Her red lips parted ever so slightly and Corwyn could smell the same sweet flower aroma dancing on her breath. He could do nothing but stare dumbly at the two nutmeg planets before him – the whole of his universe as far as he could fathom.

"Six sisters also came to Midlandic shores:
Adina, Alanna, and Ella – sights to behold,

169

Mortal minds to enlight, inspire and mold.
Hannah, Keely, and Lena the other three–
Delight of men and mortals be."

"I don't understand," Corwyn managed to pull away a bit from the orbit of the two tawny worlds before him.

"I was here when you came searching those many years ago. I saw you and was pleased with you, but you had yet to learn patience. You left before I could give you my blessing and it has taken me a while to track you down…but now that I have, I want to inspire you and give you a gift that will enrich your life and never let you return to where you have been before."

"Now, follow my lead." At that the woman took Corwyn's hands and began to dance.

It was slow at first, a simple, almost methodical step, but soon it started to increase in speed. A steady allegretto prancing in time with the sound of a fiddle that Corwyn suddenly heard wringing out its giddy notes from afar. He tried to look around as he twirled about in the sward, to see where it was coming from, only to see nothing about save the woman with whom he danced. It was almost as if the sound was the wind about him – a living source of delight in itself.

"You won't find this band, young bard," the woman answered Corwyn's searching eyes. "They are another part of the gift. Now keep in time, it's going to get a little faster."

She was right.

Following the fiddle a flute made its presence known. Higher pitched, it picked up the melody of the fiddle and carried it to an allegoric beat, which was echoed in the couple's dance.

Around and around they spun, two dust devils on top Maiden Rock.

Corwyn was lost in the face of his companion as it blurred away from him; a dreamlike state falling upon his waking mind. Suddenly, all around him had changed, radiating a kind of unimaginable beauty. In this enchanting haze, as he spun about, he now saw things that he'd never be able to describe fully: a palace of splendor on top of a flower-laden hill where beautiful women and men played lyre and lute, flute and drum – frolicking in wild delight. A place of never-ending beauty and tangible love, a place he would never be as long as he walked on Tralodren.

The longer he danced the more he felt himself becoming infused with a creative passion that rivaled everything he'd felt and known before. A passion that spoke to him of higher things than that which he thought he knew to be true already. He saw ideas flashing in his head, images and colors; heard songs as ancient as the world's foundations and as new as the birth cry of a child.

Around they danced to the beat of a disembodied drum, thumping out a rhythm that was unnatural but glorious. What was happening to him? The woman let go of one hand to spin herself around the bard in a dervish and yet the beat increased. The dance became fevered, faster than anyone could dance without error, and yet the bard felt as if he could go on forever, as if he was prancing about on air instead of earth. Indeed, his hostess was so unearthly in her motions that the bard felt as if he *was* dancing with more a figment of his mind rather than flesh and blood.

Then his mind was awakened and his eyes finally saw. Understanding came; he knew that before him was a Muse. He was sure of it, for when his mind widened to that truth he saw her shimmering eyes, her radiant hair, and glistening skin. She was of eternal youth and health – infused with the timeless quality of the arts and music as to be an embodiment of all they represented – all they are.

The bard could think no more.

Before him danced the handmaiden of his goddess and he was dancing with her!

The song gained still more instruments. A lute and bagpipes… What strange melody was this that pushed into his heart and let loose a sound that none have heard yet craved all the more? The bard couldn't say. It was too far beyond him. This was the stuff of legends; fireside stories of yore where the fantastic paired with the possible… and he was in its midst!

He now saw things in a new light – a new light that intensified the colors of all things around him. The rocky earth had now turned a rich ochre hue, the green an almost neon flare of verdant. The sky above blazed down in a sapphire light and the white satin clouds melted away to flow with the tears that welled up in the bard's eyes.

And still they danced.

How much more of this prestissimic movement could a man stand?

Yips and yells came to his ears then; a frantic, invisible, jubilant host accompanying the music in time.

And they spun.

Gold and white, silver and brown spinning as a top or tornado above the hill and shrine. The bard's breath was almost pulled from his lungs in astonishment when he saw the flaming gold sun fall away with the azure sky to be replaced with the dark satin of night and the pinpricks of frozen crystal stars.

The Muse tittered at the wide-eyed stupor of the bard.

"Most mortals would let their lust for beauty consume them – control them – rather than learn to appreciate it and to nurture it in themselves and others. You, though, are different, Corwyn. You fight back your carnal lusts even as you move to embrace me and what I represent: pure beauty and creativity made manifest through love.

"You're a rare treasure, Corwyn Danther. For you grasp the true nature and power of our goddess. I knew this then as I do now, and had you not run off before we could meet, we would have had this conversation fourteen years ago.

"Now you see the truth of things like few can or have, and that is very attractive to me. That truth has drawn me to you, mortal bard. You are a man after my own heart," the Muse pulled him close once more. He could smell a new sweet fragrance about her now, like cinnamon, and vanilla, nutmeg, and honey, mixed with roses and sugared cream.

It was then, when the bard felt as if he would surely die if he continued this mad event, everything stopped and was silent. His mind unlocking from the spinning, hazy whirlwind, Corwyn could, for the first time, come to understand just what had been happening and what was being spoken to him. His eyes turned their gaze below. He was high above the world, in the night sky of space looking down at the clouds themselves as if they were fleeting things beneath his notice. The silence of the whole setting was in itself grand and beautiful as was the view: a blue sea with floating white islands of misty cotton...

"But why–"

"Shhh."

And with that she kissed him.

At first Corwyn was shocked, but that shock soon turned to delight as this was not the mere kiss of any fair woman but the kiss of a *divinity* – the very lips of Causilla in a way. This embrace of lips was a passion he'd never forget. It didn't carry with it a physical fire as did a mortal kiss, but rather a mental and spiritual flame that blazed across the parched landscape of his being.

Consumed with this passion, Corwyn again saw visions, but these were of himself and what he was going to do in the days and years ahead. Music and adventures, tales and companions – some he had met already, some he would meet in time to come. All these pictures and still more flooded his mind, but the more powerful aspect of the kiss was the quaking that overtook his heart. He felt like he would explode from the creative energy screaming inside him for release. New ideas for songs, tales, and more flooded his brain and throat and embedded themselves in his skull... and then...

And then it was over.

Their lips parted ways and the Muse smiled. The bard tried to reach out for more, pursing his own lips forward, attempting to grasp onto the fleeing crimson, satin ribbons of his companion's lips but was held back by the Muse who waited for Corwyn to open his eyes in a sleepy, drunken fashion before she spoke.

"Know that Lena calls you blessed and has favored you. From this day forth I will be your patron, Corwyn. For love of Causilla and by her decree I have come to you and done these things.

"Your heart is true and love, pure. Your actions thus far demonstrate this more than adequately. You are a follower that delights my goddess and me; I am more than pleased to be your patron." Lena released the bard to hover alone in open space.

"Wait," Corwyn reached out with a desperate hand, his frame still wracked with the Muse's fire.

"We'll meet again, Corwyn, have no fear." Lena's eyes sparkled brighter than the stars about them. "For now you must rest and be about what you have to be about. There is much to do in this life of yours, much to see, and you only have a short span of years in which to do it." Lena then started to fade from before his eyes like gossamer in a breeze.

"A short span?" the bard feebly questioned.

"Well, short compared to the way I measure time," she winked and was gone.

Corwyn let the soundless environment where he now hovered reflect off him then looked down again. He saw Tralodren below him and was amazed again. He would never forget the vision of the planet as the gods see it for as long as he lived. Even as he observed the sweeping white mists of clouds he saw that they were growing more blurry – fuzzier in his vision. He felt lightheaded too…

Trying to regain control, he closed his eyes…

A moment later he opened them and found that he was on the grassy hill beside the shrine. Sitting up slowly he noted his lute and walking stick rested beside him. The only figure left on the hill top, his vision beheld the world around him in the familiar contrasts and hues he had come to understand as normal; the glamour Lena had imparted now seemingly absent along with her presence. Sitting up further, a white rose tumbled from Corwyn's chest into his lap. The bard picked it up and placed it up to his nose. It smelled of vanilla and cinnamon, honey, nutmeg, and sugared cream, mixed with the flower's own subtle fragrance.

Corwyn inhaled deeply then smiled.

Where Dreams
go to Die

1

Fat drops of rain splattered off Corwyn's sopping brown cloak and onto the muddy road around him. The formerly hard-packed surface of the thoroughfare had turned to a soupy, meandering puddle that was quickly mutating into a small creek. The bard had the pleasure of sloshing around in the muck for the better part of an hour and was suffering for it.

Every piece of his outfit either hung against him or dragged him down as if he wore a coat of chains rather than his simple light garb; even his boots were filled with a shallow lake that splashed about his toes with every step. He only kept the hood of his cloak up as it helped keep some of the water from getting into his eyes. This didn't hinder much, however, as the formerly expansive covering now clung to his head as tight as his slicked back reddish-blonde hair beneath it. The drenched cloak also offered little protection for his cherry wood lute. The instrument rested on the bard's back under the cloak, making him appear like a hunchback as he pressed on through the weather.

This drenching wasn't something he enjoyed, but at least he was thankful it was still light enough to see. The storm wasn't so severe as to totally blacken the sky, only cover it with charcoal gray puffs of leaking clouds. Corwyn was alone in his travels as he trudged onward, hoping for some place safe enough for him to spend the evening and dry himself by a fire before he caught cold or worse. He'd been hoping for such a place to appear for sometime now, but the countryside of the kingdom of Romain offered him no such thing. As the rain seemed to be staying, night growing closer, he continued increasingly onward – desperate for relief.

The storm had risen up fairly quickly and was upon the bard before he could do little but endure it. Thankfully, the storm was just heavy with its downpour and not riddled with lightning or strong winds. It seemed Endarien, the god of the sky, was being a bit merciful.

Being a flat land given to grass and rich crops, much of the kingdom of Romain was sparsely populated away from the kingdom's hub – it's capital city – bearing the same name. After leaving the small village of Willowdale, about half a days journey behind him, Corwyn could expect to find only a few hamlets and family farms; common folk under the heel of one of the two duchies that enforced the king's control.

The bard looked a little ways down the road and spied more flat rolling land soggy from the perpetual showers. It seemed there was no place to keep him from drowning. Not even a lone barn or granary to allow him a decent rest. He sloshed the puddle that was the road with his walking stick – an aged and worn broken branch of oak. Guess he just had to keep going a little while longer and pray to Causilla that he wouldn't come down with anything too severe.

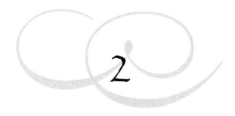

2

After another hour had passed; it seemed that the weather was far from relinquishing its hold over the darkening heavens. However, Corwyn had finally spied a tattered old building off to the side of the road. It was a little distance from him, but close enough to get to before it grew too dark. He was uncertain, though, as to what it was: barn, granary, an old home, maybe even an abandoned shrine. All he could tell was it had four walls and a roof and appeared sturdy enough to hold back the rain, so he put toward it with a fresh sense of urgency.

As the embers of day that had managed to tint the smoky clouds a dull slate gray started to fade, a cold wind started to rustle about the bard's heels. This serpentine gale made Corwyn shiver as his ankles felt as though they were being encircled by manacles of ice.

The sooner he made it to this presumably drier locale the better.

En route, Corwyn caught sight of a simple graveyard out of the corner of his vision. Resting to the right of the road, the same side as the building and in close proximity to it, the graveyard was settled a bit back from the road. The bard studied it for a moment as he passed. It was populated with surprisingly well maintained headstones and manicured grounds, hemmed in by fieldstone walls that sprouted a few dandelions, patches of wild flowers, and clover bent low in the rain. It had no gate, however, only an empty break in the wall to allow access.

Corwyn found himself slowing just a bit as he passed to marvel at just how well groomed it all seemed. Even in the present landscape, without a soul around for miles, this graveyard was kept up as if it was visited everyday, which the bard knew for certain it was not. He also wondered, only for a moment, though, (because getting free of the weather was his first concern) how so many had come to be buried here when the bard hadn't seen any sign of house or farmstead for quite a long while. He let his eyes wander just a little longer as he briskly strode past, studying the rectangular plot and the basalt statute at its center: a hooded figure with a set of keys in one hand and a measuring scale in another – Asorlok, the Lord of Death himself.

A sudden low grumble from above brought the bard's head heavenward. A quick glance ahead told him that the old building, which now looked more like a rough and common inn, was just a few yards away. He also noticed that there was some smoke coming out of a stone chimney on top the shingled roof. Had that been there all along? There was some illumination coming from inside too…he *knew* that such illumination hadn't been there before. Despite this, it was still a dry place in which to wait out the rain, so the bard pushed such nervous questions and observations from his mind.

The building was certainly rustic, pushing a hundred years if Corwyn had to guess, but like the graveyard, it was well maintained. It was also definitely an inn. A two-story, medium-sized structure that would allow for just about the right amount of travelers who would ramble through this part of Romain. The worn oak door was inviting enough, more so the slick shingled overhang that kept the steps leading up to the portal dry. Corwyn ducked underneath and pulled the clinging hood from his head. Shaking his drenched hair, he let loose a shower of his own.

Now that he was closer he could peer inside the old glass windows to see that there were outlines of people amid the dingy glow of what could only be firelight. Not too many shapes beyond the glass, but enough to convince him that there was some life in the old inn. He thought he could even see a large fire as well, deep in the bowels of the structure, and jumped at the chance to sit before it.

The door opened under the bard's hand with a creaking grind as Corwyn moved inside. Immediately, before he crossed the threshold, he felt the warmth and smelled the smoky aroma of the fire run to meet, then caress him. As he adjusted his eyes to the interior, he noticed a motherly woman coming toward him. She was a Telborian of later middle age, no more than fifty years, Corwyn guessed. She was plump and rosy cheeked, looking like anyone's loving mother as she neared the wet bard with a cheery disposition.

"Well aren't you just soaked to the bone?" even her words were maternal and disarming.

Corwyn noticed her garb with slight wonder. She wore a plain parchment colored dress that reached to her ankles. A sash of red was tied about her waist in a slipknot, the ties of the sash falling on her left side. If the bard didn't know any better he would have sworn he was looking at a priestess of Asorlok. However, he didn't see a medallion of the death god, which he thought all priests of any god were required to wear, and began to think that maybe he was looking at a follower instead.

"We better get those wet things off yah before yah catch your death," the woman's stubby fingers started to remove Corwyn's cloak. He let her. He saw no need in trying to keep it right at the moment.

"Thank you," he tried to get a closer look at the woman as she slopped off the cloak, carried it to the back of a wooden chair, and moved it closer to the fire where it could dry.

"My goodness, you must have been in that storm for quite some time."

Corwyn then saw that there were indeed people around the fire. Two people, a man and a woman; they seemed to pay little notice to the bard's arrival in the very empty and seemingly seldom used common room.

The motherly woman came back toward him with a grin. "You are just a walking puddle, aren't you? Best go upstairs to the first door on your right and you'll find some clean, dry clothes to change into along with some towels. Then come right back down to the fire to drive off any cold you might still have in you."

"I'm very thankful for your hospitality," Corwyn bowed his head to the woman, "but I don't have much coin on me. If I could just take a moment or two by the fire – long enough to dry my clothes and wait out the storm – that would be all that I'd request."

The woman chuckled, waving the bard's words away by means of a 'shooing' hand swipe. "You don't have to pay anything here. This is a Wayfarer's Inn and I'm happy to provide what service I can to those who have grown weary on the road they travel."

"Wayfarer's Inn?" the bard asked.

He'd heard tales of them from other bards and travelers over the years but didn't know where they were located; in truth, none really did. Like most faiths, those that followed Asorlok – the Asorlins – were divided into different sects. Unlike some faiths, there were no harsh emotional attachments to the divide. Since Asorlok was seen as a god of death, decay, journeys, and the afterlife, it was only natural that his followers would see a certain aspect more to their liking than others.

Some worshipped the god as he was presented, entire and pure in his complete godhead. Others identified with him more as the god of travelers and journeys, for after all, life itself was a journey toward death and death was a journey through the afterlife. These followers took it upon themselves to build roadside resting places to honor their god by helping those weary from travel. At least that was the extent of the tales, which Corwyn saw now seemed to be true. Though who could have found this place so far into the empty plains, the bard couldn't say.

"Yes, a place for the weary traveler to rest a while," said the woman. "And a place for folks to stay back a cold chill from soggy garments." She then made another effort to shoo Corwyn upstairs as if he were a stray cat. "Now off with yah. Get those soggy things off."

"Very well then," Corwyn felt a little uneasy resting in a place dedicated to the god of death, but realized he had to be a bit more practical about the matter. It was either dry off here and wait out the storm or go back out in the muck and rain and trudge about for who knows how long until he might find another suitable place... *if* he found one.

He decided to stay at the inn for the time being, as he climbed the steps to the upper level and to what he hoped would be some decent dry clothes. Although he wasn't too wild about changing into used clothing (for he was sure that was what awaited him above), he would take what he could he supposed, as long as it wasn't too shoddy of dress and had the semblance of being clean.

He was a bard after all, and though not geared toward the higher end of the scale when it came to his daily garb, he didn't want to be wearing one hundred year old hand-me-downs either. He supposed he would have to see what was presented him before he judged the matter further.

Corwyn neared the top of the stairs and made his way to the first door he saw on the right. It was slightly ajar and opened into a rather simple room, lit with a lone candle on a brass stand resting over a worn wooden nightstand. The only other things he saw were a bed and a chair. On the bed he saw a selection of garments all folded in a neat pile and sorted by type (shirts, breeches, belts, etc) and some folded towels as well. He moved closer to look at what was there, dripping all the way. He was surprised to see a shirt similar to one he was wearing and a pair of pants, which would also fit him.

"Just leave your wet clothes on the chair to dry," the woman's voice came up from below.

It startled Corwyn, but he quickly recovered.

Closing the door, he slopped his outfit over the chair just like he was told to do and then started to towel himself dry. Corwyn took to dressing himself with some haste into the drier clothing as it was still a bit drafty and he wasn't yet warmed from his stay inside. To his surprise, he found what he had chosen not only fit him like a glove but was of a newer make as well – as if it was just stitched together a few days ago.

The bard kept his boots, though, tipping them upside down to spill out the small pool gathered inside. He wasn't keen on the sparse selection of shoes (some wooden, some leather) and one pair of rather tight looking boots. Instead, he let his wet feet go bare to air-dry, taking his boots and drenched socks along with him to the fire.

Downstairs, he smelled the welcoming aroma of mutton stew, though he hadn't smelled it before when he first arrived; by the time he reached the bottom of the steps he saw the woman again smiling up at him with clasped hands.

185

"Don't you look handsome now?" She was like a mother looking over her son who had managed to dress himself for the first time. Her eyes then fell to the still muddy boots clasped in the bard's left hand. "Couldn't bear to part with those, eh?"

"I've just broken them in," the bard chuckled.

"Come to the fire now and warm up," she motioned to the fire pit like a nervous mother thinking of the well being of her child; he joined the two others that were gathered there, but they still hadn't taken much of an interest in the new arrival.

Corwyn looked toward the fire, then back at her again. "You sure this isn't going to cost me anything? I could certainly offer up something for the clothes and fire."

"It's all free for those who find there way to this inn," the woman declined the offer. "Now go sit in front of that fire. Should have some stew ready for you soon."

Corwyn did as he was told, not wanting to offend the woman's kindness or faith, for he realized that in a way this was part of her service to her god; to refuse her hospitality would not only be rude but a possible insult to her faith as well.

"Sounds good," the bard made his way to the fireplace, which continued to call him to sit and rest with each pop and crackle of the burning logs.

"Hello," Corwyn addressed the two figures seated in opposing chairs, framing the fire, as he took a seat on a wooden bench between them and faced the crackling logs.

The man, who sat at his right, had the look of about seventy or so odd winters to him. He said nothing. The woman sat off to his left. He figured her to be about thirty. She nodded politely as the bard joined them.

Both of them seemed to be worn out from a long journey. Haggard and road weary, they sat around the fire in a half awake, half asleep state which made the bard feel a bit uneasy as he took ownership of the backless bench. The fire was very welcoming and freely gave all the warmth it had. Corwyn placed his wet socks and boots close to the blaze to begin drying them out.

After a few moments he felt the cold and moisture that had soaked into his bones begin to dry up along with his drenched hair and skin like steam rising out of a cup of hot cider. The whole process was very soothing. The sound made by the rain on the roof, like horse hooves galloping down the road, was so hypnotic he didn't even realize he had fallen into a similar trance as the two other patrons near him until the matronly innkeeper pushed a large wooden bowl brimming with mutton stew into his lap.

"Here you go."

Corwyn looked up at the woman with hooded eyes. "Thanks."

"I'm sure you're famished from your trek in that rain so eat up," she handed the bard a wooden spoon after he had comfortably placed the stew on his lap.

"Might be good for you to get to know some of your fellow patrons here as well." She stood to her full height again, which wasn't more than a few fingers above five and a half feet. "Travelers to this inn are very unique indeed and have a good many tales to tell those who would listen."

Corwyn stirred his stew, "I don't doubt that."

"So I guess I can start with you then, eh?" Corwyn turned his head up toward his hostess, who was starting to leave. "Who are you?"

"Molly Darkwode, priestess of Asorlok and keeper of this inn and the graveyard beside it," the priestess pleasantly turned back to the bard to answer with a curtsy.

"Corwyn Danther," Corwyn nodded his head in greeting.

"Corwyn, eh?" A pleasant expression twisted across Molly's face. "I've heard of you, I think. Some say you're the most famed bard in all the Midlands."

"Well, that's yet to be proven," the bard dug into the stew. He was rather hungry he realized – especially now that he had the fine smelling bowl right in front of him to tempt his senses. To his delight he found it to be quite delectable. He hadn't known that mutton stew could taste so good.

"This stew is wonderful," he spoke between bites.

"Just something I've found that seems to help the travelers who come here get filled and whole before they move on again," Molly motioned toward the two others gathered around the fire. "If you're a bard then you must listen to these travelers' tales."

"I *must*, huh?" Corwyn asked between bites.

"I think you'd find them most interesting and entertaining."

At that, she left the bard alone with the two others and his stew, which he kept eating as he looked toward the younger woman.

She gave a weak smile.

Corwyn returned the grin.

Now that he managed to get a closer look at her, he noticed that her dress seemed to be a bit older than what he thought was in fashion at the time. Maybe she had come in the rain too and had changed clothes to stave off any cold as he did...

"Is it true?" the young woman spoke up in a soft voice that shattered Corwyn's ponderings like glass.

"Is *what* true?" Corwyn asked after swallowing.

"That you're a bard?" She surrendered another meek grin.

"Yes. I'm a bard," he sat little taller on the bench, letting his stew cool a bit more.

"Then you must hear me," her eyes had grown suddenly desperate and hollow, almost like he was looking into the sockets of a skeleton.

"Why's that?" The bard absently stirred the stew with his spoon. He didn't know if he was comfortable with the desperation in her voice and face.

"I've been told that bards like to hear tales and songs and then tell them to others and I have a song that has to be sung." The desperation hadn't left her eyes and was now joined by a swelling excitement, making for a very odd mixture indeed.

"Most do, yes," Corwyn was getting a bit nervous now and it was harder to keep it from showing. He didn't know what to make of this woman who had all the marks of a potential lunatic growing with each moment. Who else but a mad woman might wander into this lonely inn hidden away from the known world?

"Then hear mine please, I beg you." The woman leaned forward on her chair, which caused Corwyn to quickly slide back a little more from the woman. He would have pushed the bench back with him from his sudden jerk, but it was quite heavy and didn't budge.

Seeing Corwyn's reaction, she sat back apologetically. "Please, I mean no harm it has just been so long since anyone has heard my song and I so wish someone to hear it before I go."

A strange, icy pang jabbed its way into Corwyn's heart. The bard actually found himself pitying the woman. Somehow the fear of her had faded as pity rose to replace it. With a slow breath, the bard told himself to be still…for now. It would probably rain for a while longer (the horses on the roof had not even slowed to a trot yet) and he was still a little damp... What harm could he cause by listening to her? In the very least it would help pass the time a little better than just staring into the fire. And there wasn't any real danger to his person…at least as far as he could tell.

"All right, please share your song."

Instantly, the woman's face lit up, but the deadness of the eyes still remained. Even in the midst of such seeming joy and relief at having her request met, the hollowness refused to depart. That look would never be forgotten by the bard either as he would be reminded of it in his later years by others he would encounter from all walks of life... For a long moment the woman was silent, merely staring at the bard with the same, overjoyed expression – motionless.

"Everything okay?" Corwyn asked with some trepidation. Though she was calmer than before, the bard wasn't sure what to read of her actions.

"I-I just have to find a way to start. I haven't sung it in so long I don't know how to start," the woman's countenance fell slightly in her mental struggle.

"How about we start with your name since you already have heard mine? That should help ease us into some parley," Corwyn took another spoonful of stew.

"I'm Jenna Gridley," again a weak smile rose up on her face.

Corwyn swallowed, "Pleased to meet you, Jenna."

"So what's your song about?" Corwyn tried to prompt her mind in an attempt to encourage words to start flowing. It was a common enough tool to use with others who had developed stage fright, which was what he thought to be the case with Jenna.

"Well, it's a love song really," Jenna blushed.

"Tragic?" asked the bard.

"I guess so."

"Those make the best kind," Corwyn smiled, swallowing more of the mutton stew before he put it back down on his lap to give Jenna his full attention. "There's something about love and loss that seem to endure a tale and song to the heart."

Neither said anything for a moment.

Jenna fidgeted with her hands as they rested on her lap, unsure of herself and of where to begin, Corwyn supposed.

"Rest easy," he said. "Take a deep breath, close your eyes, forget anyone is here, and sing your song."

Jenna feebly nodded and did as the bard advised, scrunching her eyes tight at first, then letting them loosen a bit as she let out a heavy, hard, breath. When it had been expired, she looked much more peaceful.

Then she started to sing.

Corwyn had heard many a song of love and sorrow in his career thus far but none quite as elegant as this. The tone was earthy and grounded in personal experience that, when mingled with the higher voice of the singer, seemed to blend together into a wonderfully surreal expression. Indeed, the song enraptured the bard. He clung to every verse and followed the narrative tale that told of true love between a young man and woman who lived during the Shadow Years. The man was a warrior for the army of Gondad, the Origin City of humanity, and he had to follow the army in its bloody wars for many a year, leaving his love behind him all that time.

She waited for him (didn't they always in such tales?), living on nothing but her love for the young warrior, for she could not eat or even sleep in his absence. The man, for his part, spurned the advances of the army camp wenches for his true love, which he was uncertain he'd even see again.

The war raged on; their love held true, yet they were not fated to see each other alive. The young man was killed in battle, whispering the name of his love on dying lips. This wind carried it to the ears of the young woman, who then knew that her true love was dead. Heart stricken, she threw herself from a cliff so that she could be with her love in death because she could not bear to be without him in life.

A tragic tale, and quite common in most circles the bard had heard, but the song and the way it was told endeared itself to his heart. It was something like which he had never heard before, and there was some other quality that he couldn't quite place that added so much more to it than what the song alone had said... Jenna opened her eyes to see Corwyn smiling back at her.

"That was quite lovely."

"Thank you," Jenna blushed.

"So are *you* a bard?" asked Corwyn.

"No," Jenna waved the question dismissively away with her hand like it was the silliest thing she'd ever heard, "I'm no bard, but I do have a song or two in me to sing. At least that was what my father always said."

"I'd say your father was right."

Jenna's blush deepened with her smile that for once wasn't so meek as those that had crossed her lips in the past.

"Well," Jenna rose from her seat, "thank you for listening, and if you could perhaps pass it on in your travels I would be most grateful. I'm going to retire now. If you will excuse me," Jenna left the two men with a curtsy followed by a slightly hurried gait.

"Good night," Corwyn nodded.

Jenna swung her head around as she faded from his sight in the shadows created by the fire, "Gods bless you."

And then she was gone.

Corwyn thought about the strange woman, thought about her even more odd and sudden departure for another moment, all the while enjoying his mutton stew. It had cooled while he had listened to the song but was still warm and oddly enough, even more flavorful than when last he had taken a bite. His thoughts on the matter were interrupted, however, by the other person around the fire.

"I have a tale for you if you'd be so kind as to listen," the man suddenly spoke up.

Concealing his startled look as he swallowed more stew, the bard then spoke. "This seems to be a night for sharing tales. If you have something to share I'll certainly not stop you. After all, it's great weather for tales to be told."

"Aye, so it is," the old man gave a nod of his aged head in Corwyn's direction. His voice was gravely and worn like an old wheel rut that had worked itself deep into the road.

"I have a myth to tell," the old man seemed to come alive from his previous inactive state, but his eyes were as dead as Jenna's. The bard noted this in passing interest. In truth, Corwyn thought he probably looked the same to him. Now that Corwyn had rested a while he'd found out just how much his recent soggy journey had taken out of him.

"A myth?" Corwyn's interest piqued as he tended to like such tales. "About what?"

"'Tis an older myth, that's for sure. I doubt many, if anyone, has heard it but me." Then the old man grinned a wrinkled grin. "Since I made it up mind you."

"So a very rare tale indeed then," Corwyn released a lopsided grin. He was more at ease with the man than Jenna. His presence and manner, once he started to talk, was actually very engaging and grandfatherly.

"It has a meaning too," he sat back down in his chair, getting comfortable before he started to spin his yarn, "just like all myths do."

"The best ones usually do," agreed Corwyn. "So what's it about?"

The old man's eyes sparkled mischievously for just a moment before they dulled again. "Just hold that horse a little longer from bolting out the barn. You'll hear it in a moment..." the man then drew into his mind to think of the tale, get the beginning figured out and then the rest of the tale from there. In truth, he hadn't told it for some time and wanted to make sure it was right. When he had finished gathering his thoughts he turned back toward Corwyn. His face now had the familiar look of a practiced storyteller – a grandfather telling stories to his grandson – as he began his tale.

"Back when the world was still a bit new, Dradin and Causilla had come down to a city they wanted to see worship them as their patron. This city was just getting started, as most were in that ancient day, and each god came to offer something that would advance the city to higher levels of civilization. These gifts, of course, were predicated on the understanding that the citizens would make them the patron of their city.

"This event wasn't new, as it had been repeated in other cities by other gods, but this time Dradin and Causilla had taken up a contest between themselves as to whose gifts were the best for mortalkind. To be fair, each god would present their gifts to a city and then let a mortal judge decide which of the gifts was good for them, and thereby declare the god who gave it the victor of the contest.

"So was their agreement.

"The honor assigned to judge this contest, was given to a simple sage who was reported to be the wisest in the city and therefore the best suited to make such a judgment of these divine presentations.

"The first to present their gift was Dradin. He offered to shower the city in knowledge and learning – to make it the envy of the world for the insight they would all possess. He said he would grant them all incredible amounts of knowledge and they would be as wise as gods in many areas.

"This was a tempting offer indeed, but the sage waited to hear the counter-offer presented by Causilla. She, for her part, offered much too. She said she'd enrich the city with art: sculpture and song, illustration, and painting, tale-telling and so much more. This too was a very generous offer, for both truly wanted to have the city as their own.

"While the sage had no knowledge of this pact between the two gods, he was still a wise man and did not want to take a chance with this city in what he saw was a hard, possibly dangerous choice between the two deities and their lavishly generous offers. So he bided his time as best he could while he thought through each offer.

If he chose Dradin, then their city would be a home to scholars; if Causilla, a home for the artisans. But he wondered what the real benefit would be for the citizens themselves, for this sage knew that a city was far more than scrolls and sculpture. It was composed of the people who called it home; they were the ones who gave the city life and were the blood in its arteries called streets...

"Finally, the two gods pressed the sage for an answer, for they felt they had waited long enough and knew not why such generous offers would go so long unanswered. So the sage told them his reply, to which both deities were amazed:

"'You offer much, Dradin, for books and scrolls, and the knowledge they contain, are a good thing and needed for any city to thrive; but if there is no people in the city to read the books or absorb the knowledge they bring, then of what use are they? So while you offer a very generous boon, I will have to decline such a gracious gift.

"'You offer the arts, Causilla, and they too are wonderful to behold. Towering statues of heroes gone by, drawings of family and friends, plays and songs and dances...but if there is no one in the city to enjoy the plays, to hear the songs or appreciate the art, then what good are these things? So too your offer I must also decline.'

"Each god was perplexed by this answer and asked the sage to explain himself, for they had never foreseen such a result as possible – for any mortal to turn down their charity as had he. The sage then explained his reply:

"'Please take no offense at what I have chosen to say, great ones, for I have my reasons, which I will now share. It occurred to me as I pondered your offers that I came to understand the nature of the city in which I live – what makes it up and why any city can be called great or alive in the first place. For a city is not a collection of buildings or laws or art or knowledge; it is a collection of people. People are what make any city great.

"'Tis true that just laws and righteous living improve and indeed prolong the successful existence of a city, but if there could be such a thing as laws existing without people then there would be no city over which they could govern. This was what I understood while I thought over your propositions.

"'While we could have great art or knowledge, what would they be without the blessing of people to enjoy these things? For a piece of art is just an inanimate thing; little difference than a tree or rock. A book or scroll is the same. A citizen though – a mortal – is far more important than these things and actually elevates these inanimate items rather than these things elevating them.

"'And that is why I have to refuse both your offers. They do not add to the true worth of the city.'

"When the sage had finished speaking, both gods were dumbstruck and left in peace to think about what was said. The city where the sage lived thrived throughout his lifetime and beyond."

And so the man ended his tale.

"Do you understand the meaning?" His wizened face looked straight into the bard with his strange, dead eyes.

"I do," Corwyn nodded. It would have been pretty hard not to miss such a blatant meaning in the telling, though he had to admit it had been a nice myth, even if it was freshly crafted. With some polish and tweaking to its flow and rhythm the bard was almost certain–

"Then it's yours," the old man interrupted Corwyn's thoughts, "use it well for I never will."

Corwyn was a bit distressed by this comment and was going to ask more when the old man stood up and made his way away from the fire. "'Tis time I go back to sleep," he said as he passed.

Corwyn could do nothing but watch him go. He felt uneasy with the whole matter now; something didn't sit well with him and he didn't know how to deal with it. He didn't even know what to say save a weak "Thank you."

The old man stopped in his tracks, turned to the young bard and repeated in a serious voice with those same dead eyes reflecting the fire light back at Corwyn like hollow glass balls, "Use it well." Then he was gone from the firelight; lost in its shadows.

Corwyn ate the rest of his stew in silence, contemplating the stories he had just heard, until sleepiness came over him. It had been a long trek through the rain and he had finally come to feel warm once again. And with that warmth, a full belly, and even the rain above him, sluggishness overtook his frame. He didn't realize how tired he must have been until he felt his eyelids grew heavy as he watched the fire.

He thought he could hold out a little while longer till the sleep increased its hold; get himself thoroughly dry before he asked for a room for the night. He was wrong. His lids fell shut and he couldn't open them any longer as the darkness of sleep washed over him.

Corwyn awoke to a dead fire and to a darkness that soon grew less dense as his eyes adjusted to it. He found himself still on the bench where he had sat the night before only he was by his lonesome now. He marveled at how he had managed to stay on it through his slumber, when he considered it had no back to keep him from falling backwards. Thank Causilla for small favors. He could tell it was morning from lack of the storm's hard downpour and by the muffled chirping of birds he could hear outside the building.

Rising from his seat, he stretched, discovering that his body wasn't as sore as he thought it would be from slumbering in such an awkward position. He didn't see Molly anywhere. Looking around the whole area only showed a dark, silent interior that made the hair on the back of the bard's neck stand up. How had such a place lost so much life in just one evening? Then the door swung open spilling in the light of day.

The bard put a hand up to his eyes.

"Ah good," came the familiar welcoming tone of Molly's voice. "I thought you might be up now. I've made breakfast for you outside, should you care to take any.

"Hope you didn't mind sleeping on that bench. I was going to wake you to get you to a room, but you just seemed so restful and you needed the sleep, so I let you sit there. It was a small miracle, though, that you didn't fall."

"Yeah it was," Corwyn lowered his hand now as the plump frame of his hostess came into full focus; fat dimpled cheeks welcoming him to a new day. "I actually slept fairly well. Causilla

197

knows I've had far worse places in my life where I've come to slumber.

"Breakfast does sound good," the bard made an effort now to straighten out his crumbled clothing and run a hand through his reddish-blonde locks, "just give me a moment to clean up and I'll be right out."

Molly nodded, "There is some water in a basin up on the last door on your left" she pointed to the stairs, "a fresh towel too and anything else you might need."

"Thank you," Corwyn nodded then proceeded to make his way up the stairs, dry boots and socks in his left hand.

"When you're finished, you can come join me in the cemetery. That's where your breakfast has been prepared."

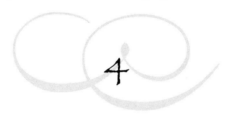

C orwyn found the new day much to his liking. The air was fresh and clean from the recent storm, and the small songbirds that made the grasses and stringy trees around the worn road and Wayfarer's Inn their roost, greeted him with a playful melody. The still, wet grass licked at his now dry but mud-caked boots and cuffs of his borrowed pants.

The cemetery was just outside the inn, a mere trot from the door to the low stonewalls encompassing it. As he walked, Corwyn looked again at the dark statue of Asorlok. The figure didn't seem as ominous as it had the night before. Indeed, any hint of darkness it might have had was washed away in the storm. Now it just looked like a time worn, stone statute; frayed from elements and forgotten by all.

Molly was at the base of this statue, the soft, damp grass that encircled the sculpture covered with a red cloth. The hostess sat upon the cloth alongside a platter of what looked to be sausages, a hunk of cheese, and round loaf of a dark rye bread. A pitcher rested in between all this food, which Molly was reaching for when Corwyn approached.

"Good morning," she smiled then poured what looked like milk into two wooden cups.

"When did you have time to make this?" The bard drew near to the cloth and then stopped. "I didn't hear or smell any of it."

"I cooked it outside since it was such a nice day and I didn't want to wake you," she returned the pitcher to its resting place beside her.

"Are the others going to join us?" The bard sat down on the outside edge of the cloth, the farthest edge both away from and across the statue of the god of the dead.

"No," Molly handed the bard a wooden plate and copper fork and knife, "they've already departed."

"Strange place to have a picnic." Corwyn looked about the gravestones that were now about level with his gaze as he sat between them.

"I think it's a bit restful and reflective," said Molly. She had started to cut off some pieces of cheese – it appeared to be goat cheese to the bard's eye – from the large chunk.

"How so?" The bard was curious but not uneasy with the comment. He figured such a statement in part from an Asorlin. They were followers of a god of death and graveyards were part of the domain the deity ruled over. Besides, he'd come to the opinion that he didn't have any reason to fear this woman. She was too pleasant – too maternal – to mean him harm and he didn't feel anything but restful in this cemetery.

"There are very few places you can go that are unaffected by time." Molly offered Corwyn some chunks of the cheese, which he took. "You can walk through the woods but that is always changing, always moving and growing because it's alive." Molly offered him some sausages and some of the rye bread that the bard also received gladly.

"But a cemetery is dead," Corwyn took a bite of the bread. The slice of dark rye was still warm and very good.

"Yes," Molly now filled her own plate, "here time has stopped – there are very few places like it on Tralodren."

"And why is that good?" Corwyn bit into his sausage and discovered it to be venison. It too was warm and flavorful. If anything could be said of his hostess, she certainly knew how to cook.

"It's good for reflection," Molly began to eat as well now. "Sages study dead things and learn from them and I think we can and should do the same from time to time."

"Study *corpses?*" Corwyn questioned.

Molly chuckled. "Not corpses, but ideas. They study dead ideas, nations, even years and learn from them. I think it wise we look back and think about the days that were and see what we can discover and learn from them so that our days to come might be brighter."

"Forgive me," Corwyn spoke after taking a swallow of his cold milk (and how did she get it cold and keep it that way while out here anyway?), "but I have never heard of death priests being so philosophical."

Molly smiled. "Not all of us are. I'm of a sect who sees Asorlok as the god of journeys. For life is just one long journey toward death, which is itself just another journey.

"It is as I told you last night; I keep this small inn as a resting place for those on their journey and maintain the cemetery beside it. That is what my beliefs have led me to do. Others of my faith have different ideas about what Asorlok would want of his priesthood and they pursue that agenda."

"I see," Corwyn bit off some more of the bread, and chewed it down enough to get some more words out of his mouth, "so why don't you wear your medallion like all the other priests do?"

Molly finished chewing the rest of her bite of sausage before she answered, "I'm of a slightly different conviction than my fellow Asorlins. I wear the medallion only when such occasions call for it."

"I see," Corwyn washed the rest of his curiosity away with another swallow of milk.

"So who is buried here? What town I mean? I didn't see any on my travels."

"Not too many anymore, that's true enough." Molly motioned for the bard to look at the headstones around them. "And as you can see it is filled to near capacity anyway." Corwyn did see that it was indeed filled – the low stonewalls keeping the headstones from seemingly overflowing into the countryside.

"No villages nearby then?" Corwyn asked.

"Not for many a mile," Molly took a bit of her sausage.

"So who is buried here?" Corwyn pressed while finishing his venison sausage.

"Those who came to find their way here," Molly cryptically answered, then finished off her sausage.

"I don't understand," Corwyn shook his head at her answer.

"This is a special cemetery, Corwyn. It houses the dead who found their own way to it. It called out to them when they were yet alive and pulled them here. Not everyone who is dead is buried."

Corwyn was getting a bit uneasy with all this talk now. He wasn't the most avid fan of death priests. Who was anyway? But this talk was not taking an avenue that he could handle. "You're starting to get cryptic on me now..."

"Yes," she finished her cup of milk, "I am, aren't I?" Molly pointed to a headstone to the left of Corwyn's shoulder. Following her direction a bit sheepishly, Corwyn peered at the worn rock marker and then read the writing carved upon it with great amazement.

"Jenna Gridley?" the bard was beside himself in bewilderment. "But I just spoke to her last night and this headstone looks to have been here for fifty years at least."

"Seventy-five actually," Molly corrected.

The bard had a rather unpleasant thought. Corwyn spun his wide-eyed head back to the chubby woman; cold sweat dripped down his back. "So those two people who I talked with last night they—"

"I do many things here in my service for Asorlok and one of them is to help the dead buried here. They might not know it when they are buried but they were dead long before they were ever lowered into the ground. No matter where they're buried, though, those who have been called wind up here."

Corwyn's face showed the inner perplexity that wrought itself in his stomach, mind, and heart.

"Don't worry about trying to make sense of it," Molly batted the thought from the air with a hand stroke then took another draft from her cup, "it won't change your path anyway. You're not destined for this graveyard and those like it which dot the land as Asorlok wills."

"So you killed them and I was talking to their ghosts?" Corwyn was getting ready to jump back and away from this woman. This was the best scenario his reasoning could provide.

"Nothing of the sort." Molly motioned for calm from the young bard. "Peace. I am not as black-blooded as the tales told of my faith lead many to believe. They kill themselves long before they are buried and find their way here."

Corwyn kept a weary eye about him now, but stilled his breathing and heart enough to at least appear calm to Molly. He would give her the benefit of the doubt...for now. Her hospitality and kindness deserved such a chance, he surmised.

"What happened to you last night with those two patrons?" Molly asked.

"I was sitting by the fire and they spoke to me."

"What did they say?" Molly studied Corwyn as he spoke.

"Jenna," Corwyn shot another glance over to the tombstone which bore her name, shivered, then continued, "wanted me to hear a song she had composed, and the other—" Corwyn stopped to try and recollect the man's name.

"He never gave you his name, but you can find the headstone of Devin Jilth just fine if you go wandering to the eastern corner of the wall," Molly interrupted.

Corwyn continued, "Well, he wanted to tell me a myth he'd made up." Corwyn's appetite was gone. All he wanted to do now was keep a watchful eye on the woman before him. Pleasant and rosy-cheeked she may be, but that could hide a more diabolical nature...at least he wasn't taking any chances. Open-minded or not, this was still an uneasy matter to be discussing – and in a *cemetery* of all places.

"They and many more like them have waited for a long while to share what they have kept locked up inside them," Molly looked the bard straight in the eye. Corwyn felt the touch of that gaze all the way to his spirit.

Corwyn started to inch a little further away from the priestess.

"I beg your pardon, but–"

"I'm not here to harm you, Corwyn. Be at ease. I'm trying to teach you something if you'll let me."

The bard capitulated to the request, waiting for an opportunity to flee at a moments notice should the need arise. He had grown very agitated in his inner person in the last few moments and yearned to be free of this place all together.

"Where do you think the greatest wealth lies?" She then asked as she finished off the final sausage on her plate.

Corwyn thought about it a moment, then gave an answer, "I suppose the greatest wealth would be what the Ancients collected in their capital."

Molly chuckled and shook her head, "A creative answer but not the best by far nor the truest."

To illustrate her point Molly pulled out a small copper coin emblazed with the mark of Romain; a lion done in profile ready to pounce toward the left of the coin. "This is just a hunk of metal, like all coins we use. It's a means of exchange – nothing more. It only has value because a good many of us ascribe value to it.

"Should you take it into a strange and savage land where they don't welcome it, you will find just how impractical it is. For you can't use it to protect you from the elements, it doesn't keep you warm, you can't even eat it. It's just a means of exchange because we say it is. It has value because we say it does."

"Here there is more treasure than the world can fathom," Molly motioned around the cemetery. "Here you'll find poems, songs and tales, ideas for new weapons and defenses, new inventions to ease the toil of mortalkind, and many, many more amazing finds.

"They're here just laying in wait for someone to use. Sadly, many who had been given these ideas in the first place let them die with them instead of using them."

"So this graveyard is the richest spot on Tralodren," Corwyn was making sure he understood what he was being told. His unease was lessening as revelation dawned in his mind.

"Not just *this* graveyard, but *all* places where mortals have died before they had a chance to share the ideas they'd been given." Molly stood up now and dusted the few rye crumbs from her skirt. She motioned for the bard to join her, which he did… hesitantly.

"You weren't expecting a philosophy lesson today, eh?" Molly chuckled pleasantly, as suddenly as the bard had reason to be uneasy, he relaxed with her once again. She had an incredible manner of being able to disarm.

"No, I wasn't."

"I think you will benefit from *this* insight, however." Molly motioned to the gravestone of Jenna, "When Jenna was buried she was dead years before that.

"That song she shared – she had a few more, and some ideas for other ventures – was a seed that she carried and which needed to be planted outside herself to grow. She didn't plant that seed, though, or the others that kept it company inside the dark dungeon where they were held deep inside, until she died."

Molly turned to take in the bard now with serious eyes, "Do you understand?"

Corwyn wrinkled his brow. "I didn't expect I'd ever hear a death priest taking about the importance of *life*."

"Just because you are awake and moving doesn't mean you are alive. Many people are awake, they go about their day, but they are far from alive in the sense that they embrace the fullness of living. Those who don't live while alive end up leaving behind a rich trove of treasure for others to exploit, should they wish."

"You mean their unplanted ideas and dreams?" Corwyn dusted off his clothes now from the few crumbs still remaining on his person. "So that's what you do here then? *Exploit* those treasures?"

Molly smiled. "My order is a misunderstood group, but you already know that. What I do here is twofold. First, I help travelers on their journeys, as with you and yours. Second, I guard over this cemetery and give rest to those that lie here. However, only those who wish to have their seeds sown after their death wind up here and at other localities as Asorlok wills."

"So no one is ever actually buried here?" Corwyn looked around the cemetery in the bright sunlight once more.

"No, they find their way here *after* death, Asorlok willing, and then to people like you. Though people die and their spirits pass on, not all ideas are so easy to perish; they struggle to live on for a chance at being reborn. And so I tend those ideas and pass them on to those who can give them life so that they too can achieve a sense of purpose in the world."

Corwyn looked over toward the gravestone of Jenna once more. Things were aligning in his head – this was all making more sense than before. "That wasn't really Jenna who I spoke to last night, nor Devin... It was just their ideas – the song and the myth."

The bard looked back up at Molly as she spoke, "It was *part* of them, but *not* them. That is all you need know." She nodded her approval, like an instructor taking pride in the work of their student finally being able to expand their thinking into a larger understanding.

"They wanted to have a chance to pass on their unsown seeds. Fear and other obstacles, self-made, imagined, and real, had hindered them while they lived – but they wanted to have their seeds scattered to grow after death. Some were given to you to sow last night."

Corwyn nodded his head slowly as his understanding deepened upon this revelation.

"They are a part of you now, Corwyn, as much as your own ideas are a part of you." Molly began to pick up the picnic breakfast as Corwyn looked up at the statue of Asorlok, eyes fascinated by the keys he held in his hand. The keys, that legends told, opened the thirteen gates to the afterlife. A god of journeys...

"How many more are here?" Corwyn at last broke the silence. "How many more ideas?"

Molly had nearly finished picking up when she looked up to the bard to give answer, "More than you can birth in your lifetime." Her words were simple and flat. "You had your fill last night. Best you move forward on your *own* journey now."

The bard became silent once more as he pondered. He stood there for a little while longer, how long he didn't know for this place felt timeless somehow, with only the birds signing and the sun shining down upon him. When he did begin to register the passage of time, he noticed that Molly was gone, as was the food and red cloth they had sat upon. Corwyn looked around and saw no one anywhere. Disturbed by this and the sign that the sun was getting closer to late morning, he made his way to the inn.

Once inside he found Molly behind what would have been a bar area with a bundle of red cloth and a hat in front of her. The bard's walking stick was resting beside the counter beside them. Again the inn was odd to the bard as it was devoid of anyone at all. Even the air seemed dust covered and ancient, wizened from lack of use. This sensation was far from sinister. Rather, it was a bit exciting as it had the hint of stumbling into a forgotten room or hidden ruin that still glimmered with the prospect of finding some lost treasure nearby.

"I suppose you will be on your way now," she greeted him with a smile.

"How long was I out there?" Corwyn motioned with his thumb over his shoulder as he walked further inside the inn.

"Long enough, I think. I packed up some victuals for you," she placed a plump hand on the red cloth wrapped package before her. "Got your gear ready for your trip as well. If you start out now you should make a decent enough village by nightfall."

"So are *you* real, then?" The bard drew closer to the counter.

Molly smiled, "Real enough for you. When I do die I'll be in Sheol working with my fellow priests in service to our god. For now, I tend to mortals and their needs as I am best able."

Corwyn nodded at her reply. He knew that he wasn't going to get any more out of the woman and so satisfied himself with her answer. And did it really matter anyway? He supposed not. Not now at any rate. The road was calling to him again and he was looking forward to joining it once more. Looking over the items on the counter, he studied them more closely.

"I didn't have a hat when I came. The gear is mine. So is the walking stick but–"

"You have one now," she handed the hat to the bard.

Corwyn took and then looked down at his clothes. "I just slept in these clothes one night. They shouldn't be soiled–"

"Keep those too," Molly swiped Corwyn's words out of the air with her hand. "It's the way of this place. Those who come, should they need new clothing, take up what others have shed before. I'll wash it and get it ready for the next traveler who finds his way here. I thought you might like a hat though. It should help keep the sun from your eyes and face."

Corwyn picked it up with a gentle hand. It was constructed of lightweight straw and possessed a medium cylindrical crown with a medium-sized brim expanding out around it, curving up a little more on the sides than the front or back. A simple, thin strand of leather fell out from inside the crown as the bard picked it up to reveal itself as a chin strap, should the wearer wish to fasten it more firmly to their person or even rest it on their back.

"Try it on," Molly motioned the hesitant bard to follow her encouraging instruction.

Corwyn looked at the hat for a moment more than donned it on his head.

"It suits you," she shot him a crooked grin.

"I think you're right," he found himself saying aloud. For some reason he knew deep inside that it did indeed feel right for him to be wearing it. If anything, it fit him like a glove and somehow made him feel better about the journey ahead, though he didn't quite know why.

"Then you must be off," she handed him his walking stick in one hand, gear in the other. "You have many more things to do I'm sure before you die. Folks who live life, like you, often do."

Corwyn gratefully took the items offered him.

"Thanks. You sure I don't owe you anything?"

Molly shook her head. "You've done more than enough for those who needed your aid.

"Good journey."

Corwyn nodded and then made his way out the door, new hat on his head. Once he had cleared the porch and had started down the road, he was tempted to turn around and get one last look at that strange place that had harbored him. When he did he found, much to his amazement, that nothing at all was present save a wide expanse of rolling plains.

The inn and the cemetery next to it were gone.

Corwyn shook his head and laughed. He wasn't the least bit surprised. After all, Molly had said he had found the inn... or had the inn found him? No matter, it had passed now and he wasn't going to go about trying to figure out how the workings of the god of death and his priests happened. He had enough of a time keeping abreast of his own faith.

It was late morning, though, and if he wanted to get anywhere by nightfall, as Molly had said, he would have to get moving, and so he did. Before him the sun-brightened road stretched onward and the bard followed. Walking stick in hand, new hat on head, he continued his trek. Birds gave him a sweet melody to enjoy the scenery and the inn faded into a pleasant memory. As he walked through the still damp and slightly muddy road he hummed a melody of his own. It was of a song about a tragic love affair between a soldier in the army of Gondad and the woman who loved him...

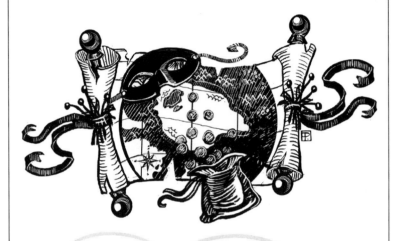

Charity for
Halflings

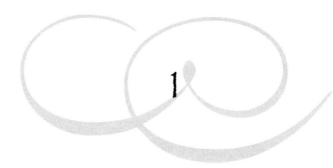

1

"**S**tupid waste of time." The dwarf's words were caustic and seethed in the pleasant early evening air. He walked beside a younger Telborian who, with walking stick in hand, made a move to out distance the dwarf with a few quickened strides. About a foot taller than his dwarven companion, the reddish-blonde haired young man returned comment to his friend's dour assessment.

"True, the ruins were less than what we were led to believe, but it was still interesting to see the land," Corwyn was enjoying the soft wind that tickled the grassy fields surrounding the road. Some soft fluttering cries of birds filled in the background as the chirp and chatter of grasshoppers and occasional crickets filled out the forefront of this natural symphony.

"There's nothing here but grasslands, Corwyn." The dwarf, whose name was Fredrick, waved his hand to the right side of the rough road they traveled. "Grasslands and farms and the ruins weren't even *ruins*."

Fredrick picked up his speed a bit to become even with the bard's gait. It was a bit harder to do after the hours he'd been on the road toting a stuffed pack on his back, but he managed nonetheless.

They were traveling Riverford Way: a dusty, wheel rut worn, dirt road that flowed out of the city of Romain, capital of the kingdom of the same name. The road flowed through the Grasslands of Gondad and then the southern portion of the kingdom where it then became lost in a mixture of trails, smaller footpaths, and a handful of other roads, which networked together at the outskirts of Romaine's influence. The road took its name from Riverford, which was the first town outside the royal city. It was to Riverford that Corwyn and Fredrick were returning after their fruitless search for some ruins now a good bit of travel to their south.

The kingdom of Romain was a rich land in Talatheal. Sister to the kingdom of Elandor to the north, Romain reigned over some two hundred fifty miles of rolling grasslands ending in the Marshes of Gondad. The land was more than fertile and had been for generations. This provided a steady harvest for the kingdom of all manner of agricultural splendor as well as abundant livestock.

This made King Morgan and Queen Engrain, the current rulers of Romain, proud. They were always trying to find something about their kingdom to upstage Elandor. Both kingdoms had a competitive streak in claiming that they were the greater of the Telborian kingdoms. Stemming from the first argument that each was founded by refugees fleeing fallen Gondad, (the Origin City of all Telborians), it later escalated into each claiming to possess the mandate of rule from the ancient city as the reborn version of said Origin City.

These conflicts had since ceased – battles giving way to less violent joust and tourneys where national honor could be had via the sword and lance of the best knights of each kingdom, but the political competition still thrived to some degree with all the nobles of both kingdoms. But this too was much more like a sibling rivalry than the violence of yester years. However, this didn't mean there wasn't competition internally between the ranks of royals who ruled over the lower classes. This was especially true when it came to marriage between noble families.

When it came to marrying off their lines to prospective suitors, it quickly became a game of skill to make the best match from the "ancient Telborian stock". This was crucial to ensure a higher degree of pedigree for the royal blood, which congealed in the various strata of these two kingdoms.

Romain was well known for its produce – chiefly grain – that it was able to ship off in boatloads and cartloads all over the continent. A powerhouse in crops, it was weaker in the area of lumber and some mineral means, namely stone, which it had to trade for with various kingdoms and independent cities. Corwyn wasn't thinking of this, though, as he watched the scenery unfold around him in an ever expansive procession.

Fredrick had been correct. The trip back, as well as to their destination, wasn't much of a sight. Mostly grasslands, there wasn't much along their route, save the odd stretch of farmland where the first green buds of life were jutting up from the brown soil, as it was already late spring and moving into the beginnings of the summer. A few clumps of trees, lonely and clustered in isolation, popped up here and there but besides that it was nothing but fields of tall grass and the dull brown road which grew more of a chocolate shade the lower the sun fell in the sky.

"Well, they *were* ruins–" Corwyn tried some more optimism to balance the dwarf's pessimistic decrees.

"Corwyn," Fredrick's orangish-brown eyes shot him a glance as if he were a father correcting his son's folly, "They were two piles of rocks and a pillar. Two *small* piles of rock. That is not what I would call a ruin."

"What would you call it then?" the bard's lips parted in a smile.

"A rock dump." Fredrick nodded a bit to his answer as if to give it more weight and thus assure a sense of greater authority to it. Like most dwarves, he was gray-skinned; a charcoal sort of hue, and stockier than others who might share his size, which Corwyn knew to be a little bit below five feet though Fredrick continually proclaimed it as five feet even (though most dwarves didn't make it above four and a half feet in height). A hill dwarf from the Grifftmacht Clan, who made their home in the hills of the same name that nestled around eastern edge of the Diamant

Mountains, he was serious of face, having deep lines etched around his mouth, eyes, and cheeks from a studious and strident life.

Unlike the mountain dwarves, hill dwarves were a bit more open than their higher dwelling kin. Adaptable to other races and choosing to interact with them, they were not as conservative in many mannerisms and ways, but still held to the same tenets of the dwarven ideal: family, honor, and tradition. Thought by many other races to be the more "liberal" of the dwarven camps, hill dwarves seemed just as dutiful and dedicated as their mountain cousins. For in truth, despite the hill dwarves' openness to outsiders, they were very similar, if not identical, to their mountain kin in just about everything else.

Corwyn sighed.

"I suppose we should reach Riverford by tomorrow night if we can keep up a good pace." The bard's blue-green eyes turned toward the road ahead of them, which seemed to spread out for an indefinable span as the prairie spread out and ever onward.

"Well at least we didn't get into trouble." Fredrick's voice now took on a slight sympathetic air, which anyone else who didn't know the dwarf as well as Corwyn, would think sounded more like pity than empathy. "We don't need a repeat of that Rockshire incident. I hear the Duchess here has it in for bards to begin with – don't want to cause any ruckus here now either."

"You still can't let that go, huh?" The bard shook his head in disbelief. "That was four years ago."

"Four years is nothing to a dwarf. You humans are like hummingbirds – always running to and fro trying to cram as much as you can into the short span of years you are allotted on this world while we dwarves take all things with the stride of ancestral wisdom." Fredrick had taken on his familiar 'scholarly tone' that the bard, and many others, had the privilege of seeing from time to time whenever the dwarf would expound upon the virtues of dwarven culture and ideals.

"Ah yes," the bard chuckled to himself, "Fredrick the wise sage speaks again. Well, no one told you to come with me, Fred. You could have stayed back at the inn."

"I came to protect you. You know that. You have this foolish notion to not arm or even armor yourself when you go out on these explorations. Someone has to keep you breathing should you run up against something or someone who wants to do you in."

"Of course," Corwyn turned toward the dwarf with an ear-to-ear grin. "And you wouldn't want your meal ticket to get away from you either."

Fredrick's eyelids lowered a bit as his face took on a more serious expression once more; the light mirth that had moments before danced about it melted away into charcoal gray skin. "Hold on there. There's nothing wrong with making sure you stay alive to keep on performing. I'm not the only one in the troupe who benefits."

"No, that's true…" The bard had turned his mind to the road once more. It was best to change the subject lest he have to calm an angry dwarf the rest of the way to Riverford.

"Besides," Fredrick spied the bard's garb, "if you allow strangers to dress you, it just proves to me how *much* you need my help."

Corwyn still wore the hat and coat he had received from Molly, along with the other clothing he had attained in his short stay in the Wayfarer Inn. To him, it seemed fine attire to go exploring in; he wore different dress when he was performing. Like all good bards, Corwyn knew the advantage of showmanship, and that much of showmanship came down to appearance and presentation.

"I told you how I got them." Corwyn turned out to the field of grass to his left and watched it dance in the cool evening breeze.

"I know." The dwarf huffed as he tried to continue to keep up with the bard's longer stride. "That's what worries me. How do you know she didn't just get them from corpses? She could have looted that graveyard you told me about and then just piled it up."

Fredrick jabbed a thick finger at the bard as he spun around to speak. Fredrick was quicker than Corwyn, however, and cut the bard off just as he opened his mouth to make his reply. "That's your problem. You're just too trusting. She could have been chatting with some murderer or one of them folks who likes to snuggle up to dead bodies but you just trust them all the same."

"You sure you're not a mountain dwarf?" Corwyn asked with a grin. "Did they mix up what clan you belonged to when you were born or something?" Corwyn was amazed at how much this recent episode in his life seemed to cause Fred so much worry. Corwyn had thought it an incredible encounter – something that would stay with him for the rest of his life. Apparently Fredrick didn't share the same understanding, and Corwyn made a mental note to be a bit more careful about sharing some things with the dwarf that might cause to put him in a similar mood. He was also unsure if he should have shared his trip to the Northlands with the dwarf. He hadn't been so forthcoming with his encounter with Lena, though, and for that he was a bit thankful given what he knew now regarding Fredrick's reactions to the other stories of his recent adventures.

"The hat might be a bit much." Corwyn tapped the rim of the woven object affectionately. He had grown to like it over his recent journeys – it had seemed to grow into him, or he into it – and it was starting to feel like a part of his natural body.

"That might be an understatement," Fredrick snorted, "you look like a pirate."

"A *halfling* pirate," he added after a moment of reflection.

"Say what you will about it, I like it. However, I won't be so base as to comment on *your* attire." Corwyn joshed.

The dwarf was dressed in simple garb. A dark green, long sleeved, knit woolen tunic, dusted from many a mile on the road, covered much of his body until brown canvas pants flowed out from under it to end in cordovan brogans; travel soiled white cotton stockings jutting up from the shoe and under the pant legs.

A wide chestnut girdle, the same color as the dwarf's shoulder-length thick, straight hair, sported a silver loop on its left side, from which a deadly looking polished steel mace swung in rhythm to his steps. Opposite the mace, a baselard dagger rested snug in its own sheath, affixed to the wide belt. Corwyn smiled to himself when he recalled that the dwarf hadn't even had to do so much as put his hand on the pommel of either weapon once.

"If you think you're funny, you can carry the backpack all the way to Riverford." Fredrick shifted the weight of a yellowish-brown, woolen backpack on his sturdy frame with a huff.

"I wouldn't dream of upsetting you, Fred," Corwyn teased the dwarf.

"Hmph," the dwarf let out a huff of hot air, which fluttered his tawny braided mustache. Fredrick wore a full beard, but kept it shorter and rounder than some of his fellow clansman. The braided ends of his mustache were the only thing that was more traditional in his clan, these being dyed a brilliant green hue.

"You up for a show again then?" Corwyn changed the subject.

"You ready to perform again so soon?" Fred kept his eyes on the road. The straps of the backpack were digging into his shoulders and under his arms, but he put the dull ache to the back of his thoughts. They'd be resting for the night and could put up with the annoying throbbing that encircled his arms until then.

"Why not? Riverford, Spole, or even Romain would be fine places to put on a show."

"*Spole?*" Fredrick snidely snorted in protest. "It's a *village,* Corwyn. Hayseeds and sheep. You think you can get any coin from them?"

Fredrick shook his head slightly upon pondering what he saw as a dismal prospect. "Riverford would be a bit better, but not by much. At least they have a decent tavern hall to put on a fair performance…maybe gain some goodly coin…"

"I'm thinking more about increasing my notoriety in the area." Corwyn's eyes leisurely strolled over the surrounding landscape.

"We haven't been this far into Romain in a while, and with my most recent absence, things needs to be stirred up again." Corwyn could smell the earthy, sandy scent of the grasses and pockets of wild prairie flowering plants that had started to spring up along the road.

"Your recent *vampire* absence?" Fredrick cocked an eye and eyebrow up at the Telborian bard.

"Yes," Corwyn darted a look over to the dwarf and then back to the road again, "*that* absence."

"Pity the halfling lived through it all," the dwarf mused aloud as he tried to find something of interest in the fields along his side of the road. He didn't. "That must have been some long voyage back home."

"Longer than I cared for," the bard confessed. "I'm sure it will be even longer for the others on their way back to Breanna."

"Maybe you should skip the small potatoes crowd and go right to King Morgan himself for a show," Fredrick brought them back to the previous thread of their conversation. "I'm sure he and Egrain would like the entertainment, and it would shoot you farther up the ranks of bards, if you're worried about having been knocked down a peg or two."

"No, not right yet. I'd rather be asked by the king than invite myself."

"Dreaming big, eh?" Fredrick let out a ripe ruckus of mirth.

"Why not? You'll always get what you expect," the bard answered with the solid strength that was the basic foundation of his philosophy. A philosophy which the dwarf had to admit always seemed to come true for the young bard ever since he had first met him some six years before. Corwyn's convictions were so strong about this one sentence tenet because it had always come true for him. Whatever he said he tended to get or have happen to him. Just how or why this happened was beyond Fredrick. Be it luck, the favor of Corwyn's goddess, or something else all together, he was unsure. Not being a follower of Causilla (he was a follower of Drued, god of the dwarves, though he still respected the goddess of music) he was just happy to be around Corwyn when the things he spoke came to pass. Pragmatism was the dwarf's worldview, and it was made even more solid with the steady income that association with Corwyn afforded.

"Hmm," the noise from Fredrick's mouth and nose was more like a grunt than meaningful words. "So you're for Riverford?"

"If we get there at a decent hour and there is a place to have some performances, sure." The bard waved to a dirty farmer some distance away who was walking in a field of wheat. The farmer stopped to look back at the two odd fellows walking past and then returned the wave before getting back to his work of hoeing his field.

Fredrick raised an eyebrow with a short glance at the bard and a headshake of disapproval upon seeing the farmer's response. "And if it's a hayseed pig stall?"

"If we can't get a decent place then we'll move on to Romain I suppose, but I want to have at least one performance in the area before we head back toward Haven and winter comes," Corwyn replied.

"Well, the others will want to do something, that's for sure. They've been getting bored out of their minds, I'm sure, while we've been off chasing old wives tales…" Fredrick grumbled.

Corwyn stopped his walk, stomped his simple broken limb walking stick into the ground before him, and turned to the dwarf. "You're still mad about the money, aren't you?"

"What do you think?" It wasn't really a question but a flat rhetorical statement. "They said it would be *filled* with treasures." Fredrick likewise stopped his movement to cross his arms with a huff.

"Oh come on, Fred," Corwyn rolled his eyes, "you didn't *buy* that part, did you?"

This was an old dispute between them. Fredrick looking for the business side of things – gaining the most coin he could from every venture and performance they undertook – and Corwyn looking more toward the adventure and performance itself rather than the monetary return. The tiff was harmless enough; each knew the other wouldn't budge on their position. Once in a while, however, they still had to let themselves butt heads over the matter.

"You certainly bought the idea of some ruins being out here quick enough," the dwarf countered, orangish-brown eyes stern as stone.

"That at least sounded plausible. There are a lot of ruins all over this Duchy. You can't expect them to all have treasure though – not if they are so close to civilization. They're bound to have had their fair share of looters a long time ago," the bard reasoned with the dwarf.

"So why go then if not for profit?" Fredrick's gray brow wrinkled.

"There's more to ruins than digging for cash…" Corwyn began his part of the old argument again.

"Oh no, here we go again," the dwarf rolled his eyes with a low moan. "The talk about how one travels and explores to learn and develop a better understanding of themselves and the world about them."

Corwyn stopped to look straight into Fredrick's eyes.

He continued the stare for what seemed like an endless span of years. It wasn't a hard stare – a cold thing that beat with malice covered in crusty, jagged rage – but a silent, contemplative gaze. The sort of look a philosopher might give his student to let him hear the weight of the words he'd just spoken as to gauge their effect; come to a clearer insight into what lay within one's inner thinking. Finally, Fredrick could take no more.

"*What*?" The dwarf lifted his hands, palms up, above his shoulders in surrender.

"You don't think we learned anything today?" The bard raised a lone eyebrow.

"Sure we did. We learned: don't trust people who say they know where some ruins are and then take your money when the ruins turn out to be a rock dump," the dwarf griped.

"You didn't learn anything from the surrounding terrain or the travel itself?" the bard continued his questions.

"Only that we should have paid for some horses for the trip or maybe a coach or wagon. The walk was long enough and fruitless as it was and seems a waste. At least with horses we could have gotten it over with quicker." Fredrick turned to move back down the road once more.

Corwyn sighed then joined him.

"You know, if you don't start to learn to enjoy life a bit more you're just going to get more sour with age." Corwyn's tone and delivery reminded Fredrick of a mother telling her child if he contorted his face into some sort of grimace it would end up staying that way.

"I'm a dwarf," Fredrick grumbled again without looking toward the bard who moved up to his side. "Don't expect too many miracles."

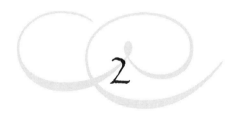

The darkness drew deeper and soon night had fallen around them before they could properly set up a resting spot for the evening, leaving the two of them to wrestle with their gear near a small cove of lanky maples. Fredrick continually huffed his displeasure at not being able to see clearly through the waning light in his endeavors while he set up a makeshift bed. Corwyn was already reclining against a tree, hat cocked low over his eyes.

"Should be a nice night," Corwyn could smell the sweet fragrance of ripening fields in the distance.

"Still can't believe they don't have anything but farmlands out here." Fredrick finally succeeded in his endeavors. "You think they'd put in a hamlet here or there. It doesn't seem to be an efficient use of all this open space."

"They're farmers, Fred. Be thankful that they and the others like them are out here else you wouldn't be able to get all that rye bread you enjoy."

"I'm sure I'd adapt if there ever was a shortage," the dwarf grumbled into his beard as he lowered himself against a tree trunk and his simple bed.

"I think it's quite enjoyable."

"This from the man who thinks searching for rock dumps is rewarding." Fredrick adjusted himself to a comfortable position.

Silence fell between them only intermittently broken by the chirping crickets and the occasional rustle of leaves above their head.

The silence rested over them for a little while...

It rested but then was broken by the cracking of a twig under heel and an intrusive, nasally voice that immediately caused the crickets to fall still.

"Stand and deliver your money or your life."

Fredrick was the first to open his eyes, looking up in the moonlit surroundings at what appeared to be some six or seven short forms of darkness standing at the base of the spindly maples.

"Corwyn?" Fredrick looked to the half slumbering bard beside him, "I think we have company." The bard was still fully awakening to the understanding of the situation.

"I said stand and deliver, vermin." The nasally tone was punctuated with the impact of a crossbow bolt into the trunk of the maple just above Fredrick's head.

Fredrick rose with a growl, mace in hand and scowl etched deeply into his face.

Corwyn was now fully awake and standing as well, easily towering over all the figures gathered about him. Indeed, these new shadowy visitors were even shorter than Fredrick.

"Keep your ground dwarf or you will soon find yourself to be like the dog that chased the porcupine," the nasally voice of the shorter figure snapped back. Neither Corwyn nor Fredrick could clearly see any of the cloaked figures amid the greater darkness of the night.

"You're *highwaymen*?" Corwyn asked the one who he believed to have addressed them, and therefore he assumed their leader. He motioned for Fredrick to keep back.

"Not just *any* highwaymen; you have the pleasure of being robbed by *Jocque's Blackguards*, the most *dashing* and *deadly* brigands to claim this territory as their own." The smaller, dark figure, the one with the nasal pitch whom Corwyn took to be their leader, stepped a little closer. Both the Telborian and dwarf could see little under his hooded frame but his crossbow, which was now reloaded with another bolt and aimed in their direction.

"Now kindly hand over your valuables and you can return to your slumber with your lives." There was wicked mirth in that tone now. Corwyn also detected something else familiar in his tone in the way he was speaking Telborous. Corwyn was sure he was a halfling. Having been on a ship with the first halfling he'd ever met, he had a great amount of time to get to know the race that much better, and was sure that these highwaymen were halflings.

"Halfling Highwaymen?" Corwyn pondered aloud, "I never heard of that happening in these parts of Romain before."

"*Halflings?*" Fredrick shook his head with disgust. "We're being robbed by *halflings*? This is so humiliating."

"No, your *outfit* is humiliating," the lead halfling, probably Jocque himself, Corwyn surmised, snapped back his tart reply to the dwarf. There was a low murmured chuckling by the others at this statement that further elevated Fredrick's rising ire. "Hand over the valuables or we'll take them from your corpse."

"Get behind me, Corwyn," Fredrick boldly stepped forward, his right hand tightening his grip on the hilt of his mace, "I'll have them running home to whatever rock they crawled out from under before they can even become a threat–"

The halflings focused their crossbows as one on the dwarf.

"No, Fred." Corwyn placed his hand on the right shoulder of the dwarf and pulled him back a bit, adding weight to his words.

"Don't be stupid, Corwyn," Fredrick didn't take his eyes from the lead halfling who he knew was laughing at him now because of Corwyn's action.

"You should take your own advice, Fred." The bard kept his hand on the dwarf's shoulder but the former pressure it exerted was now gone. "It looks as if they outnumber us five to one. Bad odds… even for you."

"You probably don't even have an accurate count – it's too dark to see how many there are." Fredrick huffed now in frustration, which rustled his mustache, keeping his gaze still ever forward should the halflings seek a chance at getting a drop on the dwarf.

"Exactly." The bard directed his gaze down to Jocque, his crossbow, leading the others, still straight at Fredrick. "How do we know you won't kill us if we cooperate with you?"

"You have my word as a gentleman," Jocque bowed his head to the bard. Neither Fredrick nor Corwyn could see any more of his face for the halfling's hood was deep and the shadows, even in the growing moonlight, were quite dark.

Fredrick snorted, "The word of a *halfling*? That's about as good as wearing armor made of meat to defend yourself from some starving bears."

There was a frigid stillness that followed Fredrick's verbal assault. It was jagged like a shard of glass and Corwyn could feel the tension cutting into them. Tension that was bringing small halfling fingers to pull harder on the trigger of their crossbows.

"We shall see whom mocks whom when this is over, you disgusting mound of hair and dirt." Jocque's voice had grown more nasally as it swelled in rage; the nearly undetectable accent growing slightly more noticeable too. "We may be thieves but we still hold to the old traditions which made us great – like bathing."

Fredrick's knuckles in his right hand quickly turned a pale white.

Corwyn's hand grew weighty once more upon the dwarf's shoulder.

"Now start handing over your valuables. We haven't got all night," Jocque advised with a slightly calmer voice.

Neither Corwyn nor Fredrick moved.

"Oh dear," Jocque moved closer, bringing his crossbow level with Fredrick's face, nearly right on center with the dwarf's nose. Corwyn's white-knuckle grip was barely able to restrain the dwarf. The bard could feel the dwarf's whole body getting ready to pounce. "Do you need me to clean out your ears with a good blast of bolt?"

"You can't take them all in this darkness, Fred," Corwyn repeated with hushed words, "you're bound to get a bolt stuck in you somewhere and you know that I'm not the world's best healer."

Frederick chortled under his breath and into his beard, "I know."

"I'm running out of patience, gentlemen, and losing my willingness to let you live." Even when the halfling tried to be genteel it came off as base and crass, grating on both Corwyn's and Fredrick's nerves.

Corwyn's hand left the dwarf's shoulder. To his amazement, Fredrick stayed put. Perhaps he wasn't that far gone into his need to bash heads as the bard first suspected.

"I have an idea," the bard whispered back to the dwarf, "just follow my lead."

"Great," Fredrick grumbled into his beard.

Corwyn turned his attention fully to the face of the leader; at least where the hooded halfling's face was presumably looking. "I'm afraid we don't have any great amount of valuables to hand over."

"Don't give me that," Jocque's tone was growing more crass as his patience diminished. "We can all see you have coin, given how you dress, and you don't look like these dirty hayseeds so hand it over...*now.*"

The other cloaked halflings drew closer, surrounding Corwyn and Fredrick in a semicircle, allowing the two to better define the number of their foes, which did indeed appear to be ten. If their cloaks hid much from view, their crossbows were in plain sight; steel tipped bolts twinkling like deadly stars in the moonlight. And all were ready to find a home in the bodies of the taller mortals before them.

"We have a splattering of coin," Corwyn moved into what Fredrick recognized as his performance voice, "but there is something more valuable than anything we carry on our person, which I've kept hidden in my shirt pocket.

"If you will let us go with the small bit of coin we have, you'll find something more valuable instead. For I've heard it said how noble your race is, and I would plead for that same fine quality to be extended to us this night."

"What are you, some kind of priest?" The other halflings chuckled at Jocque's mocking.

"Hardly," Fredrick whispered into his beard. He still held his mace and stood his ground, ready to act at a moment's notice as he witnessed Corwyn's laying a plan for their move. Just what that move might be, Fredrick was uncertain. He did know, however, that it wouldn't involve bashing anyone's face in with his mace.

Pity.

"Check his pocket then. I could use some amusement tonight." Jocque motioned to Corwyn with his crossbow. A halfling at Jocque's left followed his direction, leaving the others to come up to stand beside the bard. The height difference was more than comical; like a small child trying to rob an adult.

"Hand it over...slowly." This halfling had a froggy voice that further added to what might be seen as the sheer surreal comedy of the event. His face was still hidden by his hood but Corwyn could see the hint of a scruffy, flabby face bobbing in and out amid the hood's shadows. He couldn't help but notice the tang of sour wine and the same stale tobacco of which Charles de Frassel had been so fond.

He didn't like the similarities.

"Very well." Corwyn did as he was told, reaching inside his shirt pocket to retrieve – to slowly retrieve – a folded up piece of paper.

"Don't give them that, Corwyn." Fredrick grumbled in the dark, seeing now the way this performance would take place and the role he needed to play.

"Shut up, Hairy." Jocque ordered the dwarf with a jab of his crossbow in the dwarf's general direction, and then turned to the froggy-throated halfling again. "Bring it here."

The halfling did as he was told, fetching the paper from the bard with one hand (keeping his right firmly affixed to his crossbow; finger on the trigger) and backing away from the taller Telborian as if he were some wild animal – one best not turn his back to until he was once again beside Jocque. The lead halfling snatched the paper away from the other and began to unfold it with one hand, the crossbow in his other hand still pointed toward Fredrick though now it wasn't so direct, having fallen just a bit limp as he looked at the parchment.

"So what is this?" Jocque peered up from the opened parchment after looking at it briefly.

"A map to some ruins," Corwyn answered flatly.

"Big deal, now you're just wasting my tim–"

"Ruins we were told that were filled with treasure." Corwyn quickly added.

"Shut up already, Corwyn," Fredrick pretended to be fuming. He was delighted to see Corwyn's timing and delivery was as perfect as usual.

"No *you* shut up you mop-faced, soiled rag wearing cave dweller," Jocque sneered under his hood. "Your friend is trying to save both your lives and you are just making it harder for him to keep us from filling you full of bolts."

Jocque took a closer look at the paper, now turning it about in the moonlight to try and get a better view. "So this is a treasure map then, eh?"

"We were told that it would take us to some ruins filled with treasure," Corwyn meekly addressed the lead halfling.

"Seems to be not that far from here," Jocque looked up toward the bard, studying him with a hawkish gaze. Corwyn could then see a faint glimmer of a face under the hood. It appeared middle-aged, clean-shaven, dark-eyed and lined with the years of a hard life.

"No, maybe a day at the most of travel." Corwyn was studying the situation closely as if it were a performance he was tailoring to best suit the needs of his audience.

"Riches, eh?" Jocque held his gaze on the bard. Corwyn could see the outline of his deepening smile in the hood along with a black domino mask helping to cloak his identity, which the bard was sure the others were wearing as well. Not that it would do much to cloak their identity from authorities since halflings aren't known for being able to blend into the much taller general population of the land. Perhaps it was for theatrics…

"All yours if you just let us go," Corwyn continued his performance.

"Why not kill two birds with one stone," Jocque motioned the other halflings forward with his crossbow. "Empty their pockets of any coin."

The others rushed forward to do just that, small childish hands pilfering what they could from the backpack resting against the trees and their taller victims, while two others watched and waited a little bit behind them with their weapons ready to fire at the first sign of any retaliation. These too had the sickly sweet and half decomposed smell of sour wine and spent tobacco, with one or two reeking of fresh ale.

"You sure I can't–" Fredrick fought hard to keep his growing rage caged.

"No." The bard's statement was as stern as steel.

Fredrick sighed in bitter frustration over the matter then resigned himself to the fate, all to the best of his acting abilities. He let the two halflings on either side of him dig through his pockets, patting him down to make sure they didn't miss anything. Corwyn fared the same.

"I'll give you your lives, but not on a full coin purse." Jocque folded the map and placed it under his cloak as he watched his band complete their work in mild satisfaction.

"You're more than fair." Corwyn complimented as the halflings finally stopped their groping over his person.

"Oh please," Fredrick grumbled as the brigands finally left him as well. "These are halfling thieves we're talking about here. Not that there is much difference between halflings who *aren't* thieves, mind you. It runs in the veins of the entire race."

"You could learn much from your friend, shaggy," Jocque made a motion for the others to leave. "How to dress for one thing – he has good taste there at least. Especially that hat.

"We'll leave that for you since you understand good fashion sense."

Corwyn nodded in appreciation. "You're too kind."

"Yes, I am," Jocque gloated. "So I leave you two your lives, as promised, and you have given me a rich trophy it would seem. A fair trade, yes?"

"Oh yes," Corwyn was quick to enthusiastically nod his head in agreement.

"Don't follow – no bold actions and you'll see the dawn once again."

"Fare thee well, gentlemen."

And with that, all the halflings scattered like black mice into the night.

After some time had passed and each believed the halflings to be gone from the surrounding area, Corwyn and Fredrick relaxed.

"Now, you had to admit that was more fun than beating them up," Corwyn grinned.

"Hmph." Fredrick started to rummage around his gear, which had been scattered along with Corwyn's around the base of the trees. "More fun for *whom*? I would have really enjoyed kicking the little slugs around some."

"We should get moving to get some more distance between us once they find the ruins." Corwyn joined the dwarf in his rummaging.

"I didn't like losing my coin either," Fredrick had just about packed everything up and was making ready to leave, "or getting groped by those wretched dogs."

"You still couldn't have taken them Fred, no matter how good you think you are. You couldn't see how many you were facing, and they had the advantage of surprise, and probably knew the terrain much better than either of us. Besides, we have more in Riverford, Fred – a lot more than we gave to those halflings."

"It's still lost coin." Fredrick finished picking up the rest of his belongings.

"Think of it as charity." Corwyn's rosy optimism was near insanity to the dwarf.

"*Charity*?" Fredrick looked Corwyn in the face as the bard was finishing packing up the rest of his items.

"Charity." The bard repeated as he stood to his full height. They had both gotten some rest before their robbery and he supposed they could make it to a nearby village before dawn.

"To *halflings?*" Fredrick held his gaze at the bard, uncertain of what to make of such a decree.

"Can you think of anyone who needs charity more than halflings?" Corwyn adjusted his hat and started to walk away from their camp, walking stick keeping time with the bard's strides.

Fredrick let the matter drop, turning around to don the backpack once again before hurrying off to follow after the bard. He could feel the straps digging into his flesh again but he would be more than able to bear it knowing that the halflings were going to be disappointed in their quest for treasure.

"Least it's a nice night for walking," Corwyn let out a relaxed breath when Fredrick had caught up beside him.

"Well, that map *finally* did do us some good," Fredrick did his best to match the bard's even strides.

"And you played your part quite well," Corwyn shot the dwarf a small grin.

"It took me a moment to follow your lead, but when you pulled out the map everything came into place." Fredrick returned the grin. He was quite pleased with his own performance as well.

"So you're not upset any more about this little trip then, I take it?"

"I'm not thrilled at having myself robbed by halflings, but I can have the pleasure of picturing that little twerp's face when he sees his ruins in all their glory." Fredrick shifted the weight of the backpack on his shoulders. "That will give me a warm night's rest when we're in a nice inn in Riverford."

Fredrick's tone became more scholarly. "You see what I mean now about you having to change your wardrobe? If you start getting compliments on your dress from halfling highwaymen, then you might want to rethink your sense of style."

"You could have a point there, Fred," the bard simply eyed the road before him, doing his best to hide the smile creeping across his mouth.

"What do you mean *could*?" Fredrick looked up at the bard with a studious eye.

"Let's leave that 'til we get to Riverford." The smile at last escaped the bard's hold, spreading over his face faster than wild fire with dry tinder.

Sellswords and Snake Oil

1

Hammond made his way through the tall grasses that he let grow wild behind his barn. The late afternoon sun had come to wash over the swaying tawny stocks, giving them a bronze cast and covering the rest of the world in an amber hue as it faded into the softer tone of early evening. Tall enough to equal a man in height, the wild prairie that was The Grasslands of Gondad was a rich and still somewhat wild tract of land. Hammond's farm was, to many, one of the last spots of civilization before the ancient grasslands reclaimed the landscape.

Hammond was a middle-aged, sun-kissed Telborian with a balding head, covered by a wide brimmed, straw hat. A farmer by trade, as was his father before him, he was looking forward to what seemed to be a promising harvest this coming year. Like many other small villages in this part of Talatheal, Plainsview fell under the jurisdiction of Romain. The kingdom held a weaker hold over this outer edge of its territory, however, given Plainsview's great distance from it. The chief export of the kingdom was grain and the villages and towns from whence most of it originated were found in the plains. The harvest to come would indeed be a very fruitful and therefore profitable one if the previously favorable weather held. Happy with the state of his fields, from which Hammond had just returned, he was looking forward to the evening meal his wife was preparing. He had worked up quite an appetite.

Before he went inside he wanted to do a few last minute things in the barn while he still had some light. Like many in the area, Hammond and his wife, Marion, did their best at being self-sufficient. To this end, they had some simple livestock beyond two oxen for plowing: chiefly a cow, some chickens and a few pigs. These they kept in a separate pen beside the barn. The rest of life's necessities they couldn't get from their fields or animals, they bought in town from the local goods shop. And so it was the way for the rest who lived in Plainsview for they weren't simple serfs, as had been the case in the kingdoms hundreds of years ago, but freemen who were able to profit from their livelihood. Of course they didn't farm large tracts of land either, but together their combined acreage was a force with which to be reckoned.

Hammond had nearly reached the one story, wood-worn structure that was the barn – cleaning stray pieces of prairie grasses from his person as he neared – when suddenly he heard a strange noise.

Instantly he froze in his tracks.

He hadn't heard anything similar in all his thirty plus years of living out in the plains. Hammond wasn't sure what it was. It had sounded like an animal of some kind but it had a strange quality about it that set the farmer's spine a tingle. Turning around, Hammond noticed a section of the tall grass through which he had just come start to rustle. Whatever made that noise seemed to be drawing closer to the edge of the grasses.

Hammond couldn't see anything on the path that he'd cleared by his daily trek to check his fields, and that just added to his unease. If something was that large (judging by the way the grass was swaying it seemed to be of good size), then he should have seen some aspect of it – for it had to be close.

He didn't, though, and after a few minutes the movement stopped. Standing for a moment more, the farmer's fear began slowly to fade. In short order Hammond reasoned the threat, if there had been any, had passed and he had more important things to attend to than staring at a bunch of prairie grass.

Hammond continued his trek to the barn but he didn't get further than a few steps when again came a noise from the grass behind him. This time it had a more "sinister" quality to it. How and why Hammond knew this and ascribed this quality to the sound he didn't know; he only knew that it seemed to fit the sound's nature. A nature that again made him feel it originated from something other than an animal.

Hammond checked behind him again, this time raising his hat above his tan, sweaty brow in hopes of getting a better view of the scene. It was probably just a raccoon or maybe a coyote. There were many of them out here this time of year. It wouldn't be the first time he'd have to chase away some critter before it could make a mess of the small garden his wife kept near the house or harass the chickens.

Only Hammond already knew it hadn't sounded like a coyote. From the noise coming out of the grasses, which he noted were definitely showing signs of something large making its way through them, he was certain this was something that could pose a significant threat. He was still amazed that he hadn't seen it by now, seen some glimpse of its body through the trembling green and tawny stocks; but some part of him – a part that was growing stronger with each heartbeat – didn't know for sure if he wanted to see what was making that noise.

Then suddenly the movement stopped.

Hammond felt some cold beads of sweat form on his forehead to match the ones already present on the back of his neck. Then came a low, body- trembling growl. It rolled out to meet Hammond from the prairie like a pack of hungry coyotes. Hammond knew most animals shunned humans – only the dangerous ones made a press for them. And this beast seemed far from shunning the Telborian farmer.

Hammond took a step back.

The growl grew closer this time, the unmistakable sound of the thing being almost upon him. Hammond still couldn't see what was threatening him.

Hammond took another step back.

He had a pitchfork and sickle in the barn, if he could get to them in time perhaps he might be able to put up a good fight and scare the thing away. In most cases such a move would cause a more emboldened animal to flee. Hopefully the action would be as successful in *this* situation. Deciding to make a run for the barn while he could, Hammond turned around to sprint just as the thing in the grass leapt out at him.

Hammond only saw it out of the corner of his eye, but that was long enough to fuel his feet with a fire they hadn't had even when he was a younger man and used to race his friends to the local swimming pond.

"Marion, bolt the door!" he shouted out to his wife, hoping she would hear him inside the house more than five hundred yards away. He knew just from seeing the creature, even from the corner of his eye – it would be foolish to try and take it on with a sickle or pitchfork. No, this was something against which the hands of common man would not so easily prevail.

He altered his course to the barn in mid-stride, praying to whatever god would listen to give him the strength and protection to make it to his destination. He also prayed that Marion had heard him too and done as he ordered. He'd have little time to check during his run; hoping as well to keep and pull the attention of the creature with him all the way to his destination so as to keep both his wife and homestead safely out of its clutches.

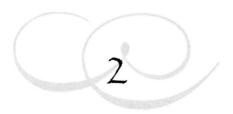

2

I t was early evening when Fredrick and Corwyn entered into Plainsview. The reddish-umber sky was like velvet in the thick cloud cover above, aiding the night's further hold over the surrendering day. Corwyn and Fredrick had been on the road now for the better part of the day, making their way to the smaller village which sat between the wilds of the Grasslands of Gondad to the west and the more cultivated lands that made up the hamlets, villages, towns and cities of Romain to the east.

It had been a few weeks since they had made their way off Riverford Way, favoring some more rural thoroughfares and villages over the more populous locales. Because of this decision, Corwyn had let the other musicians he had previously hired go, much to Fredrick's dismay. Corwyn didn't have any real plans of doing larger shows the further west he traveled. Why Fredrick stuck around, Corwyn wasn't quite so sure.

He knew Fredrick often felt compelled to protect the bard in fear of him getting into some trouble; he knew that both doubted he would have any such difficulties the closer he drew to the grasslands. Whatever reasoning the dwarf used, he had been Corwyn's constant companion as they made their way to what Corwyn disclosed was his next object of interest: exploration of the Grasslands of Gondad for ancient ruins. He planned to spend the rest of the summer in search of something from the ancient Imperial Wars that took place in the area over three thousand years ago.

What he might find there Corwyn didn't know. It could have been a "rock heap" as Fredrick called the last set of ruins they discovered or it could be something truly of note. For now, the bard was simply enjoying the journey. Soon these scant villages would be hamlets and then nothing more than sporadic farmsteads, if anything, and then the wide open plains named after the ancient empire that had once had ruled over them.

Plainsview was nothing really of note: a small scattering of wooden structures at rest around a central village square with a few smaller buildings scattering toward the outside of this timber and plaster cluster. Unprotected by walls, the village was open to the sprawling swath of fields and grazing lands around it that spread out for as far as the eye could see (thus the reason why the village was called Plainsview). Most of the population was nestled around the small piece of concealed civilization; farmers, herdsmen, and the various folks who kept those endeavors alive lived outside and around these scattered central buildings in an ever decreasing number the farther one moved into the grasslands.

A simple wooden sign, stained reddish-brown from exposure to the elements over the years, swung back and forth in the growing darkness' soft, cool breeze. The rusted chains on which it hung were attached to an equally worn post at the entrance to the village. Painted neatly in Telborous, the sign declared that this village was indeed Plainsview – if anyone had any doubt – and had a population of three hundred.

Fredrick curled his lip as he passed the sign.

"Hayseeds," the dwarf muttered beneath his breath. He'd been seeing too much of these rustic settings for his taste of late.

Corwyn ignored his remark. He knew Fredrick enough to know when to let things slide and when to take him to task. While the people in the village were not that well off, they were far from backward savages. He also knew that the dwarf didn't really dislike the people who lived there, rather the lack of coin they'd be willing to part with if he and Corwyn should perform.

"Tonight we should have a nice bed to sleep on," Corwyn was delighted at the prospect of getting a soft place to rest his head. The past two nights they had found rest in the open stretch of land beside the road. This had been true for much of their journey over the past week.

"One without lice I hope," came back the dwarf's biting comment.

Together the bard and dwarf walked along the hard-packed dirt streets, which were relatively empty save for one or two lone figures peering up at them with polite grins. Some other suntanned faces nodded their heads, tipping their wide brimmed hats in passing. The odd wild child bubbling with laughter and boundless energy scurried about here and there as well. These children soon found others who joined them in running up and down the street and between houses, shouting and screaming their joy at being allowed to play before they'd have to retreat indoors with the coming night.

Other than these things, Plainsview was relatively silent. The few shops present in the village were also along the main street, before it branched off into a few pigtail curls of more residential streets, but were now closed. However, Corwyn and Fredrick weren't so much interested in these as they were in finding a room to rent for the night.

"You could have stayed back at Riverford with the others," Corwyn reminded the dwarf as he had done now on several occasions.

"Hmph," was all the dwarf cared to share in reply.

"There we go," Corwyn's attention was turned toward a slightly shabby looking two-story building. Another worn sign swayed over the doorway. This one was also written in Telborous, though not as neatly as the sign into town had been, declaring it to be Plainsview Crossing. "I just hope they have some rooms."

"And clean beds," Fredrick was insistent. Though the dwarf wouldn't admit it, he was getting tired from constantly lugging the backpack he had carried since their encounter with those halfling highwayman a few weeks back. It still dug into his shoulders at times and took its strain on him after so many miles. It would be good to simply get the thing off his back and have a chance to rest his feet for a little while. He just would have preferred to have some place more civilized in which to take that rest.

As they drew closer, the sound of more people could be heard rolling down toward them. This inn also doubled as an ale house and food hall for most of the population who, when they might grow bored on their own parcels of land or managing their stock, could come and have a home cooked meal and fellowship with the local community.

"Something smells good," Corwyn was enjoying the fragrant wafting of meat and other savory aromas emanating from inside the inn. Fredrick ignored the comment, keeping to his own thoughts and attitude to himself.

Once inside, the noise was a rumbling ambiance that mingled with a soft and oddly timed spike of laughter and bawdy cheer. Here and there, scattered amid ten round tables, sat a good portion of the townsfolk – some with hot meals, others with mugs of ale. Further in, near the back of the inn, more sat along the wall on single stools, plates and faces staring into the plain knotted wood panels before them. Elsewhere more gathered around a bar – a fair number of men and women resting against and seating near it, eating food and downing drink.

"Hungry?" the bard asked his shorter friend, already knowing the answer. The smells were even richer and more overpowering inside. The deep earthy, savory, and carnal aroma mixed so well with the spices and seasonings that the bard's stomach was eager to be filled.

"Starving," the dwarf quickly replied.

"Let's get a room lined up before we get our food," Corwyn made his way toward the bar, which was the least crowded spot in the inn for the moment, and placed his walking stick to rest against it, catching the eye of the middle-aged woman who was working behind the oaken counter. Wide hipped and attractive in a maternal way, the short, graying Telborian grinned up at the taller Corwyn. She reminded the bard, for an instant, of his recent encounter with Molly in another inn in what seemed like a long time ago and farther away than he knew to be correct.

"What can I do for you?" Her smile was stained from years of tea drinking and a few odd evenings with the pipe, but her face was plump and jolly, like a happy grandmother.

"My friend and I need a room to stay the night and a meal."

"Just for one night, then?" The woman looked from Corwyn to Fredrick in an approving manner. "Sure thing. You can have the room on the right at the top of the stairs."

Corwyn started to dig into the coin purse tied to his black leather belt. "How much will I–"

The woman behind the counter put up her plump hand to stop the bard from saying any more. "Don't worry about that right now. It will be taken care of tomorrow – a fair rate I assure you."

"Thank you." Corwyn didn't press the matter even though he could feel the hot stare of Fredrick urging him to do just that.

"You won't need a key either as we don't have any reason to lock our doors here," the woman added with a reassuring smile.

"Probably nothing worth stealing," Fredrick muttered beneath his breath.

The woman pointed out the way up the flight of stairs toward the back of the room. "You can go right up there now if you like; it's all ready for you."

"Get me an ale," Fredrick told the bard. "I'll go put this backpack away and be down in a moment." The dwarf made his way toward the stairs at the absolute back of the inn, thankful to almost be free of the heavy pack.

"I suppose you'll be wanting something to put the meat on them bones from such a journey," the woman drew Corwyn's attention back to the bar. "You're nothing but skin and bones, you are. If you don't put some muscle to that frame you might even blow away."

"Now we can't have that now, can we?" Corwyn grinned.

"How about a mug of ale and..." he looked around for a sign some inns kept posted near the kitchen to help travelers know what meal options where available to them. After a few short minutes of searching he didn't see any such sign.

"Took the sign down to freshen it up," the woman answered the bard's unasked question and searching eyes. "It's time for some summer dishes."

"All right, then; do you still have cider?" he found the woman's dull blue eyes again.

"Sure do."

"Spiced?" Corwyn smiled.

"No problem," she grinned.

"Okay, then hot spiced cider and a mug of ale," Corwyn took a quick look about the place letting his eyes take in what the other patrons were eating. "What's a good dish you'd recommend?"

The matronly woman seemed to take some small delight in getting a chance to share her thoughts upon the matter. "Well, we do have a fresh run on rabbit seeing how it's summer and all."

"Rabbit sounds wonderful." The bard turned himself around to face the woman once again.

"Two of the same then?" she inquired.

Corwyn started to unsling the worn cherry wood lute he had resting on his back. "Yeah, though could you put some extra bread on one of the plates?"

The woman nodded her head as she left to enter the kitchen.

"Thanks." Corwyn proceeded to place the lute down beside his stool, feeling better to have the weight off his shoulders. Turning himself fully around, arms resting on the edge of the counter, the bard took in the room once again. This time he studied it with a more thoughtful gaze.

Trained over the past fourteen years as to how to read a crowd, Corwyn knew that Fredrick wouldn't be too happy as the bard's assumptions about the people of the village proved true. They were hard working, pragmatic folk who didn't seem like they would wish to part with any of their coin, should they have any, for even a simple evening's entertainment.

Sighing, he removed his wide-brimmed straw hat and set it on an empty stool beside him – Fred would just have the other empty stool to the bard's right if he knew the dwarf as well as he thought. Moving his walking stick to rest against the stool to his left, he made sure the right stool was clear for the dwarf's return. In the meantime he could let his mind wander and rest a bit from their day's journey, running a hand through his medium-length, reddish-blonde hair as he did so.

Corwyn would probably have to buy some supplies tomorrow before he headed out into the open wilderness. He figured there wouldn't be that many more opportunities to stock up for his trek into the grasslands and so would make sure to get what he could. Once supplied, he would be able to enjoy the sights and sounds of the prairie for the rest of the summer.

Few bards did what Corwyn did and they suffered for it. While many wanted the glitter and gold from their shows, forsaking the more common elements of the area in which they performed, Corwyn took to understanding the common elements more than the uncommon as they tended to give the truest picture of the area as a whole.

Most bards would just come into a city or town and cater to the group who paid them their coin and then leave. While Corwyn did this too, he also wanted to give something beyond the dutiful nature of bard and paying audience to the larger population as well. This entailed getting to know them better and in turn getting to learn more about the area itself. By taking up this approach, the bard had been able to gain a wide swath of information that put him head and shoulders above most of his fellow bards. It was one of the handful of things that were contributing to Corwyn being called, The Famed Bard of the Midlands.

"Get me my ale?" Fredrick's voice brought Corwyn back from his thoughts.

"That was fast," the bard looked down to his friend who was now devoid of the backpack and weapons. "Got some seats too," Corwyn nodded to the stool he'd kept for the dwarf.

"It's just a backpack," the dwarf made himself comfortable on the empty stool to the right of the bard. Fredrick was a practical fellow and had a strong conviction that it was totally pointless and stupid to wear armor and carry weapons in safe public places, and so had also dispensed with his mace and dagger. He thought people who kept their armor and weapons on their person were just being showy, cocky, or looking for trouble. "What did you get for food then? I'm famished."

"Rabbit," the bard joined him in sitting at the counter; turning away from the patrons he had recently been surveying.

"Extra bread?" Fredrick's orangish-brown eyes gave the bard an inquisitive gaze.

"As if there were any doubt," the bard grinned. "How does the room look?"

"It's livable." The dwarf made himself comfortable on the worn wooden stool.

Corwyn was a bit taken back by the dwarf's change of tone. He wasn't expecting the charcoal gray-skinned man to be so mild in his criticism, due to his normally prickly demeanor.

It was at this time the woman returned with a piping hot wooden mug of spiced cider and an amber frothed tankard of ale. "Your dinner should be up in a little bit," she set down the two mugs to their respective persons, her years of service giving her the unspoken inkling as to who would drink what, and moved off toward the kitchen once more.

"So what of the morrow?" Fredrick took a draft from his ale, getting some of the foamy head matted into his mustache, which he preceded to wipe away with the back of his hand.

"Get some supplies and head off into the wild." Corwyn took a sip of his steaming cider. It was still too hot to take a full drink but from what he could taste, he knew it was almost just the way he liked it.

Suddenly the door flung open and a wide-eyed man rushed inside.

"It's a *monster!*" his shout strangled all other conversation in the place dead, "I saw a *monster!*"

All present turned to consider Hammond, the local farmer, who was not known by the patrons to be given to flights of fancy. His face was flush from a run and his chest heaved through the words he tried to speak over his obviously winded frame. His wheat colored tunic was dark with sweat under his arms, back and around his neck and his face was lined with rivers of perspiration that had freshly formed after his bursting into Plainsview Crossing.

"There's a monster loose in the prairie!" Hammond continued through some huffing breaths.

"This should be interesting," Fredrick told Corwyn as the two watched a slender, older man rise up from among the patrons and stand next to comfort Hammond by putting a hand to the farmer's sweaty shoulder.

"Take a moment to collect your thoughts and breathe," this older man, who was named Bryan, then turned to the patrons. "We'll give Hammond a moment and then look into this matter, but we shouldn't start jumping to conclusions before we know the facts."

"Who's that?" Corwyn asked the woman behind the counter, "Your magistrate?"

"Mayor," the woman responded but kept her face looking toward Hammond, eager for his answer. "Oh that poor, Hammond," the woman continued more to herself than anyone else in particular, "must have been something quite frightful, to get him into such a way."

"Don't even start thinking about it," Fredrick warned Corwyn.

"Thinking about *what?*" the bard raised a lone eyebrow in question as he faced the dwarf.

"Monster hunting." Fredrick could see the wheels in Corwyn's mind turning already. The grasslands had been one thing, but a chance to hunt down a monster almost thrown right into his lap…

"Aren't you jumping to conclusions a bit?" Corwyn knew what the dwarf was thinking. They had been traveling together too long now for the bard not to. "Let's just hear what's said," then he added some logical argument that even Fredrick would have a hard time going against, "we still have to eat our meal and rest a bit from the journey. Think of it as some entertainment as we fill our bellies."

Corwyn was right, Fredrick couldn't argue with that logic. "Fair enough."

Having had a moment to catch his breath, Hammond began telling his tale to the room. All were silent as he spoke, not wanting to miss a single detail. They knew that Hammond was not a man given to lies or exaggerations and so they worried about what new danger just might be outside their doors.

"I was outside by the barn, looking to finish up for the evening when I heard a rustle in the grass. I thought it was an animal at first and so paid it little heed. However, it grew louder and the sound it made…and when I heard the roar of the thing…" Hammond's face went white and he found it hard to remove his tongue from the roof of his mouth.

Bryan reassuredly patted Hammond's shoulder, "Give it a moment more, Hammond. You take all the time you need."

Hammond nodded, but strength was already returning to him and his face was regaining some color; his tongue once more under his command.

"It came out of the grasses and it had to be the ugliest thing on Tralodren. It was large too – had to be about ten feet long and at least half that in height.

"I wasn't armed and didn't think that I could fight it off anyway. So I did what I could do: run. I'd hoped the beast would follow me and leave Marion alone but I didn't look back once I crossed the creek and made my way into the village."

At this there were some murmured conversations as each present started to debate the issue and what it meant for them.

Fredrick wasn't one to do such things, though, and continued to finish up his meal even as Bryan raised his hands for silence.

That silence was granted him.

"Good people of Plainsview; let's not get too dismal in our outlook and conversation. I suggest we select a group of men who can be trusted and are of an able arm to go out and seek the matter out. Perhaps this matter is not so dim as to hold back the chance of ridding ourselves of such a creature."

"Not so dim in the least," a new, strong voice drew all eyes to two armored men who entered the common room. Each wore armor that had seen some battles and seemed to be of a strong frame and resolute face. Both were Telborian, of average height, and had rugged tan faces. Their hair was of a brown shade and of medium length and they were each armed with a short sword at their side. In many ways both were the spitting image of what most folks would think of when the word "hero" came to mind.

"You've nothing to fear now that we're here," this comment came from the slightly older of the two men. Both men entered further into the inn.

"And who are you?" Bryan asked the question on the tip of everyone's tongue.

"I am Victor and this is Thomas," Victor motioned to the other man. He too was of a strong face but with green eyes and an open face helm that covered much of his head.

"Forgive our intrusion but we couldn't help but overhear your conversation." Both men came to stand before the mayor and Hammond now as the they measured the armored men before them. "We have been traveling the grasslands and other parts of Talatheal, searching out this very creature. We have been hunting it and others like it for many years with great success."

Fredrick jabbed Corwyn with his elbow, causing the bard to lean over to hear the dwarf's whisper. "This all seems a little odd, don't you think?"

"Just a bit," Corwyn's suspicions were piqued.

"Have you now?" Bryan shared Fredrick's slight unease with the situation but, unlike the dwarf, he was trying to be more diplomatic in his questioning. "So what has brought you two to Plainsview?"

"The hunt," Victor returned. "We have been following this Blight Demon now for–"

"*Blight Demon*?" Hammond's eyes grew wide in fright.

"Aye," Victor nodded, "the creature you saw had to be a Blight Demon."

"How do you know?" Hammond managed to calm his fears, but it was still a hard battle and the run from his land to the village had taken more out of him than he knew. Now that the adrenaline was starting to leave his body, he felt more sore and tired than afraid.

"Was it like a great serpent with the head of a wolf and four arms like a man and legs like a centipede?" Victor asked.

Hammond's face went white as he ceded some ground to fear once again, "I saw a *demon*?"

"Not just *any* demon," Thomas' mellow voice filled the room, "but one who is known to be a cruel creature carrying curses to all who would strike at it and has been known to blight the land it lives in for sport.

"No normal weapon has been known to stop it, for the weapons of mortalkind are useless against those of cosmic origin. That is why we carry enchanted blades," Thomas gave the sword at his side a quick pat, "with these we have seen many a Blight Demon fall into Mortis."

More murmuring erupted from the others at this disclosure.

"You believe this?" Fredrick had finished up his meal.

"I'd be more inclined to believe it if I could see them in action. Something doesn't seem entirely true with this whole situation," Corwyn took some of his food as he thought, "it's like I'm watching a play or something."

"Yeah, they *are* laying it on a bit thick," Fredrick's eyes squinted to get a better look at their armor and swords, but the weapons were sheathed and he was too far away from them to get much in the way of finer details from his gaze. "And I, for one, would like to see those swords."

Corwyn swallowed, "So then you agree. We should go with them when they go after this Blight Demon."

"I never said that," Fredrick's defenses sprung up with the furrowing of his brow.

"But this is something of interest, wouldn't you agree?" the bard persisted. "And," he added in softer, more tempting tones, "it would keep us at least one more day from the grasslands."

Fredrick sighed, "Yeah, I suppose we could." But then the dwarf added with a sharp wagging of his index finger, "You'll need someone to protect you too since you'll probably carry little more than that stick of yours to fend off this *demon*."

"I've never seen a demon either," Corwyn took another draft from his cup. It had cooled now to a respectable temperature for the bard's palette, "should be interesting."

"*Vampires* not interesting enough for you?" the dwarf snorted.

"Good people," Victor's voice and hands were raised up to hush the rising din of conversation. "We are more than willing and able to help you rid your village and fields from this threat. As I've said, we've done it before and we have no qualms about doing it again.

"We just ask for a room and some food to sustain us while we search out and ultimately defeat this foul demon. There would be no risk to your lives and by the same time tomorrow this threat to your property and livelihood will be eliminated.

"What say you?"

The room fell silent as all eyes turned to Bryan who was weighing the matter in his thoughts. He had lived many years and been a wise mayor appointed by King Morgan, but also loved and trusted by the people he governed. After a further handful of minutes of internal debate, the mayor acquiesced to the two armed men.

"You have the permission you need to stay in this inn and be provided with food and supplies, provided that you hunt for this creature and you allow some other men to serve as witnesses with you on your hunt.

"Should we face a similar threat again, it would be wise to have others skilled in the knowledge in how to contend with it since we might not have others like you who would come so readily to our side to fight."

Victor nodded.

A smile was on his lips, the hard look of the warrior melted a bit and made him appear friendlier, more approachable. "A very generous offer, we accept."

"Let us just get unpacked from our journey in a room and then we can begin talking with you and those you wish to have accompany us." Thomas, who had followed Victor, was already making his way toward the bar. "We'd also like to speak with the man who first saw the demon, to learn what we can."

"What room might you have for us?" Victor addressed the woman behind the counter.

"Top of the stairs and second on the right is yours," she pointed out the direction as best she could from her position.

"Thank you," Victor made his way toward the stairs, Thomas at his heels, "we shall return momentarily."

As they passed, both Corwyn and Fredrick took a moment to better size up these traveling heroes.

Both were unsure of what to make of what they saw.

"They were pretty full of themselves," Fredrick spoke his mind to the bard.

"They were pretty confident," Corwyn had finished his meal and they both sat upon their stools, backs resting against the counter as they waited for the two men to come back downstairs.

"*Cocky* is more like it," Fredrick huffed.

"Perhaps, just a little," Corwyn conceded. "But sellswords have to appear to be capable of handling any situation if they want to get paid."

Fredrick turned to Corwyn in disbelief. "It was practically *dripping* off them."

The two had been waiting now for a little over half an hour for Thomas and Victor to walk down the steps and discuss matters of their upcoming hunt with the mayor. Since they had gone to their free room, word spread like wild fire among the village and so the inn was now standing room only as all were not only curious about the new comers, but worried about the new threat that might very well be lurking in their midst.

Some good news was that Marion had been found safe and sound in the house where she had been locked up, per her husband's orders. She was reported to be fine but still worried about leaving the house less the Blight Demon get her en route to the village. Hammond thought it for the best she remained where she was, for he'd soon see her tonight when he returned home (for Victor had assured him that both he and his wife would be safe for the night) and probably the next day when Victor and Thomas came to investigate the location where he first encountered the demon.

"Seems the whole village has turned out," Corwyn ignored Fredrick's last comment as he looked over the people milling about and talking about the two men and the creature they said only they could kill. He knew better than to debate the matter of confidence versus cockiness any further.

"Still seems a bit odd," Fredrick kept vocally pushing his train of thought. "These two guys show up shortly after that farmer starts yammering about some creature–" the dwarf looked up at the stairs for the sixth time since Victor and Thomas left. "What's taking them so long?"

"Relax, Fred," Corwyn tried to calm the dwarf, "they'll come down when they're ready." The bard turned to look toward the flight of stairs. He had heard the sound of approaching footsteps. "Here they come. We'll have our answers soon enough."

"I hope so because their weapons didn't look any different from any other swords I've seen." Fredrick watched the crammed bodies in the room congeal around the foot of the steps; filtering out to the front. "Did you notice that their armor and swords weren't that marred either?"

"They did look rather clean," Corwyn agreed as Fredrick was drawn to the two sellswords with renewed study. "Course if their armor and swords *are* enchanted, they might not get nicked and dinged like regular armor and weapons I suppose."

"You think?" Fredrick spun on his seat to see that Corwyn was already facing him and shared the uncertain look on his face.

"I don't know," returned the bard as the same bodies who pressed toward the stairs parted to allow Thomas and Victor, now armor and weaponless, to pass.

Silence followed in their wake as each patron was stilled by their presence, hopeful to hear every one of their words. For the tale presently being circulated around the village had come to embellish these men with supernatural powers. Indeed, one must have such a boon if one claims to be able to slay demons.

"Would you even know an enchanted weapon if you saw one?" Corwyn smirked, already knowing the answer to his question as Victor and Thomas walked past where Corwyn and Fredrick sat. Even without their armor the two men struck a fairly heroic stature.

"Well I – humph," the dwarf huffed in frustration as Victor and Thomas moved on toward the front of the room where Bryan and Hammond waited.

Both Victor and Thomas wore simple tunics and breeches and leather shoes. They seemed commonly dressed for some fabled warriors and didn't appear that different in attire than many of the others who called Plainsview home, save their attire was a bit cleaner and newer than the rest of the populous. The only thing that set them apart was a simple looking copper headband that encircled Thomas' head.

When Thomas and Victor had made it to the center of the room, wherein the mayor and Hammond had risen to greet them, a strong silence fell over all assembled. This lingered for but a moment until Victor's strong voice shattered it to dust.

"Good people, I see word of our arrival has caused this inn to swell with a great many bodies," Victor's voice sounded like the gold-tinted timbre of a practiced politician. "Let me just say firstly that there is nothing to fear. We have tracked these creatures all over this land and dealt a swift deathblow to each and every one we've encountered.

"Your children and wives and crops will be safe and secure." At this there was some pleased murmuring amid the group. This quickly died down though as Victor continued his speech.

"For the benefit of the newly arrived, I am Victor and this is Thomas. As I have said, we have been successful in the tracking and killing of these Blight Demons now for many a year. We have gained our success by mastering the use of the enchanted weapons and armor that we carry and use for hunts against such foes.

"Tomorrow, if you'd have our help, we'll travel to where this demon was seen, track it down and slay it before evening."

At this Victor turned to Bryan who took up the conversation, speaking to the two men loud enough for the rest of the assembly to hear him. His voice wasn't so golden, but it was the fatherly tone of a friend whom many had come to trust. "And if we'd have you, then what would you have from us other than what you have already stated?"

Thomas smiled mildly and gave answer, "We would ask what we have before, that we be given some provisions and a place to rest our heads while we are in Plainsview."

"Nothing else then?" The mayor's bushy white eyebrows framed his studious dark blue eyes as he pressed the two men.

"Nothing else," Thomas' kind face deepened in its sincerity.

Once again, murmuring erupted around the room.

"Sellswords," Fredrick spoke the word in disdain.

"Sellswords that don't mind getting paid in room and board," Corwyn was watching Victor and Thomas with greater interest than before. "Now *that* is a bit odd, don't you think? Most fight for coin only and would have little qualms about asking these people for some gold or silver to do their work. I wonder why they aren't pressing the matter."

"Maybe they know that they won't get much of anything out of them if they squeezed and so they just took what they could get." Fredrick offered his pragmatic if slightly cynical thoughts.

"You still want to go with them?" the dwarf asked.

"Yes," Corwyn nodded, "it would be something unique for sure." The wheels in Corwyn's head were turning faster and faster.

"Just thought I'd give it one more try," Fredrick turned back to the bard with a disapproving frown. "You might change your mind one of these days."

Corwyn's eyes narrowed as he tried to size up the two men speaking with the mayor. "I can't help shake the feeling that something is a bit off with all this – that it doesn't feel totally right for some reason."

"So you don't trust them?" Fredrick's face brightened at the thought of Corwyn joining him in not liking Thomas and Victor. Perhaps Corwyn's mind wasn't totally made up yet after all and

260

the dwarf could persuade him to stay away for once and just go on his own way without sticking his nose into another matter that happened to cross his path.

After all, if Corwyn didn't think something was right with this than Fredrick might be able to get him to avoid it instead of investigating it. He knew it would be a hard sell to the bard but was willing to make the effort if he could get him out of following after the sellswords. For if Corwyn went, then Fredrick would have to join him, and he would rather be walking around in towering grasses than accompanying some men he not only wasn't too keen on but didn't trust that much either.

"I think–" Corwyn was cut short as the mayor raised his hands for silence and began to speak.

"I've already said that if we are going to allow these men to help slay this monster than we would want to have some men accompany them, to not only witness the deed but to learn how to protect the village should another demon appear in the future.

"Since they have first made their offer I have thought it over and decided to allow them to conduct their hunt if all we have to offer them is some provisions and a room for the duration of their short stay.

"However, I wonder who among you would be willing to accompany Victor and Thomas as they hunt for this demon?" At this the room fell still.

"We will," Fredrick and the rest of the room turned around to see Corwyn's raised hand.

"*We* will?" Fredrick kept his voice low but the bard could still hear the caustic heat behind it. "You're *volunteering* me?"

"You already said you wouldn't let me go alone unarmed against a Blight Demon. So if I go you go, right?" Corwyn grinned at the dwarf's gruff expression.

Fredrick let out a defeated sigh.

"Who are you two?" the mayor seemed amazed to see even more visitors to the village.

"I'm Corwyn Danther and this is Fredrick Grenze."

"Corwyn," Victor's eyes lit up as he put the name to a face, "I've heard of you. A bard of some repute, if the stories can be believed."

"The ones based on reality can be," Corwyn returned with a whimsical smirk, "you probably shouldn't put too much trust in the rest."

"You really would wish to watch us work?" Thomas took a good look at the bard and the dwarf beside him, hands adjusting his copper headband as he spoke. "You think you could handle seeing the horrors that we've come to deal with more often than we'd care to count?"

"Sure," Corwyn didn't even bat an eye, "I might learn something useful."

"Okay," Victor seemed reluctant to take him on. He gave a sideways glance to Thomas who, after adjusting his headband one last time, returned the gaze to his friend.

After this wordless exchange between the two men, Victor continued. "Just make sure you stay out of our way when the danger comes. We can't vouch for your safety. It will take all of our concentration to hunt the Blight Demon we can't divert any of our efforts to watch out for your welfare as well."

"That's why *he's* coming along," Corwyn gestured to Fredrick.

The dwarf grumbled into his beard.

"You aren't from the village though," the mayor continued. "I wish to have someone from the village attend. Someone who would still be here after you all have left."

"I'll be present," Hammond spoke up. "They'll have to follow me to where I saw the creature. I'll be with them the whole time."

"So you will," the mayor nodded approvingly, "but I was hoping for one more to assure us at least two faithful witnesses. Who else will come volunteer?"

There was some softer muttering and more than a few faces that suddenly veered their gaze down toward their shoes, but one hand raised itself up above the heads of those gathered. Then a voice came forth to join it.

"I will."

"Ganatar, bless you for your courage," the mayor admonished the young, tawny-haired and bright-faced man who had volunteered.

"Then it seems to be decided," Victor took charge of the room once again, something that seemed rather easy for him to do, "we have terms and now Thomas and I will have to speak with Hammond to get a better idea where to start, and talk with those who will accompany us on the morrow's hunt."

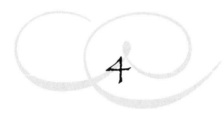

A short while later the din of the inn had quieted as the crowd of patrons thinned. Many of them returned to their farms and lives before it got too late claimed, the fear of what might be lurking out in the darkness fueling their rapid return to their own interests and family.

Those who remained behind were the ones usually given to such activities; those who lived near or in the village itself. While none came up to disturb the two warriors, the bard, dwarf, Hammond, and the young volunteer named Harold; they still spoke of them in their own conversations and gave them a glance here and there throughout the evening. It was enough to know that men were doing something about this situation and to let them handle it. After all, it appeared that Victor and Thomas had the bearings of some solid enough fellows and the two other strangers – the bard and the dwarf – seemed capable as well. All the better for the villagers who were relieved that they didn't have to accompany the others to Hammond's land. Many were surprised at Harold's eagerness to volunteer but left him to it. It saved them from having to make the choice instead.

"So you're really Corwyn Danther?" Victor had finished shaking the bard's hand after Corwyn had introduced himself.

"Yes," Corwyn assured him.

"From the tales I've heard, I would have thought you to be a bit taller and more rugged," Victor grinned. "I guess you can't believe everything you hear then, eh?" Victor then focused his attention on Fredrick. "And you're, Fredrick?"

"Yes, Fredrick Grenze," Fredrick took the hand offered him and shook it once with a strong, forceful grip. His orangish-brown eyes were watchful and heavy in their observation, but not threatening.

"He's a fellow I just can't seem to shake," Corwyn tried to smooth off some of the dwarf's rougher edges with some light humor, "he also plays in the band when we perform."

"So he's a bard then too?" Thomas seemed reserved, like his mind was elsewhere on something; as if he was thinking heavy thoughts and had to focus just to keep abreast of the conversation.

"No," Fredrick took Thomas' hand and offered him the same shake and look as he had Victor, "I play some instruments but I'm not a bard."

"I see. So you're a musician then." Fredrick and Corwyn both thought they saw a little bit of relief in Thomas' face as he heard Fredrick's answer. "So what instruments do you play?"

"Pipes and flute mainly," Fredrick flatly answered.

"I see," Thomas concluded the conversation by turning to Harold. "And who are you?"

"Harold." He took a seat at the table they had all gathered around after shaking Thomas' hand. "I just help out with Jeffery's leather shop here in town."

"It seems you're a man not easily frightened then," Victor took a seat then as well, followed quickly by the others, "if your eagerness to volunteer is any indication."

"I don't know about that," Harold's face flushed, "I just thought if someone was going to volunteer it might as well be me. I don't have any kids or even a wife."

"I don't think it will get that grim, Harold," Corwyn tried to calm any fears Harold might be entertaining.

"No, it won't," Victor agreed. "We'll do the hard work and if you keep a safe distance from us you'll be able to see all you need to and not even get your ankle sprained."

"You'll have no complaints from me there," Hammond added, "I don't have any wish to face such a monster again."

"I've never seen a Blight Demon before," Corwyn turned to Hammond, "can you tell me anything about what you saw?"

"Only that it had to be from the Abyss, for such a thing isn't natural in the least and had the stench of evil all about it." Hammond's face had taken on a slight pallor as he spoke.

"What do you mean?" Corwyn gently pressed.

Hammond shook his head, the pallor of his visage increasing. "It's something I'd rather not revisit."

"Nor should you," Thomas butted in, "Blight Demons are a terrible thing to see in the flesh and we'll not have you relive such a horrid thing. Time enough to see the thing on the morrow. For now let your mind be at rest."

"Laying it on a bit thick aren't you?" Fredrick's gaze rolled up into Victor's face. He couldn't hold the thought back any longer.

Victor's eyes scrunched down a bit as he addressed the dwarf. "What do you mean?" They weren't angry but certainly discerning, like the gaze of a card player trying to discern his opponents' hands.

"Oh come on," Fredrick half snorted, half laughed. "You've been preening the whole time – ever since you walked in the door. I'm surprised that you guys *get* any work. You're probably the showiest sellswords I've ever seen."

At this the table fell silent.

It was an uncomfortable silence for many but Fredrick kept his eyes focused on the two sellswords opposite him just the same.

He was one who tended to call things like he saw them. And what he saw was some heavily theatric sellswords.

"But sellswords would want money," Hammond's voice was small as he thought aloud and through the awkward silence. "These men have merely asked for some supplies–"

"Because they know you folks don't have two coppers to rub together," Fredrick interrupted.

Again there was a momentary silence.

Victor and Thomas shared a meaningful look, one Corwyn and Fredrick recognized, although the intent behind the look remained a mystery. It did seem to give them some plan of action, however. Victor started to speak in a measured and strong voice.

"We make our living on the kindness of others for our actions, this is true, but not in the way you might think." His eyes burned for a moment into Fredrick's charcoal gray face, this time there was a bit of anger behind Victor's green eyes. "We're wandering warriors who are trying to stop a grave threat to innocent lives." Victor's gaze proceeded to sway over all at the table, making sure he spoke to each one gathered there as if they were the only one in the conversation; hitting home the emotional footing of his speech all the harder with each personal visual exchange. To these he showed no hint of anger, just strong conviction. Corwyn was impressed.

"These Blight Demons are a real threat and do intend to and even *have* done some great harm to many places and people. We'd sooner stop them than stop to find ways to earn food, supplies, and shelter. So it is a truth that we live by our swords, it is truer to say that we live by our actions in helping the poor people who are oppressed by these demons."

"Well I for one won't hold anything against you," Hammond spouted out with strong conviction of his own. Fredrick knew, as did Corwyn, that the matter was settled for now and that the dwarf would be opposed in pressing the matter any further. So much the better, thought Corwyn, since Fredrick was often a bit too rough for most people and the bard didn't fancy this discussion becoming an argument.

"Thank you, friend," Victor's reply to Hammond sealed the matter.

"Can we move on now to other matters?" There was just enough of a condescending tone in Victor's words to make Fredrick's beard hairs bristle, but he let the matter drop, much to Corwyn's amazement. "The night will be over soon and we have a few more matters to discuss."

"Fine," the dwarf huffed, "so what is the plan then in catching this thing?"

"Well," the mood instantly changed as things got down to business, "we will have Hammond lead us to where he saw the demon tomorrow morning and then track it from there."

"That's it?" Fredrick was unimpressed.

"Pretty much," Thomas was nonchalant about the matter, focusing his attention on Corwyn more than Fredrick. "We track it down and dispatch it to Mortis."

"So you can kill it with just your enchanted weapons then?" Corwyn was intrigued by the concept.

"It's the only way you can kill a Blight Demon this side of the Abyss," Victor nodded. "Pity the poor fool who tries any other way."

"How did you come by your weapons and armor?" Corwyn saw an opportunity to find out more about the two men and took it, "That certainly has to be a great story."

Victor and Thomas turned to each other and exchanged another silent exchange.

"I think I'll let Thomas tell that tale," said Victor, "it is an interesting thing indeed."

"Well," Thomas began like a man accustomed to telling a good story, though he still seemed preoccupied as he spoke, "We received our weapons and armor from the same wizard who taught us the nature of the Blight Demon.

"It was about five years ago now when we came upon the first demon – nearly took us to Mortis right then and there. Had it not been for the aid of the wizard we wouldn't be here talking with you today."

"A fortunate turn," Hammond cheerily commented.

"Indeed," Thomas gave a toothy grin to the farmer, "had it not been for Elias and his aid, we would not be able to fight the demons as we do today."

"So this Elias *gave* you these items?" Corwyn was trying to get the full meaning of Thomas' story, sorting through it in his mind to make sure he understood all that was being said. It was something he had been trained to do as a bard. Many things in a tale went unsaid, and it was the job of good bards to hear these as well as the spoken, to add as much depth and understanding to what was really be said in its entirety. Such insight did much to add to the richness of a bard's later performance.

"Yes, he did," Thomas seemed to lose his train of thought as he moved his attention back to Corwyn. He quickly regained it, however, and continued his tale. "He wanted to because he was too weak and old to use them in battle against the Blight Demons. Upon seeing the threat these demons posed, we dedicated ourselves to stopping their scourge over the land."

"I've never heard of Blight Demons before," Corwyn continued his mild form of interrogation, "where do they come from? I thought demons and other cosmic races were all kept from Tralodren by divine decree."

"True," Victor took up the bard's question. "but a few have seemed to find their way around the decree, focusing on Talatheal to work their evil."

"Talatheal only?" Corwyn was more curious now than before. "Not *all* of Tralodren?"

"Yeah, that's the odd thing," Victor continued. "They can only come here through a weak spot in our reality in Talatheal. At least that's what Elias came to discover.

"I don't know why, but something in certain areas draws them out of the Abyss and here. So we've been tracking them down as best we can and taking them out as soon as they appear.

"In fact, Thomas and I had a feeling that we were getting close to one when we were coming to the inn to look for a room to spend the night and heard your story," Victor turned to Hammond. "Seems we got here just in time."

"Yes," Hammond was again enthusiastic in his agreement, "and I'm glad you did too."

"Us too," Victor agreed. "You don't want a Blight Demon hanging around any longer than necessary."

"We'll need to hear your story, though, Hammond, if you're able to share it," Victor gripped Hammond's shoulder as he saw the pallor return to the farmer's face. "We don't need you to relive it, friend, just share what lead up to and followed it – and let us ask you a few more questions."

Hammond nodded through thin lips. His face wasn't as pale as before, but it wasn't the same healthy shade it was before the questioning began. "I'll do what I can, if it will help."

"Thank you," Victor removed his grip from the farmer's shoulder and motioned for the woman behind the counter to come take their order. "However, Thomas and I have been on the road all day and have yet to have any real food rest in our guts.

"Once we've eaten, we'll hear what you can share. Then, tomorrow we can all make our way to your farm and dispatch this demon before noon."

"You seem pretty confident of that," Fredrick carefully considered the sellsword.

"Experience is a good teacher," Victor coolly replied.

Just then the woman from behind the counter came to stand before the table and started to take their requests for supper, which would be free of course, thanks to the benevolence of the mayor and townsfolk of Plainsview.

269

"Finally a chance to get some sleep in a bed," Thomas put his boots beside his bed as he made ready to enter underneath the thin, woolen sheet covering the simple yet welcoming straw-stuffed mattress. Their room was sparse but they were thankful nonetheless given the abundant amount of travel in the less than civilized places they had endured up until now.

The night had wound down into pretty straight forward information sharing, and after Victor and Thomas had heard what they needed to hear from Hammond, and finished their good sized meal, they told the rest gathered to simply meet them outside the inn at daybreak to begin the hunt. Both men then retired to their room.

"And don't forget the food," Victor also had made himself ready for some shut-eye and was already pulling his own sheet up to his chest. "Haven't had that much food for quite some while," he pleasantly recalled the good-sized steak, heaping pile of mashed potatoes, and tankard that never seemed to go dry.

"And on the house too," Thomas now had settled into bed and was ruminating over the evening meal. "Too bad we can't stay here longer."

"Yeah, well take what you can get while you can," Victor finally found a cozy place in the mattress and was ready to welcome the warm, soft arms of slumber about him. "You going to wear that to bed too?" Victor commented on the headband that still encircled Thomas' head.

"Just a precaution," he told the other. "You never know what might happen and it is better to be prepared."

"You still that spooked?" Victor fixed his gaze above him to contemplate the timber-lined ceiling.

"Aren't you?" Thomas too stared toward the ceiling as he spoke, moonlight illuminating the interior through a plain, open window. A deep purple hue covered all with a cold silver highlight brought on by the lunar illumination. "I still can't believe we have *Corwyn Danther* here."

"You did well enough," Victor flatly replied. "And if we do our job right all will be well. We were able to even put down that uppity dwarf too. So just relax."

Thomas wasn't swayed by Victor's confidence, "But still, it's *Corwyn Danther*. He's said to be pretty good—"

"He won't be any trouble to us, okay," Victor returned with a bit of irritation to his voice. "How long have we been doing this anyway? We're not fresh out of the crib here by any means and we can both think on our feet. We already proved that tonight. Besides, we'll be done with this all before noon and loaded up with some new supplies and then back on the road."

"I guess you're right." Thomas still didn't sound that convinced but knew better than to argue with his friend about it any more. If he had any doubts he would have to work through them on his own.

"You just rest that mind of yours," Victor added, "We're going to need it tomorrow."

"Yeah," Thomas gave up.

"You can stop the melodrama," said Victor, "it isn't going to be that bad. We're going to have a great time with this whole hunt and be on the road again to greener pastures before nightfall."

"I hope so," Thomas closed his eyes to rest, "I don't want to be having to just scratch by when winter comes. And it would be nice to take a break from all this for a little while."

"We will," Victor still spoke to the ceiling, "and with any luck we'll be over in Waves Rest by then and in a safe, sound, warm place of our own." Victor finished the conversation as both quickly fell into a restful sleep as the travel and fresh air blowing in from the open window did much to increase their need for rest.

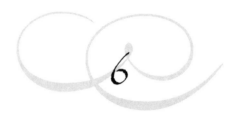

The next day came too early for all setting out on the hunt. Fredrick wasn't too keen on rising so early but did his best to be less grumpy than usual as he readied himself, strapping on his dagger and holstering his mace. He hoped to get this over and done with so he and Corwyn could be back on their previously planned excursion. To him it had become a colossal waste of time, and the attitudes of the sellswords, not to mention his opinion of them, had the dwarf wanting little, if anything, to do with them.

Hammond and Harold were waiting outside the inn before Corwyn and Fredrick had even made their way down. They were eager, if not a bit fearful, of what the day would hold. That fear, however, lightened some after Corwyn and Fredrick joined them to wait for Victor and Thomas.

"I hope they can deal with this demon before noon," Hammond fretted aloud with the first light of dawn breaking down upon all gathered, "I don't want to have to leave Marion alone to the mercies of such a beast."

"I just wish they'd hurry up and get out here," Fredrick kept his eyes pegged on the door. "I told you we didn't have to get up so early, Corwyn. They're *still* not ready." The dwarf crossed his arms with a huff. "We could've had breakfast while they were preening."

"You'll survive, Fred," Corwyn was taking a look around as the soft rays of dawn set the buildings and sky above them in a warm glow. He didn't take his lute with him, leaving that in their room but donning his hat and attire from the day before, walking stick included. He felt ready to begin even if he was a bit hungry himself.

"Don't worry about food," said Hammond. "When this demon has been slain I'll be more than happy to entertain you all with a meal in celebration."

"Thank you for your kind offer," Corwyn said to Hammond. "We'd be happy to join you."

"Course we have to find and kill the thing first," Fredrick started to tap his boot heel to the earth in a rising frustrated rhythm, "and that would mean we'd have to have the two *slayers* here to do it."

Just then the door opened and Victor and Thomas walked out. Each was finishing up what looked like a rather large sweet roll as they came to join the others, dressed again in their full armor, swords strapped at their sides.

"Good day," Victor greeted those gathered with a partially full mouth. "Are you all ready?" He finished the last of the sweet roll with one ravenous bite.

"We've *been* ready," Fredrick growled, angry eyes staring at Thomas as he consumed the last of his corpulent sweet roll with deep delight.

"Sorry for the delay," Victor wiped his hand on his pant leg. "Doris, our kindly innkeeper, wanted to give us something to keep up our strength before we left. She didn't want us fighting on an empty stomach."

"How kind," Fredrick's face had turned to a stony scowl.

"I thought so," Victor agreed as he came to stand in the midst of them, ignoring the dwarf's tone and countenance. "So where is your farm, Hammond?"

"This way," Hammond pointed out the way.

"Then lead on," Victor motioned for Hammond to start walking in the direction he indicated. "With any luck we should be done with this deed before late morning."

"Let's hope so," Fredrick grumbled as he took up the rear of the group. "I don't want to waste anymore time than we already have."

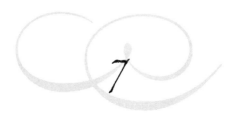

7

"So you ran from this spot here?" Victor asked Hammond who had brought them to his farm and close to the spot where he'd seen the demon.

"Yes," Hammond nodded shamefully.

"Nothing to be ashamed of man," Thomas slapped his back. "You could do little against such a creature and you did well to warn your wife and run for your life. If you had tried to face it you'd probably be dead now."

"So you say it came out of the grass?" Corwyn was making his way toward the very spot from where the demon emerged. "I don't see any depressions or signs that anything the size you said this thing was made his way through here recently, if at all."

"I thought the same myself," the farmer joined Corwyn at the edge of the prairie grasses. "But I can't deny what I heard and saw."

"Well," Thomas moved to join Corwyn and Hammond, "that's the mystery of the Blight Demon for you; they don't often leave much of a trace behind if they don't want to, and very little even if they do."

Corwyn turned to peer right into Thomas' face. "Really?" This was a somewhat unbelievable thing for him to accept. But with demons and magic and what he'd experienced these past few months, the bard had become more open-minded to a whole host of possibilities that many might toss away upon first hearing. Corwyn could see his questioning nature unsettled Thomas a bit, but only momentarily.

"Really," Corwyn observed the far away, concentrating look in Thomas' face for a second before it returned to its previous expression.

"Then how do you track them?" Corwyn held his ground, seeking out what he could from the other's unease. The bard didn't like the fact that Thomas seemed so uncomfortable with the question. Of course part of him thought it could have been that Thomas was a fan – he had mentioned he'd heard of Corwyn before...however, Corwyn thought it was something else that brought about the slight unease.

"We do so," Victor made his way over to the two of them, disrupting the tension, the rest following behind him – Fredrick last of all, "with the skillful training that Elias gave us."

"Well then," Fredrick motioned Victor forward to the tall grasses, "have at it."

Victor squatted down, searching things out with his hands and eyes. Thomas quickly joined him in looking over another part of the same area. Harold watched this all with intense energy, not wanting to miss anything.

"What are you doing?" Harold tried to get a better view of the sellswords' actions by shifting his previous position.

"We're checking for the small signs that we have been trained to locate," Victor didn't stop in his investigation as he gave his answer. "They will tell us how long ago the Blight Demon was here and if he might still be in the area."

"I see." Harold increased his concentration of the two men in their work.

"Do you see this?" Thomas asked Victor.

"Yes, I do." Victor took a note of the spot Thomas had indicated. Though it seemed like plain ground, the two sellswords treated it like a sacred find.

"Then it can't be that far away," Thomas rose.

Victor joined him.

"If it isn't that far away," Fredrick wondered aloud, "shouldn't we smell it or see it or something? Don't demons make noise? I thought they were supposed to stink too – brimstone, right?"

Victor again turned to Thomas with another nonverbal exchange.

"Not necessarily," Thomas said at last. "They are known to be experts at hiding, even in plain sight."

Hammond's face had gotten a bit paler, "Then are we in danger now?"

"No," Victor began to scan the area around them with a steely-eyed gaze, "not yet."

At these words Hammond drew closer to the rest of the men and took on an even paler shade to his countenance.

"He's here, though," Thomas drew his sword, "and we'll find him."

Victor also drew his sword as both he and Thomas made their way into the grasses, "He won't be that hard to find." Before the tall stalks had nearly swallowed them whole, Victor turned around saying: "Wait here."

"But I was told to witness the event," Harold protested.

"It's too dangerous," Victor resumed his course, disappearing among the grass. "I don't want to have to worry for your safety when we're contesting with this demon."

Harold made a move toward the grasses but then stopped abruptly. It was probably better to do what they said. After all, they were the experts and he certainly didn't want to be the cause of their injuries or the Blight Demon's escape.

Harold sighed.

"This is fun," Fredrick's pessimism was darker than usual.

However, Corwyn was ever ready to counter it. "Let's make the best of what we have here, Fred." Corwyn turned his attention to Hammond. "So you farm wheat here, Hammond?"

"Ah yeah," Corwyn's question caught Hammond off guard. He was still dreaming of terrible situations just waiting to befall them all when the Blight Demon reared its horrid head out from beyond the grass like it did before. "I've had this land now for years, got it from my father and his father before him – all the way back to King Shayne."

"So you're the descendant of serfs?" Corwyn continued the conversation attracting the attention of the others like bees into a flower patch.

"Yes, but now we're freeman," Hammond's stature improved with his statement. It was something to be proud of, for in historical terms, the freedom afforded such folk as Hammond was still somewhat new.

"As it should be," Corwyn's words further straightened the farmer's stance. "I think that's one of the best things to come out of the Telborian kingdoms. They really have learned a good lesson from the other independent cities."

Suddenly there came a noise from the grass.

"All of you keep back we've–" Victor couldn't finish his sentence as a terrible roar engulfed his words.

Hammond's eyes grew wide. He knew that sound. "The demon!"

All attention was instantly diverted to the grass before them.

Harold too was filled with fright, though Corwyn and Fredrick seemed more curious than outright frightened. All stayed put, however, as there arose a great clamor from the grasses, which now were swaying violently as the two men took action against their foe.

"What do you think?" Fredrick asked Corwyn as he kept his gaze locked forward, drawing his mace for good measure.

"It's too early to tell," the bard watched the troubled grass.

There were more shouts from the two men as they struck with their swords, or those outside the grass imagined them to be doing, since none could see what was taking place in the thin tawny and green colored, reedy stalks. There came more horrid sounds, pain-filled, blood-curdling screams and howls that did indeed sound unnatural. The thing making them, however, could still not be seen. That was until it shot out from above the grasses in a wild spasm of agony.

"Drued's sweet beard," Fredrick cursed.

The three humans with him were silent with the spectacle.

The Blight Demon was just as Hammond had said it was: a wolf-headed, serpent-bodied, human-armed thing with the legs of a centipede on its lower serpentine half. Fredrick was more than a little amazed and just a tiny bit frightened at such a sight, though he wouldn't admit that even to himself at the moment. For now he was focused on those four muscular arms that ended in deadly claws and that maw of sharp teeth. He wasn't looking forward to fighting the thing if it came down to that and, in truth, wasn't so sure how he'd do against it. He wasn't going to admit to himself now or later, either, that he had just had that thought.

The demon was wounded and all could plainly see the marks left by sword blows and the resulting blood pouring down its arms and body. The Blight Demon's cruel eyes took in the others with a hot rage and made a drunken lunge for them but couldn't get that far as Victor jumped onto the demon's back and drove his blade to the hilt into the demon's hide.

The force of the strike and Victor's added weight, made heavier by his landing, forced the demon to the ground with a crash. He pulled his sword free with a heft that caused the dying demon to thrash about in death throes and then at last grow silent. This thrashing and crashing of the fallen demon resulted in it landing outside the prairie grass for all to see. There were even telltale signs of its throes and landing; crushed grass and the like.

"Is it…?" Harold couldn't finish his question.

"Yeah," Victor gave the demon a kick with his boot, "it's dead."

"And before lunch too," Thomas walked out of the grass with a small lopsided grin.

Fredrick looked both men over, "You two don't seem any worse for wear." And in truth, they didn't. Not a single drop of blood could even be found upon their persons. Only their swords were coated in red ichor. Fredrick further noticed they didn't even look winded from their efforts.

"Like I said," Victor patted his armored chest, "the armor helps keep us safe."

Victor cleaned his blade by wiping it on the shorter grass around him. "I wouldn't worry too much, Harold, about missing anything. You won't be bothered by any of this fellow's friends."

"Why is that?" Corwyn asked, still taken aback a bit by the whole spectacle.

"We sealed the fissure that it had escaped from," Thomas now had come to stand before the bard.

"How convenient," Fredrick started to make his way over to the slain demon. He was still taken back by the appearance of such a creature, but something still didn't sit right with all of this. Something the dwarf couldn't quite leave alone. "What do you plan on doing with it now?"

"It will rot rather quickly," Victor met the dwarf halfway to the demon, blocking his path forward. "Once life has left the body it has taken, and the fissure it has used to escape into our realm has been closed, the body dissolves into nothingness rather rapidly."

"I've never heard of such a thing before," Fredrick was filled with unbelief, pushing past Victor to get a closer look at the slain demon. Again, the dwarf felt like he was looking over something that couldn't have been real, yet it was right in front of his face. It was a strange disconnect that ran about his mind between his logical thinking and his irrational fears. The slain demon looked like something out of a nightmare more than tangible reality. Perhaps that was true. This was a creature from the Abyss itself, the realm of nightmares made flesh.

"Amazing," the dwarf half whispered to himself.

Suddenly a cry of pain took all away from their thoughts and conversations to see Harold slumped on the ground clutching his leg.

CHAD CORRIE

"What is it?" Corwyn ran to his aid. He didn't need Harold to tell him what was wrong – the shaft of a bolt stuck out of his lower left leg. "He's been shot," Corwyn told the others.

"Shot?" Fredrick stopped his inspection and ran to Corwyn's side, the others following his lead, forming a human shield around the downed villager.

"Can you stand?" Corwyn offered his hand to assist Harold.

"I think so," Harold tenderly took up the hand and hopped about his good foot, letting the other dangle free, cringing through clenched teeth all the while.

"We can take him inside," said Hammond, "and tend to him there."

"Here," Corwyn gave Harold his walking stick; the wounded man took it gladly. Together Hammond, Corwyn, and the stick managed to help Harold hobble toward Hammond's home.

"Who's firing at us?" Frederick walked along side them scouring the place with his gaze. "Can't be sloppy hunters," Fredrick could see nothing around them in the flat landscape.

Victor and Thomas were silent as they took up the rear; their own eyes surveying the landscape.

Just then another bolt shot through the company, narrowly missing Victor's shoulder before it stuck itself into the ground a little ways behind him.

"*Who's* shooting at us?" Fredrick growled in frustration as he still couldn't pinpoint the source of the attack.

"Make a run for the house!" Corwyn hurried his aid to Harold, lending him his shoulder to lean upon as they increased their pace.

Victor and Thomas tore out from behind them toward Hammond's home. "We'll secure the way," Victor informed them as both he and Thomas accelerated their mad dash for the house.

"Can you make it?" Corwyn addressed Harold.

"Yeah," Harold's face was sweaty and a bit paler than before but his eyes still held a firm fire. Together they made it to the door of Hammond's home.

"Here," Corwyn helped Harold get inside, "hurry."

Fredrick was the last inside, and the door was slammed shut behind him. All heard the telltale sound of another bolt making its way into the door's hard wood exterior with a heavy thud, seconds after it had been slammed shut.

8

"Hammond?" Marion made her way into the main room of the house that served as the kitchen, living room, and dining room. She entered from the bedroom that was separate from the larger, common room. Her face was a mixture of surprise and uncertainty.

"Marion!" Hammond ran to his wife, taking her in with a strong embrace.

"I heard some screams, is the demon dead?" She returned the suffocating embrace of her husband, unsure of what to make of it and the gaggle of folks who now found themselves in her home.

"Yes," Hammond released her, "it's dead, but not all the danger has passed."

"What do you mean?" Marion pulled herself away a bit from Hammond's embrace. There was an edge of fear in her voice as her gaze turned to take in the strangers who accompanied Harold. "My goodness," Marion's brown eyes grew wide in alarm upon seeing the bolt sticking out of Harold's lower leg, "Harold, are you all right?" Marion detached herself from Hammond to travel over to Harold's side.

"He should be okay," Fredrick was already looking at the bolt shaft in the man's leg with experienced eyes, "you better have some rags and water handy to wash the wound when I pull this thing out – and a chair."

"How did this happen?" Marion asked no one in particular. She couldn't yet take her gaze from the wound.

"We don't know," Corwyn turned away from Harold to address the question. "Someone out there was using us for target practice."

"In Plainsview?" Marion was flabbergasted. "I don't believe it."

"This bolt is real enough," Fredrick returned. "I still need a chair for him too," the dwarf raised his gaze toward Marion.

Hammond took a simple wooden chair from around their table and brought it to Fredrick. "You best get that water and those rags too, Marion," he told his wife. "We'll have time to sort this all out after we attend to Harold."

Marion nodded and quickly hurried away to do just what her husband had advised, rummaging around the room for a wooden bowl which she filled with water from a pitcher on the table and then ran off to the bedroom. A short moment later the sound of fabric being torn crept into the main room of the house. When she returned Marion found Harold resting on the chair, his wounded leg suspended out straight, resting on Fredrick's shoulder as he squatted before the wounded villager. The dwarf's thick hand was already on the shaft, gingerly testing it as he sought a good grip. "This is going to hurt some," he cautioned, "but it will be over quickly."

Harold clenched his teeth and tightly scrunched his eyes shut.

Fredrick yanked the shaft from Harold's leg in one smooth movement.

Harold let out a yell of pain then fell silent as blood began to seep out of the wound.

"Where's that water and those rags?" Fredrick half demanded, half asked.

Marion hurried to bring them to him, and then turned to the ashen-faced Harold. "Why would anyone attack Harold? He's one of the nicest men I've ever known."

"That's a good question," Corwyn looked up from Harold, focusing his attention on Victor and Thomas who stayed close together near the door. "You two know anything about this?"

"Why would we know anything about some madman with a crossbow?" Thomas seemed more nervous and distracted than usual.

Just then the only window in the room, close to the table where everyone had gathered to watch Fredrick treating Harold, shattered as another bolt flew through the plate glass to land on the table beside the pitcher of water.

"Gods of Gray, Light and Dark," Fredrick cursed as he shook bits of glass from his head and beard, being careful to not let any shards get into the wound he had finished cleaning and was now starting to wrap with what appeared to be some torn bed linen. "What now?"

"My window!" Marion was quick to reply.

"Get away from the window," Corwyn advised, but they were already on the move. Hammond assisted the movement of Harold –pulling back the chair on which he sat – as Fredrick balanced his leg, taking care to keep the bandages he'd nearly finished dressing from coming lose. They brought Harold to rest against the wall beside the broken window.

Corwyn noticed that there was a piece of parchment wrapped around the bolt that had stuck in the table, and he made a swift effort to pull the shaft free from the wood, then joined the others in their new location away from the broken window.

"What's that?" Hammond's eyes sought out the parchment wrapped bolt in the bard's hand.

"The answer, I hope, to what's going on here," Corwyn unrolled the parchment from the shaft and began to read aloud:

"To those inside.

"We wish no ill toward you but only to the two scoundrels you harbor in your walls. Release unto us Jarn and Gavin and we will leave you in peace. Should you not release them to us then we will be forced to take more drastic measures to secure them and cannot vouchsafe your lives.

"You have the quarter of an hour to decide."

"*What* do they want?" Hammond looked over to the bard in confusion.

"Jarn and Gavin," Corwyn looked at the parchment again, putting together his thoughts.

"Never heard of them," Harold replied.

"There, that should hold you," Fredrick finished his work on the wounded man's leg. Now that his wound was dressed, Harold seemed to have lost some of his previous pallor.

"Thank you," Harold returned.

"Bounty hunters," Fredrick had risen from his work, and was placing another chair for Harold to rest his leg on as he spoke.

"Bounty hunters?" Marion drew closer to her husband in fright. "What would such men be doing in Plainsview?"

"I think I might have an idea," Corwyn fixed Victor and Thomas in his sights.

The sellswords exchanged another silent, sideways glance.

"What are you getting at – you aren't saying..." Hammond started to follow the gist of Corwyn's logic, as were the others, as they came to rest their eyes upon the sellswords.

"What's *really* going on?" Corwyn asked Victor and Thomas.

"I suppose it's little use pretending any longer," Thomas removed his helmet as he spoke.

"Shut up!" Victor let loose some pent up nervous frustration.

"No," Thomas rested the helmet under his arm and then removed the copper headband from his head, "We knew we couldn't keep this up forever." When Thomas removed the headband, the semblance of the two warriors changed. No more were they men of hard muscles and deeply tanned skin, but were softer in aspect and less rugged, more city-dwelling than wilderness-hardened men; pale and more rounded of frame.

Thomas appeared now as a middle-aged, green-eyed, bookish fellow. Victor's brown eyes were tired and lined with anger that did little to accent his thinning black hair and lined face.

Marion gasped at the sudden change but the rest of the men held their amazement, only reflecting it with eyes which flashed wide for but a moment.

"So then the Blight Demon isn't real either, is it?" Corwyn's voice was low and purposeful.

"No." Thomas shook his head. "I'm Gavin, and he's Jarn. We're bards from Romain."

"*Con men* is more like it," Fredrick's rebuke caused some anger to bubble up in Jarn.

"We make our living the best we know how," Jarn passionately defended his actions. "No one gets hurt and we keep what we do as much on the level as we can."

"On the *level?*" Fredrick raised an eyebrow. "How can one deceive another honestly? How do you dupe someone and keep your integrity?"

Neither of the two con men had an answer.

Corwyn took up the conversation. "What are these bounty hunters, if that is indeed who they are, about in asking for you?"

"Have to be bounty hunters," Fredrick said. "If it were Remani then these two would be dead a long time ago."

Gavin turned to Jarn, and seeing that he wasn't going to get much help from him, took up the task of providing the bard with his answers. "They must have been sent from Romain. A while back we duped a noble woman there. We had Jarn pretend to be royalty and get her to fall in love with him. Course before the wedding could come we took what loot we could and made our way out west into the wilderness."

"No one gets *hurt?*" Corwyn repeated Gavin's words back to him as an accusatory barb. "So she's sent some bounty hunters after you."

"So it would seem," Gavin sighed.

"And you were going to play us for fools as well?" Hammond grew enraged, held back from throttling the two men by his wife's pleading restraints. "I trusted you – we all did – and I even invited you into my home and here you were playing me for a fool by this whole Blight Demon matter, looking to fatten your purses and backpacks with the blessings of this village?

"I should string you up myself!"

"Hammond, peace," Marion consoled. "Fighting won't solve anything right now."

"No," the farmer agreed, "but it would make me a lot happier."

With some more pleading and coaxing, the farmer's wife managed to cool his heart and head while Corwyn continued his interrogation.

"How did you create that creature anyway?" asked the bard. "Probably the same way you altered your appearance, right?"

"With this," Gavin held up the band he had taken off his head, "we've been using it for years now."

"Why don't you just give away *all* our secrets?" Jarn snipped.

Gavin turned to face him, "I don't see any way out of this or anything we can do at the moment. We're already found out, so why keep up the charade?"

Jarn's jaw locked tightly into place at his friend's chastisement.

Gavin continued. "We got it from a wizard."

"Elias?" Corwyn was beginning to put much of the puzzle pieces together now.

"Yeah," Gavin played with the headband in his hand as he spoke, "that was one of our first jobs. We took this with us," he indicated the circlet, "and have been using it to great success ever since.

"All you have to do is put it on your head and concentrate on what you want to appear and it happens. The more believable you can make your thoughts and the harder you concentrate, the more real it can seem to become."

"So then where did you get your weapons and armor or were they stolen too?" Fredrick joined the inquisition, his tone hard and pointed.

"We *paid* for these," Jarn finally spoke with a tone that was both deeply defensive and aggressive. "And no, they aren't *enchanted*. But the circlet wasn't doing that much *good* in the hands of the wizard either. He was using it to trick young woman into his bed by making his wrinkled, stooped body seem young and attractive."

"So what I saw was an illusion?" Hammond asked all present. "That creature out there was never real?"

"Yes," Gavin cautiously nodded. "The first time you saw it we were hiding in the grass and the second time we put up a good fight and made you think it was slain. It would have rotted away very quickly as we had lunch and been gone before we left on our way."

"Because there's a limit to the circlet's influence," Corwyn surmised.

"Yes," said Gavin, "it only works well in close relation to the person you want to dupe."

"Maybe when you're done answering their questions, Gavin, you can tell them your life story too," Jarn mocked his partner. "This isn't getting us any closer to getting out of here."

"Sure it is," Fredrick smiled a mirthless grin, "all we have to do is open up that door and toss you out."

"And condemn us to *die*?" Jarn was wide-eyed in his rebuttal.

"Sounds fine by me," the dwarf added nonchalantly. In truth, he wouldn't mind being rid of them at all, especially folk who made their living on lies and robbery of others.

"So you think you'd be killed?" Corwyn moved closer to the two con men. "You think this woman would want you dead rather than alive?"

"I don't know," Gavin was truthful in his answer, "If we aren't killed they'd probably take us back to Romain and Lady Stephanie's house."

"Where she could kill us there," Jarn's sardonic tone cut the tension-thick air that was falling upon all gathered.

"Are you sure it's Lady Stephanie and not Elias that sent these men after you?" Corwyn dismissed Jarn's cutting remark.

Gavin nodded, "Lady Stephanie swore revenge, we heard, and Elias is dead."

"And *no*," Jarn jumped into the fray before anyone else could respond, "we didn't *kill* the wizard; he died of old age a few days after we left."

"We don't really know if these men *are* bounty hunters," Corwyn turned to Frederick, "or even how many men there might be."

"Who else *could* it be?" the dwarf offered up his defense of the idea. "Even *they* think it's plausible," the dwarf waved a hand toward Gavin and Jarn.

Corwyn looked to the con men again. "You don't have any other ideas who this might be then?"

"Why do *you* care?" Jarn snapped. "What concern is it of yours?"

"Because these people don't seem to care about hurting innocent parties to get at you, and I for one don't wish to be at the lethal end of a bolt simply because I happened to be standing next to one of you." The firmness in the bard's voice stilled Jarn's caustic tongue.

"Why are we even *debating* this?" Fredrick grew slightly irritated with this whole exchange. "They have confessed already and we don't have all day here. Let's just throw open the door."

"We can't go back; you know that," Jarn pleaded; his previous defiant and sarcastic manner mellowed and humbled.

"You can't go back to face the consequences of your actions?" Corwyn took a good long look into Jarn's soft brown eyes. "Why shouldn't we let you reap what you've sown? You almost succeed in tricking some villagers out of their hard earned provisions, got an innocent man wounded and made sport of another for your gain.

"Why should we help you do anything but get what you have earned from your escapades?"

"Because, we can make it worth your while," Jarn was quick to answer, his eyes alight and voice taking on a velvety smoothness that revealed his training as a bard. "We can pay you handsomely."

"You would seek to *buy* us off?" Hammond was disgusted with such a proposal.

"You won't have to farm anymore," Jarn pushed the matter forward without even carrying about the farmer's dislike of the matter. "You help us get out of here and we'll make sure you get your fair share."

"You must think me a real idiot to fall for that," said Hammond. "You may have fooled me with that demon of yours but you won't fool me a second time."

"You can't–"Jarn started to reply.

Fredrick made his way forward, "Enough of your whining already. Are you going to get out there or do I have to throw you out?"

"Okay," Gavin lifted his palms to the dwarf, trying to push for more time and calmer heads, "hear me out here. All you have to do is buy us enough time to let us escape and we'll use the circlet to make it appear like we're giving up. We'll lead whoever is out there away from you. That way you'll be safe and we at least have a chance."

"Right," Fredrick's smile was less then genuine. "and a halfling likes to do an honest day's work."

"You can watch us from the doorway," Gavin hurriedly returned, "you have my word."

"The word of a con man?" Fredrick snorted, "I'd be better off trusting a fox to guard a hen house. Why not let them get what's coming to them?" The dwarf looked over his shoulder to Corwyn.

"Sounds fair by me," Hammond added, "they should answer for all the innocent people they've made fools of and stolen from."

"Let's not get too hasty in judgment now," Gavin cautioned, "at least *think* about my idea."

"To run and hide?" More color had returned to Harold's face along with some energy for his sharp toned rebuke. "Seems to me that's all you've *been* doing."

Jarn was about to speak up but was hushed by Gavin who still had the cooler head of the two. "We were actually worried that you might catch on to things, Corwyn. When you said who you were we both couldn't believe that we'd have to pull off on our best performances in front of a well-known bard.

"I'm surprised we did as well as we did. But that doesn't change *what* we did and all I can do is plead with you, one bard to another, to have mercy on us and let us go our way."

Corwyn took in the two bards turned con men with a calm expression. "If you run now you're going to keep running for quite a while, maybe forever. Why not just give up and deal with the consequences of your actions?"

"Because that might *hurt,*" Jarn's sarcastic words jabbed into the heart of the conversation. "I have kind of grown *attached* to my head and wouldn't be too *keen* on *losing* it."

"And that is what you think awaits you?" Corwyn understood their reluctance if what they said was true. However, he wasn't so sure if it was the truth and so continued to search their face and frame for tells. Since it seemed that he was to be part of the final choice as to what would be done with the two con men, he wanted to be sure he had all the facts…and had them correctly understood.

"Most certainly," said Gavin.

"Then I can see your concern," Corwyn had concluded their belief in what awaited them with Lady Stephanie was indeed true.

He could clearly read it in Gavin, who seemed to be the more transparent and least deceptive of the duo. "But you still should do what is right. What kind of life will you live if you have the specter of capture and a possible death looming over your days?"

"A longer one," again Jarn was quick to put forth his thoughts.

"You're jeopardizing the lives of everyone here and you'd do the same to all those you come across in the days to come should you make good your escape," Corwyn motioned around at those gathered in the room. "Not only would you be conning them out of their livelihood but also risking their lives now as well. Harold here is the first of many in that line. Had that bolt been aimed higher..." The room grew silent for a minute as all let the conjured thought rest in their brain.

"It seems like you have afforded us little freedom then," Gavin seemed resolute in his fate. "Is this how you *all* feel?"

The rest nodded their agreement with Corwyn's previous statement of preferred action.

"I see," Gavin became more crestfallen.

"And hand over that circlet too," Fredrick held out his hand. "We don't want you playing any tricks now either."

Gavin looked to Jarn who cautioned him with his eyes, but Gavin seemingly ignored them.

"You can hand it over or I can take it," Fredrick's eyes lit up at the prospect of getting a chance to ruff up the two con men. He was still hungry from this morning and more than happy to vent his frustration on them by taking the circlet by force.

"Fine," Gavin handed the circlet over to the dwarf's eager hand.

"And now out the door," Fredrick began to rudely push them to the doorway then pushed himself between them to stand before the door and open it for them, smiling as he did so. "Here you are then."

Jarn looked to Gavin with a dark countenance that was just about ready to boil over into deep wrath. Gavin was not so visible in his displeasure, but Corwyn could tell it was there just the same. Both moved to stare out the doorframe into the wide open space before them.

"Well, we haven't been stuck full of bolts yet," Jarn observed, "*this* is promising."

"Remove your armor and weapons," a deep voice came out of nowhere, startling the two con men.

For a moment both remained still.

"I said remove them," the command came again but with an edge of steel that caused the two Telborians to understand the speaker was willing to back up his words with hard action if they didn't comply.

The two did as they were ordered, starting to take off their armor and weapons as the same voice continued. "You weren't too hard to track down. We lost your trail outside Romain for a bit but found it quickly enough. All we had to do was follow after the tales of these two sellswords slaying demons, dragons, and ogres. You really should have changed your ruse a bit. It might have given you more time to get out of the kingdom."

"I told you," Gavin had finished disarming himself.

"Shut up," Jarn grumbled. He too was defenseless.

"Now walk out...slowly," the voice commanded.

Gavin gave one more pleading look to the others in the room, hoping that someone would have a change of heart.

They didn't.

Sighing deeply, he followed Jarn outside into the late morning.

"Now," the voice gained a face, the stubble-speckled, hard lined, face of a balding Telborian, coming out of from a patch of lower lying grasses scattered toward the edge of the front yard, "walk this way."

Hammond, Marion, Corwyn, and Fredrick watched Jarn and Gavin make their way to the medium-sized man who held a cross bow leveled at them. Before they had walked more than five steps, six more rough looking Telborian men came up behind the con men from their positions scattered around, behind and near the house.

"Keep walking," one of the other bounty hunters flatly advised. All carried crossbows, loaded and ready to fire at a moments notice.

Jarn gave Gavin another silent stare as they moved farther ahead.

Gavin nodded.

Suddenly, both men made a run for it.

It was a foolish thing for they hadn't gotten more than ten feet when they were stuck full of bolts from behind.

Three bolts through each bard.

Three bolts aimed with deadly skill for their vital organs.

Gavin and Jarn were dead before they hit the ground.

"Idiots," Fredrick dryly commented.

Corwyn shook his head.

Fredrick saw this and was amazed, "You're actually *sorry* they got what was coming to them?"

"They deserved to reap what they had sown, but as long as they lived there was still a chance for leniency, for mercy – for repentance." The bard watched the bounty hunters approach the bodies, making sure they were dead by kicking them with their feet. When they were sure of their demise they began to tie their hands and feet.

"But who would have granted them mercy?" Hammond asked as he comforted his wife, who had buried her face in his shoulder at the sight of the two men being killed before her.

"That's probably what *they* thought," Corwyn mused.

"We have no ill will wished for you," one of the seven bounty hunters who had shot the con men addressed those in the doorway, as he stopped to gather up the armor and arms of the slain men. "We've got what we came for."

"Where will you take them?" Corwyn asked the bounty hunter.

After sliding the swords into his belt and then putting the rest of the armor into a brown, woolen sack, he spoke. "To Romain. Our client wishes to pay us for our troubles. Though she would have paid us more for them being alive, she will be satisfied with them dead."

The gruff looking bounty hunter slung the sack over his back then flung a gold coin in Hammond's direction. The farmer almost missed catching it out of sheer surprise, but got a hold of it in the end. "For the window," the gruff Telborian nodded as if he'd been a friend repaying a debt.

None said anything, merely watched the seven men make their way toward the east – toward Romain. The two bodies they now carried between them like a couple of freshly killed deer, as they silently made their way out of those in the doorways line of sight.

When the last of the bounty hunters had made their way from their eyes, those remaining started to move; Marion to finish up the lunch she had started (an attempt to occupy her mind so she didn't have to think on the image of the con men's death); Hammond to see to Harold. Only Fredrick and Corwyn remained.

"This might come in handy," the dwarf was playing with the copper circlet in his hands, turning it about as he looked it over with a favorable eye.

Corwyn said nothing, merely kept his gaze to where he had last seen the bounty hunters.

Fredrick noted his friend's silence and stopped his study of his newfound possession. "Let it go, Corwyn. There was nothing more that could have been done. You said it yourself; they reaped what they had sown."

"But as long as they were alive there was a chance they could have been reformed."

Fredrick snorted. "Maybe I should give *you* this circlet. It would conjure up something more real than a reformed con man. Hey–"

Corwyn peered down to his friend. The dwarf was holding up an empty hand that had once held the circlet. "It just disappeared." Then the dwarf's anger rose. "They *conned* us *all*."

Corwyn looked out at the plains again with a grin. "They were probably doing it the whole time."

"This isn't funny, Corwyn," Fredrick chastised the bard upon seeing the bard's grin.

"No," Corwyn kept his gaze distant as he spoke. "But they learned a lesson that will take them to the truth soon enough... and maybe even cause them to amend their ways."

Fredrick shook his head. "At least they'd gone." Fredrick then joined the bard in inspecting the front yard and flat spreading land beyond. "Still, it would have been nice to have had that circlet," he sighed. "Well, at least now I can finally get something to eat." The dwarf started to leave the doorway then stopped and turned to Corwyn once more, "You coming?"

"I'll join you shortly," Corwyn kept his gaze out toward the distant horizon. Fredrick could see the bard wanted a moment to himself and left him to it. Once the dwarf had left, Corwyn let out a small sigh, then in a soft voice prayed:

"Watch over them, Causilla, and bring them to the truth before their deeds come back to haunt them. If they truly are bards then they're in your care and I leave them to you to reconcile to the High Patroness of Bards. Save them from themselves before it's too late and place them on the right road to walk for everyone's good."

Having said his peace he left the doorway to join the others inside, where the rich smells of a fine meal began to fill the whole house, joined with good spirited conversation.

APPENDICES

APPENDIX A:

CORWYN DANTHER'S TIMELINE

The following is a simple chronological list of the various events that have taken place in the life of Corwyn Danther – both prior to and as revealed in the stories collected in this book. While not inclusive of all the events of his life, they do touch on the more monumental or pivotal moments that have shaped his life thus far.

734 P.V.   Born in Haven, Talatheal.

746 P.V.   Travels to Maiden Rock for the first time.

747 P.V.   Travels to Argos, Belda-thal to become trained as a bard.

757 P.V.   Corwyn completes his training in Argos and returns to Haven where he then later travels the Midlands, mainly Talatheal.

759 P.V.   *Rainer's Legacy*

760 P.V.   *Maiden Rock*
              Where Dreams Go To Die
              Charity for Halflings
              Sellswords and Snake Oil

Appendix B:

The Crown of the World

At the top of Tralodren, beyond the Northlands, lies The Crown of the World. Many myths and tales have been spoken about this place and little in the way of exploration or solid factual insight has done anything to confirm or deny these tales. Further, the wild rumors and assumptions of sailors, sages, philosophers, and priests have only added to the uncertainty of just what is there or is supposed to be there.

Many hold that Tralodren is a world rich in water. Following The Great Shaking that helped to define recorded time, the great landmass that had once been the only continent on the planet was shattered into the continents and islands that now populate the Northern Hemisphere of the globe. Speculation has been put forth that there are lands formed by more fragments, to the South beyond The Boiling Sea. But as to how many or how large they might be and with what they might be populated remains to be seen or fully discovered or explained.

Tales do tell of the monstrous races getting a great hold over the Northern Hemisphere from a migration from the south. Sages, scholars, and some priests have put forth that there would have to be a sizable chunk of land beyond the bubbling waves; not as many continents as is known in the Northern Hemisphere, but a good handful for certain to be home to such a large horde that made their bloody migration up into more civilized lands.

The other side of Tralodren, the reverse of the known world as it were, is open to wild speculation and debate. None know what is there for certain, but the prevailing beliefs, generated by those who have sailed the waters in times past, have said it is an empty, vast, massive ocean, and called it The Great Ocean. While it is true that none have been able to circumnavigate Tralodren, it has been a widely held belief by a great many sages and educated persons that the concept of The Great Ocean is the actual and real nature of that half of the world.

There are some that hold to there being all sorts of fanciful things there such as a virgin continent rich with all the good things that had been lost and exploited during the times of the Ancients and The Great Shaking which followed, to a land filled with dragons and other horrors waiting to awaken to come attack those on the other side of the world, to some even more esoteric theories about gateways to other planets and planes and realms. Until someone succeeds in sailing from one side of The Great Ocean to the other, we will never know. And since many aren't that keen to do such a thing, it shall remain a mystery for quite a while longer.

With The Crown of the World, however, there has been record of travels and trips to the outer rim of this place that is said to be the top diameter of the globe. While here too, none have ventured too far beyond the outer rim of this territory, it has been consistently reported that it is quite cold and a very inhospitable place. Some have said it is so cold that large chunks of ice float about the waves like islands, and that the water has even been known to nearly freeze the closer one came to the center of the Crown.

However, what lies at the exact center of this region is still unknown, as none have sailed to it in fear of losing control of their vessel and falling into the empty waters on the other side of the world. How this could be is uncertain, but it is a common enough fear that keeps all who have sailed there (the handful of those who sailed there rather) from proceeding any further.

As with the other exotic locales of Tralodren, there are a handful of ideas as to what might lie beyond and within this area. Some have said it is the resting place of Perlosa, who looks to it a sort of vacation spot she likes to go in order to govern the waves and icy reaches of the planet. Others hold a great beast lives there – perhaps even a Titan some say – who is imprisoned there for his crimes against the gods. Some hold it to be a land that is a sacred spot that is told to hold enchanting virgins eager to meet men who might sail by, the lair of a great dragon, or a whole host of other things, depending upon who is telling the tale.

What is known for certain, however, is that the area hasn't been that well explored and seemingly won't for quite some time given the fears of most of the sailors plying their trade on the waves these days.

– An excerpt from "A Basic Primer of the Land" by Elliott Nedlah, a sage in the employ of the King of Romain.

Appendix C:

The Muses of Tralodren

The following child's rhyme tells a story of the Muses insofar as their current locations are concerned.

The Rhyme of the Muses

Thirty-six maidens to inspire and delight,
By goddess' command get up and take flight.
Six to the South to plant seeds in the sand,
Six to the Midlands – fire the hearts of man.
Six more to the North to mix beauty with ice,
Six more to the West to champion virtue ov'r vice.
Six to entertain the gods alone.
Six to stand beside the goddess' throne.

Six maids traveled South to spread their charms,
Who were greeted on the shores with open arms.
Jasmine. Kira, and Amrita are all flames in the mind,
Bala, Jaya, and Leela – beauty and grace divine.

Six sisters also came to Midlandic shores:
Adina, Alanna, and Ella – sights to behold.
Mortal minds to enlight, inspire and mold.
Hannah, Keely, and Lena the other three–
Delight of men and mortals be.

To the lands of the North six more sisters found rest,
Erika, Linne, and Mia enjoyed the frozen wastes the best.
The three other sisters wasted not their gifts in the least,
Thyrmi, Vaja and Ursa's divine mission never to cease.

Now to those in the West six others were sent,
Sharing with all their gifts wherever they went.
Alison, Ashley, and Kimi voices sang out o'vr the land;
Sachi, Calista and Deka finding favor with mortal man.

Six Muses would stand beside Causilla's throne;
These always calling Delecta their home.
The rest to wander the realms of light;
To travel in darker realms would be as a blight.

So Causilla has blessed the cosmos with her gift
And in so doing the spirits of all did she uplift.

It is widely known that Causilla, goddess of beauty, love and
arts, fashioned thirty-six beings at the creation of Tralodren to
further spread the beauty of creation and her nature to all who
would receive them. Twelve of these she took for herself – to
inspire her own realm and the greater cosmos; the other twenty-
four made their home on Tralodren.

What makes Muses so unique is that unlike other divinities
and gods who have to hide their true nature and power through a
guise of flesh, the Muse is present in their full nature on the planet.
This means that they have a great deal of power and ability at their
disposal – more so than any other divinity.

To this end, each Muse has sought to use her talents to the
betterment of her charges and not for her own selfish gain (though
a few have crossed that line in the distant past when their judgment
was clouded by love for a given charge, mortal or even divinity).

Muses appear as the loveliest of human maidens, but have been
known to take a separate guise of other races when and where it is

needed. Their true form reflects the purest nature of each, which is breathtaking to behold and beyond words to describe. Their main purpose, though, is to help spread the nature of their creator in and through their given charges wherever they can. To this end they will work with people from all walks of life to accomplish what they feel is in the best interest of their goddess' mission.

The Terrestrial Muses

In the beginning of creation the Muses had full range over all of the land of Tralodren – for it was one super continent at that point in time. After The Great Shaking, the current landmasses appeared, to which the Muses cast lots to see where they should go and whom they should adopt as their charges.

Thus the twenty-four terrestrial bound Muses were divided as follows:

Midlands

The six Muses who found their way to The Midlands were Adina, Alanna, Ella, Hannah, Keely, and Lena.

Adina: Assigned to the mysterious Wizard King Islands.
Alanna: Assigned to the Northern landmass of Arid Land.
Ella: Assigned to Colloni.
Hannah: Assigned to Draladon.
Keely: Assigned to the Southern landmass of Arid Land.
Lena: Assigned to Talatheal.

Northlands

The six Muses who found their way to The Northlands were Erika, Linne, Mia, Thyrmi, Vaja, and Ursa.

Erika: Assigned to Troll Island.
Linne: Assigned to Frigia.
Mia: Assigned to Baltan.
Thyrmi: Assigned to Valkoria.
Vaja and Ursa: Both assigned to The Crown of the World.

The Southern Lands
The six Muses who found their way to The Southern Lands were Jasmine. Kira, Amrita, Bala, Jaya, and Leela.

Jasmine: Assigned to Belda-thal.
Kira: Assigned to Doom Maker's Island.
Amrita: Assigned to The Isle of the Minotaurs.
Bala, Jaya, and Leela: These three Muses have been given lands beyond the Boiling Sea, from which the monstrous races and Minotors once sprang. Just to what place beyond the Boiling Sea each has been assigned, no sage, priest, nor philosopher can declare with any certainty.

The Western Lands
The six Muses who found their way to The Western Lands were Alison, Ashley, Kimi, Sachi, Calista, and Deka.

Alison: Assigned to Breanna.
Ashley: Assigned to Cardinia.
Kimi: Assigned to Irondale and Black Isle.
Sachi: Assigned to Napow.
Calista; Assigned to Rexatious.
Deka: Assigned to The Pearl Islands.

The Celestial Muses

As already stated, twelve of the thirty-six Muses were taken by Causilla to do her will in the cosmos, starting with her realm, Delecta; allowing the other six to find a place of their own. Six of these twelve have come to serve as Causilla's personal handmaidens, while the other six have been given special status where they are posted in the cosmos.

The six who attend to Causilla are: Aznii, Deshi, Havaa, Khazmia, Maali, and Carine.

The six who remain and where they are posted are as follows:

Jelena – *Civis*
Nadia – *Paradise*
Vanya – *Bios*
Vanda – *Avion*
Vondra – *Elucia*
Kasia – *Sooth*

APPENDIX D:

BARDS OF TRALODREN

*T*he following is an excerpt of an essay written by Petra Crates, a somewhat famed Patrician bard from the last century around the Western Lands, namely Rexatious. In the essay, Petra provides some decent insight into what bards do and are believed to do in Tralodren. Though a little dated, this work is still useful in gleaming some basic information about bards and the bardic traditions on Tralodren in general.

What is a bard? Well, I guess you can say we are of a curious sort who love to travel. We have a hard time being in one place for too long and not being able to do something creative would drive many of us wild with boredom. We are a people who are creative, yes, but are more in love with the act of creation than the item that is produced by it. Is it any wonder we are thought of as we are?

Far from lay-abouts and wandering vagrants, we are very dedicated workers to our craft... though each other's craft is far from certain and uniform as one might think it should be, when compared to the other endeavors of mortalkind. "Surely," one could say, "the blacksmith makes tools for the same purpose and in the same manner; the baker always makes his loaf of bread like so; the cooper always plies his craft to similar tasks, so why is the bard so different?"

My dear friend, it would be foolish to try and label the works of my fellow brothers and sisters as so certain in progression of nature to their craft that you would expect such uniformity. Are all songs alike? Are all stories told the same way each night around the fire – even by those who don't share in the Bardic Order? Why then put us in the same category?

Bards work with things that are organic – songs and tales, dance and music and art and so many other wonders and blessings Causilla has showered down upon us. To us we have been given the light of jubilant energy in which to craft such pleasing and inspiring works not only for our benefit but also for all those around us and who might later delight in our creation.

This is what it is to be a bard. But then how does one become a bard?

Now that, my friend, is an interesting tale.

To become a bard, one is not necessarily born into it as some might have you think. Those are the flashier of my fellows who are trying to both elevate their station and probably make some more coin off of your donations as well. A bard, truth be told, is just a man like any other (though we have a great many women in the order as well) who feels that this is the life he wishes to lead.

Just as I'm sure there are some that want to be blacksmiths and bakers and oddly enough yes, politicians, there are those who wish to become bards and so follow their desire as best they know how. Many will never raise to the level of skilled performer that better known bards have come to be known by over the past few generations. Instead, these will be meager men of simple means – more musician and street performer than accredited herald of the goddess Causilla – and not that keen on getting so great an audience in even the largest of cities. Rather, these fellows are the ones who often work for the true bards – those who have had a great deal of training.

How does one get training?

Good question.

As I have said, the average fellow might be a great artist, singer, tale-teller, etc., but he might not be able to find a way to get proper training and so never rise to that higher level of recognition of accomplishment that all bards crave and need to further their careers. So it is this training that is the dividing point between a great many. It is also a dividing point for it is a costly education offered in select areas over the world.

Like with mages, the bard has to learn his art. Instead of magical academies, the bard has a college which he attends. More frequent than the magical academies but not as common as the tutoring schools for the masses to better learn their reading, writing, and simple math, these bardic colleges can be found in just about any land.

There are two types of bardic colleges from which a bard can learn. A general school, which applies basic musical principal and understanding, provides voice and instrument training and even instruction in performance and dance. The other is a more specialized school that, while it teaches the same things as the general school, also instructs the student in the ways and understanding of Causilla and the spiritual nature behind their profession.

Naturally, these schools are found in or in close association with Causillinites, so it should come as no surprise that many temples also house a section for bardic instruction; priests actually serving as teachers to the young bard.

So does one need to go to college to get training? No, not really, but it is much easier to advance in your career if you did so. There are tutors and older bards who have now retired, and take on students to keep bread in the oven and on the table, and so one could find a way to instruction that way. However, should you do so, you lose out on the great contacts and connections the colleges afford you.

I'm far from one to say which is better, as I've had friends who've gone to college or self-funded their way to their dreams by the various tutors, and both turned out fairly well. They're not famous, mind you, but don't have to sing for their suppers every night either.

So once you have your training then what do you do?

Well, once you leave the college and get good enough on your own so people actually would want to listen to you perform, you can opt for a wide selection of things. Many bards find that being universal in their approach helps at first, but hinders then later on. Hinders them because they aren't known for anything, being a jack-of-all-trades but not really a master of any thing in particular. If you want to do birthday celebrations and weddings and other events, then that's great, and you could do very well, but you won't get your name out there beyond that.

Instead, many bards soon look to find a niche where they do well. This is probably something they had training with in college and/or are inclined to with the gifting given them by Causilla. In either case, many take to finding out what their niche is and look to develop it and exploit it to the best of their ability.

What are some of these niches?

Writing various stories and plays; dancing, a whole host of musical stylings, to even playing a certain musical instrument, and simple storytelling. There are a whole host more and just as many bards to fill them, but that is how many bards get a start at standing out from among the crowd and raising up to some new levels in their careers.

To this end, many have done well and found a decent life, but still more add the final element of touring to their talents and do even better. This isn't to say that the other bards don't travel from town to town, but they just don't do it as an overall strategy for both bettering their performance and increasing their notoriety.

It's a bit more grueling for those who take on larger tours of whole regions and/or even nations, but it gets your face and name out there and a fresh audience out before you with each new stop. Better still, if you're *really* good, you can generate excitement for your upcoming event before you even get there. All this plays to the advantage of the bard who knows how to do it right and play to his strengths. A little showmanship goes a long way too and helps bring in a better name recognition and fatter coin purse.

So what does that mean? That all bards are people who chase after coin like a hound to a rabbit all over this world? I'll let you be the judge of that but for myself I can think of no greater service to offer mortalkind than the sound of music, a tale to pass and inspire and teach, a song to lift the spirit, a joke to awaken a smile on a crestfallen face, or even the simple retelling and reminding of what is great in life to those who might have forgotten or needed to be reminded again.

Yes, this is Causilla's blessing of the bard.

Chad Corrie is the author of four novels and one graphic novel – all of which take place in **The World of Tralodren®**. Chad makes his home in Minnesota.

Visit Chad on the web at: *www.chadcorrie.com* for all the latest updates and insights into **The World of Tralodren®**, podcasts and other projects and events.

We hope you enjoyed this anthology. Be sure to check out other works by Chad Corrie and those of other AMI authors. Your comments and thoughts concerning this book or Aspirations Media are welcome.

www.aspirationsmediainc.com

If you're a writer or know of one who has a work that they'd love to see in print – then send it our way. We're always looking for great manuscripts that meet our guidelines. Aspirations Media is looking forward to hearing from you and/or any others you may refer to us.

Thank you for purchasing this Aspirations Media publication.